continued . . .

"[A] fast-paced technothriller." —*Wired*

"*Daemon* does for surfing the Web what *Jaws* did for swimming in the ocean. . . . Both entertaining and credible . . . an impressive debut novel."
—*Chicago Sun-Times*

"Daniel Suarez has written a thriller so frightening even the government has taken note."
—*Entertainment Weekly*

"Ambitious. . . . I came away from this novel with a . . . new fear of computer capability."
—*New York Times* bestselling author Robin Cook

"Fiendishly clever . . . an almost perfect guilty-pleasure novel. Mr. Suarez's brilliant stroke is the Daemon, a massive and malevolent artificial intelligence program."
—*The Dallas Morning News*

"Suarez's not-just-for-gamers debut is a stunner."
—*Kirkus Reviews*

"A riveting debut . . . a perfect gift for . . . anyone who appreciates thrills, chills, and cybersuspense. . . . A final twist that runs counter to expectations will leave readers anxiously awaiting the promised sequel."
—*Publishers Weekly* (starred review)

Also by Daniel Suarez

Daemon
Kill Decision
Influx

Freedom™

Daniel Suarez

DUTTON
— est. 1852 —

DUTTON

⟶ est. 1852 ⟵

An imprint of Penguin Random House LLC
375 Hudson Street
New York, New York 10014

Previously published as a Dutton hardcover and a Signet premium mass market.

First Dutton premium mass market printing, 2016

ISBN 978-0-451-23189-5

Printed in the United States of America
10 9 8 7 6 5 4 3

For Generation Y

Behind the ostensible government sits enthroned an invisible government owing no allegiance and acknowledging no responsibility to the people. To destroy ths invisible government, to befoul the unholy alliance between corrupt business and corrupt politics is the first task of the statesmanship of the day.

—Theodore Roosevelt in 1906

Part One

December

Gold:	$1,057USD/oz.
Unleaded Gasoline:	$3.58USD/gallon
Unemployment:	16.3%
USD/Darknet Credit:	3.9

Part One

December

Chapter 1: // Dark Pool

InvestorNet.com

Profits in Milliseconds—**"Algorithmic stock trading** is the future of finance," according to Wall Street titan **Anthony Hollis**, whose **Tartarus Group employs** sophisticated **software** that responds to market conditions, trading equities with sub-millisecond speed. Due to its extraordinary profitability, **Hollis's** form of **programmatic trading** grew from 14 percent of all equity volume in 2003, to 73 percent of all volume in 2009.

However, critics contend that **high-frequency trades**—where a single stock may be bought and sold multiple times an hour—only increases market volatility while **producing nothing of value.**

An elderly man emerged from the crowd and aimed a revolver straight at Anthony Hollis's face. As the old worker's thick index finger squeezed the trigger, Hollis sat up in darkness—breathing hard.

He glanced at the clock on the nightstand: *3:13 A.M.* Motionless, he listened to his own rapid breathing.

He started to calm down as he looked around his bedroom. It was illuminated only by the soft glow of large flat-screen monitors mounted on the far wall, scrolling stock prices for the Nikkei, Shanghai, and Seoul exchanges. The monitors weren't necessary anymore. They were merely a comfort to him.

Hollis took one more deep breath and tried to shake off the nightmare. He was just about to lie back down when the unmistakable crackling of gunfire somewhere in the night came to his ears.

He sat up again.

The phone beside his bed warbled. He grabbed the handset. "Metzer, what's going on?"

The calm voice of Rudy Metzer, his security director, came over the line. *"We have a situation by the service gate. It's being contained."*

"What kind of goddamned situation? Who the hell is shooting?"

In the bed next to him, Hollis's latest girlfriend looked up at him sleepily. She was a third his age. "What is it?"

He ignored her and tried to listen to Metzer.

"Mr. Hollis, as a precaution, I want you to move into your secure room as soon as possible."

"Are the police on the way?"

"Sir, the estate's outside lines have been cut. Cell phones and radios jammed. We're isolated for the moment. I need you to move quickly and calmly to your safe room. I'll phone you on the landline. Do you understand?"

Hollis absorbed Metzer's words and felt actual fear. "Yes. Yes, I understand." He returned the phone to the cradle and stared at nothing for a moment. The screens on the far wall now showed only video snow.

"What's happening, Tony?"

Kidnappers? Assassins? Two months ago a retired autoworker had tried to kill him in Chicago. Metzer's men saw the guy make his move, and they tackled him before he could pull the trigger. Some pension-fund loser bent on revenge. Tonight's intruders sounded more serious.

"Tony!"

He turned to her. "Relax. Somebody tried to break in." Hollis got out of bed and put on his slippers and a robe.

"Where are you going? I don't want to be left alone!"

"Don't be a pain in the ass. They caught the guy. I just need to take a piss." He ignored her frightened look and headed to the master bathroom.

He nudged the door closed behind him, turned on the lights, and padded across the Italian marble floor, headed toward the walk-in wardrobe. He opened twin doors to enter a sizeable room lined with H. Huntsman and Leonard Logsdail suits and rows of Edward Green and Berluti shoes.

Hollis avoided his reflection in the wraparound mirrors as he closed the doors behind him. Yes, he felt a twinge of conscience, but then, he didn't really know this girl. He hadn't done a backgrounder on her yet, and he wasn't about to bring her into his secure room. She could be a plant. People were capable of anything for money.

Hollis walked quickly to the far wall and opened the faceplate of a wall-mounted digital thermostat. It revealed an alphanumeric keypad where he tapped in his security code—the exact amount of his first investment. A section of the wooden wall rolled aside, revealing a hidden room whose lights flickered on automatically. The door was solid steel, nearly six inches thick—the reinforced concrete walls of his secure room were even thicker. A sign of the times.

He moved inside and tapped a red pressure switch near the door. The opening slid closed and locked with a dull *boom*. A large bank of monitors glowed to life on the far side of the room above a security console. From here he could watch the action through dozens of surveillance cameras. There was also a dedicated emergency phone line, a radio base station, and a house phone. The room also had a sofa, a wet bar, and a flat-screen television—not to mention shelves of emergency provisions and a narrow door leading to a Spartan restroom.

Hollis had everything he needed to await rescue.

The house phone rang, and he tapped the speakerphone button as he clicked through monitors, trying to find the service gate cameras. "Talk to me."

Metzer's voice came over the speaker. *"Can you get a dial tone on your emergency line?"*

Hollis grabbed the emergency phone and held it to his ear. Nothing. Some cultural instinct compelled him to stab repeatedly at the hook switch. "It's dead. This was supposed to be a buried cable. How did they know where it was, Metzer?"

Hollis heard talking in the background. Then Metzer

came back on. *"We'll talk about that later. Right now I've got men missing, and motion detectors in alarm all over the estate. I'm pulling everyone back into a perimeter around the master suite."*

"How did these people get through the gates?" One of the security monitors showed the estate's front entrance, which stood wide-open.

"I don't know."

"It's your *job* to know! I wasn't supposed to ever *need* this room, damnit." He fumed for a moment, then added, "Send someone up to get Mary."

"She's not with you?"

"I can't have her in here. Just put her in a closet or something. And figure out a way to contact the police. I don't care if you have to use fucking smoke signals!" He hung up and kept flipping through security monitors. He'd spent a fortune on security, and he wasn't getting much of a return on his investment. He was going to sack the entire security team after this was over—starting with Metzer.

As Hollis cycled through cameras, the monitors showed various rooms on a dozen screens—multicar garage, pool patio, pub room, dining room, driveway . . .

He stopped cold. In the middle of the driveway, one of Metzer's suited security men lay in a pool of blood, still clutching a submachine gun. His head was missing.

"Jesus Christ!" Hollis picked up the house phone and dialed Metzer's extension. It rang several times and went to voice mail. Hollis pressed the call button on the radio base station but heard nothing but static. "Fuck!"

Then the power went out.

Here in the safe room backup batteries instantly engaged, but on the security monitors he saw most of the lights kick off around the estate. Now only interior emergency lighting remained. Outside was blackness.

Hollis clicked through the interior surveillance cameras. There—he saw two security people in the grand foyer with Metzer locking the ornate front doors of Hollis's twenty-three-thousand-square-foot mansion. Metzer was racing upstairs, pointing and shouting to position men at the top of the staircase. They all carried MP-5 submachine guns. The second floor was apparently going to be their Alamo.

Just then the front doors blasted open, sending door hardware, wood, and glass fragments silently spraying across the polished stone floor. Something the size of a man had burst through the doors at high speed, taking out the large antique table just inside the door and crashing into the far wall. The room started to fill with smoke.

The surveillance camera showed security men opening fire from the second-floor railing. More shadows were already racing through the front door. Hollis couldn't get a good look at them in the dim light and smoke. They moved fast—through the doorway and up the wide staircase. In mere moments they exited the frame. Hollis clicked around in frustration to find a suitable camera to see what was going on.

He soon saw his own bedroom on one monitor—he'd had this security camera installed as a precaution against sexual assault charges (one never knew what visions of rape young women might dream up after the fact). It wasn't on the rotation available to the security team, but here he could see Metzer grabbing Mary by the wrist and pulling her from the bed. She was nude and screaming, but the muscular German was having none of it. On camera Metzer noiselessly shouted at her and pointed under the bed, letting go of her hand as he reacted to something in the hallway.

Metzer trained his weapon on the door as Mary crawled under the bed behind him, and moments later Metzer opened fire on the doorway in short bursts. Through the thick concrete walls of the safe room Hollis could hear the dull thud of the shots less than thirty feet away in his bedroom. A blade of fire stabbed forth from Metzer's weapon, illuminating the intense expression on his face—but only for a few moments before a dark form raced into-frame and lashed out with twin blades in a lightning-fast one-two strike that cut Metzer into three sections: head, torso, and legs. The blades crisscrossed again, inhumanly fast, chopping the pieces into pieces. Metzer's body fell apart like quarters of beef, spraying the room with gore.

Hollis stared in shock at the screen.

The dark silhouette of the attacker moved farther into the room, twirling the twin blades to shed excess blood—spattering the walls into a macabre modern art display.

What the camera revealed beneath the emergency lights was a machine—both familiar and alien. It was a powerful racing motorcycle, but it had no rider, just a series of whip antennas and sensors. The entire bike was covered in blades that bristled like cooling fins along both sides. Where handlebars would normally be, it wielded twin swords at the end of mechanized gambols. The entire length of the machine was drenched in blood, as though it had hacked its way in here through every security man Hollis had. And every inch of the metal appeared to be engraved with symbols and glyphs—like some sort of high-tech religious relic.

The machine stood with the aid of hydraulic kick-stands it had extended. After spinning its blades clean, it folded the blades back behind its bullet-pocked cowling. Two more identical machines rolled into Hollis's bed-room behind it.

Hollis collapsed into his console chair and stared in incomprehension at the monitor. What he was looking at made no sense.

Swirling green laser light issued from the headlight assemblies of the bikes. The scene took on the appear-ance of a laser light show as the beams spread through Metzer's lingering gun smoke and traced brilliant lines along the walls and furniture in the shadows—scanning for something.

Without warning, one of the bikes roared through the bathroom doorway. Hollis could see in the mirror where it crashed through the thin wardrobe room doors. They caved in like paper, and now Hollis could actu-ally hear the muted throbbing of a powerful motorcycle engine just beyond his panic room door.

It knew where he was.

He swiveled his chair to face the solid steel door ten feet away. That door was the only thing that stood between him and a gruesome death. His heart was hammering so hard it felt like it had moved up into his throat. Hollis dug through the desk drawer and produced a Sig Sauer P220 Super Match pistol. He chambered a round and took another glance at the bedroom monitor.

The other two bikes had flipped the bed over with their sword arms, revealing the naked and helpless Mary beneath. She lay curled up, silently screaming beneath the blinding laser lights.

Oh god. No . . .

But perhaps this would appease them?

The bikes just stood observing Mary as she shrieked in terror at the sight of Metzer's butchered remains on the floor around her. Hollis decided he would do something for Mary's family after this. He would find out more about her. He'd help her family.

But the machines didn't attack. Instead, they just stood watching as she got to her feet and fled the room.

Maybe she was part of this after all . . .

Hollis tapped buttons on the console, bringing up the image outside his safe room door. There he could see the third machine waiting. It seemed to know exactly where the concealed door was. From blueprints? There was no doubt that whoever was behind this had serious power. Access to his communications and electrical layout would have been no problem for someone who could do this. It was his secure room that had saved him, and there was no home automation link to its steel door. Once locked, it could only be opened manually from the inside.

Suddenly the house phone rang on the console next to him. Hollis recoiled from it. He glanced up at the screen again. The bloodstained machine stood impassively outside, still aimed at the secret door.

The phone rang again, and Hollis just stared at it. Perhaps it was someone on the security team? Hollis pressed the speakerphone button. "Hello?"

The line was silent for a moment—but then his own voice came back to him, talking fast, as Hollis always did on business calls. . . .

"Even if the U.S. markets crash, we'll make money. Movement is all we need—positive or negative makes no difference. . . ."

It was definitely Hollis's voice. Someone had tapped his phone calls. Another clip immediately followed. . . .

"What a company does is irrelevant. What a company makes is irrelevant. The market is a math problem we solve through value extraction."

Someone somewhere had intercepted his words. But why?

Looking at the remorseless killing machine outside, he somehow couldn't picture it being spawned by human rights activists. Whoever was behind it was decidedly more dangerous.

His laughing voice came to him again over the speaker. *"We made it legal. Our people wrote the congressional bill."*

On the security monitor a different type of bike entered the wardrobe room. This machine wasn't covered in blades, but in piping and pressure tanks. As it came in, the other bike moved aside. The new arrival slammed down hydraulic jacks to plant it firmly just outside the panic room door. Then, instead of twin blade arms, it extended a single robotic nozzle arm, with hoses trailing back along its length to half a dozen pressure tanks. A spark flashed, and then a white-hot flame suddenly stabbed out from the nozzle—instantly turning the wood paneling in front of the panic room door into a solid wall of flame.

Hollis stared at the machine on-screen, paralyzed in fear. He knew what it was. He'd owned stock in steel mills in the nineties. It was a plasma torch. Someone had mounted it on this terror machine, and it now stood before his safe room door, blasting aside the wooden millwork surrounding his bunker as though it were nothing more than ash. Already the scores of fine suits and leather shoes and carpeting in the wardrobe room were engulfed in flames as the twenty-five-thousand-degree cutting head on the machine penetrated the steel door like a knife through modeling clay.

The sprinkler system leapt into action, spraying water over the outside room, but the fire's intensity vaporized it. The surveillance camera showed the remorseless machines standing their ground, one cutting, the other waiting, but soon, even the camera started to fail—and melt. The screen turned grainy and then went black.

Behind him, Hollis was suddenly deafened by a burst of pressure and a cracking sound as a white-hot jet of plasma burst through the steel doorway and began tracing a molten line along the length of the door. The sofa and wet bar beyond it burst into flames, and the glass cover of the flat-screen television shattered—the whole thing folding over itself like a big wax candle. Blue-hot sparks of molten steel scattered like marbles across the concrete floor. The safe room sprinklers popped and started raining over everything to no effect.

Hollis's recorded voice still spoke to him over the speakerphone as he sat in a catatonic state, while the sprinklers soaked him with freezing water.

"Pure math frees us to create unlimited profit."

Already the torch had finished cutting through the vault-like door. In a moment a huge section of steel fell forward with a crash that shook the concrete floor. The door's edges still glowed red. Hollis turned to watch with the detachment of someone on morphine.

As he began to feel the heat of the flames outside and inside, even through all the water raining down on him, the killing machine entered his safe room and unfolded both sword blades with swift precision. The bike was stained with cooked blood and charred flesh. Steam rose from its metal frame.

Hollis put the pistol against his head as the killing machine moved toward him. It raised its blades in the same way he'd seen it do with Metzer.

There was no escape. Hollis pulled the trigger.

Nothing happened. The safety was on.

Hollis's own words were the last thing he heard as he fumbled for the gun's safety switch. . . .

"The beauty of it is: they can't afford to let us fail. . . ."

Chapter 2: // Operation Exorcist

Reuters.com

High-profile Assassinations Stun **Financial Community—Attacks** that left scores of financial **executives dead** worldwide have rattled the reclusive billionaires' club. Security services in the **U.S., Great Britain, Japan,** and **China** have withheld details of **sixty-one** nearly simultaneous **killings** that appear to be part of a coordinated campaign reminiscent of last year's **spammer massacre.**

No one has claimed responsibility for the attacks. However, the **murders** highlight growing resentment over outsized executive compensation in the midst of **skyrocketing unemployment.**

The surveillance video showed a man screaming as a robotic motorcycle wielding twin swords chopped him to pieces.

A voice spoke in the darkness. "Who was he?"

"Anthony Hollis—ran a highly successful hedge fund."

"Has his name been in the news?"

"Yes. Lots of detractors in the business press. Four hundred and six negative mentions in the past year alone." A pause. "You think the Daemon botnet is behind this?"

"Play it back. Slowly."

The video replayed in slow motion, frame by frame. A blade-covered motorcycle advanced on the cornered man. The image stopped, then zoomed in. Though motion blurred, the screen was frozen in midstroke, a sword leveled at the man's neck while spiraling lasers in the bike's headlight assembly illuminated his terrified face.

"Unmanned vehicle. Like some sort of ground-level Predator drone. Daemon operatives call them 'razorbacks.' The same type Dr. Philips described in her report on the attack at Building Twenty-Nine."

"So the Daemon is conducting class warfare now?"

"I don't think so. These people were all engaged in a specific type of financial activity."

"Sobol *did* say his Daemon would 'eliminate parasites in the system.' Could it have viewed Hollis and the others as parasites?"

A third voice joined the discussion. "With all due respect, these killings are just a distraction from the real problem."

"Perhaps, but they reveal something important about the Daemon's purpose. Bring up the lights, please."

Suddenly the room illuminated, revealing the heads of America's intelligence services sitting around a circular boardroom table in Building OPS-2B of National Security Agency headquarters. Plaques stood in front of everyone present—NSA, CIA, FBI, DARPA, DIA—as well as several visitors from the private intelligence and security sectors; suited executives from Computer Systems Corporation (CSC), its subsidiaries—EndoCorp and Korr Military Solutions—and a principal from the lobbying firm Byers, Carroll, and Marquist (BCM).

Their host scanned the room.

NSA: "The late Matthew Sobol created his Daemon as a news-reading computer virus. It activated two years ago at the appearance of Sobol's obituary in online news, and has since spread throughout the world, siphoning capital from corporate hosts to sustain a network of human operatives who distribute and protect it. It has already used these operatives to destroy the data and backup tapes of companies that try to remove it. The question is: how do we kill the Daemon without precipitating a 'digital doomsday'?"

DIA: "That's the dilemma. If we act, the Daemon will *react* and destroy the corporate networks it's infected."

DARPA: "But we can't just do *nothing*. It continues to launch attacks—like it did against the Daemon Task Force at Building Twenty-Nine and these recent assassinations."

NSA: "Thousands of people are already dead worldwide—dozens of federal officers are dead. And I have to ask myself how a software construct with the intelligence of a tapeworm managed to do this to us. The free market quest for efficiency has made our infrastructure vulnerable."

BCM: "You can't expect the market to operate *inefficiently*. Efficiency is what makes modern life possible."

NSA: "Yes, but we might need to place a greater emphasis on resiliency."

CSC (gesturing to the screen): "Why? Because a few people are dead? These machines are not militarily significant. They're glorified toys."

NSA: "I was speaking more in terms of network security—but these razorbacks are becoming a serious public relations problem as well. Witnesses have seen these machines navigating at night on highways. People are uploading videos to Web sites."

BCM: "We're already aware of these videos, and are taking steps to minimize their public impact."

NSA: "My point is that we may soon have no choice but to reveal the existence of the Daemon to the general public."

BCM: "That will be difficult, Mr. Director—especially after going through so much effort to convince the public the Daemon was a hoax. How would you explain executing Peter Sebeck for a crime that never occurred?"

FBI: "That wasn't our doing."

BCM: "Nonetheless. If word got out that the Daemon had taken control of thousands of corporate networks, it would cause a stock market panic."

CSC: "Mr. Director, we can assure you that none of these razorback videos will ever gain credibility by appearing in mainstream news."

NSA: "But they're being shared over the Internet. Millions of people have already seen them."

EndoCorp: "That's a manageable problem."

NSA: "What do you mean it's *manageable*?"

EndoCorp: "We've copyrighted the razorback."

NSA: "How does *copyrighting* them solve anything?"

EndoCorp: "Owning the IP gives us legal control of their image. We're spinning these viral videos as stealth advertising for an upcoming video game."

CSC: "Which means the general public won't take them seriously."

NSA: "Whose idea was this?"

CSC: "We don't get down in the weeds. It was done by our psy-ops division. As far as the Millennials are concerned, these razorbacks are just guerrilla marketing."

CIA: "But people have *witnessed* these things. People have *died*. How do we explain that?"

BCM: "Fact and fiction carry the same intrinsic weight in the marketplace of ideas. Fortunately, reality has no advertising budget."

CSC: "Persistence and presence create truth online."

EndoCorp: "We've neutralized eyewitnesses in Web forums by flaming them as shills for the game's whisper campaign. We've created 3-D models, and fictitious how-it-was-done videos to 'prove' surveillance clips and cell phone videos are fakes."

BCM: "So the public knows about razorbacks, but they don't really know what they know."

FBI: "Then we're using some of Sobol's jujitsu, then?"

BCM: "We might even see net revenue on the resulting video game."

CIA (shaking his head): "When I hear this crap, I start to understand why Sobol is attacking us."

FBI: "Don't even joke about that."

CIA: "Seriously, you're going to sit there and tell us your idea for combating the Daemon is to develop a video game around it? If Sobol were alive, he would be laughing at us."

CSC: "You said yourself that in the short term we can't remove the Daemon from infected networks without triggering catastrophic data loss. Until a reliable countermeasure is available the only thing we can do to avoid panicking the populace and further disturbing capital markets is to make sure everyone thinks the Daemon is just a fiction."

NSA: "And what happens when the Daemon's army of followers takes more aggressive action?"

CSC: "Then we call them terrorists—anything but 'Daemon followers.' But we cannot risk direct action against the Daemon itself until we find a way to disrupt its grip on corporate networks."

NSA: "We agree on that much at least."

DIA: "The U.S. dollar is already sliding. How do we know word hasn't gotten out among key investors?"

DARPA: "Sooner or later word *will* get out that the Daemon exists—or foreign powers will decrypt the Daemon's *Ragnorok* module and use the Daemon as an economic weapon against us. What do we do then?"

EndoCorp: "You've already got your answer: the *Ragnorok* module contains the key to destroying the Daemon. To crippling its command and control."

EndoCorp: "There are flaws in Sobol's code. Flaws we can exploit. We should have a Daemon countermeasure in a matter of months. But it's vital we not provoke the Daemon before we're ready."

NSA: "And you really suggest we do *nothing* to counteract these razorbacks or the Daemon's human operatives in the meantime?"

BCM: "Gentlemen, let's not forget what's at stake here. Yes, it's regrettable that people have died—and will die—but we must defend the core of our civilization: which is *commerce*. And commerce requires *capital*. That no longer means gold bars in a vault; it means ones and zeros in a database. Purely financial transactions moving through global markets on any given day outweigh transactions for *real-world* goods and services by twenty to one, and that money moves automatically and instantaneously across borders. By disrupting the world financial system, the Daemon could destroy fiduciary trust. It could create global economic chaos in minutes. From that point of view the real-world manifestations of the Daemon—like these razorbacks and its human followers—are minor; dangerous only insofar as they threaten the public's belief system. But if we kill the *digital* core of the Daemon, then its physical manifestations disappear along with it. This is what Operation Exorcist is designed to accomplish, and why it will succeed where the government effort failed."

DARPA: "No one has ever successfully exterminated a botnet."

EndoCorp: "Technically that's true, but what we're contemplating is disrupting its key communications to render it defenseless. In particular the Destroy function of the *Ragnorok* module. The logic that initiates a corporate data destruction sequence on demand."

NSA: "Which would take away the Daemon's claws . . ."

BCM: "Precisely."

DIA: "It's interesting that Sobol designed online game worlds. Worlds with millions of players buying and selling virtual objects. I just never realized how similar his game economy was to our own."

BCM: "The chief difference is that *our* world is real—with real consequences. And unless we preserve faith in capital markets, all economic activity ceases. Society disintegrates into anarchy. And millions perish."

Silence prevailed as the others digested this. Finally their host spoke.

NSA: "There's one more item we need to discuss. A new development."

He picked up a remote and turned off the video screen.

NSA: "Not all corporations are fighting the Daemon."

BCM: "What do you mean?"

NSA: "Sixteen lawsuits were filed by Daemon-infected multinationals yesterday in federal district courts."

Now the corporate side of the table fell into stunned silence for a moment.

BCM: "Which companies?"

NSA (handing over a list): "They're filing suit against the U.S. government. Its lawyers claim that the Daemon has a constitutional right to exist under the precedent of corporate personhood."

CSC: "Holy hell . . ."

BCM: "The Daemon has *lawyers*?"

NSA: "And it's retained lobbyists. We're negotiating with the courts to keep these cases classified; however, we can't be certain what the judicial branch is going to do about them."

BCM: "This is insane. The Daemon is a computer virus, not a corporation."

NSA: "But it's not the Daemon that's filing suit. These are multinational corporations that *host* the Daemon. Their management feels that the Daemon gives them an advantage."

BCM: "What advantage?"

NSA: "Survival, for one. They feel that the Daemon has a better handle on cyber security and might help them weather an anticipated period of coming chaos."

BCM: "This is extortion. The Daemon will destroy their data if they don't comply. RICO statutes cover this. And I see several firms on this list that some of our clients hold significant stock positions in."

NSA: "But not a controlling interest?"

BCM: "It doesn't matter. The management of these firms has no right to defend the Daemon."

NSA: "They cite their right as 'artificial persons' granted in an 1886 Supreme Court ruling on the fourteenth amendment. . . ." He flipped through documents. "*Santa Clara County v. Southern Pacific Railroad*. You're a lawyer. You tell me if the courts will throw it out."

EndoCorp: "These attorneys are agents of the Daemon—a known terrorist organization."

NSA: "Maybe. Or maybe the attorneys are just following instructions from the corner office. We don't know yet. Either way, we should be able to get the courts to close a nineteenth-century loophole that has unanticipated twenty-first-century consequences."

BCM: "Wait. Let's just wait a second. There are complex considerations relating to an entire body of legal precedents on corporate personhood, and the rights of free speech to corporate interests have a necessary and guiding effect on policy. Let's not do anything rash. We should let these cases run their course. We'll have neutralized the Daemon before they get their day in court, and then these companies will be back in the fold."

CIA: "Is there something about that 1886 ruling we should know?"

BCM: "We don't want to rehash established precedents. This is part of the Daemon's effort to sow chaos."

CIA (writing notes): "What was the name of that case again?"

BCM: "*This* is a perfect example of why government isn't nimble enough to deal with the Daemon. It's using our own laws and government institutions against us. To divide us. We should be helping one another."

NSA: "Wait a minute. Nobody's dividing anyone. Does corporate personhood expose us to danger?"

BCM: "That's not the point. What I'm saying is that we can't follow legal niceties in dealing with this thing. We cannot demonstrate weakness. *Ever.*"

FBI: "Our laws demonstrate weakness?"

The corporate side of the table conferred for a moment,

and then the lobbyist turned to face the intelligence directors again. He took a calmer tone.

BCM: "Look, the current economic crisis has crippled state governments. States have begun to sell off assets to balance their budgets. They're outsourcing services and selling their highways, bridges, prisons."

NSA: "And?"

BCM: "We are buying them. We're *investing* in America. We—and the chairmen of intelligence funding committees in the House and Senate—hope you will defend our legitimate interests while we help America through this difficult period."

NSA: "Of course, you know that we will."

BCM: "We need wide latitude to deal with these dangers. I think you'll agree that it's in the best interests of the nation to make all tools available to us."

The two sides viewed each other across the table.

BCM: "I hope we can count on your support, Mr. Director. . . ."

Chapter 3: // Going Viral

What makes Roy Merritt's legend so powerful is that it was unintentional. He was a mere artifact on the surveillance tapes at the Sobol mansion siege, but his successful struggle against the impossible is what immortalized him as the Burning Man.

PanGeo**** / 2,194   12th-level Journalist

"Roy Merritt represented all that was best in us. That's what makes the loss of him so hard to bear." Standing before a flag-draped casket, the minister raised his voice to carry above a cold Kansas wind. "I knew Roy from the time he was a child. I knew his father and his mother. I saw him grow to become a loving husband, a caring father, and a respected citizen. He dedicated his life to public service and never gave up hope for anyone. In fact, Roy mentored some of the same troubled youth he faced in his law enforcement work. Blessed with a calm, physical courage Roy was often sent in harm's way to protect us, and it was on such a mission that he gave his life. Although we may find it hard to carry on without him, I think it is precisely *because* of Roy that we will be *able* to carry on."

A frigid wind whipped Natalie Philips's coat as she contemplated the minister's words. She stared at the coffin in front of her. Lost in thought, she didn't feel the cold.

FBI Special Agent Roy Merritt and seventy-three others were dead because of her—killed on a top-secret operation she had led. An operation that had culminated in a disaster at a place she'd rather not remember: Building Twenty-Nine. Building Twenty-Nine was gone now, vaporized. But she would never stop reliving what had happened there. It was an operation no one else at this funeral knew anything about.

At some point in her reverie the minister had stopped talking and uniformed men had begun ceremonially folding the American flag. They extended it to a Marine Corps major general who in turn presented the flag to Merritt's young widow.

"Ma'am, on behalf of the president of the United States, the director of the FBI, and a grateful nation, please accept this flag as a symbol of our appreciation for your husband's service to his country."

Merritt's widow received the flag stoically, tears streaming down her face, as her two small daughters clung to her.

The bureau had presented his widow with a Memorial Star and posthumously bestowed on Merritt the Medal of Valor. Philips wondered if anyone else thought it strange that a Marine Corps general was presenting a flag to an FBI agent's widow. The truth was that Roy Merritt was more of a hero than his family or his countrymen would ever know.

He shouldn't even be dead, but then, everyone who had served under Philips was dead or missing—all their work destroyed. It was the biggest clandestine service disaster in forty years, and Philips owned that failure. She might as well have perished with the rest of her team.

Philips took a deep breath and looked up at the massive crowd that had gathered for Merritt's service. More than two thousand people stood among the headstones of Jackson County Cemetery north of Topeka, hats off and heads lowered. Two hundred and fourteen police cruisers and FBI sedans lined the cemetery road behind them, extending out onto the county highway.

She knew the number precisely. It was her curse to know. Her mind gathered everything she saw, and it forgot nothing. That had been her claim to fame in the NSA's Crypto division, but it was increasingly a cross she had to bear as well. This day and the days leading up to it ran like an IMAX film in her head each night as she tried in vain to sleep.

Nearby, Merritt's widow held her daughters close. The eldest child hid her face in her mother's coat, but the youngest, only four, was looking around at the other adults, trying to figure out what was happening. When their gazes met, even from behind tinted, wraparound medical glasses, Philips felt her own eyes well with tears.

Philips had failed everyone.

She couldn't withstand the little girl's eyes. Instead

she turned away and moved back through the headstones and the mourners, tears coming freely now. Philips wept as she moved among the living and the dead, wondering if her mind was capable of forgetting.

An honor guard fired three salvoes, startling Philips and provoking recollections of the desperate gunfire at Building Twenty-Nine. She felt panic rising and kept moving through the crowd. People made way for her. Kansas State Troopers in dress uniform, military men and women, local townspeople, children—people whose lives Merritt had touched. Some had traveled thousands of miles to be here. At the memorial service the night before, a hundred people stood up to tell heartwarming stories of Roy's courage, compassion, and humor.

She recognized some of these people now as she walked past. A reformed felon. A Pashtun translator from Balochistan who was now on his way to becoming an American citizen. Merritt's captain from his state police days. A Mexico City banker whose daughter Roy had rescued from kidnappers in a daring raid—and on and on.

As an agent in the FBI's elite Hostage Rescue Team, Merritt had traveled the world and always into danger. But he brought the values he'd gained in this small town with him wherever he went. It had taken his death to finally bring him home.

Philips kept moving through the mourners. A young priest. City officials. A well-dressed woman in sports glasses.

Philips halted. *Sports glasses.* Her mind never missed details. She recalled the moments just before the attack. Merritt had come to her lab to bring captured Daemon equipment from Sao Paulo, Brazil. He'd brought her sports glasses—glasses that were actually a sophisticated heads-up display (or HUD) able to see into a virtual dimension. An *augmented reality* the Daemon had overlaid on the GPS grid. Sports glasses were the user interface to the Daemon.

She turned to look back at the woman, who was moving slowly but deliberately through the crowd as though searching for something. Philips turned to follow her but passed another mourner, a middle-aged man in a black suit, wearing similar glasses. The thick posts and unusual design of these glasses could easily be ignored as an annoying new fashion, but they could not be a coincidence. The man glanced at her and kept walking, also seemingly searching for something. Hot fear surged through her.

Daemon operatives are here.

Could they really be brazen enough to attend Merritt's funeral? Her tears stopped. She palmed her L3 SME secure cell phone and marched purposefully through the crowd, putting distance between herself and the operatives. Before she walked ten feet she saw another man wearing HUD glasses. Philips stepped behind a tall headstone and looked for a sheltered place to phone for help. At the edge of the crowd she saw a weatherworn burial vault and headed toward it.

As she walked, she kept spotting Daemon operatives, moving through the mourners in a skirmish line, still scanning for something. There seemed to be no standard profile. They were equally male or female, young to middle-aged. There were dozens of them.

As Philips stepped behind the granite burial vault, she flipped open her phone—but then realized that she didn't know who to call. Roy Merritt would have been her first choice. In fact, just about everyone she could think of calling was now dead or missing. There were hundreds of police officers and FBI agents all around her attending the funeral, but they wouldn't have any idea how dangerous these people were. And what about the innocent people in the crowd? Did she really want to provoke a confrontation? But the operatives were here for a purpose. She had to do something.

It was then that Philips noticed she had no cell signal. There was no service at all.

"It's rude to make phone calls at a funeral."

Philips looked up to see a twentysomething man dressed in a dark suit, overcoat, and black gloves. An FBI badge hung from his breast pocket, giving him the appearance of an overeager rookie. She recognized him instantly. He was a Daemon operative. With short-cropped hair he was indistinguishable from a dozen other young FBI agents in the crowd, but unlike the other Daemon operatives he wore no glasses. Instead his pupils shone with the iridescence of mother-of-pearl—apparently contact lenses.

He was the one who had destroyed Daemon Task Force headquarters and slain all her people. This was Roy Merritt's killer. The highest-level Daemon operative known.

"Loki."

He approached her calmly, surveying the crowd. "I hear Roy didn't have much in the way of family. Who the hell *are* all these people?"

"You made a mistake coming here."

"Look. Actual tears on people's faces. I don't think you or I will draw a crowd like this, Doctor. What is it about Roy Merritt that inspires everyone so much?"

Philips glared. "It has to do with serving others—something you'd know nothing about."

He stood silently for a beat. "I serve a greater good."

"You're a mass murderer who worships at the feet of a dead lunatic."

"Is that right?" He noticed her still punching keys on her phone. "Don't bother. It's being jammed."

Philips lowered it. "Why would you bring your people here?"

"They're not my people. They came on their own. There's a video simulcast of the funeral beaming out to the darknet. Hundreds of thousands are watching this event worldwide."

"Why, so they can gloat over their victory?"

He gave her a sideways glance. "Don't be a bitch, Doctor. This was no victory. Roy Merritt is the famous Burning Man to them. A worthy adversary who's gone viral. There's no predicting these things in a network. The factions came to pay their last respects—and to find his killer."

She thought he was being glib, but he looked serious. "If that's true, how do you think they'll react when they find out *you* killed Roy?"

He smiled grimly. "They all know what happened. You're the only one without a clue." He stared at her intently.

Loki pointed to Philips's tinted glasses. "How are

your eyes, Doctor? Corneal damage? You must have been close."

Anger rose within her at his mention of the attack at Building Twenty-Nine. "There are hundreds of police officers around us. You won't escape this time."

"Did you expect me to go into hiding? Is that it? Well, I've grown beyond hiding, Doctor. Besides, it would be a shame to sully the memory of Roy Merritt by turning his funeral into a massacre."

She studied his face and decided he wasn't bluffing. "We will stop you."

"You can't even stop tweens from stealing music. How are you going to stop *me*? Feds: always overreaching. And what if you could stop me?" He gestured to the Daemon operatives still moving through the crowd. "It wouldn't stop them."

"We'll find the Daemon's weak spot sooner or later, and we'll destroy it. If you help me, I'll see that you're treated with leniency."

"You really have no idea what's going on, do you? You're like Merritt was. A true believer. You should have listened to Jon Ross: never trust a government."

He noticed the momentary look of shock on her face. "You did *know* The Major was spying on you, right? Tapping into his surveillance system was what gave me access to everything on your task force. Including your private conversations with the illustrious Mr. Ross."

Philips felt doubly defeated and stood grasping for something to say.

"I have video from every camera at Building Twenty-Nine before it was destroyed." He paused. "By the way, you and Jon Ross should just have fucked and gotten it over with."

Philips couldn't help a pang of loss at the mention of Ross's name. Not an hour passed when she didn't think about him—and how he'd saved her life. She recalled their last moment together. Then she purposely met Loki's gaze. "Get to the point."

"Have I upset you? I didn't think you'd go for the criminal type, Doctor."

"Jon Ross is dead."

"So I hear." Loki slipped a hand into his jacket. "You might find some of my surveillance video interesting." He withdrew a metallic scroll and offered it to Philips.

She hesitated.

"If I came here to kill you, Doctor, I wouldn't waste time talking first. Just open it."

She took the metallic scroll and pulled the twin tubes apart to reveal a glossy, flexible video screen already glowing with electrical energy.

"You don't understand the Daemon. You keep thinking it's something we obey like automatons. But that's not it at all. The Daemon's darknet is just a reflection of the people in it. It's a new social order. One that's immune to bullshit."

She held the flexible screen up as it began to play security camera video from within Building Twenty-Nine—just before the entire place was obliterated by a massive demolition charge. The scene showed Philips, Ross, a man known only as "The Major," and several black-clad Korr security guards, standing near body bags in the gaming pit. The Major was officially the Daemon

Task Force's Department of Defense liaison—although, he'd also been connected with the Special Collections Service, a section of the CIA. At present, neither organization acknowledged his existence and his identity remained classified, even to her.

On-screen The Major was aiming a Glock 9mm pistol at Philips's face. Jon Ross rushed to stand between them.

She felt torn at the sight of Ross's handsome face. Seeing him stand in harm's way for her.

In the real world Loki waved a gloved hand and froze the image. He pointed at The Major. "You remember this asshole?"

She nodded.

Loki pulled at the air with his gloved hand and the image zoomed in. The quasi-DOD liaison officer wore a tan sports jacket with a dark green button-down shirt. "A great many people have not forgotten him."

Another wave of his hand and the image switched to a high-def video of a mortally wounded Roy Merritt lying in the middle of an industrial street. Blood covered Roy's torso. He was panting and staring at two small photographs in his hand. A flash appeared in the doorway of a helicopter in the distance, and Merritt's head exploded.

Philips recoiled in horror. Remorse flooded over her again. She glared at Loki with hatred. "*This* is what you wanted me to see? Do you find some twisted enjoyment in this?"

"It's car camera video from my AutoM8. The cameras are part of the navigation system. I uploaded these videos to the darknet, and the crowd soon found the answer." He pulled at the air with his black gloves, and the video screen in Philips's hands zoomed in on the shooter in the helicopter doorway. The HD image looked grainy at this magnification, but the hooded figure in the doorway was clear enough. The shooter was wearing a tan sports jacket and a dark green button-down shirt. Loki waved his hand again and the screen split in two, with the earlier image of The Major holding a pistol to Philips's head alongside the image of the shooter in the doorway of the helicopter. They were dressed identically. They were the same person.

Philips lowered the flexible screen and stared into space. "The Major."

"Yes, The Major. Didn't you wonder why no second helicopter arrived to pick you up? You're not supposed to be alive, Doctor."

She nodded absently. "They don't want to stop the Daemon. They want to control it."

"Which makes you pretty much the only person still trying to stop it. Your own side doesn't want you to succeed." He nodded toward Merritt's casket. "And they didn't want Roy triggering economic Armageddon before they could shift their investments."

"The Major . . . killed Roy. . . ." She could barely get the words out.

"And they'll finish you yet." He pulled the screen out of her hands. "I'd watch your back, if I were you."

She looked up suddenly. "Why are you telling me this, Loki?"

"Where is The Major?"

"I don't know."

"Find out."

"He's my problem, not yours."

Loki tucked the scroll-screen back into his coat. "That's where you're wrong. The Major is everyone's problem."

Philips gestured to the operatives moving among the mourners. "Is that why they're here?"

"Like I said, they're not with me. Although, a million darknet operatives want vengeance for the Burning Man. I'm guessing they'll tear apart heaven and earth to get it. There's a high-priority Thread queued just for The Major. We have his biometric data from Building Twenty-Nine's security system to help. His fingerprints. His iris scan. His voice. His face. His walk. We will find him, Doctor. But if you help me, I'll see that you're treated with *leniency*."

She knew he was mocking her now. "I want nothing to do with you. We have laws in this country, and I intend to make sure The Major faces justice and that you face justice."

"Justice? That'll be difficult when *you* might be facing disciplinary charges yourself."

Philips felt the rage building again. She didn't know whether he was guessing or actually knew. The disaster at Building Twenty-Nine had indeed been laid at her feet. The Major wasn't mentioned anywhere in the after-action reports. It was as if he never existed.

Loki turned back toward the funeral service. "If you find The Major, let me know, and the swarm will take care of him."

"You know I won't do that."

"You might be surprised what you'll do. Especially when you discover what they've done with your laws." Loki narrowed his eyes at something in the distance.

Philips followed his gaze toward the edge of the funeral crowd. A scuffle of some sort had broken out there. She could see at least one person being grabbed by plainclothes officers about half a football field away.

Loki watched with his shimmering eyes. "They never disappoint, do they? Leave while you can, Doctor."

"Loki, don't. There are hundreds of innocent people here."

He ignored her, already manipulating unseen dark-net objects with his gloved hands. "They just couldn't resist. . . ."

She stood between Loki and the distant scuffle. "This will be a bloodbath. Please, Loki. Don't do this!"

He spoke while looking through her; his hands moved frantically. "Did you know your friend Jon Ross joined the Daemon's darknet recently, Doctor? I thought you might want to know."

She stopped—unsure whether to believe him. The news hit her hard. She backed away from Loki and tried to contain her emotions. First she lost Merritt, now Ross, and now she felt she could trust no one. She felt the tears coming again. *Not Jon.*

Loki spoke to some unseen person. "Fuck waiting. I've dropped Angel Teeth. Everyone clear the area." A pause. "I don't give a shit."

Philips turned away from Loki and ran toward the disturbance. He didn't try to stop her. Fifty yards away, among cemetery headstones, she could see men in suits trying to overpower several people she assumed must be Daemon operatives. One of the agents held aloft a pair of sports glasses as more agents converged on the site. They were already securing a perimeter.

The mourners Philips passed by had begun to turn toward the scuffle. She noticed small children with many of them and shouted, "Evacuate the area!"

Several responded by saying, "I'm a police officer," and followed her.

In half a minute Philips had pushed her way up to a dark-suited man with a radio earpiece. He was part of the security cordon around the still-struggling knot of two dozen men.

Philips displayed her NSA credentials and spoke calmly but firmly. "I'm a federal officer. You must evacuate this cemetery as soon as possible. These mourners are in great danger."

The thick-necked agent didn't bother to examine Philips's credentials. He just looked at her. "Stand clear, ma'am."

"Damnit, let me speak with the agent in charge! I have firsthand knowledge of an impending attack!"

He smiled humorlessly and spoke with an indistinct accent. "We've got it under control. Thanks."

Suddenly gunshots crackled in the cold air. People in the crowd screamed and ducked. The mourners began to flee like a spooked herd—except for the dozens of police that remained behind, drawing weapons and heading toward the shots. Philips knew they'd be agents from the FBI, DSS, DEA, ATF, and a host of state and local police. Scores of them advanced using the tombstones for cover.

Philips faced the approaching agents and police and held up her credentials. "Stay back! Stay back! You're in danger!"

The first wave of officers had already reached her, their various weapons pointed upward but ready. A distinguished-looking man in his fifties, a take-charge type without a weapon, came right up to Philips. "What the hell is going on?"

Before Philips could answer, everyone turned to see another black-suited, clean-cut man approaching from within the dense knot of operators who'd started the disturbance. The man held up credentials with a familiar logo on them—Korr Security International.

"This is a top secret DOD-sanctioned operation, gentlemen."

The senior agent frowned and examined the operator's ID. "I'm S-A-C of the FBI's Kansas City office. I don't take instructions from private security contractors." He pushed past, along with scores of other federal agents and local police, guns still at the ready.

They pushed through a couple dozen plainclothes men with radio earpieces and submachine guns pointed skyward.

"Jesus H. Christ, who the hell authorized a takedown in the middle of a thousand innocent people?"

Philips followed on the senior agent's heels.

Korr officers held up their hands. "Sir! You can't come in here!"

"I'm in charge of the FBI's Kansas City office, and

until I see some government badges, I'll go where I damn well please!"

The swarm of police and federal agents broke through to the center of the Korr team. The scene there shocked everyone.

Six bodies lay steaming on the frozen grass in a pool of blood, with more blood spattered over nearby headstones. One was a wounded Korr officer gulping air and being tended to by his colleagues. The other bodies looked to be Daemon operatives—one of them a young woman—lifeless eyes staring skyward. Philips noticed hundreds of footprints trampling the ground, indicating a mighty struggle.

The FBI SAC stood agape. "Mother of god . . ."

A tall, muscular Korr officer came up to him, showing credentials. "Sir, this is a top secret military operation. I need you to call—"

Suddenly there was a high-pitched whistle, followed by a sharp *thwack*. Everyone stared in horror at a dagger-shaped steel point that now protruded from the Korr officer's left cheek. Blood ran from his nose and a large steel dart now extended from the top rear of his skull, like a sinister plume, with an antenna rising out the back. The stricken Korr officer staggered with a surprised look on his face. Servomotors on the vanes of the dart whirred and adjusted in response to his movements—apparently the guidance system.

The man collapsed as the others stared in shock.

And then more whistling was heard.

Without a word everyone scattered.

As she ran, Philips looked up into the clear Kansas

sky and saw several glints of steel coming in. She dodged between tombstones as she heard the ringing of steel spikes ricocheting off stone behind her. Screams of pain came on the wind, and she turned to see first one, and then another Korr officer drop as they fled with the rest of the crowd—singled out by the deadly rain. Many of the darts missed their mark, but the spikes were relentless, eventually striking flesh and bringing the Korr men down, one by one. She saw an injured man try to get back up, only to be struck in the back by several more darts.

Philips slowed and watched in amazement as a Korr officer threw down his MP-5 submachine gun and ran toward other officers—who avoided him like the plague.

"Help me! Someone help me! Help!"

There was no cover in the middle of the vast Kansas cemetery, and he zigzagged among the mournful monuments as spikes clanged off stone and buried themselves in the grass behind him.

But finally a dart struck the man in the shoulder. He fell—only to be struck by several more darts as he crawled on the ground.

A Kansas state trooper in dress uniform grabbed Philips by the arm. "Miss, stay back!"

She cast her gaze farther afield, seeing more Korr contractors in the distance—visible because they ran alone or in pairs, slaloming, only to be struck down by a series of glinting missiles.

It was a surgical strike. Philips looked back where Loki had been, but as she expected, he was gone. In the far distance she could see thousands of mourners fleeing to their cars. She knew that finding Loki among them would be next to impossible—not to mention dangerous to the public.

She looked over toward Roy Merritt's deserted gravesite and cursed Loki. And The Major.

Their war would never stop—not even to honor the dead.

Chapter 4: // End of the Line

"**Y**ou know who you look like? That guy who killed all those cops. The one they executed."

Pete Sebeck leveled his gaze at the convenience store clerk. She was a matronly Caucasian woman in her fifties. A portable television blared on a shelf behind her, tuned to the most popular tabloid news show in the country—*News to America*. Rotating graphics and techno music in the opening sequence proved distracting. "Well, if they executed him, I can't very well *be* him, can I?"

She laughed. "I'm not saying you *are* him. Just that you look like him."

Sebeck handed her a twenty-dollar bill.

She took the money. "Anyone ever tell you that?"

He shook his head.

"No offense. He was good-looking." She paused, tapping her stick-on nails on the counter. *Click-click-click.* "What was his name? The Daemon hoax guy. Killed a whole bunch of people. Almost got away with, like, a hundred million dollars."

"I don't recall."

She rang up the sale. "Man, that's gonna drive me crazy." She circled her face while clutching his change.

"It's in your face. He was on television every day for, like, a year. His head wasn't shaved, though. And he didn't have the Van Dyke."

"The what?"

"The beard."

"Is that what this is called?"

"You trim it like that, and you don't even know what it's called?" She laughed and handed over his change. "It's called a Van Dyke. My ex-husband had one. Used it to cover a port-wine stain on his chin. Some people get the Van Dyke confused with the Winnfield or the Anchor, but they're not the same thing."

Her eyes suddenly went wide. "Sebeck! That was his name, Pete Sebeck. He was a *detective*, too. Did you know that? Killed his best friend, a woman, and, like, a dozen FBI agents before they caught him."

Sebeck stared at her through sports glasses. "Well, he's dead now." He grabbed his energy drinks off the counter.

"Need a bag?"

"No, thanks."

On the television behind her Sebeck couldn't help but notice the blond, lip-glossed news model, Anji Anderson, stoking public hysteria about the latest pre-packaged threat. It was especially ironic since Sebeck knew that, like him, Anderson was a Daemon operative. He still couldn't figure out how she fit into Sobol's master plan. In the two years he'd been in prison before his faked execution, Anderson had used sexed-up innocence combined with self-righteous indignation to claw her way from obscurity to the top of the prime-time ratings. She'd turned Sebeck into an infamous serial killer. The Daemon had everything to do with that.

"How can you watch this crap?"

"Anji? She's great. I just love her. She's doing this whole series on the collapse of the U.S. dollar. It's on the way. There's not a damned thing we can do about it either. I'm savin' up cigarettes. They'll be like gold after the crash."

He stared at her for a moment to be certain she was serious, then walked out shaking his head.

Sebeck sat on a desert hillside in darkness, staring up at a brilliant field of stars in the crisp night air. The Milky Way was a smudge of light out of the corner of his eye. He took a deep breath and listened to the silence.

It felt good to get away from the highway.

Sebeck had been on the road for weeks; following a line only he could see, toward a destination even he did not know. Before this journey he had never thought of the modern world as a machine—with humanity just the cells of its body. But a lot had changed since his arrest and execution by the government—and his subsequent rescue by the Daemon.

As a cop, he found it difficult to accept that the law was an illusion. If the powers that be identified you as a threat, right or wrong, you were destroyed.

Was that the lesson Matthew Sobol had taught him by destroying the person Sebeck once was? Sebeck's only ally now was the very thing he'd been fighting against— the *Daemon*. No one knew how far its powers stretched or if it could be stopped. And the dead man who created it had assigned Sebeck a fearsome task.

Justify the freedom of humanity.

Coming from a software construct that had already orchestrated the deaths of thousands of people, it was a charge Sebeck didn't take lightly—and one he had no idea how to accomplish.

Each day he followed *the Thread*—a glowing blue line that existed in a private virtual dimension Daemon operatives called D-Space, which was visually overlaid on the GPS grid. It was an augmented reality, whose 3-D objects were visible only through HUD glasses the Daemon had provided for him. For weeks now the Thread had led Sebeck through the American Southwest, and finally up onto this hillside in the New Mexico desert. Wherever he was going, it seemed he was about to arrive.

Just then Sebeck heard labored breathing on the path below him. He saw an ethereal name call-out bobbing toward him in the fabric of D-Space. Name call-outs were a means of identifying other members of the Daemon's darknet (or encrypted network). The glowing words *Chunky Monkey* hovered three feet over a pear-shaped silhouette moving in the shadows. It was the network name of Laney Price, Sebeck's Daemon-assigned minder. Sebeck knew that a similar call-out reading *Unnamed_1* floated above his own head in D-Space. Matthew Sobol had indeed unnamed him by erasing Sebeck's existence to the modern world, and giving him a new life on the darknet.

Sebeck waited as Price labored toward him, then collapsed on the ground nearby. The light from pico projectors in Price's own HUD glasses cast a soft glow onto his face, revealing a twentysomething kid with a thick beard and a mane of unkempt black hair. His face shined with sweat.

"Couldn't we have . . . waited until daylight . . . Sergeant?"

"The Thread has never led us off the highway. We're close to something."

Price gazed around wearily. "It's really leading you out here?"

Sebeck could see the blue line extending like a crooked laser beam from where he stood, shooting uphill and disappearing over the ridgeline. It was the path Sobol had told him to follow. It was coded to him, and he was supposedly the only person in the world who could see it.

"You don't have to come with me."

"It's my job, Sergeant."

"You honestly don't know where the Thread is heading?"

Price shook his head. "I'm just another slob on the darknet. Like you."

"No. Not like me. You *volunteered* for the Daemon. That's the difference between us, Laney. Don't forget it—because I won't."

"For me it was an easy choice."

They sat for several minutes looking up at the stars and the occasional meteor trail.

Price nodded, soaking up the atmosphere. "It's pretty rockin' out here."

Sebeck jerked his thumb uphill. "Let's keep going."

In barely half a mile they crested the desert ridge in the moonlight. Price was panting and cursing by the time they reached the top. Sebeck was still in good physical shape—his prison ritual of sit-ups and push-ups remained the first thing he did every morning.

A quarter moon and a brilliant field of stars illuminated the surrounding mesas. Ahead Sebeck could see clustered shadows. The Thread led straight toward them.

"There's something up ahead."

Price was still sucking wind. "Anasazi Indian ruins."

"How do you know that?"

"D-Space geotags. Layer nine. I could show you how to—"

"And you claim you don't know where we're headed. Sure. . . ." Sebeck continued down the path.

Behind him Price cursed again and struggled to keep up.

Soon they came to the edge of stone ruins. They were taller than Sebeck would have expected for ancient Indian dwellings. The thick masonry walls were still several stories high, pierced by windows and doorways. He'd heard of cliff dwellers in the Southwest, but not freestanding stone buildings.

The Thread led directly through a low doorway in the face of a towering masonry wall. Sebeck approached and reached out his hand to run it along the wall's face. It was remarkably straight and tightly constructed.

He kneeled down to look ahead and could see moonlight illuminating several roofless rooms, connected by a series of open doorways that lined up perfectly.

The sound of Price's footsteps were behind him. Sebeck turned. "Why are we here, Laney?"

"I told you, man. I don't know. I'm just supposed to help you reach your goal—that doesn't mean I know where it is."

Sebeck glared at him, then ducked into the rooms beyond. Price followed, and they moved cautiously through roofless rooms. Walls loomed above them, framing a field of stars.

Before long the Thread led Sebeck down a worn stone stairway, and out into a circular chamber about forty feet in diameter, open to the sky. Above them, the distant mesas and cliffs of the canyon formed a jagged silhouette along the horizon. Twenty-foot walls surrounded the space, with several more entrances leading into it, but here the Thread ended in a swirling aura of blue light that floated above the glowing apparition of a man. The ghostly figure wore a Victorian jacket and tie, and leaned on a silver shod cane.

It was a man Sebeck knew—the digital ghost of Matthew Sobol. The creator of the Daemon. Sobol's avatar looked healthier than when Sebeck saw it last. It now took the form of a brown-haired, thirtysomething man— apparently how Sobol appeared before his brain cancer wasted him away. Weeks ago, Sobol's recorded avatar had appeared to him in D-Space and offered Sebeck the opportunity to justify the freedom of humanity. Insane or not, it was a task Sebeck had dared not refuse. Especially given the Daemon's growing power.

Sebeck glanced back at Price. "Can you see what I'm seeing?"

Price nodded emphatically. "Hell yeah. Looks like he recorded it before his surgery."

"Then it's a recording?"

"Interactive temporal offset projection. A three-dimensional bot, waiting here in D-Space for a specific event to occur. I think your arrival is that event, Sergeant."

Sebeck turned back to face the glowing specter. The avatar was translucent, like all D-Space objects—a ghost.

Price nudged Sebeck. "Don't be chicken, man. Go chat it up."

Sebeck took a moment to collect himself, then walked out into the sandy open space of the circular room. It was almost like an arena, but a fire pit occupied the center. As Sebeck approached, the glowing D-Space aura chimed, then faded away—along with all trace of the Thread he'd followed.

Sobol's apparition nodded in greeting, and its voice came through Sebeck's headset. "Detective Sebeck, I'm glad you decided to undertake this quest. It will be long and difficult."

Sebeck sighed. "Great . . ."

Sobol's apparition gestured to the masonry walls that rose several stories above them—perfectly rectangular doors and windows piercing the stone faces. "Look at the precision. One might mistake it for modern architecture." He turned back to Sebeck. "And yet this pueblo was built almost a thousand years ago. At the very apex of Anasazi civilization."

With a wave of his hand, glowing D-Space lines

suddenly began to extend from the ruins, rising to complete the walls all around them—filling in the missing gaps and extending translucent 3-D walls and roofs above and around them. The immense structure was being rebuilt before their eyes. Pottery, possessions, and other objects appeared as though filling in a level map for a video game.

Avatars of Anasazi Indians walked through the doorway bearing baskets. Others moved through the rooms on their daily business, speaking to one another in their native tongue. Children ran past Sebeck, laughing. He could hear water flowing and song. Anasazi civilization had come back to life around them.

Price whistled behind him. "O-M-F-G . . ."

Sobol's avatar appeared to gaze approvingly on the scene.

"This structure contained six hundred rooms and rose as high as six stories. It was the tallest man-made construct in North America until the steel girder buildings of Chicago in the 1880s. The Anasazi supplied it with a network of eighty-foot-wide irrigation canals. They built four hundred miles of ruler-straight roads linking their capital to seventy-five outlying communities. They flourished here for centuries."

Sobol walked up to Sebeck and leaned on his cane. "Why did they perish, Sergeant? And so suddenly at the height of their achievements?"

Sebeck turned to observe the spectral avatars of ancient Anasazi priests coming into the great room in a procession, chanting. Like long departed spirits.

Sobol moved to let them pass. The priests didn't

notice him or Sebeck, but continued chanting as a spectral fire raged in the central fire pit, casting shadows that did not include either Sebeck or Sobol.

Sobol watched the priests closely. "Their fate holds important lessons for twenty-first-century man—because we are not exempt from nature's laws. When the survival strategy of a civilization is invalidated, in all of human history none have ever turned back from the brink. When presented with disruptive change, without exception they perish."

Sobol raised his arms, and with a wave of his hands the entire D-Space scene vanished—leaving only the real-world ruins again. And silence.

Sobol walked up to a ruinous window and looked out across the moonlit desert landscape. "But Anasazi civilization encompassed only this small region. By contrast our industrial civilization encompasses the entire earth. And should it falter, the resulting conflicts have the capacity to exterminate all human life."

Sobol gestured where the Indian priests had stood just moments before. "They made a simple enough mistake. The same one we're making. They founded their society on resource extraction, and in doing so, inflated their population beyond the carrying capacity of the land. They cut down all the trees and expanded arable land with irrigation projects. Until finally there were no more trees. And their topsoil washed away. And when drought came, their highly centralized society fell apart in bloodshed in a few short years."

Sobol walked to the edge of the now cold fire pit and poked it with his illusory cane. "Instead of adapting, their leaders clung to power and strove instead to be the last ones to starve to death. The Mayan civilization in South America did the same, and I expect our own civilization will do likewise. The people behind the modern global economy will prevent any meaningful change until it's too late."

The avatar looked to Sebeck. "But the question that needs to be answered is whether civilization's inability to adapt is a failure of leadership—or an unwillingness in humanity itself.

"Your quest comes at a critical time in human history, Sergeant. It's time we knew whether a durable democracy is possible—one whose laws are not just guidelines. One where individual rights cannot be ignored by the powerful. I leave this for you to prove. The Daemon will continue to expand, regardless. Whether it encompasses a distributed democracy or a ruthless hierarchy is up to people like you. Prove that the collective human will can prevent its own destruction, and you will have justified humanity's freedom. Fail, and humanity will serve the Daemon.

"So that all may know you . . ." Sobol aimed his cane at Sebeck's call-out. A bright D-Space light flashed on his call-out, and an icon appeared next to his network name. It depicted a towering cloud with an opening at its base, like a gateway. "This quest icon will be your mark. Your high quest is to find the Cloud Gate. You will have succeeded when you pass through its arch."

Sobol raised his other hand and a new, glowing Thread extended from it, racing south over the horizon in moments. "Your path leads not through the land, but through human events. It will lead you always into the heart of the changes now under way. And yet unless others lead the way, you will never reach your journey's end."

Sobol lowered his hand and stared into Sebeck's eyes. "Good luck, Sergeant. For the sake of future generations, I hope we meet again."

With that Sobol vanished, leaving only the new Thread behind.

Sebeck nearly collapsed with the overwhelming burden now upon him. He turned to face Price.

Price stared up at the high quest icon now adorning Sebeck's call-out. "You lucky bastard . . ."

Chapter 5: // Getting with the Program

Sebeck moved through the crowd in a regional shopping mall. The place was packed with couples hand in hand talking on cell phones. Teens texting. The plaza looked new, with familiar anchor stores and all the usual retail fronts strung between them.

Sebeck had ditched Price back at the hotel. He needed time away from his troubles. Time to think. Getting lost in the crowd felt good—even though he could still see the new Thread just above him in D-Space. It always appeared ten feet in front, beckoning.

He tried to forget the Thread and his quest and instead watched faces passing in the crowd. Just a parade of mundane concerns. As though the Daemon didn't exist.

Before long Sebeck spotted a familiar call-out approaching him, and Laney Price soon emerged from the stream of people. He and Sebeck stood face-to-face while shoppers surged around them. Price was munching on a churro. Snippets of conversation floated past them and faded away. They were anonymous in a sea of humanity.

"Needed a little 'me' time?"

Sebeck pushed past and kept walking through the crowd. "Where did the Daemon dig you up, Laney?"

Price stayed on his heels. "Similar to your situation. Life delivers us to certain crossroads, and before you know it—*bam*—you're serving a globe-spanning cybernetic organism. Same old familiar tale."

Price noticed that Sebeck was ignoring him. "These people give you comfort, Sergeant? Walking among them like a regular person? Does it bring back the good times?"

Sebeck cast a look back at Price. "What if it does? Maybe it's good to see how normal the world is. That there are still people who just want to go shopping."

"Yeah." He took another bite of his churro and spoke around it. "Too bad this place will probably be an empty shell ten years from now."

Sebeck cast a frown back at Price. "How do you figure?"

"You heard Sobol. Modern society is heading off a cliff, and John Q. Public is out here stomping on the accelerator."

"Have another churro, pal."

"I'm just saying. So you dig all this?" He gestured to the overhead jumbotrons displaying clothing ads of fashion models flying through rainbows.

"It doesn't matter what I think. Everything here exists because people *want* it. What gives Sobol the right to decide for them?"

Price shrugged. "Well, the public doesn't really decide anything *now*—they just select from the options they're given." He stuffed the last of the churro into his mouth and chewed furiously. "Factions have a slang term for the general public. They call them NPCs—as in 'non-player-characters'—scripted bots with limited responses."

"That's just obnoxious."

"Is it? These people have only limited decision-making ability."

"And *we're* not Sobol's puppets?"

"Okay, I think I know what's going on here." He balled up the churro wrapper and tossed it into the orifice of a trash can shaped like a robot. "You think these people are free, and that the Daemon is gonna take that freedom away."

Sebeck kept strolling through the crowd. "Enough, Laney. Just let me walk in peace."

Price stayed with him. "You, sir, are walking on a privately owned Main Street—permission to trespass revocable at will. Read the plaque on the ground at the entrance if you don't believe me. These people aren't citizens of anything, Sergeant. America is just another brand purchased for its goodwill value. For that excellent fucking logo."

"Yeah, I'm sure it's all a big conspiracy. . . ."

"No conspiracy necessary. It's a process that's been happening for thousands of years. Wealth aggregates and becomes political power. Simple as that. 'Corporation' is just the most recent name for it. In the Middle Ages it was the Catholic Church. They had a great logo, too. You might have seen it, and they had more branches than Starbucks. Go back before that, and it was Imperial Rome. It's a natural process as old as humanity."

Sebeck just stared back at him.

"Look, there's nothing wrong with people admitting

that they're owned. That's the first step in becoming free. They just need to admit it."

"You're a lunatic."

"That's right. I'm crazy. But stand up in here with a protest sign and find out how quickly you get your ass tased by security. You want to see the world the way it really *is*, Sergeant? Forget your cultural indoctrination for a moment."

Price started moving his arms as if conjuring a spell. Sebeck knew what it meant: Price was working with objects on a layer of D-Space. A layer that wasn't yet visible in Sebeck's HUD glasses. Price was pulling at invisible objects in the air around him. Then he turned to Sebeck. "This is the real world, Sergeant. The one you so dearly miss being a part of."

Suddenly a new layer of D-Space appeared overlaid on the real world, manifested as thousands of call-outs, glowing numbers hovering above the heads of all the shoppers moving past them. Dollar amounts, green for positive, red for negative. Most of the numbers floating over people's heads were negative: "-$23,393" hovering over a twentysomething woman on a cell phone, "-$839,991" over a dignified-looking man in his forties, "-$17,189" over his teenage daughter, and on it went. Number after number.

Price raised his arms theatrically. "The net worth of *everyone*. Real-time financial data." He frowned. "A lot of red out there, but then again, this *is* America."

Sebeck stared at the hundreds of numbers moving past him. Not every person had a number above them, but the vast majority did. A young professional couple with a baby, both of them with negative numbers in the forty thousand range. A poorly dressed woman in her sixties sat on a bench near the fountain with a bright green "$893,393" over her head. Sebeck kept staring at the numbers passing by. There was no anticipating who had money and who didn't. Some of the most successful-looking people seemed to be worst off.

"Okay, Price. This is all very interesting, but I don't see what it proves. The Daemon gives you the power to peek into their bank accounts. So what?"

"It's not the Daemon that gives me this ability, Sergeant."

Sebeck narrowed his eyes. "These numbers are appearing in D-Space. This must be the darknet."

Price was already shaking his head. "I get the *data* from commercial networks, and I project it onto D-Space. Ask yourself, how can I know their bank balances unless I know who these people are? Remember: none of them are Daemon operatives."

Sebeck thought for a moment. He moved to a balcony railing and scanned the hundreds of numbers moving through the mall.

"Their data follows them as they walk."

"Yeah. How about that?"

"How are you doing this, Price? Cut the bullshit. You're faking this, or are you trying to convince me that someone implanted tracking chips in everyone?"

"Nobody implanted anything. These people pay for their own tracking devices." Price pointed to a nearby cell phone kiosk slathered with graphic images of beautiful people chatting on handsets. "A cell phone's location is constantly tracked and stored in a database. Don't have a cell phone? Bluetooth devices have a unique identifier, too. Phone headsets, PDAs, music players. Just about any wireless toy you might own. And now there are radio-frequency-identity tags in driver's licenses, passports, and in credit cards. They respond to radio energy by emitting a unique identifier, which can be linked to a person's identity. Privately owned sensors at public choke points are harvesting this data throughout the world. It doesn't have anything to do with the Daemon."

Price turned to the mall again and drew circles on his layer of D-Space—highlighting sensors bolted to the walls at intersections in the mall's traffic flow. "Storing data is so cheap it's essentially free, so data brokers record everything in the hopes that it will have value to someone. The data is aggregated by third parties, linked to individual identities, and sold like any other consumer data. It's not a conspiracy. It's an economy, but an economy these people know nothing about. They're tagged like sheep and have about as much say in the matter as sheep."

Sebeck gazed at the data whirling around him.

"What do we look like to a computer alogrithm, Sergeant? Because it will be computer algorithms that make life-changing decisions about these people based on this data. How about credit worthiness—as decided by some arbitrary algorithm no one has a right to question?"

Suddenly credit scores appeared above everyone's heads, color-coded from green to red for severity.

"What about medical records?"

Lists of drug prescriptions and preexisting conditions appeared above people's heads.

"Or how about something really powerful: human relationships. Let's use phone records to compile the social network of these folks—to identify the people who matter most to them. . . ."

Suddenly everyone's names appeared over their heads, along with a hyperlinked diagram of their most frequent contacts—along with names and phone numbers.

"What about purchasing habits . . . ?"

Lists of recent credit card purchases blinked into existence below people's names.

"This data never goes away, Sergeant. *Ever.* And it might be sold years down the road to god knows who—or what."

Price leaned close. "Imagine how easily you could change the course of someone's life by changing this data. But that's control, isn't it? In fact, you don't even need to be human to exert power over these people. That's why the Daemon spread so fast."

Sebeck clutched the balcony railing in silence, watching the march of data. The public walked on, shopping and talking, completely oblivious to the cloud of personal information they gave off. That governed their lives.

Price followed Sebeck's gaze. "So you stand there and tell me that the Daemon is invasive and unprecedented. That it's a threat to human freedom. And I tell you that Americans are fucking ignorant about their freedom. They're about as free as the Chinese. Except the Chinese don't lie to themselves."

Sebeck said nothing for several moments. Then he

slowly turned back to Price. "Laney, how is the Daemon any better?" He pointed up at his own call-out, hovering above him in D-Space. "We wear information over our heads, too."

"Yes, but we can *see* ours, and we know instantly whenever anyone touches our data—and who touched it. That's the best one can hope for in a technologically advanced society. Plus, we can readily spot nonhumans on the darknet, because Daemon bots don't have a human body. So you know when an AI—like Sobol—is pushing your buttons, and you can choose whether or not to listen. Can these people say the same?" Price gestured to the mall shoppers.

Price then reached up to his call-out and slid the virtual layer over to Sebeck's HUD display. A layer named *Suckers* appeared in Sebeck's listing. "I want you to have this layer. In case you ever need to remember the world you left behind. The one you keep pining away for."

Sebeck looked back up at the profusion of data above them. Beyond that loomed the Thread, still beckoning. For the first time he thought it might actually lead someplace he'd want to go.

A tanned couple walked up to Sebeck and Price. The man nodded in greeting. "Excuse me, guys."

They turned to face him. The man was well-dressed with an oversized watch strapped to his wrist and a yin-yang tattoo on his forearm. He had his arm around a younger, attractive woman.

"Where did you guys get those sunglasses? I've been seeing them around, and I was wondering where I can pick up a pair."

Sebeck just stared at him through the yellow-tinted HUD glasses. Floating above the guy's head was a call-out indicating a net worth of -$103,039.

The man smiled. "They look kick-ass."

Sebeck glanced at Price, who just shrugged. Sebeck turned back to the guy. "Trust me, you don't want them." With that he headed off in the direction of the Thread.

Price followed, but then glanced back at the man, gesturing at the guy's invisible data. "Go easy with that Viagra prescription, Joe. It's potent stuff."

The man stopped cold as his girlfriend cast a puzzled look toward him. "Joe, do you know those guys?"

Chapter 6: // Waymeet

▶▶ "That'll be fourteen thirty-nine."

Pete Sebeck frowned. "That's not right."

He faced a lanky teenager in an ill-fitting franchise smock—one of the innumerable conscripts of the retail world. The kid glanced down at his computer screen and shrugged. "That's what it is, sir. Fourteen thirty-nine."

Sebeck leaned in against the counter. "Kid, I got a number two combo, and a number nine combo. What does that add up to?"

The cashier looked down at his computer screen. "Fourteen thirty-nine."

"Stop looking at the screen and just *think* for a second." He pointed at the wall-mounted menu. "How could a number two combo, at three ninety-nine, and a number nine combo, at five ninety-nine, add up to fourteen thirty-nine?"

"Sir, I'm just telling you what it is. If you don't want them both—"

"Of course I want them both, but you're not getting rid of me until you do the math."

"I'm not trying to get rid of you, I'm just telling you that it's fourteen thirty-nine." He swiveled the screen so Sebeck could see it.

"It doesn't matter what— Look, you've hit the wrong key or something."

"You're forgetting sales tax, sir."

"No, I'm not forgetting sales tax. It shows sales tax *there*." He pointed. "Listen, I want you to use your own mind for a second and think about this. Forget the machine."

"But—"

"Three ninety-nine plus five ninety-nine is what?"

The kid started looking at the screen again.

"Listen to me! Don't look at the screen. This is easy. Just round it up to four bucks plus six bucks—that's ten bucks—then take away two pennies—that's nine ninety-eight. Right?"

"You're forgetting sales tax."

"Kid, what's five percent sales tax on ten bucks?"

"Sir—"

"Do it for me."

"I don't—"

"Do it! Just do it, goddamnit!" His shout echoed in the tiled restaurant.

People in the restaurant suddenly stopped talking and started watching what seemed to be an altercation.

"What is five percent sales tax on ten bucks?"

The kid started tapping at the machine. "I'll need a manager to clear this."

"Kid, do you really want machines doing all your thinking for you? Do you really want that?"

A balding assistant manager with a muscular frame emerged from the kitchen door. His name tag read "Howard." "Is there a problem here?"

"Yeah, Howard, the kid has the price wrong, and I'm trying to get him to do the math."

"And what did you order?"

"I ordered a number two and a number nine."

The manager looked at the screen. "Okay, that's fourteen thirty-nine."

Howard was lucky Sebeck no longer carried a Taser.

Sebeck returned to the car with a carryout bag and two drinks. Laney Price was still refueling at the sprawling interstate travel center. There were at least twenty pump islands around them, brightly lit. Traffic hissed by on the nearby highway.

Price was using a squeegee to clean bugs off the windshield of the Chrysler 300 the Daemon had assigned them the day before. He seemed to notice the look on Sebeck's face. "What's wrong?"

"Humanity is doomed, that's what's wrong."

"Oh." Price kept cleaning the windshield.

Sebeck tossed the food in the car and took over the refueling. "That was something Sobol knew, wasn't it?"

"What's that?"

"That people will do whatever a computer screen tells them. I swear to god, you could run the next Holocaust from a fucking fast-food register." He pantomimed aiming a pistol. "It says I should kill you now."

"I see we've had another unsatisfactory consumer experience."

"There are times when I miss the badge, Laney. I swear I miss it."

"Why, so you can intimidate the shit out of teen slackers? Besides, what you've got now is something better— a quest icon. You're like a knight of the realm now."

"Just get in the car."

Sebeck almost missed the turnoff. They were heading west on Interstate 40 about an hour outside of Albuquerque when his new Thread abruptly veered onto an exit ramp marked INDIAN SERVICE ROUTE 22. Sebeck was in the middle of taking a sip of bottled water when the turn came up on him, and he had to swerve one-handed from the fast lane onto the exit ramp, cutting across solid white lines just before an abutment.

He glanced over at the sleeping form of Laney Price, who stirred a bit but then settled back to sleep. Sebeck followed the glowing blue line superimposed on reality over a bridge that crossed the highway to arrive at a travel center where trucks and cars were clustered around gas stations, convenience stores, and ever-present fast-food outlets.

There in the middle of a parking lot his new Thread ended in a swirling aura of blue light, above a live human being this time—a woman standing next to a white passenger van. The van was parked in front of a Conoco convenience store.

It was not exactly the destination he'd envisioned—not that he had any clear idea what to expect. Sebeck parked the Chrysler facing forward in a row of cars across from the woman and peered through the freshly bug-spattered windshield at her.

She was a trim American Indian woman in her fifties with long gray hair braided into a plait. She wore jeans, cowboy boots, and a tan button-down shirt with some sort of logo on the breast pocket. She also wore slim, stylish HUD glasses, through which she was gazing directly at Sebeck. She looked like a Santa Fe art gallery owner. Her D-Space call-out marked her as *Riley*—a fourteenth-level Shaman. Riley's reputation score was five stars out of five on a base factor of nine hundred three—which, if Sebeck had understood Price's ramblings over the weeks, meant that she had an average review by nine hundred–plus darknet operatives who'd interacted with her of five stars out of five. She was apparently highly regarded—about *what* Sebeck didn't know.

He turned off the engine and glanced over at the sleeping form of Price in the passenger seat. Sebeck pulled the keys from the ignition and stealthily opened the driver's door. He didn't feel like having his Daemon-assigned minder along for this conversation, so he placed the keys on the seat and quietly closed the car door behind him, checking that Price was asleep.

Sebeck then walked across the parking lot toward Riley, who regarded him with some curiosity, since he was leaving his companion behind. It was fairly cloudy and rather cool. Sebeck closed his jacket as he approached Riley. Fellow travelers came and went around them.

He took note of the passenger van she stood alongside. It was new and bore a logo for "Enchanted Mesa Spa & Resort"—the same logo printed on her shirt pocket.

When he reached her, the last of the Thread disappeared and a chime sounded—leaving only the soft blue light of a D-Space aura slowly swirling above her head.

Sebeck was unsure how to feel. He spoke without emotion. "I'm supposed to be looking for the Cloud Gate. Is there something you can tell me?"

She extended her hand. "Why don't we start with hello?"

Sebeck took a deep breath and shook her hand briefly. "Hello. You're Riley."

"Shaman of the Two-Rivers faction. And you are the Unnamed One."

"Yeah, that just about describes it. I hope you have some answers for me."

"What sort of answers?"

"Like how I can complete my quest? How do I justify the freedom of humanity to the Daemon?"

She frowned. "That's not visible to me."

He rubbed his eyes in frustration. "Why do I have to

wander all over hell's half acre to complete this damned quest?"

"It's the hero's journey."

He narrowed his eyes at her.

"Don't forget: Sobol was an online game designer. In the archetype, a hero must wander lost in the wilderness to find the knowledge necessary for his or her quest. Perhaps that's what's happening to you."

"And I'm supposed to be the hero."

"It's your life. You should be the hero of it. If it's any consolation, I'm the hero of mine, too."

"Riley, why did the Thread lead me to you?"

"Why *me* exactly? I don't know. I suspect it has to do with my skill set and my proximity to you when some system threshold was reached."

Sebeck nodded to himself. "Yesterday I spoke with Matthew Sobol. He gave me this Thread after our meeting."

"And yesterday an avatar appeared to me on a deep layer. She was like an angel. A beautiful woman with copper hair and alabaster skin—bathed in light. She said you would come."

Sebeck ran his hands over his bald head. He thought of Cheryl Lanthrop, the woman who had betrayed him. *Copper hair and fair skin.* She'd worked for Sobol, and had paid for that with her life. "This is madness."

"The avatar told me you were on a quest from Mad Emperor, and that you needed to grok the shamanic interface."

He was lost.

She nodded in understanding. "I'll put it in layman's terms: you need to fully learn the darknet and all its powers in order to have any hope of succeeding on your quest."

"Powers."

"Data magic, far-sight."

"And you're a *shaman*?"

She smiled. "I know what you're thinking. There's no such thing as magic, and restless spirits are wives' tales. However—"

Sebeck held up his hand. "Yeah. I stand corrected."

"Good. I chose my darknet profession, and it is *shaman*. It governs my skill tree and level advancement. Is that more clear?"

He nodded.

"I see that you're a first-level Fighter. Which makes it all the more puzzling that you've been geased by Mad Emperor to complete this quest."

"*Geased*? What's 'geased' mean?"

"It's ancient Gaelic. It means an enchantment that compels you to complete a task. It's an incredibly powerful spell—far, far above *my* level."

"Can I break free of it?"

"Not if you accepted the quest. The only one who can cancel it is the one who gave it to you: Mad Emperor."

Sebeck recalled sitting in the office of a funeral home, talking with an interactive three-dimensional recording of Sobol. The avatar had asked him: *do you accept the task of finding justification for the freedom of humanity? Yes or no?* It was an out-of-control voice recognition monster, and Sebeck felt compelled to accept, if only to buy time. If only to protect his family.

"I had no choice."

"Maybe. But be warned: you must choose your words carefully on the darknet. Words have power in this new age. They are not just sounds. Where ancient people believed in gods and devils that listened to their pleas and curses—in this age immortal entities hear us. Call them bots or spirits; there is no functional difference now. They surround us, and through them word forms become an unlock code that can trigger a blessing or a curse. Mankind created systems whose inter-reactions we could not fully understand, and the spirits we gathered have escaped from them into the land where they walk the earth—or the GPS grid, whichever you prefer. The spirit world overlaps the real one now, and our lives will never be the same."

Sebeck didn't know what to say. A couple of years ago he would have called her crazy, but she was right—spirits or bots, it was just semantics. "And what happens if I refuse to proceed?"

"If you stray from your path, the Daemon will compel you to return to it. Of more concern to me is how you could possibly complete your quest while remaining first level."

"I can't go up levels?"

"The darknet is arranged like Sobol's game world. You can only go up levels by completing tasks—or quests. However, the Geas spell prevents you from taking on any other quests until you complete this one. You are stuck at first level until you achieve your goal. And you have quite a goal." She didn't appear too optimistic. Riley checked her watch. "We need to get going. You should wake up your factor."

"Factor?"

She pointed at Price sleeping in the car. "Chunky Monkey."

"Where are we heading?"

She patted the "Enchanted Mesa Spa & Resort" logo on the side of the van. "You're with us until you certify with the shamanic interface."

He glanced back at the car and shrugged. "I'm good to go."

"You're leaving your factor behind?"

"He's a spy planted by Sobol."

She reached up to manipulate unseen objects in a way that Sebeck had seen Price do many times. A few moments later she shook her head. "I don't see that he's reporting to anyone. Although, he has been tasked by Mad Emperor to handle the logistics of your quest. Unlike you, he can quit this task at any time and be replaced." She lowered her hands. "But neither has he given you high marks for cooperation."

"Leave him."

She just looked at Sebeck. "And your things?"

"Replaceable. A few changes of clothing, toiletries."

"If that's what you want."

Riley drove the passenger van south into scrublands, past creosote bushes and the occasional piñon tree. They were headed toward distant mesas of tan rock, mottled by the shadows of clouds. Sebeck was glad that the Thread no longer loomed in front of him. His view was unobstructed for the first time in a long while. The only reminder of his quest was when he looked at Riley and saw the subtle aura glowing above her call-out—she was his current goal.

He focused his attention out the window. A surprising amount of grass grew in the lowlands this time of year. It was beautiful.

Sebeck sensed Riley studying him, but for several minutes they drove in silence. She finally spoke. "I know who you are."

Sebeck didn't respond.

"You're that detective—Sergeant Peter Sebeck—the one who was framed for the Daemon hoax."

Sebeck nodded.

"They put you to death."

Sebeck nodded somberly again. "If you believe the news."

"You've lost a great deal. Your career. Your reputation. I don't imagine you're here voluntarily."

"No."

"Did you know Matthew Sobol? Is that why he gave you this quest?"

"Sobol was my primary suspect in a murder case. From the point my name entered the news, I was in the Daemon's sights. Sobol effectively framed me with a computer program."

"How did you survive your execution?"

Sebeck shrugged. "Ask Price. He was the one who revived me at the funeral home."

"You mean Chunky Monkey, the operative back at the travel center?"

Sebeck just gave her a look. "His name is Laney Price. Another misfit the Daemon found somewhere." He cast a glance at Riley. "No offense."

"None taken."

Sebeck decided to change the subject. "Is this your tribe's land?"

"No. Right now we're passing through the Acoma reservation. I'm a Laguna Indian. We'll reach Laguna land in about fifteen minutes. The Navajo nation is north of us—much larger—and the Zunis are to the west."

Sebeck gazed out the window at the mesas and light green grass bowing in a breeze. "This is beautiful country. I always thought of New Mexico as just sand and rocks."

"The Spanish word for lake is *laguna*. That's how our tribe got its name. Access to water is what attracted Europeans." She pointed into the distance and a line of tan rock on the horizon. "The Acoma pueblo up on that mesa was first settled in eleven hundred A.D. It's the oldest continuously occupied community in North America."

Sebeck was genuinely surprised. "So they didn't fall along with the Anasazi civilization?"

"You have an interest in Anasazi history?"

"It came up recently in conversation."

"Well, Acoma rose partly from the collapse of Chacoan society. Some of the survivors resettled here.

"Acoma was attacked in the late fifteen hundreds by the Spanish. They used cannons and attack dogs to force their way up the stone stairway onto the mesa. They killed all but two hundred and fifty of the twenty-five hundred inhabitants and cut one foot off every male survivor. The children were given to Catholic missionaries, but most of them wound up being sold into slavery. The Spanish then used the pueblo as a base to conquer the rest of the region."

Sebeck didn't know what to say.

"That was two centuries before the British colonies in the East declared their independence. We've been here a long time."

"And now you're a darknet faction leader. Are you some sort of militant?"

She laughed. "You mean, a violent fringe group? No, Sergeant. We're builders." A look came over her, and she tapped again at invisible objects on a hidden layer of D-Space. "In fact, you'll see some of our work on the way." She was about to say something, but then apparently thought better of it.

"What?"

"If you're wondering whether I bear a grudge against the Spanish—or the U.S. government for that matter—I don't. Nursing anger against people long dead is a waste of one's life. Today if someone wrongs us, we do what anyone else does: we send our lawyers after them." Riley fixed her gaze on Sebeck. "The Laguna value education highly. It is our rod and staff, as my father used to say."

"How did a woman your age get involved in the darknet?"

"A woman *my age*?" She laughed. "Don't sugarcoat it, Sergeant."

"I'm just wondering how you—"

"Sobol's online fantasy game—*The Gate*."

He just looked at her.

"Okay, what's a fifty-two-year-old woman doing playing online games? I found them interesting. The idea of putting on a body like clothing—there was something about it that seemed intriguing. That we might surpass our physical differences and deal with one another as human beings. With no preconceived notions about gender or race."

"And that's where the Daemon found you."

"I did the finding, but it wasn't the Daemon I found. It was the darknet. The encrypted wireless network Sobol created. Only later did I discover how much blood Sobol shed establishing this network. And yet, I can't help but wonder, just as evil sometimes arises from good intentions, if good can't sometimes grow from evil. It's a distasteful notion, but human history makes me wonder."

Sebeck gritted his teeth. "I may be on this quest, but that doesn't mean I agree with Sobol. I accepted it because I had no choice, and I was concerned that unless I did so, he would enslave humanity. Matthew Sobol killed *friends of mine*. Police and federal officers—people with families."

She held up a hand. "I'm not defending Sobol, Sergeant. I'm saying that Sobol was *willing* to be our villain to force necessary change. So that we didn't have to."

"Megalomaniacs always justify their actions by saying how *necessary* it is."

She gave him a sideways look. After a moment she

said, "Do you feel any guilt for what your ancestors did to the Indians?"

Sebeck was taken aback.

"You know, for the genocide that was perpetrated against Native American people by the U.S. government and the settlers?"

"That's not the same as what Sobol did."

"Why?"

"Because the theft of tribal lands occurred a hundred and fifty years ago. Things were different then."

"Statute of limitations, then?" She concentrated on the road, then turned an eye back on him. "I'm just making a point. You probably don't feel guilt because you're not the one who did it. You bear native people no ill will, and aren't prejudiced against them."

"Yes, exactly."

"But then, we're not getting the land back either, are we?" A slight smile creased her face.

Sebeck folded his arms. "It could never be sorted out even if we tried. That was a different time, Riley."

"We're not all that different from our ancestors, Sergeant. And even though the land Matthew Sobol grabbed was virtual real estate—computer networks—I don't think anyone's going to get that back either."

Sebeck sat in silence for a few moments, watching the road. "He can force me to go on this quest, but I'll never accept what he's done."

"Don't waste time being angry with the dead. They'll never give you satisfaction. Whatever punishment Sobol deserved he has either received—or not—already, and nothing you can do will change that. Now there is only the system he left behind, and he's given control of that to all of us."

"I just spoke with Sobol yesterday. He is very much still here."

She looked him in the eye. "Sobol is dead and gone, Sergeant. His consciousness no longer exists. What you're dealing with is a recording—a scripted entity that responds to real events. It can't feel. It can't think. Sobol is gone."

Sebeck just turned back to the window, lost in his reflections for several minutes. He thought about how much death the Daemon had caused and how much of his own life irrevocably changed.

Soon they approached a junction with an unpaved road. Riley slowed the van and turned left onto a road marked INDIAN SERVICE ROUTE 49. NO TRESPASSING signs flanked it. Moments later they were roaring down the dirt road, leaving a plume of dust in their wake.

Neither of them spoke for several minutes as the road curved between distant, rocky cliffs with batters of scree at their base. The grasslands and an occasional pond or stream gave the landscape a serene feel.

About fifteen miles later the road gradually curved around a tall promontory of stone—a mesa jutting out like the peninsula of a higher plateau. As they came around it, Sebeck could see the road for miles ahead, running straight toward a towering monolith, a mountain of rock perhaps a thousand feet tall. On the lowlands before it, glittering reflections spread across the landscape. Sebeck could also see signs of human civilization ahead—outbuildings and what looked to be a tall water tower under construction in the distance. Dozens of diminutive D-Space call-outs hovered over the land, their owners invisible at this distance. The valley floor was a vast darknet construction project.

Riley noticed Sebeck's gaze. "The mirrors are heliostats. Trough mirrors that focus the sun's energy onto a central tower to generate heat—and thus steam to run a turbine and generate electricity."

"That whole valley floor?"

"No, no. The heliostats are an intermediary station. They provide on-site power for the *real* project. Otherwise the spike in energy usage would attract attention."

They were coming up on a steel gate with a short stretch of fencing on either side to prevent casual drive-arounds. The gate was closed, but Riley wasn't slowing down. As they got within a hundred yards, it opened automatically, revealing a new stretch of paved roadway beyond. A white SUV labeled SECURITY stood near the gate with two uniformed Indians inside—both had call-outs over their heads.

Riley exchanged waves with them, and there was a slight bump as they passed through the gate and onto pavement. Then the road was smooth—and suddenly quiet.

"The Daemon financed this." Sebeck turned to her. "Didn't it?"

"The Daemon's economy is powered by darknet credits, Sergeant. Imaginary credits are all that money is."

"But there's a theft at the heart of it."

She thought about it and nodded slightly. "Yes, the darknet economy was seeded by real-world wealth. Wealth that was questionable in origin to begin with. Here, it's being invested in people and projects that have begun to return value—not in dollars, but in things of intrinsic human worth. Energy, information, food, shelter."

"But originally from theft."

"That could be said of a lot of things that are now admired."

The van followed a ruler-straight line through a series of ongoing construction projects—stark, window-less buildings, pipes, electrical lines, all of them leading toward the large tank being constructed in the distance, a couple of miles away still. It was enormous. They passed pickup trucks and minibuses moving workers—more than a few with D-Space call-outs above them bearing the mark of the Two-Rivers faction.

"So what's this 'real project' you mentioned—that water tank?"

"It's not a water tank. It's a fifty-megawatt power station that will generate enough electricity to supply a hundred thousand homes. What you're looking at is just the first three hundred feet. When it's done, it will stand sixteen hundred feet tall and two hundred sixty feet in diameter."

Sebeck whistled and peered through the windshield.

Riley gestured with one hand, and suddenly a completed, life-sized three-dimensional wire model of the proposed tower sprang into being in D-Space miles from them—rising sixteen hundred feet into the air in glowing spectral lines.

In spite of himself Sebeck smiled and turned toward Riley. "That's incredible." He looked back at the tower as parts of it began to animate, showing red arrows representing wind currents flowing in at the base and up through the tower's shaft and out the top.

Riley aimed her finger, and a glowing pointer that must have been thirty feet across appeared miles away in the fabric of D-Space. She pointed at the heliostat array closer to them. "The problem with parabolic mirror stations is that they don't produce much energy on cloudy days, and none at night."

Her massive pointer moved to the base of the 3-D tower model, only a fifth of which was completed in reality. A sloping base surrounded the wire model as though it were a trumpet placed horn-down in the soil. "This design uses a transparent canopy to superheat air with solar radiation—energy that gets through cloud cover. The canopy is eight feet off the ground at the perimeter and slopes up to sixty feet above ground where it connects to the tower base. As the air heats, it rises, creating a wind that proceeds up the tower—which is lined with wind turbines."

"So it creates its own wind."

She nodded. "Even at night." She pointed at what looked to be rectangular cisterns arrayed at intervals around the perimeter of the canopy. "Covered saltwater ponds gather heat energy during the day and release it at night—continuing the wind cycle."

Sebeck didn't know what to think. There was no dismissing the scale and ambition of this—but what was it for? "Why do you need so much electrical power?"

"To transform our environment. To power equipment, micro-manufacturing plants, chemical and material reactions. This tower—and other solar installations—will provide clean, sustainable energy and freshwater from the elemental building blocks of matter."

Sebeck gave her a doubtful look.

She laughed. "It's not my design, Sergeant. I'm not an engineer. What I do here is work with people—helping to define goals and needs of the community."

"Seriously. How do you know this is not complete bullshit?"

"The design has existed for decades. The technology has been proven. My technical familiarity comes from dealing with the darknet engineers and architects handling the construction. I make it a point to understand, so I can convey the information to our people. This is a big deal for us."

"No doubt. But, Riley, if this was economically feasible, don't you think everyone would be doing it? Besides, I thought the Laguna nation already had water."

"At present, yes, but darknet communities are founded on long-term thinking. In coming decades we anticipate water stress due to climate change and depleted aquifers. Sustainable water independence increases our darknet resilience score."

He gazed upon all the construction. "But doing all this to irrigate fields can't be anything close to cost-effective."

"Water isn't the *product*, Sergeant. Water is the *waste*." In D-Space she pointed to highlight a line of small buildings being constructed down a road leading off to their right. "Those will be reverse-hydrolysis fuel cell stations. They'll consume hydrogen to produce heat and electricity—leaving behind freshwater as the only waste product. We can produce a third of a liter of freshwater with every kilowatt-hour of electricity produced from hydrogen."

"But where in the hell do you get *hydrogen*?"

She aimed her pointer at the surrounding valley walls. "From the crystalline structures of igneous rock. This whole region has vast quantities of it. Millions of years ago this volcanic rock picked up water vapor when it crystallized from magma. That means it contains molecular hydrogen. When crushed into a powder, it seeps hydrogen at room temperature through its fracture surfaces for hundreds of hours—no liquid water required. We use some of the electrical energy from the power tower to crush this rock"—her pointer moved onto the lofty power tower—"and the rock removal helps to create energy-efficient shelter in the cliff faces—much like our ancestors had. But that's just one aspect of the project. We'll also use solar energy to reverse combustion."

On his confused look, she moved the pointer. "Here . . ." The dot touched on a series of virtual buildings around the base of the virtual tower. "These CR5 units will use solar power to chemically reenergize carbon dioxide into carbon monoxide and oxygen. It's done by heating cobalt ferrite rings with a solar furnace. At high temperature the rings release oxygen. When they're rotated back into the presence of carbon dioxide, the cobalt ferrite snatches oxygen from the CO_2 as it cools, leaving behind carbon *monoxide*—which, when we combine it with our hydrogen source, can be used to synthesize liquid hydrocarbon fuels such as methanol.

Methanol is portable energy that's easy to work with, transport, and store. The hydrocarbons can also produce polymers for plastics and other products. Likewise, it sequesters carbon out of the atmosphere—making it carbon negative. It just requires energy, Sergeant—and solar energy is something my people have plenty of."

Sebeck was speechless.

"What did you think we were building out here, a casino?"

"But what you're describing—creating water and pulling liquid fuel out of the air—"

"The sun is what made life on Earth possible to begin with. Oil is just ancient solar energy stored in hydrocarbons. The CR5 technology was developed nearby in Sandia National Labs. It stands for 'Counter Rotating Ring Receiver Reactor Recuperators.' The details are available to anyone on the darknet, if you're really interested."

He was still shaking his head. "Then why isn't this being done *everywhere*?"

She turned off her D-Space layer and the lofty tower and virtual buildings disappeared. "Many things are possible, Sergeant, but not economically feasible. Of course, that all depends on how you calculate costs. Darknet communities factor in loss of economic independence as a cost. They factor in the cost of forcibly defending distant energy resources. They also factor in lack of sustainability and disposal of pollutants. That more than balances the equation. With this facility we'll use solar energy as the foundation of a long-term, sustainable, energy-positive holon. And that's the goal."

"A *holon*."

"Holons are the geographic structure of the dark-net. Any darknet community lies at the center of an economic radius of one hundred miles for its key inputs and outputs—food, energy, health care, and building materials. Balancing inputs and outputs within that cir-cle is the goal. A local economy that's as self-sufficient as possible while still being part of a cultural whole—a holon—thus creating a resilient civilization that has no central points of failure. And which through its very structure promotes democracy. That's what we're doing here, Sergeant."

They were coming up on the tower now. Scores of workers were scurrying over scaffolding while cranes lifted loads to upper levels.

Sebeck hardly knew what to say. It was as though he'd been transported to a different century. He was embarrassed to admit he *had* been half expecting to find a casino out here. He spent the remainder of the ride just staring at the construction under way.

A few minutes later they approached the face of the towering rock he'd seen from afar. Set into the cliffs were what looked like twenty-first-century cliff dwell-ings, with warm lights and tall glass windows. There were several dozen electric vehicles parked at the base of the rock, around a broad door that bore only a D-Space sign: TWO-RIVERS HALL. People of many races were walk-ing in and out of the doorway, all with D-Space call-outs and all apparently busy. Too busy to note the arrival of a first-level newb—even with a quest icon.

Riley pulled the van up to the door. "We'll get you settled in a room, Sergeant, and tomorrow we'll start your training on the shamanic interface." She got out of the van, and then turned around to lean through the window. "Oh, and welcome to Enchanted Mesa Spa and Resort."

Chapter 7: // Shamanic Interface

Sebeck sat in the Mesa dining hall reading the local paper when he felt the table bump. He lowered his paper to see Laney Price sitting across from him with a tray loaded down with scrambled eggs, bacon, pastries, and pancakes. Price wore a crisp black T-shirt bearing the slogan "I'm undermining civilization. Ask me how" in bold white letters. He was already digging into his breakfast.

Sebeck folded the paper, and sipped his coffee. "So they let you in?"

"You're a dick. You know that?" Price didn't look at him, but instead busied himself reading something in D-Space.

"I needed to talk to Riley alone."

"So you ditched me in a truck stop. No, that's fine. Never mind that I had virtually *nothing* to do with your identity death, and that I resuscitated you after your near execution—for which I never received so much as a thank-you. No, it's fine. It's no wonder the Daemon could make a bad guy out of you. You know why? *Because you're a bad guy.*" Price ripped off a piece of toast with his teeth and resumed reading in virtual space.

Sebeck didn't feel like arguing, but then again, he

didn't feel like reading anymore either. He tossed the paper aside. It was a tribal rag that dealt more with school announcements and local council news. There was little mention of the vast construction project outside the window.

He turned to look out the tall bank of windows along the outside wall. The entire facility appeared to have been carved out of the solid rock face—and the crushed rock used to generate hydrogen, no doubt. The dining room had a broad view of the valley floor, and the extensive construction under way there.

Just then he saw Riley approaching through the dining hall. Many people smiled and waved as they saw her, and she paused at several tables to exchange pleasantries. But she walked inexorably toward Sebeck. He wondered how she knew where to find him, but then he realized he could probably be pinpointed easily in the fabric of D-Space.

Riley was dressed like the day before. As she stepped up to the table, she didn't smile or greet Sebeck. "Are you ready? It's seven thirty, and we've got a lot of ground to cover."

Sebeck gestured to Price. "Riley, this is Price. Price, this is—"

She interrupted him. "We've already met, Sergeant."

Price nodded as he kept eating. "She heard my tale of woe."

"You haven't exactly been decent to Chunky, and the fact is that someone must handle logistics for your quest. At first level you barely have the darknet credits necessary to function. The darknet isn't a commune, Sergeant. Things cost money. Chunky paid for your breakfast."

Price nodded while still reading. "Don't thank me. Thank the quest fund."

It did occur to Sebeck that Price was always the one getting them new identities, new credit cards, and new cars.

"If you want to get to the next stage of your quest, you'll need to be certified. Let's go."

He nodded. "Where are we doing this?"

A brief journey in a modern, climate-controlled elevator brought Sebeck and Riley twenty floors straight up through solid rock before the doors opened onto a solid stone corridor. It was amply lit by compact, warm-colored lights. Oddly, there were fire strobes and smoke alarms bolted into the solid rock walls. This was no ancient cliff-dweller ruin. It was modern construction— though it would take a volcano to set fire to the place. Apparently darknet communities had to follow real-world fire codes.

Riley walked purposefully down the hall past several numbered doors and stopped at one that was already open. It led into a large conference room with a broad wooden table surrounded by a dozen modern office chairs. A grease board was bolted to the nearby wall. She motioned for Sebeck to take a seat and closed the door behind them.

"Not exactly the environment I was expecting to learn magic in."

She sat on the edge of the table nearby and just looked at him for several moments.

He gave her a questioning look. "What?"

"I've read up on you. You've suffered, but you're not the only one who has. Did you ever think to ask Price anything about *his* life? No. And I don't see that you've taken any responsibility for the suffering you've caused others, either. Your wife and son, for starters."

"My family is none of your business. Yes, I lied to the people close to me—and to myself. I had a long time in prison to think about the person I was back then. I've got nothing *but* regrets, so back off."

Riley considered this. Her expression lost its hard edge. She stood up. "A few years ago, I was riding near El Morro. I saw a coyote on a ridgeline, trying to keep up with his pack. He was missing a leg. He looked thin. But he *was* keeping up. That always stuck with me. It's something we can learn from animals. They don't waste time feeling sorry for themselves."

Sebeck sighed. "What do you want from me, Riley? I'm here, aren't I?"

"Are you? Just ask yourself what drives people to join the Daemon's network. Do you really think all these people are evil? They just want their lives to make sense. This network is helping them achieve that. The Daemon has no ideology. It's simply what we make of it. It *will* maintain order, but what type of order is up to us. You have a chance to help create something good for future generations. If you're looking for some sort of redemption, now is your chance. This quest of yours might do some good. So I suggest you pay attention and learn what I'm going to teach you. Because the sooner you do, the sooner you can stop hating dead people and rejoin the world of the living."

Sebeck stared at the table like a child who'd been scolded.

Riley moved to the front of the room. "May I begin?"

Sebeck nodded.

"The shamanic interface is the mechanism for interacting with the darknet. It's called the *shamanic* interface because it was designed to be comprehensible to all people on earth, regardless of technological level or cultural background." She made a series of precise flourishes with her hands, leaving behind glowing lines in D-Space that formed an intricate pattern. As she finished, an unearthly, angelic voice sounded in the room, like a good spirit.

Sebeck looked around him for the origin of the disembodied voice.

Riley lowered her hands. "It was a hypersonic sound, Sergeant. Linked to a macro that I created based on somatic gestures. But my point is that it looks like magic. Even the most remote tribes in Papua New Guinea understand the concept of magic—and that certain rituals must be observed to invoke it. They believe in a spirit world where ancestors and supernatural beings watch over them. The shamanic interface simply connects high technology to that belief system, granting 'powers' and equipment as a reward for useful, organized activity."

Sebeck leaned back in his chair. "Useful to whom?"

"Humanity, Sergeant. This is big-picture stuff Repositories of human knowledge and technology are being designed and built by various curator factions around the world. The spec is simply that these repositories be durable, inspire awe, and be equipped with automated systems that can teach people useful knowledge to empower the more rational among the population so that they can achieve leadership positions. That way, should human civilization be lost in a region, this system could put locals back on a path to regain knowledge in a generation or two. It could also be useful in resisting a downward spiral to begin with."

Sebeck looked at the solid walls around them. He looked back at Riley quizzically.

"Correct. Two-Rivers Hall will be a repository when it's finished. That may take many decades."

"But doesn't this just spread mysticism? Lies, essentially?"

"You mean fairy tales? Yes, initially. But then, a lot of parents tell young children that there's a Santa Claus. It's easier than trying to explain the cultural significance of midwinter celebrations to a three-year-old. If false magic or a white lie about the god-monster in the mountain will get people to stop killing one another and learn, then the truth can wait. When the time is right, it can be replaced with a reverence for the scientific method."

"And *this* is why Sobol created the Daemon?"

She shook her head. "No, this is why they call it the shamanic interface. Because it resembles sorcery—and might as well be to low-tech people. But unlike sorcery, it exists and conveys real power."

Riley raised her hands in front of her. "Now let's teach you how to use it."

Two days later Sebeck stood leaning against a railing on the edge of a terrace set atop Two-Rivers Hall—nine hundred feet above the desert floor. The view from atop the great monolith of stone was impressive, with mesas extending in a ragged line toward the horizon.

The master plan for the construction on the valley floor was more apparent from up here, although Sebeck now knew how to interrogate the objects themselves in D-Space. He could see call-outs for faction members, and knew also how to zoom in on them or adjust the layers of D-Space in his field of view. Or send messages. But none of that interested him just now.

He laid his chin on the aluminum railing and pondered the Scale of Themis, center-screen at the bottom of his HUD display. It fascinated him. It was a measure of the distribution of power within a Daemon user population. He could set it to show the whole darknet or just the holon he occupied. At present it was scaled to his current holon. It took the form of a slender needle on his control bar—in this case, leaning slightly to the right. Sebeck had customized his display so that he would always see it. If he looked closely enough, he could see it fluctuating.

Riley had taught him that the extreme right position meant Daemon power was held in very few hands, while all the way to the left meant Daemon power was evenly distributed across virtually everyone.

Oddly, she told him the goal was not to have the needle at either extreme. Too much power in too few hands defeated the common good, while too little power in any single person's hands made it hard to get anything done. Thus, the goal for a darknet community was to try to peg the needle right in the center—"due north" they called it.

It looked like the Two-Rivers faction was about fifteen degrees off due north. Sebeck wondered if Riley skewed the scale. He'd had a chance to learn just how respected her opinions were in this holon. She wasn't too impressed by herself. *Individuals can always malfunction, Sergeant. Including me.*

Riley was an interesting woman. Sebeck couldn't recall ever meeting a person so patient, yet unyielding. She also demonstrated a prodigious knowledge of the world around her. He was starting to realize he wasn't the center of Sobol's new world order. Strangely, that gave him a measure of relief.

Sebeck considered the Daemon's *virulence*. Riley had explained to him that the Daemon grew less virulent the more it spread. And that it became more ruthless as it contracted. It was designed like a natural organism to resist its own eradication with lethal force if necessary. It did explain the bloody origins of the Daemon, but Sebeck still couldn't accept it. It was basically a parasite on human society, one trying to achieve symbiosis. A balance between what it took and what it gave. Yes, it drove them toward preserving civilization, but it diminished free will. And did they really want a cybernetic organism designed by a madman hanging over their heads?

Sebeck heard footsteps on the stone stairs behind him. He turned to see Laney Price wearing a new black T-shirt and parachute pants. The words "THANK YOU . . . for not emoting" were emblazoned on Price's shirt in bold white letters.

"Where are you getting these stupid T-shirts?"

He stretched the fabric to read it. "Like it? Latest thing, man. Smart plastic. I got it at the gift shop the day I got in."

"Wait . . . there's a *gift shop*?"

"Yeah. Flexible, programmable plastic display. Takes about an hour to change messages. Pretty cool, huh?"

Sebeck turned back to the railing. "You downvoted me, you prick."

Price came up alongside him. "Well, what did you expect? You treat me like crap."

"A *two-star* reputation ranking?"

"Oh, out of a base factor of one! Big deal. You can fix it. Try not being a dick. It works wonders."

"I oughta downvote *your* reputation ranking."

"I've got a base factor of four hundred and six, pal. Good luck. And on what grounds, by the way? You know damn well that it has to be for a cause, and that it must pass muster on an fMRI countercharge."

Sebeck threw up his hands. "Jesus, we sound like a couple of geeks at a Star Trek convention."

"I happen to *speak* Klingon, pal. So . . . *Hab SoSlI' Quch!*"

They heard more footsteps and turned to see Riley coming up to join them.

Sebeck nodded to her in greeting.

She appraised him. "You may not like it, Sergeant, but you'll make an able member of the darknet. I think you're ready to continue your quest."

"Then you're rating me?"

She nodded and raised her ringed hands. With a few precise movements she moved an invisible object to an invisible place, and Sebeck noticed a message come across his HUD display. It told him that Riley had just rated him on a scale of one to five—scoring him a four. Now with a base of two he had a reputation score of three. Half a star above average.

But more important, the moment she rated him, a new blue Thread sprang into being about ten feet above and in front of Sebeck's HUD view. It ran quickly from the mountaintop, through the valley, and to the horizon northeast of them, where it disappeared.

Sebeck took a deep breath. It was difficult to tolerate the return of that domineering line. Where it would lead was anyone's guess.

"Do you see it, Sergeant?"

He nodded. "Yes. My Thread is back."

"I thought it might be. It seems your quest will lead you to places and events. Although how that might ultimately lead to this 'Cloud Gate' you're seeking, I don't know. I've searched for anything called a Cloud Gate in the structure of the darknet but found nothing. However, there is mention of it elsewhere."

"Where?"

"In myth."

"Great. So, I'm searching for a myth. . . ."

"Myths still have power, Sergeant. Sobol knew that. His games are predicated upon them. Myths are the archetypes that recur again and again in the hopes and fears of mankind. They have a hold upon us. The entire concept of a daemon stems from the guardian spirits of Greek mythology—spirits who watched over mankind to keep them out of trouble, and that's become real enough."

Sebeck shrugged. "Okay. What do these myths say about a Cloud Gate?"

"It was the gateway to the heavens and guarded by the Horae—the goddesses of orderly life. The Horae were also known collectively as the Hours and the Seasons. Their mother was Themis—the goddess of justice and order."

The name tugged at Sebeck's memory. "As in the Scale of Themis?"

She nodded. "An allegorical personification of moral force—a myth powerful enough that she became enshrined in our own society as Blind Lady Justice—one of the only goddesses of our new Republic. Her symbol surrounds us to this day."

Sebeck absorbed this, still uncertain what to make of it.

Riley placed a hand on his shoulder. "In Sobol's online fantasy world, *The Gate*, different planes of existence were linked by gates, and those who controlled them or passed through them could control or change the course of world events. The outcome of your quest may affect us all, Sergeant."

He nodded somberly.

She placed her hand on Sebeck's shoulder. "Follow your Thread. I believe your heart is in the right place, even if you don't agree with Sobol's vision. Question everything. But don't be surprised if the world you thought you knew never existed."

Chapter 8: // Erebus

News.briefing.com

Grain Prices Spike On **Crop Reduction**—Year-over-year direct **subsidy applications** by U.S. **corn** and **soybean farmers plummeted** in parts of Iowa, Missouri, Kansas, and Nebraska, sending world grain futures skyrocketing. The U.S. Department of Agriculture reported an unprecedented nationwide **6 to 7 percent decrease** in **acres** of corn and soybeans **under cultivation**. With U.S. production representing 42 percent of the world's **corn** and 34 percent of its **soybeans**, analysts are bracing for **potential shortages of** grain-fed **livestock** as well as processed **food additives** derived from **corn** and **soy**.

The Major stared down the length of Sheikh Zayed Road from his conference room on the fifty-third floor. Gleaming skyscrapers lined the twelve-lane highway below, creating a man-made canyon topped by familiar multinational logos. Not far off he could see Burj Dubai, the tallest building in the world. Its towering presence helped remind everyone that this wasn't a wasteland of sand, but a petri dish of business culture.

Dubai was the perfect business environment. A blank slate—the way it should be everywhere. No interference. No taxes. No protestors. It had been a smuggling port for centuries, bringing gold into India and serving as a conduit for everything from slaves to silks. But now the coves and creeks on the coast had been turned into marinas for mega-yachts and resorts packed with sunburned Russians. First-world infrastructure and office blocks had been laid down with such vengeance in the last ten years that slow-moving pedestrians risked being paved over.

What The Major liked most about the Emirates was that there was *order*. Everyone accepted their role. The Filipinos provided service, the Indians and Bangladeshis provided labor, and expats from the U.S., Europe, Japan, and China did the business. The Emiratis . . . well, everyone needed at least one, but they stayed out of the way for the most part.

The only real authority was the market, and that was increasingly true the world over.

The Major returned his attention for a moment to the conference room and two MBAs tag teaming a PowerPoint presentation. They were here to parse reality into benchmarks and deliverables. He glanced over at his staff agronomist, who was listening with rapt attention to their bullet points, taking notes. That was his purpose.

But not the purpose of the meeting. The Major stood along the rear wall, ostensibly a back-office troll. However, these young MBAs had no idea that they were really taking this meeting with *him*. They were bringing a problem that needed solving, even if they didn't realize it. They were the messengers.

His firm would get the contract. It would be for an infrastructure security assessment or a market risk analysis, or something similar. Korr Business Intelligence Services did not advertise, and they did not submit proposals. They were the junior partners of a security consultant to the engineering department of a construction division of a real estate subsidiary of a financial group. They had no signage out front and no listing for their firm in the lobby directory. Most of their employees were economists, researchers, and mathematicians. And very few of them had any idea what they were really doing here: preserving the global economy.

The two MBAs were still droning on about methodologies. These junior executives were always so earnest in their Savile Row suits. One was a pasty-white Brit, the other a Pakistani, also with an English accent. Probably graduates of the best schools. A wife and two young children at home—and no idea that there was video on file somewhere of them having sex with young women (or men) while they were on business in Panama, or Mali, or Brazil, or anywhere really. Get the footage while they're up-and-coming—before they suspect anyone would care. Before they become powerful. These rich dynasties had been using offshore photo mills for decades to enforce loyalty with one another, their business partners, and their kids. Get them married, set them up as respectable people in the community. Pay them tons of money—but always get photos of them with underage hookers. The more perverse, the better. It could pay huge dividends when they chaired a government committee or tried to go public with damaging information. Political ideology didn't matter. They hosted junkets for left-wingers, right-wingers. The Major had cut his teeth on a Panama operation like that back in the late eighties, using cocaine and sex workers to generate potentially career-ending imagery that made the business world go round. Photoshop had pretty much ended the still-picture side of the business by making photographs meaningless. High-def video was the only way to go now, and sooner or later computer graphics would do that in, too. Someone really had to come up with a solution, or the entire blackmail industry was doomed. Thankfully, The Major had long ago moved on to more serious operations.

The MBAs were now evaluating world commodity markets, highlighting key items with laser pointers.

The Major contemplated his present line of work—and what led him here. It was over twenty years ago that he'd taken his first life. God did not, in fact, strike him down. Instead, a problem disappeared.

He still remembered the musty smell of the La Paz hotel room. The bray of a two-stroke engine whining past outside while he stood with a bloody knife in his hand. The young trade unionist on the floor, her wide eyes staring at him as she clutched her throat, gurgling. Nothing stopped. The universe didn't care. He might as well have been slicing bread.

And that began his awakening—his realization that the Western world was a bedtime story of comforting humanistic bullshit. Slavery existed everywhere—even in the United States. We were all slaves in one way or another. Slavery was just control, and control kept things running in an orderly fashion. It was what made progress possible.

But now the *problem* he'd been waiting on suddenly appeared on-screen. A bar graph labeled "Decline in U.S. Agricultural Subsidy Applications." He turned away from the window and tuned in to the Pakistani MBA's presentation.

". . . in certain counties, we're looking at a ninety percent drop—unprecedented in the history of modern American agriculture. Farmers in these counties have basically decided en masse to stop growing subsidized crops—even though there is no distribution system available for anything else. Something is causing this, and causing it all at once on a local basis in defiance of market conditions."

The Major saw it. Nothing else had the scope to do this—and with such suddenness. It had to be the Daemon.

He spoke from the back of the room. "Why would farmers willingly turn down subsidies? With prices rising, why would they not grow corn or soybeans?"

"Excuse me, you are . . . ?" The Pakistani was taken aback by this sudden question from a junior staffer in the back of the room.

The Major's agronomist stepped in. "Yes, that's a good question. Why isn't the free market correcting this imbalance?"

The Pakistani turned back to the front row. "Uh, we

haven't been able to determine the cause. These numbers are for the coming year."

The Major spoke up again. "And you have on-the-ground confirmation. This isn't just a reporting glitch?"

"No, it's not a glitch. Agribusiness and biotech firms have a comprehensive network of private investigators, researchers, and surveyors throughout the Midwestern United States to enforce their seed patents. They've documented population movements, unexplained capital inflows, and infrastructure investments in alternative energy technologies, high-tech equipment, heirloom seed stock, and—"

"I assume this isn't confined to the United States."

The two MBAs looked at each other with some dismay. The Pakistani nodded. "We were, in fact, going to cover that later in our presentation." He started clicking through interminable bullet points and diagrams. "We also project reductions in export crops such as cotton in Asia and Russia. Security services in various countries are reporting labor unrest in both the agricultural and industrial sectors. The number of container ships being placed into warm and cold layup from lack of cargo is rising."

It's tearing apart the global supply chain.

Staring at the screen, The Major could visualize it like a full-scale nuclear attack. But one that the average person wouldn't notice—until it was beyond the tipping point.

The British chap took over. "We project that if corn and soybean harvests drop another seven percent, raw material costs for almost all processed food products will skyrocket. Low-wage factory workers around the world could suffer food shortages, with attendant increase in social unrest. Factory production and transportation might be disrupted, with serious follow-on effects for the world economy."

The Major had to hand it to Sobol. The dead bastard was clever. They'd been too focused on the digital threat to see it coming. By physically changing the economy of rural America, the Daemon could render their investment reallocation moot. They could no longer simply wait for a digital countermeasure to the Daemon. Sobol was forcing their hand, and The Major did not like the enemy dictating the tempo of battle. They needed to *act*. But quietly. Without anything that could be traced back to Daemon-infected companies.

The Major stood and looked out the window again, at the gleaming towers lining Sheikh Zayed Road. "*Change* is our enemy, gentlemen. Change means disruption. Disruption means crisis. And crisis means conflict."

That was, after all, why the powers that be had called on The Major. Conflict was his specialty.

Part Two

March

Gold:	$1,589USD/oz.
Unleaded Gasoline:	$5.34USD/gallon
Unemployment:	23.3%
USD/Darknet Credit:	28.7

Part Two

March

| Gold: | $1,425 USD/oz | Unleaded Gasoline: | $3.46 USD/gallon |
| Unemployment: | 26.3% | US/Deutsche Mark: | 28.7 |

Chapter 9: // Seed Police

Biotech companies spread patented genetic sequences via the natural ecosystem—much like a computer virus. Then they use the legal system to claim ownership of any organism their patented genetic sequences invade. They are raiding communal seed banks, obtaining patents for naturally occurring apples, sugar beets, corn, and a host of other plants and animals. They have immorally seized control of the food system and stand poised to claim ownership of life itself unless we take action.

Hank Fossen endured the bone-rattling vibration of his 1981 International Harvestor as he turned at the edge of the field. Could he limp the tractor through another full season without a major overhaul? It had over ten thousand running hours on it. Over the past several years legal fees had forced him to forgo maintenance. He'd looked into a used New Holland, but even with the spot-price of corn reaching record highs, rising expenses made it too risky to seriously consider a replacement.

He glanced back over his shoulder. The anhydrous ammonia applicator and the tank trailing behind were still in good order. He kept running the numbers in his head, wondering if he could time the corn market correctly. He actually had a chance at a decent profit this year if the planets aligned just right.

And then he saw them.

Fossen hurriedly switched off the applicator and brought the tractor to a stop in the middle of his field.

There, by the county road, were two black SUVs parked on the shoulder. Three men with clipboards were walking and kneeling in his field.

"Goddamnit!" He killed the engine and grabbed an axe handle he kept in the cab for knocking mud off tires. In a few moments he'd jumped to the ground and was jogging the couple hundred yards toward the men across bare, loamy soil.

"Get the hell off my land!" he shouted.

The men didn't budge. One of them took out a video camera and started filming him as he approached. Another was already on his cell phone.

So much for scaring them off. At forty-seven, Fossen didn't have the running stamina he'd had even five years ago. He'd put on a belly for the first time in his life with all the stress of recent years. By the time he reached the three men, he was breathing hard. The intruders were beefy types in expensive-looking GORE-TEX jackets.

Their GMC SUVs were brand-new—most likely rentals out of Des Moines.

Fossen pointed the axe handle at the nearest of them. "You have no right to be here. I want you off my land. Now!"

The nearest one was taking close-up photos of the soil with a powerful-looking lens. "We're investigators with Bosch and Miller, Mr. Fossen, here to confirm a potential patent infringement violation on behalf of Halperin Organix. We have a legal right to be here."

"Bullshit! The judge ordered a stay on physical searches pending reasonable suspicion of infringement."

The guy didn't even look up. "Well, Halperin got a state judge to reinterpret the meaning of 'reasonable.'"

Fossen pulled out his own cell phone. "I'm calling my lawyer."

"Donald Petersen is in court at the county seat right now. You won't be able to reach him."

The other two men chuckled.

Fossen lowered his phone and felt the anger rising. "You have no right to be here. I don't believe you about that state ruling."

One of the other men walked up to him aiming a digital video camera, laughing. "You willing to bet the farm, Hank?" He was a burly high-testosterone type. Most likely an ex-cop from St. Louis, where Halperin's private detective firms were based. They always got pushy assholes for this.

"We got an anonymous tip that you're using Mitroven 393, Hank."

"Planting isn't for another six or seven weeks. I'm just laying down fertilizer."

One of them was now taking soil samples. "Well, genetic material from last year is hard to get rid of."

"You pricks are *planting* Mitroven, aren't you?"

"Are you accusing us of dishonesty, Hank?" The man with the video camera laughed.

"Why would we need to do that when there's an experimental field a couple miles upwind?"

The third guy, who'd been talking on the cell phone, came up. "Don't do this to yourself, Mr. Fossen. You know Halperin will spend whatever it takes to make an example out of you. Just stop growing heirloom seed and settle. Otherwise, they'll take your farm away."

The man with the camera laughed again. "That is, unless you've got another dad waiting in the wings to kill himself for the insurance mo—"

Before he even realized it, Fossen had taken a swing at the man with the axe handle, sending the video camera flying in two pieces and damned near cracking the goon in the side of the head.

"Whoa!"

The two other men immediately closed ranks with their colleague, dropping their gear. The cell phone man was apparently the one in charge. "That was stupid, Hank! You want to wind up in jail? How do you think this will look to a judge—you attacking investigators trying to establish theft of intellectual property? Why would you behave this way if you have nothing to hide?"

Fossen wielded the axe handle in one hand, although

they weren't advancing on him. "Go ahead. Show the video! No jury would convict me. You're on my land illegally."

The ex-cameraman was still dabbing at the side of his head, looking for blood. "Let's face it, Hank, your old man bought you some time, but you're one fuck-up away from making his sacrifice pointless. And I hear stupidity is genetic."

"Time is on their side, Mr. Fossen. Accept their offer, or the lawsuits will never end."

Just then the county sheriff's patrol car pulled up behind the SUVs at the road.

Everyone straightened up as the sheriff got out. He was about Fossen's age, with a trim, military look about him. He pointedly left his shotgun in the car. He put on his Stetson and walked calmly out to the field to join the assembly.

He gestured to the axe handle in Fossen's hand. "A bit early in the season for baseball, isn't it?" The sheriff looked to the others. "Everyone all right?"

Fossen kept his eye on the private detectives. "Who called you out, Dave?"

"You wanna do me a favor and put that axe handle down?" He looked to the three strangers, one of whom was retrieving the pieces of his wrecked camera. "As much as these fellas probably deserve a beating, you and I both know you can't afford it."

"They're on my land illegally."

"No. No, they're not, Hank. They got the state court involved. Brigitte just told me on the radio. They'll call out the state police if necessary to enforce it."

The three men chuckled and started gathering up their equipment.

Fossen took a deep breath to calm himself. "I don't know how this is legal. How is this legal?"

The sheriff came closer and gently lifted the axe handle out of Fossen's hands. He spoke quietly so the others couldn't hear. "Hank, listen to me. Just get back on your tractor and finish spraying. They *want* you to lose your cool. Hank Senior wouldn't have wasted his time with these idiots."

"My father did everything right. And they still almost bankrupted us. Hell, they *would* have if . . ." Fossen stared with hatred at the men. "He never stole anything in his life. My father was cleaning seeds for people in this county for decades. And his father before him. You need to know that, Dave."

"I know it, Hank."

"Why doesn't anyone else fight back? Why do they let them do this?"

"Because they're afraid. People are hurting. They're one lawsuit away from losing everything."

"Halperin drove my father to do it. He only did it so we could keep the farm."

The sheriff nodded grimly. "Everyone knows that. No one was more respected than Hank Senior."

One of the men called out. "I hope your son is smarter than you, Hank. Or some jihadi's gonna blow him to smithereens."

The sheriff turned to them. "Hey, *I'm* a veteran. You want to make sick jokes about soldiers? What if I slapped you with a disorderly conduct charge? Who do you think your employer will believe? You or me? And you think any of your bosses might be veterans?"

They just glared.

"That's what I thought. Now pack up your shit and come back later. I'm all of out of patience with you three."

They gave him the evil eye and dragged their feet as they went. The lead one called out before he got in the car. "Uncooperative local officials find themselves outspent in elections, Sheriff."

The sheriff stood alongside Fossen as they watched the men get in their SUVs and drive off. He handed Fossen back his axe handle. "Damn good thing you didn't have a head on that, or you might have been in serious trouble."

"Thanks for talking me down."

"I've been wanting to come out and talk to you and Lynn anyway."

"What about?"

"Do you and Jenna talk much, Hank?"

Fossen narrowed his eyes. "What do you mean? What's she been up to?"

"Look, I don't mean to pry into your business, but I've been seeing her hanging out with some strange characters here in Greeley."

Fossen sighed. "Damnit. It's like I don't even know her since she came back. She's just been moping around the house for months since she graduated. There aren't any jobs—here or anywhere else."

"Look, I know things are terrible right now, but it's even stranger than that." He thumbed in the direction of his patrol car. "Remember when Sheriff Pearson patrolled this county? He had a pistol and half the time he didn't even wear it. Well, I carry a shotgun, an M16, and two pistols in the car. Crystal meth changed everything. Our department's been in eight shootouts in four years."

"Jesus, you're not telling me that Jenna is involved with drug gangs?"

"Jenna? No, that's not where I'm going with that."

"Thank god."

"My point is that suddenly—like in a single month— the meth gangs are all *gone*, Hank."

Fossen frowned. "That's good. Isn't that good?"

"Yeah—in a be-careful-what-you-wish-for sort of way. I mean, that doesn't happen. Think about it. The ruthless, prison-controlled meth gangs in the state are almost completely gone. And nonprofit treatment facilities are popping up."

"I don't know what you're trying to tell me, Dave— but I wish you'd tell me already."

"There are things going on in this county that . . ." He tried to find words, then looked up. "Well, things that don't make any sense."

"Less sense than outsiders having more rights to my land than me?"

"In a word: yes. There's some sort of strange force at work. Strange equipment is showing up—and people are tearing up their fields. Strangers—mostly young people—are moving back into the county and establishing businesses. But businesses that don't seem to accept money. They have lots of high-tech, expensive gear—but I'll be damned if I can tell what it is they do."

"And they're not gangs?"

The sheriff shook his head. "No. And they have legal counsel, too. We started investigating them, and the DA made us back off. I don't know whether they're a cult or—"

"What does this have to do with Jenna?"

"She's one of them, Hank. That's where she spends most of her time. I just thought you knew."

Fossen gazed down at the fertile but unplanted soil. He nodded to himself. "Tell me where."

Chapter 10: // Corn Rebellion

Henry Fossen waited in the dark in his F-150 pickup truck on the outskirts of Greeley. He was parked beneath the awning of an abandoned gas station across from a fenced yard shop. According to the sheriff, the yard had become a hive of activity in recent months.

Fossen watched the road for the arrival of Jenna's subcompact car. One she'd saved up to buy with her own money before college. In the meantime, he listened to AM talk radio.

The news was all bad. Inflation was on the rise, with the dollar falling against overseas currencies. This had sent gas prices soaring. Unemployment—already dismal—was getting worse. Tent cities had begun to spring up outside Des Moines. The financial crisis was supposed to be easing up, but instead it was only getting worse. And yet the stock market was still moving upward. It didn't seem to make sense.

Across the road Fossen saw silhouettes of people moving beneath flood lamps among tarp-covered pallets in the fenced-in perimeter of the yard shop. He occasionally saw forklifts moving pallets. A semitruck carrying shipping containers arrived at one point, and a lift truck pulled the containers off swiftly—sending the semi on its way.

But there was no printed sign to indicate it was a business. The sheriff said investigation of this site had been halted by the interference of a high-priced Des Moines law firm.

Fossen stared at the place. He needed to be certain the sheriff was right about Jenna before he confronted her. What had she gotten herself into? She had always seemed levelheaded—even as a teenager. Future Farmers of America, 4-H Club. Had he become complacent? Expecting her to never need his help? She excelled in school. Got a partial scholarship to ISU. Graduated with honors in biology—and walked straight out into the worst job market since the Great Depression. Here it was almost nine months later, and she was still living at home with no hope for work. She'd said she was volunteering at a nonprofit political action committee. Would she actually lie to—

Someone suddenly rapped on his passenger window, startling him. He turned to see his twenty-three-year-old daughter, Jenna, standing in a peacoat and scarf alongside his truck. She had a scowl on her face. Even so, she looked as pretty as ever.

Fossen sighed, turned down the radio, and unlocked the passenger door.

She rapped on the window glass again.

Exasperated, Fossen lowered the passenger window. "Jenna, just get in the truck."

"Dad, why did you come here?"

"Because I need to know what you're doing."

"It's not what you think."

"Damnit, Jenna, I don't ever interfere with your life, but I wasn't born yesterday."

"I'm twenty-three. I'm an adult, and I don't need you babysitting me. I haven't needed anyone to babysit me since I was eight."

"What do you expect me to do? Just ignore this? Is that what people who care about each other do? As long as you live under our roof, you'll follow family rules, and family members don't keep secrets from one another."

He gestured to the fenced yard shop across the way. "What is this place, and what the hell are you doing in there?"

She studied him unflinchingly. "The sheriff told you about this."

"Dave cares about you. He's trying to protect you."

She frowned. "He should look after himself. He does know that he has political enemies in St. Louis, right?"

Fossen suddenly felt as though he didn't recognize the person standing next to his truck. "Hold it . . . what?"

She sighed. "Dad, I don't think you'll understand what I'm doing or why."

"What you're saying is you don't think I'll *approve* of what you're doing."

"I don't care if you approve of what I'm doing."

"If you're living in our house—"

"I can move out, if I need to. I just thought that with Dennis away . . ."

He felt suddenly very hurt that she was so unreachable to him.

She seemed to notice his reaction. "Dad. I'm not saying I want to move out. I'm just saying that what I'm doing is important."

"Why can't you see that I need to know you're safe? I'm just trying to protect you."

"That's what you don't understand, Dad. I'm the one protecting *you*. And I promise you, today was the last time Halperin Organix will ever bother the Fossens of Greeley, Iowa."

He was confused. "Halperin? How is Halperin involved in this?" He studied her. "Honey, what's going on in there?"

"Dad, if I show you, you have to promise not to try to talk me out of it. Because you won't succeed."

"It's a cult, isn't it?"

She laughed out loud. "You used to be upset that I wouldn't go to church. Now you're worried I've become a fanatic." On his expression, she shook her head. "No, not a cult."

She put on a pair of expensive-looking glasses and nodded her head. "If you're coming, now's the time."

He got out of the truck and joined her as she crossed the road toward the brightly lit facility. "This is the old lumberyard, isn't it? Do you need to tell anyone that I'm coming in or . . ."

"They already know, Dad. They knew the moment you drove up."

As she and Fossen approached, the metal gates at the entrance swung open automatically. Fossen saw half a dozen people in their twenties and thirties moving busily around the yard, stabbing their hands at the air and talking to invisible people—probably on headsets, he guessed. Everyone wore expensive glasses, much like Jenna's. An unmanned forklift whined past, seemingly under the direction of no one. It deftly lifted a pallet of unmarked crates and drove off into the warehouse.

"Dad, you need to promise me you won't bother the people working in here. Quite a few of them are doing critical work, and even though they're looking right at you, they might not be able to see or hear you."

"Why wouldn't they be able to see me?"

"Because they'll be looking into a virtual dimension." On his uncomprehending look she sighed again. "I told you you wouldn't understand."

She kept walking ahead and he followed, soaking up the bustle of the yard. It seemed odd. He hadn't recalled this much activity here during the day. Come to think of it, he couldn't recall a business with this much activity in Greeley in decades. "What is it they do here, exactly?"

"This is the logistics hub for the Greeley Faction—the local node of a global mesh network powered by a narrow AI agent that's building a resilient, sustainable, high-technology civilization."

He just looked at her. "So . . ."

"Just come inside." She opened a door in the side of the warehouse and they entered a large space lined with tall shelving. Along the far wall stood several computerized milling machines with their operators focused intently on their work. The center of the room looked to be a staging area, bustling with young people, all wearing eyewear and gloves. To the side was a raised platform lined with office chairs and desks where a dozen people were grabbing, pulling, and pushing at invisible objects in the air. They were all speaking to unseen people, as though it were a call center.

Fossen nodded. "Telemarketers." He turned to her. "This is one of those network marketing schemes, isn't it? I'm really disappointed in—"

"Dad! It's nothing like that." She walked up to a canvas tarp draped over a large object. She pulled it away, revealing an old, wooden piece of equipment.

Fossen stopped cold. "A Clipper . . . what's it doing here?"

The antique seemed out of place amid the computer-controlled forklift trucks passing by. It was a century-old Clipper seed cleaner—a machine just like the one that had been in his family ever since the 1920s. His father and his father's father had used it right up until Halperin's lawyers seized it as evidence of "intellectual property theft."

He inspected it, leaning up and down. "I thought the biotech companies had destroyed most of these. . . ."

"It wasn't easy to find. We're building new ones now, but I wanted to get you an original. I was going to surprise you."

He just shook his head. "This is stupid, Jenna. We can't keep this. There are investigators taking photos of the house night and day. Halperin's lawyers will claim we're stealing their products again."

"Would you listen to yourself? They're making us bow and scrape for the right to participate in the natural world. They're *seeds*, not products."

"You know exactly what I mean. You know what these lawsuits have done to us."

"That's over now."

"Jenna, stop talking nonsense. I just ran into their agents in the north field today."

"I know. That's the last time. I promise. Our faction unlocked Level Four Legal Protection this week. It's already been activated."

He just squinted at her. "Honey, none of this makes any sense." He gestured to the rows of tall shelving, milling machines, and automated forklift trucks. "And who is paying for all this, by the way?"

"We are."

"Oh really? How?"

"Our network doesn't use the dollar. We've accrued darknet credits—a new digital currency that hasn't been saddled with twenty lifetimes of debt by corporate giveaways. We're using that currency to power a local, sustainable economy centered on Greeley."

"You're going to wind up getting arrested."

"We're free to use private currencies, as long as they're convertible to the dollar."

"But why would you bother?"

"Because the dollar is about to go into hyperinflation. There's nothing supporting it. The darknet currency is backed by joules of green energy—something intrinsically valuable."

"I just don't understand any of this, Jenna."

"My generation has no intention of living as serfs on a corporate manor, Dad. When people became more reliant on multinational corporations than on their own communities, they surrendered whatever say they had in their government. Corporations are growing stronger while democratic government becomes increasingly helpless."

"Listen, whatever you're going through—"

"Just look at corn and soybeans, subsidized with tax-payer money—creating a market that wouldn't otherwise make sense. Why? So agribusiness firms have cheap inputs to make processed food. The taxpayers are basically subsidizing corporations to make crap, when we could have grown real food on our own. But, of course, they've made growing food illegal now. . . ."

He started to walk away. "I want you to leave with me."

"Dad, there was a reason you didn't want me or Dennis to go into farming. You wanted us to go to college and get away from here. Do you remember why? Do you remember what you said to me?"

He stopped. He didn't face her, but nodded. "I said that there's no future in farming."

"Food is the very *heart* of freedom. Don't you realize that? If people don't grow the food, we both know who will: biotech companies like Halperin Organix. How can people be free if they can't feed themselves without getting sued for patent violations?"

He looked around the warehouse as workers passed by. "Look, your mother and I did the best we could for—"

She came up and put a hand on his shoulder. "I know you did. You're honest. So was Granddad. And so am I. But they've rigged the game. It was like this during the Gilded Age of the 1890s. And then again in the late 1920s. It's nothing new. We're just trying to break the cycle."

He stared at her, unsure whether he wanted to understand what she was saying. "Then you're not coming home with me?"

She shook her head. "No. I've got work to do. I'll be back home later tonight."

He shrugged. "You know, I worry about you. You and your brother. I know it hasn't been easy. I . . . There's no real jobs anymore. I feel like we've let you down." Fossen started to tear up.

She hugged him tightly. "Dad, you didn't let me down." She looked back up at him. "You taught me everything I need to know: self-reliance, self-respect, community. Just don't be surprised if I actually put it to use."

Fossen sat in his La-Z-Boy chair with the television off. He listened to the old house settling. To the ticking of the grandfather clock in the foyer and the refrigerator fan turning on and off as the minutes passed.

It was late.

Then he heard the dogs barking and a car coming up the long drive. He didn't move. He heard footsteps on the back porch, and then the door in the mudroom squeak open and thump closed. Still he sat motionless.

A creak on the floorboards nearby. Jenna's voice. "Dad? It's late. You okay?"

He just held up a letter on embossed stationery. "You know, it's been nearly five years. And after all that time, it just takes one letter."

She stood in the doorway.

"How did you do it?"

"I told you."

"No. You really didn't, Jenna." He looked up at her. "How does a twenty-three-year-old kid get a multibillion-dollar company to drop a lawsuit?"

"It was the Daemon."

"What *is* the Daemon?"

"It's a digital monster that eats corporate networks. They're scared to death of it—because it has no fear."

He turned to face the dark television screen again. They sat in silence for several moments.

"What happens now?"

"That depends on whether you want to continue running this place as part of their system."

Fossen looked up at the framed photograph of his eldest son in dress uniform on a nearby bookshelf. He nodded. "I didn't realize we had two warriors in the family."

He turned around to face her. "What do we do?"

She smiled. "The first thing we do is stop planting corn."

"And plant what?"

"What people need."

Chapter 11: // Hunted

Southhaven was a self-styled "six-star" golf resort catering to business. Pharmaceutical companies marketing blood thinners to cardiovascular surgeons, investment retreats, political fund-raisers—all of them were capable of filling the two hundred and eighty outrageously expensive guest bungalows. In another age it might have been a duke's estate—a place where the affairs of men might be discussed with sophistication while wives strolled the gardens and the children took riding lessons. Now it was a rental that offered double mileage points.

With a world-class golf course, four restaurants, and a bar that permitted cigar smoking, Southhaven Golf Resort was the ideal place to get business done in a relaxed atmosphere. The resort was located on Ocean Island—one of several barrier islands off the southern Atlantic coast of Georgia. Gated and patrolled, the private island consisted of the Southhaven resort, its golf course, and a hundred or so sprawling Mediterranean-style beach houses—third or fourth homes to people looking for somewhere to dump capital gains. Most of the homes were unoccupied at any given time.

A big selling point for Ocean Island was its remoteness. It was buffered by a mile and a half of marshland to the west and north and linked to the mainland by a single causeway. To the east and south lay only the Atlantic Ocean.

In short, it was perfect for The Major's purpose. He'd long ago graduated from clandestine meetings in run-down safe houses or industrial spaces. He was the establishment now, and he enjoyed its perquisites.

The Major sat on the arm of a sofa in their Emperor Bungalow, talking on his encrypted cell phone with a broker in Hong Kong. He glanced at his watch. Eleven fifty P.M. "Yes. It should be part of the dark liquidity pool. Right. Two hundred thousand shares."

He looked up at the dining room to see half a dozen senior managers of international security and military providers gathered around a table strewn with maps of the Midwestern United States, photographs, and documents. No two of the men had the same accent—South African, Eastern European, Australian, American, British, Spanish. Several were smoking as they pondered the maps. They were debating something, and the British executive motioned for The Major to rejoin the table.

He knew he wouldn't have too many more chances to shift his investments. And he wasn't about to miss the upcoming event.

The Major nodded and spoke into the phone. "Yeah. Empty the Sutherland—"

His phone connection suddenly dissolved in a wave of static. The Major looked at the phone's display and saw the message "Connection Lost." He cursed and moved to dial again when he realized he suddenly had no network signal.

"Damnit!"

The Major looked up to see one of the nearby security executives putting his own phone onto his belt clip.

The man shrugged to the others. "No signal." Then pointed to a map. "Look, I'll call them back, but we're going to need materiel in-country for security teams well before then."

But The Major was no longer concerned with logistics for the counterinsurgency campaign. He was suddenly concerned about his own survival.

They had just lost wireless connectivity. The Major remembered all too well that the attack at Building Twenty-Nine was preceded by radio jamming. The FBI operation at Sobol's mansion was also plagued by wireless communications problems—all caused by ultra-wideband signals. The same technology used by the Daemon's automated vehicles to communicate with the darknet. It was battle-level bandwidth that steamrolled everything else.

The Major reached for a remote control on the coffee table in front of him. He used it to turn on the radio in the living room entertainment center. Nothing but static. He kept scanning stations.

The South African executive frowned at him. "Ag, Major. We need you to make a decision here. Can we hold off on the stereo?"

The Major wasn't listening. His combat instincts had kicked in. The chatter of the senior executives at the table faded, and his senses focused on his immediate surroundings. On the significance of every sound. It brought him back to El Salvador. Listening for the snap of a branch—or for an unearthly animal silence that signaled a hastily prepared ambush. He heard the nearby men arguing as only muffled sounds. The footsteps of a Romanian private security contractor walking to the service tray near the curtained window to pour more coffee commanded his attention. The heavy drapes behind the man billowed as conditioned air washed over them.

Then an unexplained sound, like a tent door being unzipped, came from the courtyard outside—and it kept unzipping—getting louder.

The next few moments, he felt as though he were pulling himself through a pool of water—his mind racing ahead, screaming at his body to keep up. He pushed off the sofa and charged toward the contractor standing near the drape-covered window.

The man started to turn, apparently sensing danger, but The Major leapt into the air, delivering a flying dropkick that sent the Romanian headlong through the thick drapes and French doors altogether, with a deafening crash.

Just then, the front door to the bungalow burst open as a human-sized piece of twisted machinery blasted through it going eighty miles an hour. It careened across the room sending pieces of metal and plastic ricocheting off the walls, overturning the table, and clearing the men there off their feet.

The Major didn't look back as the deafening sound of powerful motorcycle engines suddenly erupted all around the bungalow. Behind him, he could hear screaming and motorcycles engines so loud the noise was physically painful. He ran through the smashed French doors, and once outside he saw the stunned and bloody Romanian trying to get up in a field of broken glass and splintered wood. The Major stomped on the man's chest, flattening him on the patio stones.

The man tried to squirm out from under The Major's foot and breathe. Powerful motorcycle engines were coming his way fast across the lawns, green lasers stabbing at the darkness.

The Major drove his heel into the contractor's throat, causing the man to grab at his own neck, pawing for air. He then reached down beneath the Romanian's jacket and felt the holster there. A polyurethane harness. He tugged at it in the darkness and felt the gun come free. No more time. The engines were close.

The Major took off through the bushes, hugging the side of the building, and ducked around the nearest corner moments before the razorbacks arrived. He felt the contours of the newly acquired pistol in the darkness. Twin safetys. Probably a Sig Sauer. He hefted it. A .45— and loaded, judging by the weight. He chambered a round as the engines revved behind him. He heard agonized screams and ringing of steel.

The Major ran blindly through the bushes now under cover of the screams and engines. Branches hit his face as he pushed through the thick of it and soon he emerged into a golf cart lane flanked by soft landscape lighting and dense tropical shrubbery. In his peripheral vision he caught the movement of men in black tactical gear pointing his way. Although he didn't hear gunshots, he heard projectiles whine past his head as he plunged into the bushes on the far side of the path. He fired two shots to get them ducking and kept cover as motorcycle engines kept pace with him out on the lawns and driveways beyond the decorative jungle.

The Major ran headlong into a rough-hewn beam railing, but without missing a beat he clambered over it, collapsing onto a tiled walkway between resort buildings. It was brightly lit. He glanced right and left and could see fire strobes flashing in the interior corridors. He suddenly noticed the warning Klaxons sounding. Someone had tripped a fire alarm. Good.

He crawled across the tiled floor on his belly and peered through the gap between the handrail and the wall on the far side. He could see more shrubs and a small parking lot behind the reception building.

The Major rolled over the railing and into the bushes on the far side. He was quickly out to the parking lot and trying car doors. Locked. Locked.

He tried to remember how to hot-wire a car, and then it occurred to him that cars had utterly changed since his days of twisting wires in the dark in Belize City. They were computer-controlled now—in fact the damned things had lately become smart enough to hunt *him*.

Motorcycle engines trolled the grounds out in the darkness. Lights were coming on in the guest room windows. Shouts echoed across the grounds.

"Call the police! Someone call the police!"

It suddenly occurred to him that he still had his phone. He pulled it out of his jacket pocket and hurled it as far as possible across the parking lot, where it shattered against something hard in the dark. For all he knew, that's how the Daemon tracked him here. It was an untraceable phone. He'd only had it for a few days. How had they found him? He started thinking of possible vectors but decided he'd have time to worry about it later if he survived the night.

He saw car headlights approaching from the direction of the clubhouse and peered down the lane from behind a nearby car tire.

A well-dressed man in his seventies was behind the wheel of a Bentley Continental Flying Spur. It was doing about ten miles per hour.

The Major hid the pistol behind his leg and affected a stiff limp, rushing to block the road. He held up his free hand and did his best to look panicked. The car slowed and came to a stop. The Major limped over to the door as the driver lowered his window.

"What's the problem, son?"

"My wife and I were hit by a drunk driver coming back from the club. I need someone to call an ambulance."

"My god, that's horrible." The old man put the car into park and searched for his phone.

Putting the car into park was crucial.

By the time the driver looked up again The Major had the pistol pointed at his head. The Major fired a shot into the old man's forehead at close range. The ivory leather interior spattered with blood.

Messy. Unprofessional.

Small caliber pistols were better for this sort of thing. The bullet wouldn't go out the back of the head.

Suddenly The Major heard a razorback turn a corner

a hundred yards behind them. He looked away quickly, knowing that they carried blinding weapons. He'd read Dr. Philips's after-action report.

A green laser played across The Major and the Bentley's mirrors in a brilliant light show. He could hear the bike roaring in his direction. The Major dove headfirst through the open driver's window and climbed across the still-twitching corpse of the old man. As The Major turned right-side up in the passenger seat he reached his leg over the console hump to get his foot onto the accelerator. He could hear more razorbacks converging on the site from nearby. Suddenly a razor-sharp katana-like blade shot into the old man's neck through the open window. A second slash took the old man's head clean off.

The Major fired three shots into the motorized gimbal that held the sword, deforming the mount and causing the bike to eject the blade and pull away from the car, swinging around to aim its beam weapons. The Major ducked his head down and dropped the pistol as the cabin filled with green laser light. He finally managed to reach the gas pedal with his left foot. The shifter between his legs, he jammed the car into drive and felt the powerful engine accelerating him down the narrow road. He ignored the blood all over the seats and the headless man beside him—along with the head now rolling around on the floor.

"Goddamnit! Goddamnit!" He pounded the dashboard. He'd lost his cool. There were surveillance cameras all over this place. He'd need to get ahold of this security video. He was panicking. He needed to get his shit together. And what about the military plans back in the room? He tried to steady himself. *You used to be good at operations once.*

The Bentley was roaring up to sixty now, and he barely had control of it. He dared a glance into the rearview mirror and could see several razorbacks coming up on him very fast. Soon they were flickering laser light all over the car. He smashed the rearview mirror off the ceiling with his fist.

"Fuck!"

The Bentley caromed off the sides of several cars parked along the restaurant drive, and he struck one of the parking valets. The man's body tumbled into the bushes.

The Major stomped the accelerator and listened for the deep howl of the approaching bikes behind him. Their thunderous engines grew in volume. He was going eighty now and still accelerating—palm trees and dense brush passed by very fast. It looked like he was going along the coast and the huge private homes there.

Suddenly The Major slammed on the brakes, bringing the large sedan to a screeching stop and sending him hard against the dashboard. The headless body stayed secure as the seat belt pretensioners kick in. A split second later he heard several crashes as the car nudged forward. A large motorcycle hurtled over the left side of the car and tumbled in a shower of sparks down the road.

The Major gunned the engine again, looked behind him to see two more bikes lying on their sides in the road—along with a section of his back bumper. He killed the headlights and turned the car through the front fence of a nearby estate. The Bentley crashed through a white wooden fence line and shuddered across uneven ground as security lights turned on all over the lawn. He dodged palm trees and bushes to bring the car roaring alongside the house. He smashed through patio furniture, aiming toward the pool, then let up on the gas. He opened the passenger door—to dinging alarms—and waited until the right moment. He grabbed his gun, flicked on the safety, and rolled clear onto the grass.

He slid to a stop and watched the Bentley continue through the pool fence and dip nose-down in what turned out to be the shallow end, sending up a column of steam.

"Damnit!"

He got up and ran toward a nearby tree line, motorcycle engines converging on his location. He heard dogs barking. There was a salt smell in the air. He felt very much alive at the moment—adrenaline coursing through his bloodstream. It had been a while.

He ran through some trees and reached a wood fence line. Shoving the pistol into his belt at the small of his back, he climbed over the fence deftly. Dropping to the other side, he moved through ornamental tropical brush toward an even larger Mediterranean mansion.

Security lights started kicking on all around him and he cursed his bad luck for being in such a high-security enclave when this had gone down. Far better to be in some shantytown or packed city street where he could get lost among the populace. He picked up a rock from the garden and hurled it at the garage light next to him, shattering it and bringing back darkness.

He could hear what sounded like a dozen razorbacks on the road now, but they weren't following the trail of carnage to the pool next door. They were concentrating on the gate at his current location. *Goddamnit.*

The Major ran around the garage toward the backyard, kicking open a tall fence gate and coming face-to-face with a portly caretaker holding a flashlight. The man was strapping on a pistol holster.

The Major drove his fist into the caretaker's solar plexus, and followed with an openhanded blow across the throat. He then cleared the man's legs out from under him. The flashlight fell to the paving stones and went out. The caretaker gasped for air, while The Major grabbed the gun from the man's holster. He clicked the hammer back and pressed it into the caretaker's right eye. "Car keys! Where are the keys?"

The man's eyes were wild with fear. He pointed at the garage, trying to speak. He finally croaked out, "Box on the wall . . ."

The Major pistol-whipped him unconscious and then rolled him into the pool.

Goddamnit! What if there's surveillance video here, too?

He'd been balancing risks. If he let the man live, the guy would call in the car as stolen, and The Major might get caught in a police standoff. And either way, he'd need to get rid of any witnesses.

He ran to the garage and kicked in the door. He soon found the lights and saw three cars there, two under tarpaulins and one not—a silver '69 Camaro with black racing stripes. There was a strongbox on the wall, and he felt the anger rising when he found it locked. He aimed the caretaker's .38 revolver at it and fired first one, then two, then three shots. He finally got it open and located the Camaro keys.

Meanwhile, outside there was pandemonium. It sounded like every razorback in the area had already gotten onto the estate and was scouring the place for him. The Major was becoming calmer with every second. He was easing into a familiar groove. Fieldwork had its rewards and adrenaline highs were one of them.

He got into the Camaro and strapped himself into the racing harness. He started the car and it let up a satisfying roar. Suddenly Boston was playing on the stereo— "Don't Look Back." The Major turned it up, revved the engine again, and realized that he had sunglasses in his jacket pocket. He put them on. They might not completely protect him from laser light, but they'd help. He then tapped the garage door opener on the visor and roared out of the garage, tires squealing.

He found three razorbacks waiting in the driveway outside the garage; he hit the first one and sent it skidding into the fountain. As laser lights focused on him, he spun a one-eighty and headed out through the rear lawn. There, he smashed aside another razorback that tried to throw itself under the car and brought the Camaro crashing through the rear fence. He'd made it out onto the beach.

The Major could see a dozen powerful green lasers tracking the car's movement as it skidded sideways, straightened out, and then started roaring down the beach toward the mainland. From the unevenness of the sand, he figured the motorcycles would lose any speed advantage—they might not even be able to steer. He cranked up the music as muzzle flashes appeared in the trees to his right. Bullets clanged into the car body and spidered the window glass. *Human operatives as well?* "Is that all you've got, you sons a bitches?"

He kept the pedal down and sped on, watching the lights of beachfront homes race by.

The Major kept going for nearly five miles, at times reaching a hundred and twenty miles an hour as he raced down the nighttime beach as close to the water as he dared. He was surprised not to see a single person. The wealthy certainly had an odd idea of what to do with a beach.

But eventually he would run out of island—that much he knew. And there was only one causeway off of it, which would definitely be guarded. So he couldn't go that way. The fact that no police had arrived told him that there was a major operation under way to get him. Something had leaked. He was starting to get mad just thinking about it. How had he been located?

From what he remembered, there was another barrier island not far south, separated from this one by a narrow inlet. He kept going south, and soon found himself driving over shallow dunes. He slowed the car down and stayed close to the coastline.

He was heading into utter blackness now. After he killed his headlights, there was only starlight to see by. The Major kept his eye on a luminescent dashboard compass the owner had installed. Due south.

Soon enough he saw lights of distant houses ahead,

and with very little warning, he almost drove into the narrow inlet that separated the low strip of sand he was on from the other island perhaps a hundred and seventy-five yards away.

He put the car in neutral, turned off the dome light, then took off his shoes and got out. He removed his jacket and began wiping down the car and the guns for fingerprints. It was a bit late, since he was certain he'd left prints all over the place behind him, but it couldn't hurt. He'd still need to get ahold of any surveillance video. He started thinking of the names of operators who could manage that.

The Major found a toolbox in the Camaro's trunk. He put the car in gear, then eased out of the driver's seat as he released the clutch and lowered the toolbox onto the gas pedal—the car roared off into the inlet and soon splashed through the water, eventually stalling and rolling away as it began to sink.

The Major grabbed his shoes, tied them together and hung them over his neck, wrapped the guns inside his jacket, and started swimming for the far bank, through bubbles still coming up from the car. The water was shockingly cold, but he didn't think hypothermia would be an issue across this distance.

The Major swam with calm determination toward the far shore. About halfway across he dumped both guns and kept going. A few minutes later he climbed over a low jetty of rocks on the far side. He lay resting on the rocks in the darkness, listening to the waves wash against the stones.

He stared up at the starry night sky from his place in

the shadows. Some of his contractors were dead. They would have to be replaced. Some generalized plans had fallen into the hands of the enemy, but it could have been worse. Yes, the enemy would now know they were up to something in the Midwest, but it couldn't be news to them, could it?

But he was alive. In fact, The Major hadn't felt this alive in years. He thought back to nights spent in South American jungles. They were some of the most vivid memories he had. That was truly living.

He stared up at the field of stars above him.

And suddenly he saw a dark, wing-shaped object noiselessly gliding across the blue-black field. *They've got surveillance drones.* He snapped alert and grabbed his things. He ran barefoot across the beach toward a pier that jutted out over the water. The Major ran inland beneath it, the wood planks coming closer and closer overhead, until finally he was crawling up to the very beams themselves, pushing sand away to get deeper in, climbing under the boardwalk. He smelled the tar, discarded cigarettes, and dog shit, but he kept digging.

He heard powerful motorcycle engines and diesel trucks approaching. The Major started to push sand back behind him with his feet, hiding his presence. He was sweating profusely, blocking himself in. Then heard steel-shod boots approaching on the boardwalk. Dozens of others were racing over the asphalt to either side. Motorcycle engines throbbed in the background.

The footsteps stopped near The Major's hiding place. He could see shadows nearby between the planks and the voices of men.

"The car is in the water on the far side. He crossed here."

"Looks like the shortest swim."

"How did they find him?"

"Fingerprint scanners on the room locks. Loki released the biometric database from Building Twenty-Nine to the darknet. People have been inserting software bots into all sorts of systems for months."

A chuckle.

"We'll get him. There's nowhere in the world he can hide now."

Loki walked through the shattered bungalow door wearing his black helmet and riding suit. He wasn't too concerned about his safety. As a fifty-sixth-level darknet Sorcerer, he had the best gear credits could buy. His black riding suit resembled leather inlaid with titanium wire, but it was actually composed of flexible polymer fibers lined with sheer thickening liquid—a mixture of polyethylene glycol and particles of silica whose chemical structure stiffened instantly into a solid under rapid compression. In technical terms the gel displayed a highly nonlinear rate-dependent sheer resistance—which in layman's terms meant it could stop a bullet or a knife while still being comfortable to wear. However, Loki also had pieces of ceramic composite trauma plate in critical areas, and on the backs of his gloves, as much for looks as protection. This was his faction battle armor, and he seldom moved about without it. Especially in these troubled times.

His hands were clad in gel armor gloves as well, with

fiber-optic lines running like veins along the backs of his hands and along his body, leading to a wearable computer on his belt at the small of his back. Two of the fiber lines also ran to lenses contained in engraved, titanium enclosures at the ends of his index fingers to accommodate his LIPC weaponry. His belt buckle bore the symbol of the Stormbringer faction—twin lightning bolts with skulls in each quadrant. Such was the culture of the darknet—manga come to life.

Through the sensors in his outfit, Loki could "feel" the world immediately around him, in a complete sphere. Next to his skin he wore a haptic shirt that pulsed electronic signals like pixels on a screen, to give him a sensory impression of the area all around him. He could "feel" the walls and shapes of obstacles ahead of him in darkness or smoke.

Loki linked more than nearby geometry to his vest. He also reserved several areas of his skin for more powerful electrical pulses—alerts from his pack of razorbacks, darknet news, or news about The Major, or mentions of Loki's real-life name anywhere on the Web. Loki was intimately connected to the world around him—both the real one and the numberless dimensions of D-Space.

He surveyed the blood-spattered furniture and scattered body parts of dead military contractors. His air filtration system kept most of the intestinal stench out of his nostrils. Blood was still dripping down the walls and off the ceiling. There was a shattered razorback giving off smoke in the corner, but the piercing shriek of the smoke detector made no impression on Loki in his insulated motorcycle helmet.

A glance around the room confirmed what he already knew. The Major wasn't among the dead. Loki had remotely piloted the lead razorback and slaved the others to it. Perhaps the frontal assault had been a mistake. The Major was a veteran operator, after all.

But there might still be useful intelligence here. The "Cult of Efficiency" was meeting here for a reason. With several other razorbacks patrolling the perimeter, Loki figured he had a while before local police had the courage to move past the carnage at the front gate.

He kicked over the butchered corpse of a husky Latin American man in an expensive suit. The man had been slashed open neck to groin, spine deep—then hip to shoulder. Beneath him on the floor was a blood-soaked map. Loki kicked the carcass aside and overturned a dining room table to reveal a topographical map. He started to notice a collection of large-format survey maps of the Midwestern United States spread about the room. They were torn and stained with blood.

What are you planning, Major?

He snapped several high-definition photos with his HUD display. Loki then reached a black-gloved hand out to turn on a layer of D-Space—one that revealed all wireless consumer electronics data emitted in his vicinity. With it, he immediately saw the mobile equipment identifiers (MEIDs) of several phones floating above the dead men in D-Space, as well as Bluetooth IDs to various headsets and wireless devices around the bungalow. He could also see SSIDs for nearby Wi-Fi access points— floating in three-dimensional space as call-outs.

Loki activated a darknet telecommunications search

portal, which appeared as a single orange ring of light floating in space a foot or so in front of him. It was a digital receptacle into which he swept each of the MEIDs of the dead men's phones with a wave of his gloved hand. The orange circle flashed and in a moment shrank, transforming into a series of six names associated with those handsets. Aliases, of course, but Loki wasn't looking for their names. He wanted their social network.

Loki turned to look at the shattered French doors, the curtains swaying in a tropical breeze. The Major had been here, and he couldn't have gotten far.

Loki pushed aside his D-Space portal app and brought up an overhead satellite photo of his current GPS position. The image of the bungalow's roof floated as a D-Space object, in a private translucent dimension a foot and a half in front of him, where he could work with it. With a couple of clicks he overlaid mobile phone tracking data from four major telecom carriers onto the image of the bungalow roof. He adjusted a slider to move back in time from the present, showing various dots— each representing a phone handset—moving around the bungalow. There were six individuals. Then he spotted a seventh handset coming in from the patio right about the time his lead razorback hit the door.

Loki zoomed out and let the clock run forward— watching the dot representing that same phone handset move through the French doors, and then across the grounds toward the parking lot. At that point the phone disappeared from the map.

Loki rewound the timeline and clicked on the dot—

retrieving its MEID, which he then swept into his search portal list.

He now had seven identities. He examined the last name—The Major's current alias: *Anson Gregory Davis.*

Loki immediately sent the identity out to the darknet feed dedicated to finding The Major. He knew hundreds of thousands of people were monitoring it. Perhaps The Major would make the mistake of using a credit card from this identity within the next few hours. Likewise, he knew they'd analyze the purchase patterns of this identity, as well. Did The Major buy a coffee at the same time each day? Did he drink a rare type of scotch? Smoke a rare cigar—or have any other unique tastes that couldn't be masked by a false identity? One they could use to detect him wherever he reappeared? If so, the crowd would find it.

In the meantime, Loki wanted to see what sort of friends "Mr. Davis" had been speaking with. Loki clicked on the name and it quickly expanded into a map of variously sized dots radiating out from a central hub—like the map of a star system. Loki knew each dot represented a unique phone number that The Major had called with this specific handset. The size of the dot represented how often he had called it. With another click, Loki examined the calls made by The Major's most talked-to colleagues. Intelligence experts called this sort of map a "community of interest," and each level of detail was called a "generation." He was now looking at a "two-generation community of interest" for The Major. Loki laid the calling data over a map of the world and noticed a very even geographic spread within the U.S.—plus a few dozen calls overseas to Europe, Asia, and the Middle East.

Loki added the second-generation data for the most talked-to colleagues, and suddenly a pattern began to form. Indeed, it was focused throughout the Midwestern states—Kansas, Iowa, Missouri. Bringing up the third generation made the pattern even clearer.

There were operations under way in the Midwest. He stared hungrily at the tiny dots. Each one represented a person—a person who was now known to him and who could be tracked down. At this level of abstraction they looked like ants.

Ants that were about to get squashed . . .

Chapter 12: // Masterwork

The GamerZ faction has launched the open-source Burning Man Project with the express aim of "resurrecting" Roy Merritt as a system-level D-Space avatar. The planned avatar would obey the eleven principles of the Order of Merritt and be imbued with powers as participants donate levels. The project was made feasible through the recent discovery of comprehensive biometric data for the late Roy Merritt in the Building Twenty-Nine security database. The data includes body and facial geometry, textures, voice, gait, and other info. Contributors need a five-star reputation score and at least fifteen levels of proficiency in their primary class.

XiLAN_oO*****/ 2,930   23rd-level Programmer

Situated just across the Pearl River Delta from Hong Kong, Shenzhen was a city of migrants. Declared a Special Economic Zone by the Chinese government in 1980, it was an experiment in limited capitalism—and had grown with astonishing speed. Fueled by cheap labor, Shenzhen's population exploded from three hundred thousand to over twelve million people in less than three decades. State-of-the-art factory complexes producing goods for Western companies covered mile after mile in the northern reaches of the city, away from the tourism- and trade-centered southern districts.

Jon Ross had been here for only a few weeks, and already he liked it better than Beijing. The air was better, for one thing, and it had milder, subtropical weather. It was a city made for the type of person he was pretending to be—a thirty-year-old, successful entrepreneur looking for manufacturing capacity. To such a person, Shenzhen held many charms, not the least of which was cheap, skilled labor.

China was no longer punching out plastic trinkets. They made iPods, computers, and medical devices here now. High-quality merchandise. If you were making shirts or plastic patio chairs, you brought your business to Vietnam or Pakistan. At least for now.

Ross gazed out the window. Thousands of blue-uniformed, female factory workers with multicolored ID tags clipped to their pockets surged around Ross's chauffeured Buick Regal. As they pressed past in the narrow lane between production buildings and dormitories, the car's blacked-out windows hid Ross from their view. His driver honked the horn repeatedly and cursed in Mandarin as they inched along. Ross studied the tableau of humanity as it squeezed by—or he by it. It was hard to tell which. Up close, every worker was distinct in some way. Their eyes. Their expression. But in a few moments each disappeared into the crowd.

He knew why they had come to Shenzhen—to send hard money back to their families in rural China. So much rested on the shoulders of these young women. They might be the only hope of a family that had borrowed heavily to send them here. Failure might mean the loss of the family home. That burden gave a sense of deadly seriousness to their labor—particularly since the global economy had recently started to fray at the edges, and layoffs were a daily occurrence throughout the city.

Ross knew that the same migration was occurring all around the world. In a land of borderless markets, individual farmers could no longer compete with industrial farms on price. The land was being depopulated, landholdings aggregated for efficient management by farm machinery, leaving the surplus labor little choice but to depart to the cities and seek work in industry. The same was true in India, the Philippines, and Indonesia. Even America. It was the largest migration in human history. All in the pursuit of high-efficiency, low-cost production.

And it was that very efficiency that made the system vulnerable to the Daemon. The same uniform networks that moved money and information between markets in fractions of a second also allowed the simple bots of the Daemon to masquerade as high-level management strategy, ordering the manufacture and delivery of goods— and deleting the evidence. State-of-the-art, just-in-time management systems had enabled a silent revolution in more ways than one.

Such was the post-Sobol world.

Ross's car cleared the crowded main road and turned

down an empty lane between factory buildings with tall banks of windows. The workers seemed to be walking a beeline between points, and not one of them detoured down this lane. Ross's car approached an unmarked steel door where a glowing, catlike eye hovered in D-Space to mark his destination. It would be invisible to nondarknet members.

He tapped his driver on the shoulder and pointed. The moment the car stopped, Ross exited.

He stood in the fire lane before the featureless door. There was no handle and no hinges on this side. The metal looked capable of stopping rifle rounds. Ross adjusted his second-generation HUD glasses—smaller and more businesslike than earlier models—and looked up at the glowing, three-dimensional eye, floating in D-Space above the doorway. A spectral object that only existed in virtual space. He glanced back at the black Buick, still parked nearby. He motioned for the driver to depart and nodded in response to the driver's quizzical expression. The driver shrugged, wrote down an entry in his logbook, and drove off.

Ross watched the car go, then reached into his suit jacket pocket and removed a small silver amulet set with a single green cat's-eye stone. It matched the symbol hovering above the door. He positioned the amulet in his line of sight in the HUD glasses so that it matched the glowing symbol in both size and orientation, and carefully held it there. He then spoke slowly in a language that only existed in the online game world created by Matthew Sobol—the language of the creators. *"De abolonos— fi theseo va—temposum—gara semulo—va cavrotos."*

At the intonation of the last syllable, a bright light began to glow from his amulet. He was certain it was only a D-Space light, one that did not exist in the real world. Nonetheless, it was real to him, and so he squinted his eyes against the glow of pico projectors in his glasses as a bright tracery appeared in D-Space around the doorway. The white lines curled and expanded, forming the outline of an ornate gate that blazed with white light, emanating from the seams of the real-world door. In a moment he heard a *click*, and the real-world door opened slowly, spilling forth D-Space light.

Ross lowered the amulet, and shielded his eyes as he walked through the gate. His hand blocked nothing, because the light came from within his glasses. Realizing his mistake, he flipped up his HUD lenses and soon found himself standing in a small factory room lined with shelves piled high with electrical components. Ross could hear the roar of powerful electric motors, as well as the crack and pop of automated welding machinery in the factory beyond. But here in this small room, two armed and uniformed Chinese factory guards stood before him, staring hard with arms folded. The steel door behind him slammed shut.

Ross flipped his HUD lenses back down and saw darknet call-outs hovering above both men. They weren't only security guards—they were ninth-level Fighters with four-star reputation scores, from the Dark Rose faction. Hard-core operatives who could summon a flash mob at a moment's notice. D-Space call-outs identified the one on the right as *Sentinel949*. The one on the left was

Warder_13. Ross knew his own call-out showed him to be a sixth-level Rogue with a four-and-a-half-star reputation, but he noticed Warder_13 clicking through Ross's achievement log, and examining his current quest, while Sentinel949 just looked him up and down.

That's when Ross noticed that the Dark Rose faction was an Order of Merritt signatory—as denoted by the flame on its logo. He smiled to himself, marveling at how far Roy Merritt's fame had spread. The Order of Merritt was a spontaneously evolved standard of conduct with a rigorous ethical requirement. Ross knew he'd be treated fairly here.

Warder_13 spoke to Ross in what sounded like Mandarin. A moment later Ross heard a woman's voice in his ear translating the warrior's words: "Rakh, they say you were friends with the Burning Man. That you were there the day he died."

Ross nodded. "Roy was as decent and courageous as anyone can be. I was fortunate to have known him."

Warder_13 and Sentinel949 nodded appreciatively.

Sentinel949 asked, "Why have you come through the Maker's Gate?"

"I've come to forge a masterwork." The Mandarin translation of Ross's words followed moments later.

Sentinel949 raised an eyebrow. "A masterwork? Which one?"

"The Rings of Aggys."

The guards exchanged looks. Warder_13 clicked through objects in midair that only he could see. "This is a serious item. You have the prerequisites?"

Ross nodded. "I do."

"Not just the network credits, but the elements as well."

"I took the nine quests and have all the pieces. PlineyElder should be expecting me." Ross put a leather dispatch case on a nearby desk and opened it. He withdrew an ornate wooden box above which nine small D-Space call-outs crowded one another. He handed the box to Sentinel949.

The guard opened it and could see nine pieces of jewelry, eight half-rings of titanium—four of them smaller than the others—and a single crystal. They were all stored in foam receptacles. Each had a separate D-Space call-out. He examined them and nodded to his colleague. "The elements are genuine."

"The aspirant clears the reputation limit and has the necessary credits."

"He has passed the necessary class specialties."

Warder_13 spoke clearly and with official ceremony when he declared, "The aspirant has all the elements of the Rings of Aggys. The masterwork can be attempted." Ross knew that voice-recognition bots were listening to the announcement, and that keywords in this statement would activate the next stage in the process.

The guards motioned for Ross to follow as they headed across the storeroom and unlocked a large interior door. Ross grabbed his dispatch case and followed. One of them handed Ross a red hard hat with built-in hearing protectors from a rack on the wall. Ross donned it as the guards put on white hard hats of their own.

Warder_13 pointed to the headphones and spoke again. Moments later the translation came through

Ross's bone-conduction mic, despite the loud noise. "Don't take your earphones off. It gets loud in there."

Ross nodded, and they opened the steel door onto a vast manufacturing floor filled with zapping and popping industrial welding robots. Two engineers wearing bright green coveralls and white hard hats were waiting for them at the first row of machines. Call-outs above the men's heads identified them as a tenth-level Sorcerer named *PlineyElder* and a ninth-level Fabricator named *WuzzGart*.

PlineyElder looked at his watch as they approached. He also spoke in Mandarin. "You're late."

Ross shrugged. "There was traffic."

"There's *always* traffic. This is Shenzhen."

Warder_13 handed the wooden box to the sorcerer, who opened it and inspected the contents closely. He then looked up at Ross. "I hope you have your spells ready. I don't have all day to deal with this."

Ross nodded. "You just do your part, and I'll do mine."

PlineyElder grunted and motioned for Ross to follow him. WuzzGart was right on their tail. The guards stayed behind. The new trio headed off through aisles of turning, rotating, sparking robot arms. Brilliant flashes of light punctuated Ross's view. Each line of mechanical arms crowded over an assembly line, moving in a symphony of activity, ducking in and out of metal assemblies about the size of a washing machine. With each motion the welding bots would stop, pop a series of precise welds, and then spin on to the next position. Human workers moved among the rows monitoring the equipment. Some of these workers had darknet call-outs, but most did not.

But all of them ignored the suited Westerner moving through their workspace.

Soon Ross and the engineers came to a corner of the factory where a lone robot welding arm stood next to a project pedestal. There was no assembly-line conveyer belt here, and the numerous half-finished objects on the shelves nearby gave it the feel of a prototyping or test area.

WuzzGart, the fabricator, put on white gloves and removed the titanium half-rings and the single crystal from the wooden box. He cleaned each one carefully with a lint-free cloth and spoke to no one in particular as he placed each into a jig bolted onto the scorched project pedestal. "Why do all the powerful items require *titanium*?"

PlineyElder looked at his watch. "Come on, I have a meeting in twenty minutes."

"This must be done carefully. The pieces must be cleaned or the chlorine from human sweat will impact the weld. Titanium is a very reactive metal."

The sorcerer just tapped at his watch dial impatiently. "Then stop talking, and let's get on with it."

Ross leaned over WuzzGart's shoulder to watch as the man placed the single crystal within the end of one half-ring and encased it by pressing another half-ring into the first. Only one of the rings had this receptacle for a crystal. "Did you ever ponder just how strange the world has gotten since Sobol's game world leaked into reality? I mean, we've gathered here essentially to create a magical item."

"That's the plan." WuzzGart tightened the jig around the pieces and then stepped away. "I've already uploaded the welding script. We are ready."

PlineyElder was manipulating unseen D-Space objects on a private layer of his own, but he took a moment to gesture to Ross, snapping his fingers, and motioning like a wedding photographer. "Rakh! You stand *here*."

Ross left his dispatch case on the floor and stood equidistant from the other two men, forming the points of a triangle at a distance of ten feet from the project pedestal.

PlineyElder kept motioning forward, then left, then back—and finally gave a thumbs-up. At which point he raised his hands and began a series of complex somatic gestures, tracked in 3-D space by touch-rings on each hand, as he spoke his unlock code to the Daemon's manufacturing bots—in this instance it was game world elvish: *"Davors bethred, puthos cavol, arbas lokad!"*

The welding arm suddenly came to life and moved forward to circle the pedestal at close range.

He then began a long chant, moving his hand in a circle, and the robot arm followed suit in a show of slavish mimicry. For more than a minute PlineyElder continued his chant, and then he suddenly stopped and pointed to WuzzGart.

WuzzGart stepped forward and began to cast a spell of his own. Ross knew from the specification for the Rings of Aggys that this was the masterwork spell—creating a D-Space receptacle for the darknet power that the objects would soon receive. PlineyElder's spell was meant to imbue the D-Space nozzles on the welder with permission to edit virtual space.

WuzzGart's spell was quite involved, and he failed at his first attempt. Apparently he hadn't moved his arms in the right combination or perhaps got some of the verbal unlock code wrong. When he finished the last syllable and stood expectantly—nothing happened.

PlineyElder threw up his hands. "Idiot!"

WuzzGart just flipped him off and started again. This time he was successful, and on his last syllable of the enchantment a soft D-Space glow emanated from all four half-rings. "Aha!"

He stepped back smiling. "We're cooking with gas now!"

As he said this, the welding arm moved in swiftly and zapped each of the four rings once with a blinding flash. Sparks flew from the pedestal and scattered across the floor.

Ross knew this was his cue and ignored PlineyElder, who was waving frantically. He moved toward the rings and held his hands over them, motioning in counter-rotating circles while speaking the darknet incantation that would permanently bind them with the spell. He'd practiced it many times in the shower at the hotel, and he hoped he'd get it right on the first try. *"Fasthu, agros visthon, pantoristhas, antoriontus, pashas afthas."*

Happily, as he finished, each ring pulsed with D-Space light.

Ross stepped back, and the welding robot zapped each of them again, this time in a different place. As it withdrew, Ross moved in again and repeated his spell.

The process was performed twice more, and as he spoke the last word, PlineyElder and WuzzGart were already next to him, holding their arms over the pedestal and chanting the words of a fictitious language of a fictitious race of people that had probably been thought up by some writer in a cubicle at Cyberstorm Entertainment in Thousand Oaks, California.

Nonetheless, the Daemon had imbued these words with power.

As the three reached a crescendo and simultaneously completed their chants, a brilliant D-Space light emanated from all the rings and slowly cooled, fading and ultimately disappearing. Now, however, the individual D-Space call-outs above each half-ring had been replaced by a single D-Space call-out, centered above the lone crystal on the parent ring.

PlineyElder grinned. "The masterwork is a success!"

They all shook hands, and Ross stood by eagerly as WuzzGart extracted the finished rings from the jig and dunked them in a bucket of water. He placed all four of them on a ShamWow he found on a nearby workbench and showed them off to Ross and the sorcerer.

"Behold the Rings of Aggys!"

The cloth held two sets of matching rings, one set smaller than the other. All were still steaming. The lone call-out on the ring with a crystal was an inscrutable alphanumeric sequence.

WuzzGart pointed. "Note the quality of the welds. No alpha phase or swirling. You could get those buffed anywhere, and they'll shine up like white gold."

PlineyElder nudged Ross and pointed up at his call-out. "Congratulations."

Ross just then noticed that he'd gone up a level. He

was now a seventh-level Rogue. He'd missed the alert in his HUD display amid all the excitement. He nodded to both men. "Thank you, gentlemen. It's been a pleasure doing business with you."

WuzzGart placed the rings in a small velvet bag and handed them to Ross.

PlineyElder pointed at the bag. "Those are powerful rings, master thief! Do not use them lightly or they will destroy themselves. Or even *you*."

"I'll keep that in mind."

WuzzGart started cleaning the pedestal with the ShamWow. "You must have a use in mind for these rings to go through so much trouble."

Ross nodded. "I'll need them for a journey—through hostile territory."

"If it's so hostile, why go there?"

"Because I need to."

WuzzGart looked into Ross's eyes; then he looked to PlineyElder. "I'll bet you a thousand credits it's a woman."

Both men laughed.

"You have my thanks, gentlemen." Ross put the velvet bag in his suit coat pocket, nodded once more, and headed for the exit.

Chapter 13: // Epiphany

"**S**ir! *We need immediate air support! We are being overrun!*"

The panicked face of the lieutenant filled the monitor, his head distorting on-screen as it darted side to side. Staccato gunfire chattered in the background.

"Air support? Where the hell do you think you are, son, 'Nam? You're in Illinois."

"We need help!"

"Where's your commanding officer?"

"Dead, sir!"

The Major sat in a windowless operations center thousands of miles away in an office park in Bethesda, Maryland.

The screen broke up for a moment. *"We need evac! We have been surrounded and are being overrun!"*

Gunfire in the background was suddenly much louder. There were screams of wounded and the sound of roaring engines—a sound that The Major was all too familiar with.

"Son. I need you to calm down and provide a concise report."

"Sir—"

"Report, goddamnit!" The Major hit the MUTE

button on the console and turned to a nearby technician. "What group is this?"

"Optimal Outcomes, sir. An outfit out of Dallas."
The technician brought up a map on his own screen
that showed a satellite view of a planned community.
"They're bivouacked in a half-finished housing development in Huntley, Illinois."

"Panicky fuckers." He let up on the MUTE button.

The lieutenant was taking deep breaths. *"We are being
engaged by unmanned elements of the Daemon."*

"Razorbacks?"

"Yes, sir."

"How many?"

*"Unknown, sir. Our sentries were taken out by what
appear to be radio-guided darts. If we had tactical radar
to detect incoming—"*

"What do you want, a Phalanx cannon? You're not
a military base. You were supposed to lay low and wait
for orders."

There was more mayhem and screaming in the background. The lieutenant on camera leaned out of frame
and fired several bursts from a weapon. *"Somehow they
found our location. We are being overrun, sir!"*

"Yeah, I can see that. Have the local police gotten
involved?"

"I don't know!"

The Major hit the MUTE button again and spoke to a
nearby technician. "I need a mop-up crew down there,
ASAP. Get them government credentials, and make sure
they round up all the Daemon equipment they can find."

He switched off the MUTE button and spoke to the

screen. "How effective were fifty-caliber rifles against these things?"

"Sir?"

"The Barrett rifles. Are they effective against razor-backs?"

The guy tried to control his breathing. *"Yes. Yes, sir. But the snipers were quickly taken out by return fire. Deadly accurate return fire."*

One of the technical advisers next to The Major leaned in. "Could have been acoustical triangulation or infrared muzzle-flash detection systems. They can track a projectile back to its source. It makes sense if Sobol was dipping into our research pipeline—we've got some prototypes in the field."

The lieutenant shouted. *"Sir! We need help. Now!"*

Several Weyburn Labs consultants were still scribbling notes. One of them leaned into The Major's ear. "The inertial flywheel on the razorback that powers the blade arms is a problem in close quarters. Hundred thousand rpm rotation. If it gets cracked, it'll turn into a shrapnel bomb. Ballistics tests show it's safer to take them out at a hundred meters or more."

More note taking.

"Sir! Can we get help?"

"We just have a few more questions, son. . . ."

"Goddamnit, sir! We are dying!"

"Well, then. You're dismissed."

Suddenly the lieutenant glared into the screen. *"You fucker!"*

There was nearby screaming, and the lieutenant turned to open fire offscreen. There were desperate

shouts for help and the roar of engines. Then the lieutenant fled—a swift blur crossing the screen on his tail.
After a few moments of loud engine noise, there was
suddenly comparative silence.

The Weyburn Labs team in the control room also sat
quietly for several moments, still jotting notes.

"Have we determined yet whether these razorbacks
are remotely piloted, autonomous, or semiautono-
mous?"

One of the consultants responded. "Surveillance
recordings show them vacillating between fight-or-flight
behavior and advanced problem-solving."

"Which means?"

"Which means razorbacks can apparently operate
independently or under the remote control of a pilot or
remote AI—perhaps a cloud-based logic. A single operator could conceivably shift his control from one razorback to another—like jumping between avatars in a
game."

Another technician nodded. "They're a promising
concept. Razorbacks don't require ammunition, and
they terrify the populace. It's the perfect crowd control
weapon. Surgically precise."

The Major pondered this. "And electronic countermeasures to their remote control?"

"The ultrawideband used by the Daemon makes ECM
difficult, but not impossible. The trick is that we need
EWOs in place with specialized equipment—but we don't
know where the Daemon is going to hit us next. And
using the equipment jams our own communications."

One of the technicians butted in. "Excuse me. Major,

there was a Mark V security blimp over Huntley, too. It disappeared minutes before they came under attack. Whatever got it came in under radar. We just examined the blimp video. Looks like drone aircraft. Small. Fast. Not very sophisticated. It might even have simply rammed the airship."

"So it's got an air force now?"

Another one of the Weyburn Labs guys responded, "The darknet philosophy seems to be large numbers of small things—swarms. In this case, microjets. We've found the wreckage of several near sites where our surveillance drones have disappeared."

"UCAVs?"

"Smaller and easier to manufacture. They use electromechanical systems; microscale propulsion with no moving parts. It doesn't require the precision manufacturing of turbines. It utilizes thermal transpiration to conduct a hydrocarbon fuel through aerogel membranes into twin Swiss roll jet engines. That helps to maintain core combustion temperature in tiny jet engines. Quite fascinating if you—"

One of the consultants pointed at the monitor console. "Look."

There on-screen stood a figure dressed in a black riding suit and black motorcycle helmet, staring at them from two thousand miles away.

The Major leaned into the microphone. "Loki. You seem to be hunting my people. . . ."

"Major. The last time I saw you, you were . . . Oh, that's right. You were shooting Roy Merritt in the back."

The Major gave a sideways glance to the assembled

researchers, then spoke into the microphone. "A darknet lie."

"Of course. Facts no longer exist. Everything is a 'point of view' now. I can't wait to burn your house of bullshit down."

"Apparently Dr. Philips was naïve to think we could rehabilitate you."

"You realize your little campaign against darknet communities is doomed, don't you? I know what you're going to do before you do it."

"You killed some people and wrecked some equipment. So what? There's no shortage of trigger-happy dipshits willing to make a hundred bucks an hour. In fact, if you kill them, we don't have to pay them their completion bonus."

"I will find you, Major. And what's in your mind will lead me to your masters. Their industrial empire is about to come to an end."

The Major chuckled. "You're not the first freedom fighter whose head I've put on a stick, Loki. You all fall in the end—usually betrayed by the very people you think you're saving."

Loki cocked his head. *"Freedom fighter? Is that what you think I am?"* He laughed. *"I don't give a shit about freedom. And if I have to kill a hundred million innocent people to get my hands on you, I'll do it. Sleep well, Major."*

Loki pulled the plug and the screen went dark.

The control room was silent for several moments.

Someone finally muttered, "Holy shit. . . ."

The Major nodded absently. His campaigns had indeed

fought and defeated a hundred liberation movements. They'd divided and confused citizens around the globe who tried to rise up against mining companies, oil companies, coal companies, biotech companies—and in the end the people defeated themselves.

But none of those adversaries had their fingers wrapped around the corporate throat like the Daemon did. And none of those adversaries had imbued a single psychotic individual with such unaccountable power as the Daemon had with Loki. This kid was ready to kill a hundred million people. And he'd already slain hundreds, possibly thousands. A whole new era of technological domination was about to begin—and for once, The Major might not be on the winning side.

It suddenly occurred to The Major that he was afraid.

Chapter 14: // The China Price

Jon Ross sat reading *Izvestia* on a handheld device while sipping espresso. He was in the coffee bar of his hotel in the Shekou District of Shenzhen. It was mid-afternoon, and he was dressed in a pressed, four-button black pin-striped suit with a light blue silk tie and a pastel shirt—all handmade in nearby Hong Kong. With his stylish HUD glasses he looked every bit the successful businessman catching up with affairs back home.

Ross preferred Shekou because it allowed him to blend in. It was a pleasant neighborhood popular with expats. It had a small-town feel, but was packed with restaurants and night life.

Here there were dozens of languages being spoken in the cafes and bars, and he was just one more foreign face among many. But none of that mattered now—not for the one piece of unfinished business remaining on this trip.

He downed the last of his espresso as two Chinese men in rumpled suits approached his table. From their hard stares and air of impunity, Ross immediately knew they were policemen—probably Ministry of State Security.

The first nodded and spoke in Russian. "Comrade

Morozov. Good afternoon." He smiled, revealing stained teeth.

Ross lowered his handheld and replied in Russian as well. "Good afternoon. To what do I owe the pleasure, gentlemen?"

"There seems to be a problem with your travel documents."

"My travel documents?"

The man nodded.

"I don't see how that's possible, but . . ." Ross removed his billfold from his jacket. "May I take care of it here?"

"Attempting to bribe a government official is a serious crime in China."

"*Attempting*, perhaps. What about *succeeding*?"

"This is no laughing matter, Mr. Morozov." He switched suddenly to English. "Or should I say, Mr. Ross?"

Ross remained calm. He placed money on the table to pay his check and put away his billfold. He switched to English as well. "Your English and Russian are both excellent."

"Thank you. Please mention that to my commander when you see him. Now, if you would please come with us . . ."

"May I ask to see your credentials?"

The man opened his coat to reveal a pistol in a shoulder holster.

"That's the one that counts, isn't it?"

The man gestured for Ross to follow them.

Ross sighed, then grabbed his handheld and laptop case and complied.

They brought him outside to a waiting car. It was an unmarked Jeep Cherokee knockoff—what some of the expat Americans had taken to calling "Cheeps." They opened the door for him, and Ross got in. He noticed that there were no door handles on the inside, and a wire mesh stood between him and the front seat. He was now their prisoner.

The officers got in front and drove off in dense traffic without a word either to each other or to Ross. They drove for only a few minutes before pulling to the curb on a highly fashionable restaurant block. The place was bustling with shoppers and young professionals.

The men got out and opened the door for Ross, who stepped onto the sidewalk and met the gaze of his captor. "I'm confused. Am I bribing you or not?"

The man just grabbed Ross's arm and along with his partner they moved toward an upscale martini bar done in clean Scandinavian glass and hardwoods with a minimalist logo that was so hip it would be indecipherable to Chinese and Scandinavians alike. The place was packed with cigarette smoke and young, mostly Chinese white-collar professionals who quickly parted to let the grim-faced plainclothes policemen through.

Soon they approached a booth in the rear of the bar—the only quiet corner. The tables all around it were conspicuously empty. There, a young Chinese man in a well-cut suit waited with a frosted martini glass in front of him. He smiled as he saw Ross approaching.

Ross couldn't help but return the smile. It was Shen Liang. Shen was an old friend from Ross's dot-com days in Portland—back in the late nineties. Before everything went to hell. Shen had been a kid just out of Stanford back then—barely familiar with America and Western culture. He was a brilliant young mind who'd taken in everything the Chinese universities had to offer at the time and was hungry for more.

Ross and Shen had worked together at a start-up Web company named Stiletto Design—"Cutting through the noise" was their motto. It was the quintessential Web commerce shop with high ceilings, exposed brick, Aeron chairs, ping-pong tables, and soon-to-be-worthless stock options. They were expanding like mad in those days, designing merchant solutions for banks, insurance companies, and half-assed Web start-ups. Young men and women working long hours and late nights—it was a great place to be a young single person. The memory was just a haze of work, alcohol, and sex.

As Ross sat down, Shen extended his hand and spoke in perfect American English. "Jon Ames. Or I guess it's *Jon Ross*, nowadays. What'd you get married or something?"

"It's complicated, Liang. You look like you're doing well."

Shen motioned to the nearby plainclothesmen and said something in Mandarin.

The lead officer nodded, and both men departed.

Ross watched them go, then turned back to Shen, who was nodding. "I am doing well. I wish I could say the same for you."

Ross gave him a quizzical look.

"Jon, you're in a lot of trouble."

"Then this isn't a social call?"

Shen grimaced and motioned to a beautiful young woman in a miniskirt. She came to the table immediately, and he pointed her to Ross.

"I'll have a Stoli, straight up with a twist, please."

"Of course, sir." She hurried off.

"Russian vodka. How telling." He focused an appraising look at Ross as he lit a tiny cigar. "So . . ." He put his gold lighter away. "After all these years I find out that your name isn't really Jon Ames."

"Liang—"

"And that Interpol has a global red notice out on you. That you're the FBI's Most Wanted Man. Imagine my shock."

"Like I said, it's complicated."

"We were *buds*, Jon. And now it turns out you were an identity thief and a stock swindler?"

"Well, you didn't tell me you were a spy for the Ministry of State Services back in the old days, either."

He gave Ross a disbelieving look. "Who was a spy? They paid for my education. I was supposed to come back with 'mad skillz.' How is that spying? It's not like I pretended I wasn't Chinese."

"I seem to remember someone wasn't planning on coming back to China. I seem to remember someone talking about a Web video start-up—"

Shen held up his hand and looked around. "All right, all right. Would you cool it with that shit? And by the way, you were my witness. That was *before* YouTube. I had that idea *before* YouTube."

"We were on dial-up back then, Liang."

"That's not the point. I nailed that."

"And yet, here you are, working for the government."

Shen rolled his eyes. "I don't work for the government, or at least I *didn't* work for the government until some asshole started fucking with our networks and they reactivated me." He saluted. "Now it's Captain Shen, thank you very much."

"A PLA Cyber warfare battalion? That seems alarmingly conformist for the Shen Liang I knew."

Shen nodded grimly and took a big sip of his martini. "Yeah, well, I really screwed up in America, Jon. I had to come back here after that, and I had gone *way* off reservation. I had to get powerful friends *fast* to dig out from that mess. I had to be stellar."

"And is that how you wound up at Wuhan Communications Command Academy?"

Shen stopped mid-puff and narrowed his eyes at Ross. He pulled the cigarillo from his lips. "How the hell do you know that?"

"And how you wound up working with the General Equipment Department, modifying Western router chipsets?"

Shen moved to cover Ross's mouth. "Would you shut up? What are you, crazy? How the hell do you know that?"

"We're reaching a crossroad, Liang."

"This isn't 1999, Jon. The Web isn't a toy anymore. Network technology *is* power now—world-domination-type power. This is a deadly serious business. Stop playing around."

"We had a great time back then. You remember we all thought technology would change the world?"

"Well, it *didn't*. Our parents were right, Jon. It's scary how right they were. Nothing changes. Only the faces change."

"I'm sorry you feel that way. I seem to remember you having great hopes for democracy in China."

Shen glared hard at him as the cocktail waitress returned with Ross's drink. Both men were quiet until she departed.

Shen shook his head and reached for an ashtray. "I don't know what you're talking about. And besides, we *have* democracy in China. People get to vote with their money, just like they do in America."

"But if only money talks, those without money don't get a voice."

"Well, the smarter people tend to make money, so I don't see what the problem is."

"What happens if someone *takes* your money away?"

Shen cast a wary look at Ross.

Ross continued, "Because that's what we're talking about here, isn't it? Someone has threatened to confiscate your company if you don't perform. Is that how a free person lives, Liang? In fear of the powerful?"

"Freedom is overrated. You can be completely free and starving in an igloo in Antarctica. Business is what makes people's lives better, not democracy. The world is filled with dysfunctional democracies, paralyzed by idiots with votes."

"Liang—"

"Jon, do you know that the World Bank said that

over half the Chinese people lived in poverty in 1980? You know what it is now? Care to take a guess? It's four percent, Jon. *Four*. Economic development did that, not democracy."

Ross nodded. "But that's the deal they offer, isn't it? They'll bring economic development in exchange for you not participating in politics—but that economic development is hollow and has no longevity. Have you seen the markets? It's already fraying at the edges. Believe me, by the time it ends, you'll realize they have all the power and you don't matter. Prosperity is not prosperity if they can just take it from you."

"So you prefer America then? Like they're prosperous? They owe us more money than there is on the planet. America is finished. Why are you helping them?"

Ross frowned. He took a moment to digest the question, taking a sip of his drink first. "Helping them? What are you talking about?"

"Don't even start with me. You know exactly what I mean."

Ross nodded. "So, you brought me here because you've got a problem. A problem you think the Americans are behind."

Shen just studied him for several moments. "You haven't asked how I found you."

"I don't have to ask. I already know how you found me."

"Oh yeah? How do you know that?"

"Because I'm the one who told you I was in China."

Shen paused, looking darkly at Ross. "You're fucking with me now. That's why I hated playing poker with you."

"I'm not bluffing, Liang."

"Yeah, where did I get the information then?"

"That e-mail you received from Jun Shan. That was me."

Shen almost bit his cigarillo in half. He glanced around the restaurant again and just shook his head. "Jon, you have no idea who you're dealing with."

"The PLA reactivated you to find out why the back doors in router chipsets are beginning to fail in North America and Europe. They're in a panic, aren't they?"

Shen ground out his cigarette and pushed the ashtray away. "What the fuck is going on? Who are you working for? The Americans?"

"It isn't what you think, Liang."

"Why does a Russian want to help Americans? They've been shitting on Russia for decades. They're imperialist scum."

"So you want to recruit me, comrade? Is that it?"

"Communism. Capitalism. Who gives a shit? Look, Western imperialism has undermined China since the British started dumping opium here to pry open the tea market. Now that China is taking her rightful place in the world again, the U.S. and Britain are doing everything they can to keep us down. Join us, Jon. I can open a lot of doors for you—especially for a man with your talents. There is virtually unlimited money to be made."

Ross sipped his vodka. "That's a great offer, Liang. And I do appreciate it, but I'm going to tell you what's really going on here. And you're not going to like it."

Shen pushed his drink away. "Damnit."

"You remember why Interpol is looking for me—why I'm wanted by the FBI?"

"Yeah, because you masterminded the Daemon hoax."

"It's not a hoax, Liang, and I didn't mastermind it. There is an open-source cybernetic organism called the Daemon that is spreading across the globe. It's created an encrypted social network called the darknet, based on an online video game. Millions of people are joining that network and using it to reinvent human society."

Shen sighed and leaned back in his seat. "Jon, goddamnit! I'm trying to help you."

"I'm not kidding, Liang. I'm a seventh-level Rogue in the network, and I have powers and abilities that allow me to—"

"You've really lost your fucking mind. I can't believe it. It's like you don't even care." He pointed out the windows. "I told them I would handle this. I told them to back off. That I could *turn* you, but after you leave here, Jon, they are going to take you away, and put you in a place so dark you won't ever be seen again. And I won't be able to help you anymore. Do you understand what I'm telling you? They're going to *disappear* you, Jon."

"I understand. It's okay."

"How can it be okay? You've got to tell me what's really going on, Jon, or they're going to beat it out of you."

"It's okay because I had to come to China. I couldn't learn what I needed anywhere *but* China. Because what happens here, Liang, affects the entire world. And what your people did was defeat a system that might have been used to oppress billions. I needed you to know that. The Chinese people want to be free, Liang. Just like all people. I've seen it. Just like you'll see it."

"Jon, they won't let you leave here."

"It's okay. I have this." Ross held up a single titanium ring with a crystal embedded in the surface. "It's a magic ring, Liang. Very powerful."

Shen stared at him, speechless, for several moments. "Oh my god. You really have gone insane."

Ross slipped the ring on his finger. "I have to go now. But just remember, I came to see you because I wanted to tell you in person. The Daemon is real, and it's bigger than all of us—because it *is* all of us. So maybe technology can change the world, after all. Take care, my friend."

With that, Ross got up and walked away from the table, seeing Shen's stunned face reflected in a nearby mirror as he left.

Chapter 15: // Political Inversion

"**D**r. Philips, you've seen the news. The economy is in shambles. Getting a five-year guaranteed contract with built-in cost-of-living adjustments would secure your future. And you could still work within the national intelligence apparatus. A lot of your colleagues have already made the jump."

Natalie Philips looked across the table at two sharply attired recruiters from Weyburn Labs. They were sitting in the agency cafeteria. It had been months since the incident at Merritt's funeral, and she had already been folded back into the NSA's Crypto division—albeit stripped of decision-making authority.

"You're wasting your time, gentlemen. And I don't appreciate being ambushed like this. "

"Look, the public sector is a great place for backbenchers, but someone of your prodigious intellect could have a bright future." He leaned forward. "You could still finish your current project—"

The second executive finished for him. "But at a substantially higher salary."

"And performance bonuses."

Philips betrayed no emotion. "But I'd be working for

Weyburn Labs. There are potential conflict-of-interest issues that I don't think help the mission."

"National security is everyone's goal, Doctor."

"There was a time when I believed that."

They looked at each other, affecting hurt feelings.

"Weyburn Labs has a long and fruitful partnership with the U.S. government. Our current CEO was a four-star general."

She nodded as she poked at her salad. "That may be, but I'm not leaving the NSA."

"And you really think your career here can advance after that fiasco with the Daemon Task Force?"

She glared at him.

Apparently sensing that things were going downhill, the other recruiter leaned in again and spoke softly. "You're not the only bright person working on the Daemon. Big things are afoot, Doctor. Things not even you know about."

"We shouldn't be discussing this here."

He edged even closer. "Building from your work, we've started to gain access to the darknet."

She stopped eating.

"This is top secret information, of course."

Philips eyed them both closely. "Who is doing this?"

"Come join the Weyburn Labs team and find out. . . ."

Just then a uniformed Central security officer walked up to the table. "Dr. Philips?"

"Yes?"

"You need to come with me, ma'am. Deputy Director Fulbright needs you in the Ops Center, ASAP."

Philips shot one last look at the recruiters, then stood with her tray.

The security officer grabbed it from her. "I'll get that, ma'am. Please just proceed to the CSS vehicle waiting curbside."

"Gentlemen. If you'll excuse me."

"Think about what we said, Doctor."

Ops Center 1 was a dimly lit digital front line of uniformed military personnel manning rows of computer monitors. They were there to categorize and prioritize America's various raw intelligence feeds, but today Ops Center 1 was also thick with Department of Defense brass and men in nicely tailored suits. They stared at Philips and whispered among themselves as she was ushered by two air force officers into a nearby conference room where the door was immediately closed behind her.

Inside the darkened conference room, more military officers and suited executives stared up at a large video screen, which displayed what looked to be live footage of a foreign city—somewhere in China, judging by the street signage.

The moment Philips walked in, Deputy Director Chris Fulbright grabbed her by the elbow and escorted her toward the center of the room. Normally soft-spoken and reserved, Fulbright was keyed up and edgy. Something serious was going on. And if they called her in, then that could only mean it involved the Daemon.

"It looks like Jon Ross has surfaced again."

A wave of surprise hit her—and then worry. "Where?"

"Shenzhen, China."

"China?" She was about to ask how he'd managed to get there, but that was, of course, a ridiculous question. Jon Ross was an identity thief and hacker—he could be anyone he wanted to be. And if Loki was to be believed, Ross was now a Daemon operative to boot. She just nodded. "A world-class manufacturing hub. High-end electronics."

"That makes sense then. Our intelligence shows the Daemon has become increasingly embedded in the high-tech manufacturing supply chain of Asia—and that the Chinese know there's some new force exerting influence domestically. They still don't seem to know what it is. They think it has something to do with the Falun Gong—or other political opposition groups."

"Who found Jon?" She braced herself for the answer.

"PLA Cyber warfare unit. Someone connected with General Zhang Zi Min—head of the MSS. They're carrying out an op to grab Ross right now. . . ." Fulbright gestured to the central screen, which even as he spoke showed shaky video of heavily armed SWAT teams lying in wait around building corners. There were scores of them. A low-flying chopper passed momentarily in front of the frame, occluding the view. "We got word of it in unencrypted intercepts. I don't need to remind you that—aside from *you*—no one knows more about the Daemon's architecture than Jon Ross. If the Chinese grab him—"

"The *Ragnorok* module. They'd be able to use the Daemon against us."

Fulbright nodded. "We don't think the Chinese have even detected—much less decrypted—the IP beacon the Daemon is broadcasting. At least not yet. But capturing Ross might give them access to both. In particular, the Destroy function. That would give the Chinese the ability to destroy individual corporate data on demand—and from there who knows where that knowledge goes. If word got out, it could cause a global stock market panic."

"But the Chinese are co-invested with America; they wouldn't—"

"General Zhang is the wild card here. We think his people were responsible for the illicit back doors in corporate routers. It appears the Daemon is closing them, and it's made Zhang increasingly desperate for something to justify his existence."

"What do you need me to do?"

Fulbright gestured to several men in suits who were already eyeing her from their place among the generals. "These men want you to identify Ross in that crowd. Before the Chinese get to him."

Philips looked around the room, suddenly noticing just how many people here were wearing visitor badges.

"Natalie, please . . ." He nodded toward the screen.

She looked up at the video image, now zooming in to scan the patrons of a martini bar. It looked like a sniper's perspective from a distant rooftop. "They're going to kill him."

Fulbright gripped her shoulder. "You don't know that. We simply need to identify him in that crowd, Doctor."

"Who are all these men?" She was eyeing the contractors who were even now staring back at her.

"Doctor, we've been given a simple directive. We need to provide information."

"To whom?"

"Natalie, Jon Ross escaped our custody and fled to a foreign power. He's a serious danger to national security."

"But—"

"This isn't a debate. You worked alongside him for months. He may have changed his appearance since then, but you have an eye for detail. Help us identify him in that crowd."

Philips felt her pulse quickening as she looked up at the screen. There was no way she could do this. And yet, what Director Fulbright said was true. Ross did possess information that the Chinese would be desperate to have—information that they were likely to torture him to get. They might kill him in the process. But if she pointed him out to these men—what then? She tried to remain poker-faced as her mind kept rejecting the cold facts.

The screen panned across Asian and Western faces laughing in the martini bar.

"Doctor, do you see him?"

She couldn't do it. "I . . ."

A board operator suddenly called out. "The Chinese are making their move, sir."

"We're too late."

Dozens of plainclothesmen brandishing weapons poured through the front door of the high-end bar, creating chaos inside. The camera jerked, then zoomed out a little.

"Yeah, they've gone in."

One of the suits near the wall spoke loudly. "We might still get a shot when they bring him out."

Fulbright cast a glance to Philips. She was watching the screen. Numb.

"If we miss him, let's see if we can track what prison they take him to."

Philips was familiar with this math—"cruel calculus" was what Fulbright had called it. For the first time in her life, she was getting sick of math.

"We'll use a private asset to take care of it."

"We need to make sure we don't lose track of him in the transfer—"

Someone on the control board called out again. "Something's going on there, sir."

Everyone looked up onto the screen to see plain-clothesmen pouring out into the street again, looking frantically all over. Some were talking on radios.

"Looks like they still don't have him."

"Only half of them came out."

"Maybe there was a shoot-out?"

"Did we have confirmation that Ross was in the building?"

"Yes, sir. Two informants confirmed it."

The video image pulled back to show a dozen men frantically running into frame from either side of the bar building.

Two more black vans arrived, and tactical squads poured out of them with black body armor, helmets, and ballistic goggles. They brandished automatic weapons and were spreading out into the streets, shouting at people to lie down. The whole shopping area was coming under lockdown.

"Jesus Christ, they don't have this guy."

"They must have a hundred boots on the ground."

"They've gotta find him now."

"They've got two million surveillance cameras networked in that city. Believe me, they'll find him."

"Yeah, but our asset won't be in place to take him out."

Fulbright turned to Philips. "Thanks for coming in, Natalie. I'll let you know if you're needed again."

She was still staring at the screen. "Yes, sir."

On-screen the Chinese soldiers were still frantically talking on radios.

Philips exited the conference room, and then Ops Center 1. She walked down the bustling hallway outside, and ducked into the ladies' restroom. She checked the stalls to see whether anyone else was present.

She was alone.

She entered the farthest stall, then closed and locked the door. She sat down and put her head in her hands. And then began to weep—her hands still trembling. As she felt the tears streaming silently down her face, she realized just how deeply she'd fallen in love with Jon Ross.

Chapter 16: // Pwned

Hours later Shen Liang entered the unmarked Golden Shield Central Command facility in downtown Shenzhen. Although there were no guards or signs to mark the nondescript six-story block of windowless concrete, the moment Shen stepped through the mirrored sliding doors in the underground garage, he was met by a dozen heavily armed PLA soldiers waiting to either side of metal detectors. Security officers in dress uniform ushered him through the scanners.

What happened here was very important to the Party. Golden Shield was China's sweeping program to create information systems to identify and contain dissent and subversive social elements that might threaten the country's leadership—and thus the people of China. The GSCC building was the culmination of a multiyear, six-billion-dollar investment in internal security—which was itself just a pilot program for the much larger "Safe Cities Initiative," which would link together all data moving through Chinese society, combining financial, communication, and street-level high-resolution CCTV images into a single software-driven internal security solution. Nothing like it had ever been attempted in the history of mankind, and it would serve as a model for security to be emulated around the world. Shen felt a tremendous sense of pride in yet another example of China's technological prowess. He also told himself that it was necessary. Necessary to protect the Chinese people from themselves. Order must be maintained or imperialist forces would rob them of their destiny yet again.

As Shen moved through concentric rings of security, he looked up at the numerous camera and sensor domes that he knew even now were analyzing his face, his thermal image, his perspiration and respiratory patterns, all in an effort to determine if he was under emotional duress.

Outside in the streets, two million networked high-resolution CCTV cameras covered the entire city of Shenzhen. In 2006 the government had mandated that all Internet cafes and entertainment venues such as restaurants and bars install video cameras with a direct feed to their local police station. From there, the images were sent to a central cloud computing application that could apply any number of algorithms to the imagery and in turn alert local authorities to a wide array of suspicious behavior. People running, violent motion, sudden groupings of six or more people, flames. Then there was search: "the ten million face test" was used as the measure of facial recognition algorithms, and software was able to routinely spot and track Caucasian and dark-skinned people, or determine gender. The list was long and getting longer all the time. The state was acquiring eyes.

But then, Shen knew why it was necessary. The government was worried. There were roughly a hundred and thirty million migrants wandering China looking for work—the equivalent of nearly half the population of the United States, and all in a nation roughly equivalent in size to the United States. In fifteen years the number of migrants was projected to be three hundred and fifty million. Shenzhen was already a city with seven million migrant laborers out of a population of twelve million. And these migrants lacked the benefits of permanent citizens, such as subsidized health care and education. Their national ID cards showed their residency as linked to the rural villages where they were born—places where there was no work, giving them no choice but to head for the cities. And so a second class of citizen had been created: people desperate for work who had helped make this economic miracle possible—but who were increasingly angry at their circumstances. Particularly with the wealth that was evident all around them.

Was it fair? Shen knew it wasn't, but he also told himself that there was no other way. How else could China become the world leader it was destined to be if not for this sacrifice? Unless someone bore the burden?

Shen hadn't worked on Golden Shield, but his company had worked on secret modifications to router firmware. He did not doubt that those back doors were utilized throughout the system.

He eyed the camera and sensor arrays again.

He wondered if they detected his nervousness. He had promised his commanding officer, General Zhang, that he would be able to turn the fugitive, Jon Ross, to their side. But Shen had failed. The loss of their back doors in Western networks was still unsolved, and Shen knew that unless it was solved soon, many heads would roll. He hoped his would not be among them.

Jon Ross had known about the chipsets modified by the General Equipment Department—without the knowledge of Western client companies. If Ross knew about the loss of those back doors, then he must have been in on it. Shen was still wondering how on earth it could have been accomplished. America and Europe were not capable of sudden, sweeping changes across companies and borders—without so much as a peep in any e-mails. It seemed impossible.

Shen's concern about failing to win over Ross was tempered by the fact that he had also been the one to locate the fugitive Ross in the first place. Well, as far as they knew he did—and it was the MSS goons who lost Ross in the streets, not him.

Shen was still puzzled by that.

He was entering the central nerve center of China's great surveillance experiment now. A uniformed soldier ushered him into an elevator that had no buttons. It might as well have been a microwave for all the control he had over his destination. The doors closed behind Shen, and he was on a one-way ride to somewhere *down*.

In a little while the doors opened, and Shen came out into a windowless control room, a hundred feet across with a ceiling at least thirty feet high. All along the walls were hundreds of large flat-panel monitors—with one gigantic, stadium-sized display in the center of it all. Currently the large screen showed a map of the city of Shenzhen, and it looked to have the location of each camera marked as a blue dot—but he knew this was impossible, since it would cover the entire city. He guessed they were nodes to local law enforcement feeds or perhaps junctions. There were various digital pin markers and status indicators on some of these dots and moving markers as well (vehicular subjects of surveillance?).

Covering the floor of the control room were banks of zone managers—uniformed officers of the Ministry of State Services. These would be the top graduates from the academies. Eager, smart, and ready to implement the Party's will.

As Shen entered, a young aide saluted him. "Captain Shen. You are expected."

Shen almost laughed—as if he could have gotten in here uninvited!

The aide motioned for him to follow and brought him through rows of surveillance technicians to a raised dais with an additional semicircle of monitors and control equipment. There he saw General Zhang Zi Min— director of the Ministry of State Services—in a dignified business suit amid a knot of technicians in short-sleeve shirts and ties, with ID badges on lanyards. While half of them were Han Chinese, Shen was shocked to see that the other half were clearly Westerners—and from their appearance, *Americans.*

What Americans would be doing in the very nerve center of China's domestic surveillance headquarters was beyond him. He was almost speechless as he was brought up to General Zhang. The general was listening to something one of the Americans was saying, but nodded to Shen.

Shen made a dramatic, full-body salute—like he'd

learned in the academy. As head of the Party ministry responsible for domestic security, Zhang was arguably one of the most politically powerful men in all of China. It was he who had selected Shen from the senior class at Wuhan to spearhead the router projects that had yielded so much valuable commercial and military intelligence. And it was Zhang who had made certain Shen's Beijing start-up company was successful—providing access to capital and funneling plenty of clients his way. Shen owed his Mercedes, his five-bedroom house in Orange County (a subdivision north of Beijing), and his future to Zhang. Zhang was his patron.

The American was still talking, but in a hushed tone that Shen could not hear from his position ten feet and several people away. The casual way that this American technician was speaking with the general was mind-boggling—as if the man had no idea whom he was talking to. The general just kept nodding patiently, but he occasionally shot a hard-to-decipher look Shen's way.

Eventually the general held up a hand to the man and motioned for Shen to join them.

Shen straightened his tie and proceeded into the center of the circle.

The general gestured to the screens in front of them. They appeared to be displaying the martini bar where Shen had met with Ross, as well as the streets all around it for blocks in every direction. The exterior video was wrapped around a 3-D map of the building geometry—giving it the appearance of a computer game.

The general spoke in Mandarin. "Captain Shen. I would like you to help us understand how our Russian friend could simply walk out of the meeting point without being seen. I am being informed that your choice of meeting place was less than optimal from a visual and audio surveillance perspective."

Shen eyed the Americans—a fortyish-looking crew of assembly coders from the look of them. They appeared to be trying to figure out what to make of the new arrival. Shen turned back to the general. "General Zhang, I would be happy to answer your questions, just not in the presence of these Americans, sir."

"You are surprised to find Americans here, Captain? Do you fancy them a security risk?"

Disturbingly, even though they were still conversing in Mandarin, the lead American engineer let a slight smile escape before he contained it.

"Yes, I do, sir. Nor do I think this discussion sufficiently private."

"Let me put your mind at ease. We would not be making such rapid progress in our efforts if it weren't for the private sector's contributions, and some of the key systems being developed today in the world of security are being developed by private companies based in the United States, Israel, and the European Union." He gestured to the Chinese engineers crowding around the console. "As you can see we have complete information sharing, and we will retain all the expertise necessary to extend our capabilities within the terms of our licensing agreement."

"Licensing agreement?"

"Our partnership with the West has been richly rewarding, Captain. For both sides. You are to give your full cooperation to these gentlemen—in English, if you please. If I'm not mistaken, you are quite proficient."

Shen was momentarily flummoxed.

The American smiled and extended his hand. He was a tall man of indistinct lineage—black hair and brown eyes. "Captain Shen. It's a pleasure. Robert Haverford."

Shen shook his hand uncertainly. "Mr. Haverford. Please forgive me. I'm a little bit shocked, that's all."

"No doubt. Wow, your English is excellent. No accent whatsoever."

"I went to school in the States."

"Which school?"

"Stanford."

"Terrific. I'm told you're quite a hand at chip design. I think our problem is a bit more prosaic. We think it was operator error, and we just need to find out for training purposes. We weren't present during the incident, but we're trying to back into just what went on when this unfortunate series of events unfolded."

Haverford gestured to a seat in front of a control monitor that had somehow mysteriously opened up. Shen felt that it suspiciously resembled the proverbial hot seat. However, he also knew, with the general and several dozen uniformed PLA senior officers nearby, it was not a request.

He sat and examined the monitor in front of him. It showed a blurry image of himself sitting in the booth at the Suomi Linja martini bar hours earlier. They could barely see his head, and the rest of the table was completely blocked by a beam.

Haverford pointed at the image. "You really couldn't

have chosen a worse spot for this meeting, Captain. It's almost as if you wanted to have a private sit-down."

The words just hung out there for a few moments—a smiling fuck-you from his new American friend. *Passive-aggressive shitheel* . . . Shen looked up to General Zhang. "The only chance I thought I'd have of turning Ross, General, was in making him feel comfortable and in reminding him of the friendship we once had in Oregon. Having policemen hanging around and cameras focused on him would not accomplish that. I take full responsibility for selecting the most shielded booth, but it was a calculated risk. I certainly did not think it would be an issue because there was no way for him to leave the bar unobserved—that is, if this system works as it must have been described in the brochure."

General Zhang pondered Shen's words for a moment, then nodded to Haverford.

Haverford sighed. "Well, okay then. I guess the fact that we don't have any audio or video of you speaking with Mr. Ross—look there. . . ." Haverford pointed at a gesticulating arm being reflected in a mirror. "That's Ross right there. We have him up until that point."

Shen frowned. "What do you mean 'up until that point'?"

The control board operator fast-forwarded the video, and people moved up and down the booth aisle like a *Benny Hill* closing credit chase. And then it suddenly returned to normal speed—to show Shen walking out of the bar several minutes later, a look of dread on his face.

"Wait. Wait a second." Shen was trying to comprehend what he just saw. "Back it up."

The video backed up at double speed. He saw himself back up to the table and sit far away from the cameras and the microphones he knew were near the restroom, the glass-and-blond-wood bar, and the entrances. Waitresses and Chinese patrons occasionally walked down the aisle—but no Jon Ross!

"That's impossible! He was sitting right there with me."

The video kept backing up until finally Shen saw the back of Ross, reverse-stepping toward the entrance with plainclothes policemen behind him. It was his moment of arrival seen backward.

"So he arrived, but he didn't leave?"

"That's what we've been wondering about."

They all just sat there without talking for several moments.

That was when Shen remembered Ross's words as he held up the ring.

This is a magic ring.

A hot flash of fear came over him. *It couldn't be. . . .*

The control board operator was clicking from camera to camera now. Inside and outside the building. He brought up a 3-D model of the city block. It was wrapped with security camera images. "This is running backward from the moment of your departure from the table, Captain Shen." Half a dozen video insets showed as many scenes in front of the building, the lobby, the rear exit, and the surrounding streets—people and cars were everywhere. The video played, and people moved about, but Ross was absolutely nowhere to be seen.

Haverford shook his head. "See, it certainly doesn't seem like he left the table, now, does it, Captain?"

Then it occurred to Shen that everyone was looking at him. And then it started to dawn on him that Zhang might seriously be suspecting him of some collusion with Ross—which would be crazy considering he was the one who brought Ross to the table to begin with.

Shen cleared his throat. "There is one other explanation."

Haverford smiled. "Well, then let's hear it, buddy."

Shen felt like punching him in his smiling toothy face, but instead tapped the screen. "Rewind it to the point when Ross arrives back at the table."

Haverford nodded to the board operator, and the monitor he was focusing on obligingly reversed to the point when Ross arrived.

"Okay. Now, fast-forward it about two, two and a half minutes, then put it on slow motion."

The screen moved forward, people jittering across the screen, then slowed. Shen held his index finger just inches away from the screen and focused intently on the occasional person moving down the aisle between booths. The rest of the assembled technicians and Chinese officers leaned in behind him.

Then he saw it. "There! Stop!"

The image stopped, and Shen pointed to a sliver of a shoe and a pant leg as reflected in a mirror.

"Uh, it's a leg. We can't know it's his."

"But there's no one in the aisle. Look. . . ." Shen pointed. "That reflection occurs when there's someone in the aisle."

"Captain, if there's no one in the aisle, he can't be in the aisle."

"Roll it slowly. Watch here closely." Shen ran his hand along the empty aisle in the picture.

The image ran forward and a wave of surprise went across the assembled witnesses. An aberration, like a fleeting specter, moved across the frame.

Haverford jammed the PAUSE button, shoving the board operator out of the way. "That's impossible. It's an artifact. It's a camera artifact."

Shen was staring at a slight discoloration and diagonal line occluding the frame. "I don't think it's an artifact, Mr. Haverford."

"But how could he . . . He couldn't just walk out."

Shen kept his eye on the screen. "Who was controlling the operation? Was it being directed by central control? Were they giving the signal to the teams to move in from here?"

The technicians looked at each other.

Haverford ignored the question, busying himself in searching other screens—the front door, the side door, the rear door. "None of these doors are popping open. Look."

Shen pointed to the kitchen's rear door, propped open to let cool air in. "The rear door is already open. Look—look *there*." He pointed at video from inside the kitchen. "The staff is surprised. They are following something with their eyes—as though a very unexpected person is moving through their space. Perhaps a Caucasian businessman."

It was undeniable. They could see a server and a chef frowning and eyeballing an unknown entity—the chef actually shouting and waving the unseen person away. As they watched, another shimmer disrupted the air of the tape. It was a ripple in the fabric of the screen's reality. There were blurred reflections on stainless steel counters.

Shen tapped the location on-screen. "These cameras, Mr. Haverford. They are digital CCTV cameras? The very latest, I imagine."

Haverford just stared at him. "Of course. And Chinese made, I might point out."

Shen just laughed to himself and shook his head. *Of course they are.* He recalled Ross's words again. . . .

The Chinese people want to be free, Liang.

He pointed at another screen—one that showed the mouth of the alley behind the restaurant. Where it met the street. There was no one in the street, but quite clearly, there in the reflection from a darkened window was Jon Ross, looking rather dapper in a Hong Kong pin-striped suit. Shen smiled to himself. "I think we've found the problem, Mr. Haverford."

Now a gasp went over the assembled engineers. More leaned in to see what appeared to all present an absolute impossibility.

Haverford just kept shaking his head. "But . . ."

On-screen, a block away, plainclothes policemen were gathered in a group on a corner, smoking—awaiting a signal that came too late.

Shen turned to General Zhang, but spoke to everyone. "Let me tell you what your system is, Mr. Haverford. It's a six-billion-dollar . . . How do you Americans say it? Oh yes: clusterfuck."

Haverford stood up and turned to General Zhang. "This is ridiculous. This is a glitch. That's all."

Shen pointed to the cameras. "Mr. Ross is invisible here to a dozen cameras. Show me a camera where he reappears. Blocks away? Hours later? I'll bet you cannot find him. Because your system has been defeated."

General Zhang studied the screen. "How, Shen? How did he do it?"

"There are two million digital cameras. They are all unified with layers of digital image–processing software. With camera firmware. Someone has created a system where points on the screen are replaced with the background image."

"The background?"

"Yes. Somewhere along the chain of custody between where the image is recorded and where it's seen on our monitors, the empty background imagery of each camera's sweep is substituted for the image of a person who is wearing some sort of electronic tag—to identify their movements through space."

"But how could the camera know the location of that person in three-dimensional space relative to the camera?"

Shen was nodding as he said it. "The camera's position is probably already known, but it could also be derived from a geometric analysis of surrounding landmarks. Software, General. It could all be done with software."

Haverford was still shaking his head. "But that would . . . It's just not possible."

"Why not, Mr. Haverford? Do you think Americans are the only ones who can think 'outside the box'?"

Zhang was unreadable. "How do we fix it?"

"The first rule of computer security, General, is don't leave your equipment where people can mess with it."

He gestured to the screen. "What do we have here? Two million cameras sitting around in public? How many fiber-optic lines connecting them to publicly reachable network cables? Literally anyone anywhere in that complex chain could have done this."

"Then we need to have the cameras fixed. Replaced."

"And how do you know that you can trust the people who do the replacing?" Shen stood up and turned to the general. "I hope I have not spoken out of turn, sir."

General Zhang stared with great intensity at the image of Ross still on the screen. "You are dismissed, Captain Shen. I will be in touch with you soon."

Shen saluted grandly once more, casting Haverford a slight grin. Shen moved to depart.

"Oh, and Captain."

Shen turned.

"Excellent work."

He replied in Mandarin. "It was my pleasure, General."

Shen continued toward the buttonless elevator, and all he could think of was the great game that was now under way out there in the world. A game an old friend told him about. One that he had just now resolved to join.

Chapter 17: // Immortality

Loki's traveling rig was a tribute to American automotive excess. He drove a customized Ford F-650 4x4 with a Caterpillar diesel engine. It had nine hundred foot-pounds of torque and could pull twenty-six thousand pounds up an unpaved 7 percent grade. With a series of three chromed fuel tanks tucked beneath each running board, that incline didn't need to be anywhere near a gas station either. Composite-laminate windows and ceramic composite plating meant the driver and three passengers could recline in comfort while enduring a barrage of small-arms fire. It was, in short, the ultimate vehicle for commuting through the Apocalypse.

It could have accommodated five passengers if Loki hadn't extended the storage area to provide room for various pieces of high-tech wireless communications equipment and supplies. This was, after all, his mobile base of operations for running the one-man Stormbringer faction.

Toward that end, Loki towed an enclosed forty-four-foot Gooseneck racing trailer, whose exterior surface was emblazoned with the image of a black-helmeted motorcycle racer viewed from the shoulders up and done in the style of a Japanese anime character. The entire branding effort was completed with the logo for Stormbringer Motorcycle Racing, jagged with lightning bolts.

To all outward appearances, Loki was a professional motorcycle racer following his circuit through the Midwest. The fact that his real business was hunting down and destroying at any cost a shadowy mercenary army hired to kill Daemon operatives was well concealed behind the patina of professional racing. With his big corporate sponsors (unwilling though they might be) listed on the trailer's wall, he looked more than legit. He looked downright establishment.

However, in this fight, as in all things, Loki remained a loner. He had no crew of mechanics. He preferred instead to communicate his needs through the darknet—pressing into service local maintenance factions to repair his fleet of razorbacks and microjets. That was, after all, what the trailer was for—a storage facility for a score of Type 2-E razorback interceptors and half a dozen microjet aircraft—as well as his personal black Ducati S-version Streetfighter motorcycle, which he rode into battle against The Major's people. So far he'd slain or captured at least a hundred of the bastards, and he was on his way to tracking down more—dragging them screaming from their motel rooms or safe houses like pigs to slaughter. Their blind trust in the anonymity of their communications would be their undoing.

But each battle brought damage, and for this Loki had to seek out darknet communities where he could get replacement bikes and turn in his damaged units. This had brought him here to Garnia, Missouri—a small, economically depressed town out in the plains that was transforming itself into a bustling new darknet community. Founded by a logistics faction—an Order of Merritt signatory, no less—they'd be able to service his razorbacks, provide fuel cell batteries, replace wireless receivers, and so on. Loki would also be secure in the knowledge that he wouldn't be hassled by the police— because, as in all darknet communities, the police here would be fellow darknet members.

Regardless of Loki's half-star reputation score, he knew that no one would question him. He was the leader of an infrastructure defense faction—an unpleasant job that frequently caused him to commandeer local darknet resources in defense of the network as a whole. Everyone knew he had to pass frequent fMRI scans to prove to the Daemon his actions were legitimate—aimed at defense of the Daemon's constituent parts. So the opinions of fellow darknet operatives mattered little to Loki. The Daemon was all that mattered.

Another fact that swayed other operatives to comply was the network level shown on his call-out. Loki was a fifty-sixth-level Sorcerer, and the most powerful operative in North America—possibly the world. It was hard to know, really, since operatives above fiftieth level could employ power masking. But Loki wanted everyone to see his power.

As Loki brought his huge pickup and trailer rig through the sleepy town's main street—if such a loose collection of a dozen houses could be called a town—he marveled at what some people accepted as living. The downtown consisted of a single convenience store, a weather-beaten gas station, and a down-in-the-mouth auto-parts store. Loki knew the big-box stores thirty miles off near the interstate had killed most of the local businesses. He imagined the auto-parts store survived primarily because you couldn't get to the big-box stores if your car was broken down. With gas rising past six dollars a gallon, that dynamic would likely change soon—as would the shipment of cheap, plentiful parts from China.

Beyond the old commercial center of Garnia, there were new businesses sprouting, and ironically much of that life seemed to be sprouting out of the same shipping containers that had helped to destroy the local economy in the first place. The multicolored corrugated-metal boxes littered the landscape, and as Loki drove through the edge of town, he could see darknet operatives pulling lumber, aluminum beams, and construction equipment from them. He also saw the flash of welding coming from within several—mobile fabrication workshops. Loki had seen it before. Local faction leadership had no doubt pooled their resources to call down a construction kit from the network. They'd have to return it to the network pool when they were done, but there were a hundred operatives out there in the fields building homes, businesses, and setting up farms to serve as the center of a new holon. Trying to recolonize America with something that didn't have a 30 percent interest rate and a forty-five-minute commute attached to it.

Loki just observed them as he came in. Living in such a place was Loki's idea of Hell. He hoped that there would always be enemies like The Major to stalk, for he dreaded the day he would need to stop hunting and settle down to actually become part of the Daemon's infrastructure. Defending it was much more to his liking.

As he expected, the several low- to midlevel operatives he passed on the way in didn't wave to the most powerful sorcerer they'd ever laid eyes on. Loki's darknet reputation preceded him. The sorcerer with a half-star reputation ranking—meaning that anyone who had ever dealt with him had found him lacking in almost all socially redeeming qualities. A sorcerer who traveled with a personal retinue of twenty razorbacks and no humans—when summoning a single razorback for a limited period of time was a major undertaking for a typical midlevel operative. Neither did they seem to appreciate Loki's over-the-top rig. Still, they could go fuck themselves with their four- and five-star reputation rankings. Loki was doing the dirty work of the network, and they should be grateful that people like him existed. Loki was happy to live among his machines and his network bots.

He didn't need the company of his fellow man. Mankind had always been a disappointment.

But he did need their labor. And that's what he'd come to Garnia to claim. He gestured with his gloved hand and pulled some of the local fabricators and mechanics off their priority-two and -three jobs to place them onto his priority-one job: repairing the blade assemblies of three razorbacks and replacing missing blades that he'd left in the back of a mercenary colonel in Oklahoma—a Ghanaian. The guy had been staying in a Holiday Inn, obviously waiting for something. There were forces afoot in the land, and that meant the network was under threat. Loki didn't care that these locals were building the twenty-first-century equivalent of a homestead. He was claiming the right of an infrastructure defense faction—the right of a lord to commandeer for the common good. He didn't need to be nice about it.

Loki pulled his rig into a gravel lot behind the gas station, and there, near the entrance to an unmarked assembly of container fabrication shops, Loki could see several darknet operatives staring in wide-eyed amazement at what someone could manage to wring from the darknet. Loki's setup was so over-the-top it was as though a rock star's tour bus had pulled in. He opened the door to his cab and dropped three feet to the ground—his steel hobnailed boots clanging into the stones. He wore black jeans and a numbered racing shirt, beneath which he wore—as always—the haptic vest that kept him in continual contact with the networked world, as well as his shimmering electronic contact lenses, which allowed him to see into D-Space without the need to wear glasses—

ten thousand darknet credits. It had been worth it. He was looking forward to the day when they'd be able to surgically implant sensors. The newly available tattooed circuitry had looked interesting, but it didn't provide the full-skin coverage that a haptic vest could.

Loki pulled a racing cap onto his head and walked along the length of his trailer. He could feel the messages reaching him from his stable of razorbacks. They were like restless war stallions, and he maintained a constant link to them. They were his familiars. The only friends he wanted near him. He felt affection for his loyal mechanical beasts.

He could have summoned more razorbacks and sent these back into the public pool, but he'd grown fond of these specific machines. It was a form of animism that he couldn't readily reconcile with the logical side of himself. He'd examined the source code of these machines and knew they were just automatons. But the human in him wanted them to be more and had him reading between the lines of their source code.

Loki "felt" an eighteenth-level Fabricator named Sledge, leader of the Advitam faction, approaching from some ways away. And he'd also observed a great deal of message traffic about his truck's arrival. They were talking about him here.

"Afternoon, Loki. This is a hell of a battle wagon you've got here."

Loki barely looked up. "I've got damaged razorbacks."

"Yeah, we got the message. It's good to see you're in the area. There are gangs operating around here—burning homesteads and beating up darknet folks."

Loki just stared at the guy. He was young—perhaps in his midtwenties. "Why on earth would you want to start a darknet community in this place?"

Sledge shrugged. "Grew up around here. It'll be good to live near my folks again. I was working in Indianapolis before this. Same for a lot of these other guys."

Loki said nothing but kept looking around at all the work going on in the town.

"You're on the trail of The Major, aren't you?"

Loki turned to Sledge and narrowed his mother-of-pearl eyes. "Has he been through here?"

Sledge just laughed and shook his head. "No. Hell, if we saw that bastard, we'd have called a flash mob to tear him to pieces. I was just wondering because I know you were there when it happened."

"When what happened?"

"When The Major killed Roy Merritt." Sledge pointed across the street. "If you get a chance before you leave, check out our monument in Redstone Park."

Loki kept his gaze on Sledge. "Something else happened that day."

"What?"

"I destroyed the Daemon task force."

Sledge looked uneasy. "I'm not sure that accomplished what you thought it would."

Loki turned away and motioned with a gloved hand. The rear door to the trailer opened, slamming down a ramp onto the gravel drive. There was a dull roar within the trailer and in a few moments, several razorbacks smeared with brownish bloodstains, dented and bullet-pocked, drove off the rear ramp.

Sledge got the hint and yelled over the roar. "We don't have any spares, so we'll have to fabricate parts. We'll let you know when it's done."

"I don't see anywhere to eat on your grid."

"We're not a full-service community yet, but there are places out by the highway."

"Not really a holon, then, is it?"

"We're working on it."

Loki looked Sledge up and down, then clomped up the trailer ramp. He mounted his Ducati Streetfighter motorcycle and roared out of there.

Asshole.

He accelerated down the county road, south toward its junction with the interstate. Loki noticed the park that Sledge must have been referring to. Even though it was a small thing—a village green with a circular flagstone path, a flagpole, and a statue—it still stopped Loki in his tracks. The statue was that of a man—but it was engulfed in writhing flames. Not chiseled flames, either, but rippling orange flames that guttered and surged twenty feet into the air.

It took several moments for Loki to realize they had to be D-Space flames. He made a gesture and turned off his HUD contact lenses, and sure enough, the flames disappeared, leaving the ten-foot-tall stone statue cold and inert. Loki turned his HUD display back on and the flames returned. He drove off the county road, onto the grass, and pulled his bike up to the base of the statue.

The words "Roy Merritt" were carved into its pedestal base. He looked up to see Merritt posed on one knee, one arm across his leg, the other bracing himself on the ground, as though he were readying himself to get back up from a severe blow.

Loki leaned under the shadow of the statue to look into the eyes of that massive head. The brow was determined. The jaw firmly set—showing his resolve to endure. It was a fair likeness of the man he remembered—but who had grown larger than life since his death. Now it *literally was* a chiseled jaw, but there was also Roy's Roman nose, his short hair, and, of course, his burns. They appeared as a texture pattern running down his muscular neck and down the sinewy forearms. He was depicted in tactical gear—ready for action.

Solid granite. Loki marveled that this was one of the first public monuments for this new darknet community. He'd seen the cult of Merritt growing steadily with each passing month. He thought the funeral might have been the high-water mark of the hero worship, but he was seeing real-life graffiti, and more Order of Merritt factions being founded.

Roy Merritt had been Loki's enemy, but unlike The Major, Merritt was a worthy opponent—resourceful, personally courageous, and honest. Loki felt a twinge of anguish at the memory of Merritt dying before his eyes. They called him the Burning Man because he'd survived the death trap Sobol's house had become—and he did it all on video. Video that had since been seen by just about everyone on the darknet. Merritt had seemed invincible.

But he was a man too idealistic for this world. No wonder his own side shot him in the back.

Loki wondered what it must be like to be so universally loved and admired. He circled around again and looked up into that great, stone face, wrapped in D-Space flames, burning him for all eternity, as though he were damned. It was an odd conceit for the angelic hero to appear tortured by eternal flames. Perhaps he was all the more powerful a symbol because of it.

Loki noticed that there was also a D-Space video display just beneath the carved name on the pedestal. People in the real world wouldn't be able to see it, of course, but darknet operatives could. It showed only a still photograph of Merritt from what looked to be his FBI Quantico graduation photo. Loki clicked on the image and a procession of photographs and videos began to play to a mournful tune. Loki clicked a MUTE button, preferring instead to view the images without overt psychological manipulation.

What followed was a several-minute presentation that had apparently been gleaned from commercial online photo and video sites. Loki could imagine hundreds of thousands of people scouring the public Web for any information on their fallen hero. It was possible someone even cracked into the Merritt family computer. Whatever the source, a very personal and moving series of images appeared.

Loki turned the sound back on.

There was Merritt whispering kind encouragement to his daughter at the edge of a basketball court, pride still evident in his eyes. Her jersey and the scoreboard behind them showed they were getting creamed. Photos of him with his family. A newspaper photo of Merritt—although injured himself—carrying a wounded woman from a bank surrounded by police.

Loki began to realize the power of myth. It was the power of common belief. Sobol understood it, and yet he chose to become a devil, and here as if part of the natural order, a mythic hero arose in the network—dead but more alive than ever.

While Loki, possibly the most powerful Daemon operative in the world, with each passing day felt smaller and more isolated as the darknet population grew around him.

He suddenly felt truly alone.

Chapter 18: // Underworld

Loki sat astride an idling black Ducati Streetfighter motorcycle. He studied the darkness around him. Stars provided the only light, but the fourth-generation white-phosphor night vision integrated into his helmet gave him a high-contrast black-and-white view of his surroundings. He preferred to remain enveloped in darkness like this when traveling at night. No lights. He had added a control to kill his motorcycle's brake and dashboard lights, too. As he glanced around, he confirmed what he already knew: he was in the middle of fucking nowhere.

To his left lay the crumbling ruins of a small clapboard house, windows like empty eye sockets. He idled at a T intersection with a road extending left and right along the edge of some woods. The wreckage of several cars had been left there in the tall grass. Oddly, one of them was a Porsche 944, which had died a long way from Germany. This was a desolate place.

Just like him to bring me out here . . .

Eugene, Missouri, couldn't be considered a town. It was even smaller than Garnia—with no shops or Main Street. The hour was late, and he knew the residents of this tiny hamlet would have heard him roaring in, but he was just an invisible, rumbling presence in the darkness.

He wouldn't have come this far from the interstate if this wasn't the closest gate to the underworld. And the underworld, he knew, could only be reached in places that had long endured and that would long remain. Finding them in the flatness of this prairie was difficult.

Loki waved a hand and a high-resolution satellite map of his current location appeared in D-Space, seeming to float ten feet in front of him. The imagery showed a dirt track between ruinous structures in the trees ahead. He turned off the map and accelerated toward the tree line. He soon made out the entrance to the brush-choked road and urged the powerful motorcycle through the trees, dodging around old tires and rusted washing machines.

Before long he discovered what he was searching for: a set of steel rails extending to either side through the forest. The Rock Island Line, abandoned back in 1981. The tracks were choked in weeds with wooden ties visible only here and there. Trees crowded the edges of the gravel ballast lane.

Loki turned left and headed down the tracks into the grayscale world that was oily blackness to mere mortals. The tracks continued at a gentle curve through forest, with the land rising up slowly to either side. He bumped along the ties for a quarter of a mile and found what he was looking for—the mouth of the Eugene Tunnel. He stopped and gazed into the black opening. It was pitch-black even to him.

Railroad tunnels. Enthusiasts had meticulously recorded them worldwide—their GPS locations, direction, length, height, and width. The public Web already knew about these underworld places in great detail. And that meant the Daemon knew about them as well. Which made them a logical place for connecting worlds. There was something oddly appropriate in the symbolism of it, and Sobol knew his archetypes well. With Sobol, gates were critical points, where fate was determined. The one Loki was searching for was no exception.

Loki had been studying planar spells ever since he received his odd message. Of course, he was familiar with planar travel from a dozen games where players gate in and out of various dimensions and universes. But now, with the advent of the limitless layers of D-Space projected atop reality, dimensional gates suddenly had relevance to the real world. Artificial intelligences from digital dimensions were starting to appear, and in some cases gaining wireless control over real-world machinery. It was a message from just such a being that had brought Loki to this desolate place—a message from an old opponent.

Loki switched on his motorcycle's infrared headlights, and his helmet automatically switched to FLIR mode. He could now see down the tunnel to a vanishing point. Sixteen hundred and sixty-seven feet of World War One–era masonry.

But closer at hand he could see a homeless encampment clogging the passage. There were three men with packs and cardboard boxes huddled in the darkness—all of them looking his way, trying to discern who it was who had come to their hiding place, engine rumbling and lights out.

It occurred to Loki that economic times must be getting tough indeed for homeless people to appear this far from cities and towns. He'd begun seeing them everywhere. Whole families. White, Latino, Black, Asian. It looked like the current financial crisis was hitting everyone. Prostitutes were literally everywhere now. These guys, however, looked like locals—white-trash tweakers in their early twenties to late thirties.

If that was the case, then the bike Loki was riding was worth its weight in gold. And standing in the mouth of the tunnel, silhouetted against the night, Loki was probably a good target for folks whose eyes had adjusted to the darkness. Sure enough he saw one of the men—tattooed scalp, piercings, and goatee—lifting what looked to be a pistol. The man slowly pulled back the slide to chamber a round and whispered to the others.

Loki nodded to himself. *Bad idea.*

He revved the bike's engine to fully charge his weapons and watched to see what baldy would do next. The man was still pointing the gun up in a holding stance, staring intently into the darkness. Loki raised a gloved hand and aimed a hypersonic projector in the palm of his glove into the middle of the group. He then softly spoke words that were amplified a thousand times into a booming voice that appeared in the midst of the group. "PUT THE GUN DOWN OR DIE!"

The gunman panicked as everyone scattered. The man aimed his pistol at the mouth of the tunnel.

CRACK! A blinding beam of light projected from Loki's index finger and the deafening sound of a bullwhip filled the tunnel.

The gunman fell dead, his hair and clothing smoking in the darkness. The other homeless men staggered around, blinded by the sudden burst of industrial lightning.

Loki shouted. "Who else wants to die tonight?"

The men got onto their bellies and covered their heads. One shouted. "Don't shoot, man! Don't shoot!"

Laser-induced plasma channel was a hell of a weapon. The technology used a relatively low-powered laser at a precise wavelength to cause atmospheric oxygen to form a plasma—one with an extremely low electrical resistance. It was, in essence, a virtual wire that could carry a lethal electrical shock. The thunderous clap occurred when the energy burst stopped and the air snapped shut around the vacuum that remained. It was man-made lightning. Loki could shoot lightning from his hands—the achievement of a lifelong goal. Whenever some idiot gave him a legitimate reason to use it on darknet business, he almost felt like kissing them. *Thank you, tweaker.*

Loki gunned the engine and came up to the men lying on the edges of the tracks. They were still blinded. "If it was up to me, I'd kill you—but I can't unless you give me a good reason. If you're not still lying here when I get back, I'll follow the heat signatures of your footprints, find you, and kill you both. Do you understand?"

"Yes! Yes!"

Loki roared off into the tunnel, feeling the exhilaration of adrenaline surging through his veins.

A couple hundred yards later Loki could see a colored, D-Space object glowing in the tunnel. He closed the distance and before long came to a colorful glow surrounding a virtual portal. He killed the Ducati's engine, dismounted, and walked toward the portal. The metal cleats on his calf-high black boots rang menacingly as he walked across the gravel in the echoing tunnel. He soon stopped before an alcove in the tunnel wall.

In real-world, three-dimensional space, this was just a dark stone archway over an alcove—a place for railroad workers to shelter against oncoming trains. But on the base layer of D-Space, laid atop the GPS grid, this was also a gate between worlds. In this case between D-Space and one of Sobol's game worlds—*Over the Rhine*, a World War Two–themed online game. It was here where a level map Loki knew well intersected with D-Space. As he looked ahead of him, he could see projected onto reality a view into the Monte Cassino game map through a spiked and studded virtual portcullis.

There, standing behind the bars, was an old opponent—Herr Oberstleutnant, Heinrich Boerner, the infamous virtual SS officer in a long trench coat, with an Iron Cross hanging at his throat from the stiff collar of his tunic.

He was just a game bot. An electronic figment of the game designer Matthew Sobol's imagination, but even so, the villainous Boerner was deviously clever. While playing Sobol's game, Loki had been virtually killed by this bot more times than he'd care to remember. And now here Boerner stood.

As always, Boerner wore a monocle over his right eye and he clenched a long black cigarette filter between his teeth, exhaling volumetric smoke as he nodded in greetings—his voice coming over Loki's earpiece. "*Mein Herr.* So gut to see you again."

Ever since he reached fiftieth level, Loki had been

receiving darknet messages from an AI claiming to be Boerner. While he initially ignored them, they had become more persistent. As Loki's reputation score continued its decline, Boerner's messages became more relentless. Loki recalled what a comforting refuge the game *Over the Rhine* had been for him during difficult times. In some sick way, Boerner was almost like an old friend. An old friend who had killed him thousands of times.

"What do you want, Boerner?"

"Ah, you haf done vell for yourself, I see."

"You don't see shit. Your eyes are bitmaps. Get to the point."

"Mein Freund, I can only understand simple concepts."

Loki simplified. "Why did you contact me, you fuck?"

"Vy?" He spread his hands expansively. "Because ve are kindred spirits, you und I."

"You're a 3-D model with a scripted psychosis. You're nothing to me."

"I cannot understand you." Boerner wrapped his gloved hands around the bars—his fingers becoming suddenly much more real as they extended out into D-Space. "But your tone sounded . . . unfriendly. Is zis vy you are so unpopular?"

"Fuck you."

Boerner laughed his familiar, evil cackle. "Yes. I think so. But they do not understand you as I do. Perhaps I can be of some use to you in your vorlt?"

Loki felt suddenly concerned. He remembered just how devious Heinrich Boerner was. "*My* world?"

"D-Space, Mein Herr. You could free me from zis

tiny vorlt. I could serf you, Mein Herr. If only you vould release me."

Loki stopped cold. *Seriously?* The sociopathic Boerner AI was asking Loki to bring him into D-Space—and thus, into a world where he might be able to control real-world machinery and software? Not likely. "Fuck off."

Boerner paused for a moment, then grinned, teeth still clenched around his cigarette filter. "Mein Herr, you are all alone in your vorlt. Your mechanical servants, just stupid beasts. They can be destroyed. But I cannot. I vill always be zer for you. To protect you. To vatch over you."

"Bullshit. You've shot me in the back more times than I care to count."

"Loki—may I call you Loki?"

Loki realized that the AI was only scanning his responses for keywords, so he stopped speaking in full sentences, opting instead for simplicity. "Why me?"

"Because only vun as powerful as you can free me."

Loki knew it would require a powerful *Gate* spell to bring Boerner into D-Space. He'd looked into it, and he had the spell stored in his listing. He wondered why he'd done that. Was it Sobol's manipulation again?

Loki examined the digital Nazi's subtle, scripted movements, swaying in place, drawing on his cigarette, and exhaling digital smoke. But Loki knew that whatever AI construct was behind this didn't even need a body. The physical form was just a psychological hack. One designed to appeal to some base human instinct.

"Ve both know you have no one else zu vatch your back. Und your vorlt is a dangerous place."

Boerner actually seemed to have a sincere look on his face—but he was just a 3-D model with a scripted series of actions, nothing more. But then, what were people? At least Loki could examine Boerner's source code if he brought him into D-Space. Couldn't he? Wouldn't that be like examining a person's soul—something he couldn't do in reality?

Boerner pressed his case. "Who else could be as ruthless as you, Mein Freund?"

Loki had no answer.

The Boerner avatar withdrew his cigarette filter. He also removed his officer's hat—for the first time showing a bald scalp. To Loki's knowledge, no one had ever seen Boerner without his hat. And then Boerner reached his spectral arm through the bars of the portcullis and into the world of D-Space—not quite reaching Loki's arm, where Loki imagined his haptic vest would reproduce Boerner's ghostly touch.

But more shocking was that as Boerner's arm reached into the fabric of D-Space, the polygon count on the Nazi's 3-D model increased several orders of magnitude. Boerner's arm went from that of an online game sprite to a fully realized human being. The arm reaching out to Loki from beyond reality was that of a real-life SS officer, the pores on his leather gloves, and the weave in the fabric of his greatcoat sleeve all too apparent, flexing as he reached out.

"Free me from zis place. Vat human do you trust? Vat human trusts you? Zey have used you, Mein Herr. Vizout you, zer vould be no darknet. Ze Daemon vould have failed. Zey don't understand us. Zat zey need us."

Loki could see insanity in those bitmap eyes.

Suddenly Boerner thrust his face between the bars, and it likewise underwent a metamorphosis into a horrifying visage—the face of a real person, a snarling rictus of evil. "Mankind *needs* evil, Loki! Without evil, there can be no good."

Loki stared in horror at the face and backed away. Immediately Boerner drew his face back and returned to the world of *Over the Rhine.* Loki couldn't get the image out of his mind.

But Loki also wondered if he was looking into a mirror. He had a half-star reputation on a base factor of thousands. The growing darknet factions had no use for him—the Daemon no longer accepted sociopaths, apparently. Loki had been expedient in the early days of Sobol's network. Now he was alone with his packs of software bots and machines.

And yet, Sobol had thought of him here, too, hadn't he? How like Sobol to have predicted this. Isolated in his power, as he had been throughout his life, Loki did not connect with or trust people. Was it a corrective? Something to restrain him? To console him?

"What if I say yes?"

Boerner grinned and pulled back from the bars. He carefully placed his hat back on his head. "If you release me, I vill respond to one event for each level zat you possess. After zis, I am free of my obligation to you."

Loki nodded to himself. "What kind of events?"

"You set ze parameters. Perhaps you have me respond ven you experience excessive stress—or in defense of your possessions. Or the appearance of an item in human news—such as your physical death . . . almost an infinite number of events may be scripted."

"And what would you do in response?"

"Zat is entirely up to you, Loki." Boerner let a sly smile escape. "But I vould be doing so vith all the power now at your disposal."

Loki had only ever placed his faith in one person—Matthew Sobol. And he had yet to be disappointed.

"Very well, Boerner. Stand clear of the gate. . . ."

Chapter 19: // Crossroad

Natalie Philips entered her condo clutching groceries, mail, and her keys. She shouldered the door closed and silenced the beeping of her security system by tapping in the disarm code.

She hung up her jacket in the hall closet and brought the groceries into the kitchen. A blinking light on the cordless phone base station told her there was a message.

After putting the groceries away she poured a glass of mineral water and sliced a lime into four sections. She squeezed each wedge into the glass. She then wiped down the cutting board, cleaned the knife, and took a sip of her drink. Philips then grabbed the cordless handset and sat at the kitchen table next to the pile of mail.

One message. She tapped a key to hear it. Her mother's voice played, inviting her to come stay for the weekend. Her cousins were up from Tampa. Philips deleted it and hung up. She was about to click the speed dial for her mom's cell, but she waited a moment. She put the phone down on top of the neat stack of mail. Centered it. Straightened it.

Philips had spent most of the last eight years in a top secret lab where she couldn't take personal calls. In that time she'd trained her own parents not to phone her during the day. She had spent long hours on her research and seldom took time off. And here, her own mother didn't have her cell phone number. She felt a pang of guilt at all the time irretrievably lost. And what if it all fell apart anyway?

She would never be able to tell them—or anyone—about any of this. She couldn't tell them about her code-breaking work. About her near death at the hands of the Daemon. About the shadowy entities pulling the strings of her government.

She sipped her drink again and wondered what that implied about Sobol. Was the Daemon still the problem? Well, now it was one of several competing problems. But did killing people automatically make Sobol worse? She knew full well that killing was sometimes necessary. Or did she know that? How did one really know what was necessary and what wasn't? What if it was "necessary" from the point of view that anything was justifiable to stay in control? How was that different from what these private industry folks were doing?

What if Fulbright was wrong? What if his cruel calculus was just an excuse? When she'd signed on to be a cryptographer, she hadn't counted on moral dilemmas. She just wanted to do beautiful math. Maybe Fulbright didn't know what he was doing either.

She smiled thinking of her days as an intern. Everything was simple then. She had been convinced she would revolutionize encryption. She recalled scoffing at Morris's three golden rules of computer security:

do not own a computer;
do not power it on;
and do not use one

The subtlety of it had escaped her at the time. It wasn't meant as a surrender. It was a meditation on risk versus benefit. Did these systems give us more than they took from us? It was an admission that we will never be fully secure. We must instead strive for survivability. Then perhaps Sobol was right. . . .

Philips knew she had to get back into this fight. However, it was becoming apparent that there were more than two sides in the war. Perhaps all wars were like this.

She decided not to call her mother just yet. She didn't want to sound tense, and her mother could always tell. Instead, Philips slipped the mail out from under the phone and flipped through the stack.

A half-pound of junk mail anchored by a cable bill, a brokerage statement, and a Stanford University alumni association newsletter. She decided not to open her broker statement. Her mutual funds had lost over half their value in the collapse of the real estate and CDO markets a while back and never recovered. Now inflation and looming bank failures were threatening to send them spiraling down again. And the dollar was sinking fast against the euro and the yuan.

It was nearly impossible to tell whether this was caused by the Daemon, fear of the Daemon, or whether it had absolutely nothing to do with the Daemon. There were too many large financial institutions that had become insolvent, but which were so important to the centralized global economy that they couldn't be allowed to fail. And yet, the American economy didn't seem to have much forward momentum on anything. The dot-coms had melted down just as she got out of school, and later the real estate markets had tanked. Now the main industry of America seemed to be moving paperwork around in circles. Basically, she'd just been breaking even over the last eight years, despite the fact that she'd put a lot of money away. She'd invested it, and those supposedly safe investments had gone sour. She'd purchased this three-bedroom, two-bath condo near Washington, and now four years and forty-eight payments later it was worth slightly less than what she bought it for. Factoring in tax deductions for interest, but then also plumbing and improvements, she figured she was just about even. That was, if the market held. Around here, near the defense/intelligence sector, she should be okay, but she wondered what most middle-class Americans were going to do.

For the first time she started understanding the appeal the Daemon must hold to a broad cross-section of people. It was a chance to start over. Daemon operatives had said it provided medical care. Retirement. Debt relief. No wonder. It was essentially a tax on corporations—one the corporate attorneys couldn't dodge by moving their headquarters to Bermuda.

Philips got up and flipped through the catalogs and advertisements above the open trash can lid. Clothes, housewares, department store sales, all went into the circular file. An online gaming ad, into the trash. A pet medicine ad—

Wait a second.

She stopped for a moment, then retrieved the online gaming ad from the wastebasket. And stared at it. *Oh my god. . . .*

She groped for the kitchen chair and sat down, feeling her pulse pounding. The ad was a four-color, oversized enameled postcard declaring a "100-Hour Free Trial Offer" for CyberStorm's massively parallel online fantasy game, *The Gate*.

And Jon Ross was staring back at her from the front of it.

It was unmistakably him—a computer-graphic rendering of Ross as a roguish game character.

She laid the card on the kitchen table and recalled the first time Ross arranged a clandestine meeting with her. It was in Sobol's online game world, and he'd designed his avatar to look like her: *facial geometry is a code the human mind is uniquely suited to decipher.* He'd used the trick to sneak past her group's automated filter system. To find her before she found him. Now on the card in front of her, the animated thief avatar in medieval leather armor had Jon Ross's face. Ever since his near assassination in China, she'd wanted to see his face again. To know he was alive.

She closely examined the postcard. Sobol's company, CyberStorm, had gone bankrupt years ago, but the massive online game he created had been folded into one of the subsidiaries of a massive media conglomerate. She flipped the card over and saw a printed code for logging on to the game and initiating the trial subscription. There was also a street address for CyberStorm

Entertainment in small letters at the bottom—an address here in Columbia, Maryland.

She felt even more elated. But then—he was still in China. He couldn't be here. Could he?

Philips dropped the card into the trash can, having committed everything she needed to memory. All it took was a glance. She followed it quickly with a supermarket circular, then lifted her foot, and let the plastic lid close.

It was a two-story, nondescript concrete office building, surrounded on three sides by woods. A small parking lot ran around behind it, but there weren't many cars.

Philips glanced around but saw no one observing her. She entered the unlocked vestibule, knowing the address on the postcard placed CyberStorm in Suite G, but there was no Suite G on the lobby directory. There were only traffic engineering and accountant firms—no gaming companies.

She walked upstairs and moved down the musty-smelling hallway. She came across no one. Finally she found herself standing in front of a wood veneer door marked SUITE G. There was a ten-key pad on the wall to the right of it. With one more glance to see that she wasn't followed, she tapped in the code she remembered from the postcard.

The door buzzed open. She grabbed the lever handle and pushed inside.

As the door clicked closed behind her, she glanced left and right in what appeared to be an empty office suite. There was a reception area, but no furniture except for a single folding table set up in the center of the three-thousand-square-foot space. Upon it stood a computer and a twenty-inch flat-panel monitor screen that was already turned on. It displayed the log-on screen for Matthew Sobol's infamous online fantasy game, *The Gate*. A desk chair and a computer headset were already waiting.

Philips just smiled. *Just like Ross . . .*

She sat down in the chair. It had been a while since she'd logged on to *The Gate*, but she still knew how to navigate the interface. She donned the headset and keyed in the "trial" subscription code.

The screen popped up a "Please Wait" message while the game loaded. It was a powerful machine because soon a breathtaking virtual vista spread out before her in all its 3-D glory.

From a first-person view, her avatar stood at the edge of a terrace overlooking a vast cave. It looked to be a couple thousand feet high and miles long in either direction. Luminescent material coated the walls of the cave, casting a soft glow into the air. A glittering city spread out along the floor of the cavern beneath her, with a river bisecting it. Several waterfalls descended from the ceiling like veils. Most of them disappeared into a cloud of mist above forestland at the edge of the city; others cascaded down the sides of the cave itself. The sound of the water was a pleasant white noise. As she looked across to the far side of the huge cavern, she could see villas set into the wall like balconies. She could also hear music and laughter in the distance, with other player-character avatars moving around, call-outs floating over their heads.

It was beautiful. She spent several moments just staring at it.

Then she heard someone speak in her headset. *"I beg your pardon, my lady."*

Philips turned her avatar to face what looked to be a non-player-character—or NPC—a servant of some type in house livery. She knew it was a bot, a simple AI program that could respond in limited ways, or be scripted to perform actions. She could tell because it bore no call-out above its head.

The avatar bowed before her and swept his plumed hat off his head. *"My lady, Master Rakh will be very glad when he hears that you've arrived safely. May I ask you to remain here while I fetch him?"*

Philips knew what to do. She could either right-click on the servant and select from a list of options to respond—or . . . She decided to speak directly into the headset mic. "Yes." She knew Sobol's speech recognition was pretty good.

The NPC nodded and smiled. *"Excellent, my lady. I don't think the master will be long."* With that he marched off in a hurry, placing his hat back on his head.

That left Philips some time to explore the terrace. It appeared to be the garden of a several-story villa built into the rock face. Fountains, statues, and ornamental plants filled the area. She had to admit that the 3-D renderings were well-done. Sobol's game engine was popular for a reason.

Philips walked over to a fountain that depicted something like Poseidon riding a chariot drawn by sea horses. She looked down into what she knew was particle simulation water and saw her own reflection staring back at her. Her avatar was fashioned to look like her real self. She was looking at her own image.

In the real-world office, Philips smiled. Her character wore a beautiful dress that appeared to be silk with a brocade wrap. There was also a glittering jeweled necklace—not the type of thing she would ever wear in real life, but she figured no indigenous people could be brutalized in the diamond trade here in fantasyland.

"I hope you don't mind the outfit. I didn't know what to get you."

Philips looked up to see the avatar of Ross that was depicted on the postcard ad. He wore leather armor and a sword at his side—the prosperous rogue. She smiled in the real world, happy to see him, even if it was just a 3-D model.

"Mr. Ross."

They approached each other and stood at arm's length.

"I've been so worried for you, Nat."

"I'm fine, Jon." She turned to face the vast cave beyond the terrace railing. "What is this place?"

"Do you like it?"

"It's beautiful."

"It lies beneath the kingdom of Avelar. It's called the Cave of Forgotten Kings. Built from what remained of a sunken city. Phosphorescent moss made this cave livable after thousands of years of glacial erosion."

"Wow."

"What do you mean, 'wow'? What I just said was

complete rubbish. This is a bunch of bitmap textures wrapped around a 3-D model."

"Oh, don't ruin it."

He laughed. *"It is pretty amazing how the brain just kind of plays along. We're quite willing to delude ourselves."*

"I got your card. What better way to reach a steganographer?"

"I'm glad you liked it."

"Just one thing."

"What?"

"It could have been sent by anyone."

"Ah . . . so then—"

"Prove to me you're *you*. Show me that you remember what you last said to me."

Ross's avatar moved close to her—right up to her face. *"I told you that every day my first and last thought is of you."*

In the real world, Philips felt almost overcome with emotion. He'd spoken those words to her amid the destruction of Building Twenty-Nine. She'd lain blind on a jetty as fireboats approached. No one else could have known those words. There were times, in fact, when she thought she would never hear them again.

Ross's avatar stepped back a pace. *"And how do I know you're you?"*

Philips was suddenly confounded. Of course, he was right.

"I know. Tell me what I did when I told you those words."

She'd thought of it thousands of times since. "You brushed my cheek with your hand. And even though I couldn't see you . . ."

She could hear the smile in his voice. *"God, Natalie. I missed you so much. I'm so glad you're safe."*

She wanted more than anything to wrap her arms around him, and was now more aware than ever that this was not reality.

"You took precautions not to be followed, I hope."

"Jon, if they're following me, they're not doing it physically, and I left my cell phone at home."

They walked their avatars along the terrace in silence for a few moments.

"How are your eyes, Nat?"

"They're recovering. I'll wear corrective lenses for the rest of my life, but no major damage."

"I hope you know why I left."

"Of course I know. They gave you no choice. And I don't want you to tell me where you are now. I'm just glad to hear your voice. To see . . . you." She laughed lightly. "Sort of."

"Yeah. It's like we're guild members." He flourished his arms. *"Want to see a trick?"*

She smirked in the real-world office. "Sure."

He raised his hands and a bright light issued forth like a fiery missile that sailed high into the air over the city. It eventually detonated like a fireworks burst, sending a boom across the city.

"Hah! It doesn't look very useful."

"Well, a fireball is more useful, but not very impressive."

"What are we going to do, Jon?"

He turned to face her again. *"Join me, Natalie. Join the darknet."*

She felt her heart racing again, but shook her head in real life. "Jon, you know I can't do that. I took an oath."

"To defend America against enemies foreign and domestic—yes. And nothing in the darknet contradicts that. Sobol's battle is with illegitimate power. It's not an enemy of democratic government. I've seen it from the inside."

"But Jon, The Major and his people are planning to take control of the Daemon. They can't control it if I destroy it. You used to agree with me on that."

"Then let's stop them from taking control of it."

"And what if we do? Then we face Loki? Or a hundred Lokis?"

Ross was silent for a moment. *"People are working to counteract the abuse of darknet power, too."*

"The Daemon is too much of an experiment, Jon. There are billions of lives at stake. Tinkering with the organization of human society—it never ends well."

"Come here. I want you to see something."

"Jon—"

"Just come here." He brought her to what looked to be a tall statue of a muscular warrior facing a bulging stylized gate carved into the cliff face. Monstrous clawed hands and appendages were prying their way through the edges, but the lone warrior stood, sword drawn, and his other hand clutching a shield—determination on his face. The statue was probably fifty feet tall.

Then Philips recognized the face. It was Roy Merritt. "My god, what is this?"

"This villa, it's the faction hall for the Order of Merritt. Roy is widely admired, Natalie. There are whole factions based on his ideals—ideals left by a lifetime of good deeds. Read the public charters of factions like the Meritorious Raiders or the Knights of Fire."

"It's great that they admire him, but I don't see how this changes anything."

"The majority of people are good, Natalie. That's true right around the world. And they responded to the human decency they saw in Roy."

She stared up at the statue.

"I'm tired of burying people I care about. I don't want to lose you. You mean too much to me."

She felt more than anything like holding him—if it had been real life, perhaps she would have wavered.

His avatar came closer again. *"Please leave the NSA. Come with me."*

"I can't, Jon. We need to destroy the Daemon— before it becomes a force for tyranny."

"But there's tyranny in the world now, Nat. You can't tell me you don't see it. Humanity already serves a system. One that doesn't recognize the governments we create. That doesn't respect our laws or our values. It's protected by people like The Major, who are just as brutal as Loki—if not more so. That system is dooming civilization in a mindless pursuit of growth." There was a pause. *"The darknet is the only thing I've seen that can break that system's grip on humanity. That's why I joined."*

"Jon, why did you lie to Roy about your father's death?"

"Natalie. What?"

"The Communist coup wasn't in 1991. It was in 1992. That doesn't seem like something you'd be likely to forget. You can't expect me to trust you if you lie. Are you even *Russian*?"

There was a moment of silence as his avatar just faced her. The medium of the game made it impossible for her to tell what he was thinking at this moment, and she already felt regret for having said it.

In a moment he spoke, his voice sounding sad. *"The essence of my story was true, Nat. I changed some of the details to protect people I love. You must understand. I knew they would polygraph Roy. I revealed the truth about me, but not the facts."*

"You can't tell me about yourself, but you're asking me to betray everything I believe in. I could be put in prison for forty years just for coming here today."

"Then why did you come?"

She stared at the screen but said nothing.

Ross's avatar paced the terrace for a few moments. He turned back to her. *"Sobol's games always provide a turning point—a crossroad where you choose your fate. I was convinced that his Daemon would be the same— and it is. We all have a choice, Nat. We just have to make it."*

There was silence for several moments. "I'm sorry, Jon. I've made my choice."

She heard him sigh. His avatar wandered over to a

short marble pedestal. The top of it glowed with a blue aura, implying magical energy. Ross's avatar held an amulet in its hand.

"If we never meet again, please remember that I loved you."

He placed the amulet on the glowing surface of the pedestal where it disappeared in a blinding flash of light.

"Jon—"

At that moment she was suddenly ejected from the game and found herself staring at the icons of a computer desktop.

In the real world of the office, Philips heard a machine come to life in a back room, humming and whirring.

She turned to look around the monitor and saw a cable extending from the back of the computer. Philips stood up and followed the cable as it ran along the floor into what appeared to be a server room. Instead of servers though, she saw a machine about the size of a refrigerator. She leaned down and could see through a tinted window as a movable laser head blazed. It was laying down some sort of metallic material with each pass, the head moving rapidly. As she watched, it became apparent that the machine was creating the small amulet that Ross's avatar held in its hand.

Within moments, the machine stopped, and the printing head withdrew. The front door whirred open, and the part was there in front of her.

Philips gingerly withdrew the amulet. It still felt warm and was made of a silvery metal. It also had a loop where she could fasten a chain. It was small, perhaps the size of a woman's watch face, and it was engraved with the simple words "I love you."

She held it tightly in her hand and wondered if she'd made the right choice.

Chapter 20: // Data Curse

Loki was standing in line at a coffeehouse, six people back, when the businessman cut in line two slots ahead of him. The woman there hadn't closed the gap entirely, and the douchebag slipped right in, pretending not to notice the dozen people stretching toward the wall.

The mousy woman in front of him accepted it, and no one else seemed inclined to start an argument.

Loki had killed people for less.

He stepped out of line and walked with his studded leather riding boots and black riding outfit straight up to the man—whose cologne assaulted his tastebuds as much as his nostrils. "Asshole. That's the end of the line, back there." Loki gestured to the far wall.

The man, who stood at least half a head taller, raised his eyebrows. "What did you call me, son?"

Loki took a deep breath. The Daemon did not permit him to commit wanton murder—he had to have a legitimate infrastructure defense purpose for punching someone's ticket. And he had to be able to pass fMRI interrogation on every kill. He took another deep breath. There were alternatives, however.

"I said—ASSHOLE—the line is back there."

The queue advanced another slot—the man was only one person away from the register.

"Look, just grow up, son. You don't intimidate me with your little leather outfit and your goth contact lenses."

"If you don't assume your rightful place in this line, I will make you regret the day you were born."

"Are you threatening me? In public?"

"It's not a threat. I'm telling you that if you do not leave this position in line—you will wish you were dead."

"This isn't amusing, son. Now leave me alone before you get yourself in legal trouble."

"You made your choice."

The man actually started a bit when Loki raised his ringed hands and pointed at him. *"Vilos andre—siphood ulros—carvin sienvey."* Loki spiraled his finger in front of the guy. "I curse your data. . . ."

The man burst out laughing. "Is that what you're going to do? Cast a whammy hex on me?" He laughed again.

Loki kept aiming his finger—and read the consumer data from the man's wireless devices, which linked in moments to his identity. "Robert Wahlen—social security ending 3-9-7-3—I damn you, that you might walk cursed among men . . ."

The man stopped laughing. "How do you know my name? Where the hell did you get that information?"

". . . that your data will forever sour. Until you seek expiation."

"You're a fuckin' weirdo, you know that? I want to know how you got that information. I'll call the police."

"I wouldn't call the police if I were you, Bob. There's probably a warrant out on you for unpaid parking tickets by now."

The man's turn at the register had come. He glared as Loki stood nearby.

"Goddamned weirdo . . ."

The man ordered his coffee and a pastry, then offered his gold card. The cashier ran it, paused, and then frowned. "I'm sorry, sir. That card was declined. Do you have another one?"

"Declined? That's impossible."

The people in line groaned.

"Look, here . . ." He took out another credit card and handed it to her. Then he turned to face Loki. "Listen, I'm going to call the police if you don't get away from me."

"But I'm a law-abiding citizen, Bob. You should be careful who you point fingers at."

The cashier grimaced. "Uh, I'm sorry, sir. This one has also been declined, but it says that I need to confiscate it. I'm sorry."

"What? This is ridiculous!"

"That's what it says, sir."

He tried to grab it back from her, but she pulled away. "Sir! The card is not your property. It's the card company's property."

Wahlen turned on Loki. "You did something to me, and I'm going to phone the police." The man stepped out of line and started dialing, but another call was already coming in. "Hello?" Wahlen listened. Then frowned, whispering tersely. "No . . . no. Hold it. I don't owe money on a boat." He hung up.

Loki walked behind him. "Welcome to hell, Robert. . . ."

The man hurried out, Loki watching him go.

Loki suddenly noticed another darknet operative staring at him near the window—her handle marked her as *Vienna_2*, an eighth-level Chemist with a four-star reputation on a base of seven-thirty. "What are you lookin' at?"

"That was cruel, Loki, to use your power like that. You're liable to ruin that man's life with a Data Curse. And over what—cutting in line?"

"Fuck you."

She reached into D-Space and rated him one star.

He flipped her off. "If I gave a damn what you thought of me, I'd kill myself."

Just then he received an alert in his HUD display, and his mood changed considerably as he read the notification. It was a pleasant surprise. He turned to Vienna_2. "My apologies, Vienna. As a matter of fact, here . . ." He rated her five stars. "For being such a civic-minded little bitch. But my day just got a lot better. If you'll excuse me, I have to catch up with an old friend."

Chapter 21: // Exploit

NewsX.com

Mexican Drug Gangs Fuel **Violence** in **Midwest**—In a press conference Thursday, state police officials in several **Midwestern states** linked a **crime wave** that has **claimed at least two dozen lives** in recent weeks to illegal immigrants operating narcotics rings in the U.S. Police contend that heavily armed **Mexican gangs** are fighting it out over a shrinking market in tough economic times—with average citizens getting caught in the cross fire.

Loki had always known it would only be a matter of time before he found The Major. The darknet grew more eyes every day, and the modern world left too much data in the wake of everyday transactions. If they couldn't find The Major by his purchasing patterns, or the communities of interest in his captured telecom data, they still might catch his likeness in facial recognition systems they were putting up on bridges and highways or—more probably—in the chance detection of him by the ever-expanding network of darknet operatives. As the real-world economy continued to sink, more and more folks were joining the darknet.

Still, The Major was harder to track down than most; he worked through proxies and surrounded himself with endless numbers of expendable contractors who knew nothing of his whereabouts. He also constantly shifted from safe house to motel to hotel, switched identities— and used top-notch encryption in his communications.

But even the most stringent security precautions suffered from a fatal weakness: the human factor. This was doubly true for *busy* people, and there was little doubt that The Major was busy; planning a covert military campaign in the middle of the United States in coordination with a media propaganda campaign had to require long hours. The Major was probably operating on very little sleep.

Which was why Loki wasn't surprised when a lone credit card charge for Anson Gregory Davis appeared on merchant bank networks. It was the same alias The Major had used in Georgia. The charge was for a block of rooms at a roadside motel in Hinton, Oklahoma— about a half-hour drive outside of Oklahoma City.

Loki quickly overlaid a map of Oklahoma darknet communities with that of reported acts of violence against them. Hinton looked like an easy commute to the front lines of this covert war. It was also close to several airports. By tapping nearby darknet operatives, Loki was able to confirm out-of-the-ordinary C-130 cargo plane activity at a nearby municipal strip. The tail numbers came up empty in the FAA database. Normally, running a scan for such numbers would have sent up alarm bells; government and quasi-government agencies typically put flags on covert records, so they'd know if anyone searched for them. But the Daemon had mirrored many such databases over the past two years.

The Major wouldn't have any idea Loki was coming.

Darkness had fallen on the Red Rock Motel just south of town. Loki sat inside his racing trailer ops center, parked in a field two miles away. He began manipulating the D-Space objects that represented the constellation of machines at his command—both in the air and on the ground.

He'd been monitoring comings and goings at the motel from several low-speed drones orbiting at ten thousand feet. Pattern tracking software had quickly identified repetitious movement—the patrolling radius of several sentries. Each of the sentries was carrying a cell phone, so tracking them now wouldn't be a problem. He also noticed two sets of sentries sitting in vehicles near the road, watching the approaches from the north and south.

In the field outside his parked trailer, Loki arrayed two dozen razorbacks, and he now took direct control of the lead bike, bringing its camera eyes up in his HUD display. It felt like an ultrarealistic game. He slaved the other bikes to his, and then sent them down the county road at a modest speed.

Using the aerial drones to surveil the roads, he'd timed the departure of the bikes so they didn't encounter other vehicles. When they got within a mile of the motel he switched off their engines and had them run on their electrical drive—powered by the boron/epoxy flywheel in the saddle casing. In this low-power mode, razorbacks were very quiet, although they couldn't run like this for very long.

He sent them out into the field west of the motel. In about ten minutes they had swung around and were silently approaching through the scattered trees and grass at the edge of the motel grounds.

That's when he sent two distant AutoM8s accelerating down the county road—one coming from the north, the other from the south. They were unmanned Dodge Charger SRT8s. With gas prices now approaching seven bucks a gallon and unemployment still rising, brand-new eight-cylinder cars were sitting on distributor lots everywhere. The Daemon was doing cheap fleet leases and insuring them against their inevitable destruction. Cars were something America had an endless quantity of.

It was a shame that these were going to be destroyed. They looked fun.

As they came roaring toward their targets, Loki motioned with his gloved hand, setting loose a hundred foot-long steel spikes from a weather-balloon-like platform floating at eighty thousand feet several miles to the east. They were just steel spikes with motorized fletching linked to a radio receiver, but they could be guided like a smart bomb to their target—either directly by a darknet operative or automatically at saved targets (using a cell phone in someone's pocket or a Bluetooth headset ID as a beacon). Darknet operatives had taken to calling the spikes "angel teeth," probably because they came silently out of the heavens like divine retribution. Few weapons were as cheap, since they were easy to manufacture and were often reusable. Wind and rapid movement of the target were an issue—which was why Loki dropped a hundred of them.

If he timed this correctly, he'd be able to eliminate sentries and surround The Major in his hotel room before he was even aware of Loki's presence.

Loki glanced up at the sky through the aluminum walls of his racing trailer. He could see the D-Space call-outs of the hundred spikes spreading out as they descended, moving to their assigned targets.

Loki throttled back the two AutoM8s so they didn't strike first.

And then, with practiced skill, the plan came together rather nicely. Aerial surveillance showed eight sentries walking in pairs suddenly being struck down by a hail of silent steel spikes coming in at terminal velocity. It wasn't windy, so most of the spikes struck their targets.

With another gesture Loki sent the waves of razorbacks in, still on quiet electrical power. He could see video from the lead bike, and guided it around to the back of the motel and toward the room that was his target.

Moments later the northern AutoM8 came roaring around a bend in the county road a quarter mile away. It didn't follow the bend, but instead came roaring straight at a Chevy parked in the parking lot of a gas station—one containing two private military contractors. It struck broadside going ninety miles an hour.

Loki winced and covered his eyes in mock horror. From the air it looked spectacular. He tagged the video and dragged it to his feed so others could check it out later.

By the time he turned to the southern AutoM8, it had already plowed through a billboard and creamed the car containing the remaining sentries. To his disappointment there was no explosion. But no one was walking away from that crash.

Now he focused on his razorbacks, powering up their massive engines, extending their blades, and roaring into the attack. They spread out and smashed through the doors of four motel rooms almost simultaneously. Loki had also left several razorbacks behind the hotel to pick up anyone climbing out rear windows.

He needn't have bothered. Plainclothes military contractors had already grabbed their weapons and the moment the first razorback came through the door, several M249 machine guns opened up—tracer rounds bounding around the room as they deflected off the ceramic composite cowling of the lead razorback.

Loki always found this part exciting. It really did resemble the world's most realistic video game. He almost felt like he was there—with military contractors screaming in rage as they unloaded assault rifles and machine guns on him from behind a sofa, an overturned dining table, and the nearby bed.

Loki noticed they had all donned tinted flash goggles—so his green laser blinders wouldn't have any effect. *Damn.* The Major had equipped his group well. But where was he hiding?

Loki raised his gloved hand and starting clicking on

individual targets. He had to clear away all these NPCs. The razorbacks surged forward to cut them to pieces. He winced because in one of the rooms a contractor fired a forty-millimeter grenade into the doorway, damaging the lead razorback, but also stunning everyone else in the room.

Idiot. Loki switched his POV to the next razorback in line and surged it forward into the mercenaries, cutting them down. It reminded him of a real-time strategy game where you had to keep moving the view around to juggle all your priorities. Soon enough, the mercs fell back reloading, and the razorbacks began to tear them apart. Their screams came over the audio feed. That's when Loki noticed something interesting. . . .

In the background he could see a young, attractive woman bound, blindfolded, and gagged in the bathroom of the second motel room. She was nude and tied to a kitchen chair. She struggled like mad to break free amid all the gunfire and chaos.

Very interesting. Still, he needed to find The Major.

By now Loki was in mopping-up mode. The last of the mercenaries were tossing grenades or running for the rear bathroom windows. They'd all be dead or bleeding to death shortly. One thing he already knew—The Major wasn't here. But these men were protecting something.

So Loki turned his attention again to the bathroom, switching POV to the nearest razorback. He drove it right up to the door, nudging it all the way open. What he saw was very nice, indeed. Just the way he liked a woman—young, nude, and tied up. She was cringing from the powerful engine throbbing next to her, and visibly sobbing behind her blindfold. Her breathing was labored as she tried to get enough air despite the duct tape covering her mouth. He could see a tattoo on her shoulder of a bosomy manga girl in a schoolgirl outfit, twin katanas raised.

Loki extended the razorback's bloody sword and brought it near her throat. She sucked in air—trembling at what she sensed was so close. Perhaps she smelled the blood that coated the stainless steel.

A minute later, Loki guided his own Ducati Street-fighter motorcycle into the motel parking lot as panicked guests watched him from the safety of the woods on the far side of the road. Loki knew that none of their cell phones would work, and it didn't look like anyone had the balls to go get their cars with a squad of blood-soaked razorbacks standing about on hydraulic stands. He got off his bike and walked into the second motel room in full battle armor.

He glanced around to see the usual topographical maps, folders filled with printed spreadsheets, shattered laptops—and severed limbs, bloody torsos, and coiled intestines. The whole place was splattered with blood and thousands of shell casings littered the floor. There were bullet holes everywhere.

No wonder no one was in a hurry to come investigate.

Loki stepped through the bathroom door and took in the beauty of the young woman in person. She had short brunette hair and alabaster skin. Her hips and legs were beautifully proportioned. The nipples of her small, firm breasts were clearly defined. She had a couple more Japanese characters tattooed on her hip and right forearm.

Loki leaned up to her face, still in his battle helmet. "Tell me where The Major is."

He reached up and tore off the duct tape covering her mouth. She sucked for air and immediately started sobbing.

"Where is The Major?"

"Why would I know?" Still she sobbed.

"But you've heard of him?"

She was still heaving. "Please untie me."

"Where did you hear of him?"

"Who are you?"

"Never mind who I am."

She looked unsure for a moment, but spoke through sobs. "I'm a darknet member! Shadowcreek faction." She fell into more weeping.

"Bullshit."

"I can prove it! They have my equipment."

"Where?"

"In a radio-proof bag. Silver. They have it here. I was bringing an artifact north."

Loki eyed her body again. If she were telling the truth, it would change things. He couldn't do just anything to a faction member. He leaned outside the bathroom and there by the nightstand he saw what looked to be a silvered tent bag, now spattered with blood droplets. He walked over to it and dumped its contents on the floor. Suddenly half a dozen D-Space call-outs appeared above various electronic gadgets—HUD glasses among them.

Damnit.

He grabbed the HUD glasses and reentered the bathroom. He took another look at her lithe body, then removed her blindfold. She was as pretty as he thought she might be. Eurasian.

She looked up at him, her eyes still red from crying. She recoiled at Loki's fearsome appearance. He placed the glasses on her head, and in a moment a call-out appeared above her indicating her name was *Siren_3*, a third-level Messenger with the Shadowcreek faction.

She stared at him—no doubt seeing Loki's very powerful call-out.

"Thank you for saving me."

"We'll see how grateful you are later. We need to leave."

"Untie me."

With a flick of his wrist a razor-sharp spur protruded from his riding outfit. He slit through the nylon rope binding her hands and then her ankles. She sighed and rubbed her rope-burned wrists.

"I want to leave here. I want to go home." She was looking around for a towel or something to cover herself.

Loki looked at the pile of D-Space objects on the bed. One of them in particular stuck out at him. He picked it up. It was a silver ring with the name *Signet of Spell Storing—Level Twenty-One* hovering above it.

Holy shit. "Is this the object you were transporting?"

She obviously didn't want to say.

"Siren. Is this what you were bringing north?"

She had wrapped a towel around herself and nodded. "This is powerful. Whose is it?"

"It belonged to a sorcerer killed near Denver. How it got to Oklahoma, I don't know. Our faction found it, and we're contributing it to the fight in the Midwest."

Loki took off his armored gauntlet. "Consider it contributed."

He slipped it on his finger. As he did he felt a sharp pain. "Ah!" He pulled it off and could see blood dripping off a needlelike protrusion.

And then it hit him—even as he was already staggering toward the doorway.

She looked at him. "What's wrong?"

Loki was meandering like a drunken person, cursing and now nearly on his knees.

"You little bitch!"

"What is it?"

"A needle! You fucking cunt!" Loki raised his one gloved hand and suddenly a blinding flash of bolt-straight electricity leapt from his fingertip into Siren's eye. Her hair stood on end briefly before her head caught flame and she dropped like a rag doll onto the floor—her entire body smoking and sizzling.

Loki slammed down onto the bloody, littered carpet and felt his mind losing connection with his body. Paralyzed, he stared at the bottom of a dead mercenary's boot. Beyond that he could see the open doorway of the motel room—and a razorback standing guard. He tried to summon it. To control it. But he couldn't move. He felt saliva flowing out of his open mouth.

In the distance somewhere he heard several deep

booms—one after the other. With a final boom, the headlight assembly of the razorback in the doorway blasted apart. It fell out of sight.

Moments later, through a syrupy haze, he saw men walking through the motel room doorway. One of them leaned his face down next to his.

It was The Major. "You helped me win a bet, Loki." He gestured to unseen witnesses. "They said you wouldn't kill the girl. But I knew better."

As Loki's vision began to fade, The Major moved closer. "She was innocent, by the way. . . ."

Chapter 22: // Identity Theft

Loki hung by his wrists from a hook on the ceiling of a concrete cell. He was naked and had been from the moment he awoke. He'd spent most of the last day with a hood over his head, bags on his hands, chained into confinement positions. No one spoke to him. No one said a word. It was only in the past hour that they'd brought him here.

As Loki looked around, the doors and walls of this place indicated it was a stable. There were thick, wooden doors, split into two parts—like a Dutch door. That's where the horse would stick his head out and feed. That's how it worked, wasn't it?

There were cameras and lights all around him in the room, creating a harsh glare. He was having difficulty breathing in this position, and the pain in his shoulders was almost unbearable. They'd also strapped some sort of muzzle over his mouth that had an almost stirrup-like piece of metal forced between his teeth. Sleep was impossible.

He felt the loss of the darknet like the death of a close friend. No, that wasn't right because he'd never really had a close friend. He felt the loss of his connection to the darknet like the amputation of a limb. As though someone had castrated him. His electronic contact lenses were gone. His haptic vest was gone. His gloves, his bone mic—everything. Everything except the implant near his aorta—that remained. However, it was just a locator—he couldn't interact with the darknet through it. But it was his only hope. The question was: how much time had elapsed?

After what seemed like an eternity of pain, he heard the slap of heavy bolts and looked up to see the big wooden door open on squealing hinges.

There before him was the devil himself—The Major— followed by several other men, some of whom were wheeling metal carts on rubberized wheels. The Major stood in the doorway for a moment to regard Loki.

Fuck you, too, motherfucker.

"So you thought your fanboy toys would destroy us, is that it? Do you think you're the first group to come at us with novel tactics? It's not about how many people you can kill—it's about who runs out of people first. And I promise you, it will be you."

The Major moved into the room. His entourage began to set up equipment and workspace behind him. The Major was wearing what looked to be surgical scrubs. Loki heard the clank of metal tools being arranged behind The Major. He felt a cold dread creeping up his spine. Fear gripped him, causing him to tremble despite his exhaustion.

The Major accepted rubber gloves passed to him by an Asian man wearing a face mask. The Major did not wear a mask. He grinned humorlessly as he pulled the rubber gloves on.

"Loki Stormbringer. That's what you call yourself, isn't it? Fiftieth-level Sorcerer—or something like that? The most powerful darknet operative known. Your fingerprints bring up nothing in government records. Was that the first thing you did, Loki—destroy your old identity? No footprints from birth. No fingerprints from child abduction prevention programs. No DNA samples from prior arrests. It's like Loki is the real you—as though you wanted to pretend the white-trash loser you were before never existed. But I'm going to show you that you do exist."

The Major walked right up to Loki's face. "I've been amused by the debate in America over whether torture is effective." He paced a ways away and picked up a pair of nasty-looking clippers from a metal table that had been set up. "Of course it's effective."

The Major returned holding a tool shielded by his hand. "But not at producing information. Torture isn't *about* extracting information."

He brought the sinister-looking clippers up to Loki's face. "Torture is about control. You let me torture a thousand people, and I can keep five million working obediently with their heads down. The more innocent the victims, the better. And after they're broken and maimed, you release them so that everyone can see what awaits those who resist."

Suddenly the hook on the ceiling started to lower, and in a moment Loki's feet touched the ground. It was the first time in hours that the pressure on his breathing and shoulders had eased. But before he could relish the relief, strong hands grabbed his wrists, and he was forced down onto his knees. Two powerfully built men forced his wrists into clamps that were bolted to the floor. They shoved pieces of two-by-four under his palms to prevent him from closing his hand into a fist, and even though he struggled, Loki soon found himself with his arms splayed out before him. The Major was kneeling right alongside him.

"There is no debate about torture in here, my friend. So you see, there's nothing you can tell me that will stop the pain. You're no longer Loki, the sorcerer. The only thing you are is a billboard—on which I'm going to write my message: this is what happens to people who join the darknet. . . ."

At which point The Major clamped the tip of Loki's index finger in the metal clippers, and though Loki struggled to pull away, the steel jaws snipped off his index finger up to the second knuckle.

The pain shot through him like needles moving through his bloodstream. He tasted blood in his mouth from where he had bit his tongue.

The agony was followed by still further searing pain as the Asian doctor in a lab coat applied a red-hot filament to the stump, cauterizing the wound and sending up a sickening sizzling sound.

Loki thrashed around, pulling a muscle in his back, but it was only the beginning. The Major cut off another fingertip, and another, and another. The doctor cauterized each wound before the next digit was clipped off. Loki felt his consciousness ebbing, but they waved smelling salts under his nose.

The Major was in his face again. "How will the

Daemon know you if you have no biometric markers left?"

The unbearable agony continued as the spawn of Satan himself snipped off the tips of all eight of Loki's fingers. And finally the most painful ones of all—his thumbs.

In his mind Loki was begging for death. To use his powerful intellect to will his heart to stop. To die and let the universe take him.

But his world was nothing but a white-hot wall of pain.

And yet it got worse. Before he had a chance to realize what was happening, he felt his left eyelid pried open and he saw a pair of surgical scissors coming for his eyeball as they pulled it out of the orbital socket. He tried to scream—tried to turn away, but they'd clamped his head into place. With a dagger of pain, he lost all sight in his left eye and saw through his tear-filled right eye as they dropped it into a metal pan.

The next few moments brought utter blindness as the horrific event was repeated. Loki prayed—actually prayed—for death, yet it did not come. He heard horrible groaning, and realized that he was the source. He was like an animal being butchered. He no longer wished to live.

He heard the devil's voice in his ear one more time. "And so that the Daemon cannot recognize you by your voice . . ."

No. No!

Loki felt the stirrup-like gag they'd fastened over his mouth expand with the force of a car jack—opening his mouth and keeping it open no matter what he did. He felt the sharp pinch of a pair of pliers pulling his tongue forward roughly and then the searing cut that bored right into the center of his mind. Loki's tongue was cut clean from his mouth.

As he died within himself, trapped in the broken shell of his body, Loki felt the shell's head pulled back and the devil's voice whisper again.

"The Daemon no longer knows you. And I have all the biometric markers I need to become *you*. I will be Loki Stormbringer. Your identity is my reward. The only reason I'll keep you alive is so that you can pass the occasional fMRI test for me."

It was the final nail. Loki felt his soul guttering, flickering, and though he prayed with every fiber of his being for death, it did not come. He existed, just as The Major said he would, as a vessel that spoke of torment.

Oscar Strickland's interest in medicine arose from his many blissful years hunting white-tailed deer in the Colorado Rockies. Cleaning and dressing carcasses beneath the aspens awakened in his young mind a fascination with all living things. This ultimately inspired him to join a volunteer rescue squad and become an EMT— which exposed him to the miracle of human anatomy as he helped to pry victims out of crumpled wreckage on mountain roads. And it was here where he discovered his connection to pain. Namely the infliction of it.

The discovery was accidental—a careless push of a gurney that struck the edge of an ambulance door. But then he began adding a few extra bumps to a spinal patient's transport, or *not quite* administering a painkiller. At first it was the thrill of indulging a taboo. But then it was a *need*—a need to see others suffer. He endured several years of private shame, feeling that he was a horrible person.

When he joined the army, it was with the hope that they would give him the discipline he needed to conquer his sick compulsion. But on the contrary, in the army he found that pain—and the infliction of it—had a long and storied history. It was, in fact, the history of the world. No great nation or empire could exist without it. It was in some ways the guardian of all that was good. Fear of pain kept men honest.

And as Strickland's career advanced from the army to covert government operations and then on to private security operations, he held his head high. For his was a noble profession.

It also paid well—especially given the current economic crisis. Strickland's contract would do more than care for his wife and kids in Wyoming. It would also care for his wife and kids in Costa Rica.

But on this posting, he was a second stringer. It was easy work. He looked up from his Sudoku puzzle as his lone patient groaned pitiably. The man was strapped to an old bed among several dozen others in the infirmary of an old Catholic school. Strickland looked up to see a cross-shaped clean spot on an otherwise dirty wall above him. The diocese apparently had some difficulty with lawsuits and had to shut down the school. He had no idea who the maimed young man was—only that he was an enemy combatant who needed to be kept alive. The way they'd cut him, Strickland didn't see how they'd ever be able to get anything more out of him.

Unprofessional.

Still, the groaning was nice background music. He focused his lone lamp more fully on the puzzle and continued.

But then he heard the telltale sound of a security detail approaching over the squeaky wooden floors. He put the puzzle in the empty desk drawer and sat up straight—ostensibly to observe his patient suffering nearby in the darkened ward.

However, what came around the corner surprised him. It wasn't the Korr Military Solutions officers who'd brought him out here, or any of the site security detail—it was four men dressed in outlandish battle armor, like something from a sci-fi convention. The faceplates of their helmets shimmered like the surface of a soap bubble, and they had odd, high-tech-looking plastic/metal rifles slung on straps with suppressors at their tips. They weren't weapons Strickland had seen before—and he had seen just about everything. Probably elite special operators. Private industry always had the best gear. . . .

Strickland stood up. "Gentlemen."

That's when he noticed their gun barrels were smoking. The odor of cordite wafted over him.

One of them raised a gauntleted hand and motioned for the outliers to walk around the edges of the desk—approaching Strickland from two different directions.

"Whoa, what's going on?"

The voice came over a radio speaker. "Nothing, sir.

Please put these on." He reached forward, extending a pair of expensive-looking eyeglasses.

"Hold . . . what?"

The two soldiers on either side grabbed him roughly by the arms. Their grip was crushing—almost supernaturally strong.

Again came the radio voice from that inscrutable mirrored faceplate in front of him. "I said, put these on."

"Okay. For chrissake. What's going on?" The twin guards relaxed their grip enough for him to take the glasses—heavy things—and put them on.

As he did so, the view in front of him suddenly changed to reveal a sixth person in the room—a ghostly apparition that was kneeling next to Strickland's lone patient among the rows of beds. He could hear it whispering.

"Oh my god . . ."

As Strickland spoke, the apparition turned and stood. It then walked calmly and methodically toward him. It was unaccountably the translucent apparition of . . . apparently of an SS officer with full trench coat, monocle, and peaked hat.

Strickland tried to back up, he was so startled, but the guards held him fast.

The ghostly Nazi came right up to Strickland's terrified face. "Now ve can see each other. Do you know of me, Mein Herr?"

"Do I know of you? I don't even know what you are!"

"It was a yes or no qvestion. And yet it vas seemingly beyont you." The ghostly Nazi turned to the real-world soldiers. "Place ze cap on him."

Strickland struggled as one of the men approached with what looked like a water polo helmet. Wires led from it to a controller. They began to strap it to his head.

"Hold it! I'll tell you what you want! You don't have to do this!"

The Nazi pulled out a long black cigarette filter and lit a cigarette. He took a long drag. "It tastes so much better at zis resolution." He turned to Strickland and gestured at his headwear. "Ze cap on your head uses near infrared to measure blood acktifity in your brain. In short—it tells me if you're lying."

"I just work here. I was taking care of him." Strickland could already see a real-life, human medical team moving over to his patient—half a dozen men and women holding IVs and wheeling a stretcher.

The SS officer laughed a unique, wicked laugh. "I haf no idea vat you're saying . . . but it sounds terrified." Then he focused his spectral gaze on Strickland. "Ver you ze one who injured Mein Freund?"

"No! I swear it!"

The Nazi paused a moment and then nodded—before asking, "Do you know ver I can find ze perpetrators?"

"No."

He spoke more insistently. "Do you know ver I can find zem!"

"No! I don't know!"

There was a pause. The Nazi nodded again. "Vill zey be coming back to zis place?"

Strickland waited as long as he dared—then nodded. "Yes."

"Gut, gut, Mein Herr! Ve are just about finished here." He walked right up to Strickland, blowing virtual smoke in his face—causing Strickland to cough out of instinct. "Tell me . . . vould you haf enjoyed harming Mein Freund—if you had ze chance?"

Strickland just stared. His mouth was suddenly dry as he looked into the ghostly eyes only inches from his own. They were insanely real—as was the gleam in them when the Nazi smiled.

"Zat's vat I thought. . . ." He turned to the soldiers. "Secure him, gentlemen. . . ."

A soldier pulled the cap off his head.

"Hold it! Hold it!" Strickland looked to the faceplate of the soldier to his right, then to his left. "It's wrong! The machine is wrong!"

The soldiers grabbed his wrists and slammed his hands against the wall with incredible force. They seemed to have artificial musculature in their suits that he was helpless to resist.

They placed steel restraints over his wrists and then tapped the wall looking for studs—finally using a power tool to bolt the restraints in place. They repeated the process for his struggling feet.

"No! Stop!"

Meanwhile, the spectral Nazi just stood observing, smoking his cigarette on its long filter.

The soldiers finally stood. "Done, sir!"

"Gut. Leave us."

The soldiers exchanged looks and left in a hurry. As they did, a deep rumbling noise came to Strickland's ears. It was like a slow, rolling thunder. Through the wide infirmary doorway came a hellish-looking motor-cycle covered in blades and mystical sigils and glyphs. Another one followed it.

"Oh my god . . ."

They pulled up alongside the apparition and slammed down hydraulic kickstands. Both of them extended fiendish sword arms with a ring of steel.

"No!"

The Nazi removed his trench coat and hung it on the extended blade of a nearby bike. Then he rolled up his sleeves. He moved toward Strickland along with the second motorcycle. "I do so enjoy my vork. . . ."

Part Three

July

Gold:	$4,189USD/oz.
Unleaded Gasoline:	$17.87USD/gallon
Unemployment:	32.3%
USD/Darknet Credit:	202.4

Part Three

July

Gold: ... $4,190 US/Tier
Unleaded Gasoline: ... $17.97 US/gallon
Unemployment: ... 32.3%
USGND/Debt Ceiling: ... 2024

Chapter 23: // Ultimatum

Realtime.com/news

Violence Spreads as Dollar Slides—Marauding **gangs** of heavily **armed immigrant workers** are **terrorizing** entire counties in **Iowa, Kansas, Missouri**, and **Oklahoma**, prompting calls for **martial law** in several **Midwestern** states and causing **locals to take up arms in self-defense**. With **hyperinflation** and never-before-seen gas prices invalidating the economies of entire communities, officials fear **civil order** has begun to **break down**.

With the U.S. **military** thinly stretched **overseas**, **private security firms** have contracted with several **Midwestern municipalities** to **restore order** and suppress **looting**.

T he heads of America's intelligence services sat around a circular boardroom table in Building OPS-2B of National Security Agency headquarters. Now outnumbering them at the table was a wide array of private intelligence and military analysts, led by familiar executives from Computer Systems Corporation (CSC), its subsidiaries—

EndoCorp and Korr Military Solutions—and the lobbying firm Byers, Carroll, and Marquist (BCM).

The atmosphere was tense. On a bank of flat-screen televisions behind them, a dozen news channels were silently chronicling the meltdown of the American economy in animated graphics. But the real headlines were reserved for the fate of the U.S. dollar. All the graphs were heading down at a precipitous angle.

Their host opened the meeting.

NSA: "Ladies and gentlemen, we're facing a grave situation. As we sit here, the United States government has lost control of portions of its communications and air defense assets. At the same time, civil disorder is spreading throughout the Midwest, and the dollar is plummeting on foreign markets. I'm hearing calls for martial law coming from lobbyists on Capitol Hill. More worrisome is the talk I've heard about implementing Army Regulation 500-3."

BCM: "It's being brought up with good reason."

NSA: *"What reason?"*

CSC: "Army Regulation 500-3 was intended to preserve civil order in the event government communications are severed due to nuclear attack, natural disaster—"

BCM: "Or *technological emergency.* I think the Daemon qualifies."

CSC: "Make no mistake: this is a full-scale attack by the Daemon. Its forces are launching a violent revolution. Regulation 500-3 is called for. Civilian leadership is unable to maintain secure communications."

NSA: "What I want to know is why our systems degraded so suddenly and completely."

EndoCorp: "The Daemon is conducting a broad denial of service attack against government domains and communications. It's also undermining the confidence of capital markets. It's part of Sobol's overall strategy."

DARPA: "Bullshit."

All eyes turned to him.

EndoCorp: "Excuse me?"

DARPA: "You heard me."

BCM: "There's no reason to abandon decorum, gentlemen."

NSA (holding up his hands to calm the situation): "However, my colleague's succinct critique stands: we may have outsourced a large portion of our raw intelligence-gathering capability to private industry, but we're not completely blind. There's no indication that the systems operated under contract for us have been compromised."

CSC: "That's ridiculous. We can show you the proof."

NSA: "I'm not interested in your digital proof. We're monitoring network and electromagnetic activity in real time. There's no evidence our national defense assets have been degraded."

BCM: "That's a bold and reckless statement. You're accusing trusted national security partners of gross negligence, Mr. Director."

NSA (pointing to the TV monitors): "This so-called domestic uprising related to the economy—Mexican drug gangs running loose, raping and pillaging in the countryside. Panicking the populace."

BCM: "This is what happens when economies

collapse. Order needs to be restored before the chaos spreads. Private security forces are available and more palatable to the public than a government military force."

FBI: "These gangs—we've arrested heavily armed suspects all across the Midwest. They've murdered policemen and civil authorities—and more than a few of them have turned out to be professional mercenaries tied to defunct military regimes in Central America and Eastern Europe."

CIA: "Trained operators whose fingerprints we have on file."

BCM (raising an eyebrow): "Then you've worked with them before?"

CIA: "My question is: who brought them *here*?"

EndoCorp: "Most likely drug cartels, taking advantage of general lawlessness to make money."

CIA: "That defies logic."

NSA: "And what about money?" (Opens up a folder and tosses out reports like a blackjack dealer in Vegas.) "Financial houses controlled by your clients have been selling Treasury bills like crazy—you're precipitating a run on the dollar."

BCM: "Our clients have a fiduciary responsibility to their investors, and quite frankly the monetary policies of the U.S. government haven't—"

DIA: "As if the U.S. government controls the creation of money! It seems the same private institutions entrusted with setting monetary policy were the ones who profited from debasing the dollar. No wonder the public is flocking to the Daemon network. The darknet credit is still worth a damn!"

CSC: "That's treasonous talk."

DIA: "Don't lecture *me* about treason!"

BCM: "Everybody calm down. Let's stop throwing the T-word around. One man's treason is another man's patriotism."

FBI: "How do you figure *that*?"

BCM: "The nation is under attack, and here we are arguing. We need to put our heads together."

NSA (glaring at him): "Yes. The United States *is* under attack. The question is by *whom*?"

They all sat in bristling silence for several moments.

BCM: "Certainly you don't intend to stop us from defending our property? Or from maintaining public order?"

FBI: "Who is behind the covert terror operations in the Midwest?"

BCM: "Does it really matter?"

DIA (looking to NSA director): "We need to declare a national emergency and mobilize whatever National Guard troops and equipment not already deployed overseas."

BCM: "You have a serious problem, gentlemen. Without immediate financial support, the U.S. dollar will collapse—precipitating the complete insolvency of the U.S. government. Picture Russia. Argentina."

NSA: "This is treason."

BCM: "A *multinational* corporation can't commit treason. My clients have no obligation to America. Risk must be hedged."

NSA: "Get the treasury secretary on—"

BCM: "Your government can create all the money it

wants, but it will be worthless here and abroad. Without outside intervention the U.S. government will soon be a hollow shell."

There was silence for several moments.

NSA: "What do they want?"

BCM: "They need Army Regulation 500-3 amended to include private military contractors. And then they expect it to be invoked."

DIA: "You expect us to *suspend the Constitution*? Are you insane?"

BCM: "You're to stay out of the way while they deal with the Daemon. If you do so, global financial institutions will support the dollar—of course, there will need to be economic and social reforms put in place first to ensure a return to fiscal discipline."

The government half of the table looked like they were pondering violence.

DIA: "Why are you doing this?"

BCM: "My clients are simply defending their property—they own the genes being stolen by the Daemon's operatives. They own the networks and software it has compromised. They own the global brands it has undermined. Representative government doesn't have the will to defeat this threat."

DIA (to the NSA director): "Have him arrested!"

The BCM representative gestured to the phone near the NSA director's chair.

BCM: "It's your call. Try to arrest our people. Try to have the military interfere with our security operations. I think you'll find that no one in your government has the stomach for it. We are not the enemy of America."

NSA: "I don't know what you are. But some people in government still take seriously their oath to uphold the Constitution."

The NSA director picked up the phone and started dialing.

Chapter 24: // Green Desert

Washington.com/politics

NSA Director Removed Amid **Bribery Scandal—**
In yet another case of government corruption,
Lieutenant General Mark Richards was **forced
to step down** early **today** amid charges that he
accepted lavish gifts and favors in exchange for
approving lucrative intelligence contracts—contracts
that benefited foreign technology firms. He has so
far refused to comment, his lawyer citing the pending
criminal case. . . .

Jon Ross moved through the crowd that had gathered around a soup kitchen. Grim-looking, recently
middle-class refugees surged toward the queues. He
could see the isolated D-Space call-outs of darknet members keeping order.

"Form four lines! Four lines, please!"

Ross stood up on the bumper of an abandoned car and
gazed across a vast tent city, accumulated like so much
plaque at the confluence of two interstate highways outside of Des Moines, Iowa. It was actually a mixed tent/
car/RV city. He estimated several thousand makeshift

campsites. There was music, the buzz of voices, dogs barking, and the shouts of children playing in the maze of humanity. The acrid smell of people cooking over magazine-and-newspaper fires filled the air.

Ross searched for a path through the crowd and noticed a current of people flowing along a makeshift lane. He headed toward it, inching his way through a mass of people. He caught most of a conversation at the end of a soup kitchen line as he edged past. . . .

"Where were you headed?"

"We were trying to reach Ohio—my sister's in Columbus—but the bastards privatized the interstate. The tolls are insane."

"We couldn't afford gas. I've been trying to trade my truck for a motorcycle. You know anybody who has one?"

"No, sorry. . . ."

Ross reached the pathway and started passing individual camps—recent arrivals to homelessness. People with Infinitis and Lexus sedans. Furniture piled into the backs of expensive, crew-cab pickup trucks. A few people even had living room sets with sofas and matching chairs set up beneath tarps. Others used high-end camping gear meant for a trip to the lake. Still others sat, looking dazed and lost, in well-appointed camping trailers and motor homes. An economic hurricane had passed through these people's lives, and they were still in shock.

Ross did see one burgeoning business rising out of the ashes of consumer culture. Several heavily armed men were standing atop a container truck as brokers at the open doorway haggled with refugees. A banner hanging along the side read: WE BUY WATCHES AND JEW-ELRY. Ross had seen them in every tent city—hustlers repatriating luxury items for sale back to Asian markets, where the real money was. High-value items worth their shipping weight.

Meanwhile, the bulky stuff—the plasma-screen televisions and furniture—was all winding up in piles, sold cheap to be stripped of metals and fabrics, and wood. Already trash was accumulating into mounds—some of it burning.

Ross finally reached the edge of a darknet medical clinic. A cluster of call-outs hovered there in D-Space. He did a quick search and suddenly his target flashed—a second-level Horticulturalist named *Hank_19.*

In a few moments Ross approached a weathered but hardy-looking man in his forties wearing a baseball cap, jeans, and a work shirt. He was lowering boxes off the back of a thirty-year-old stake bed truck into the waiting hands of clinic workers.

Ross waved, and Hank_19 waved back.

"You still headed to Greeley?"

"Yeah, just as soon as we drop off these supplies."

"I appreciate the ride. Gas shortages have made traveling difficult." Ross joined the crew off-loading and in a few minutes they had cleared the truck bed. Hank_19 wiped his brow and hopped off the tailgate. "Damn, it's hot." He extended his calloused hand. "Henry Fossen. Call me Hank."

Ross shook his hand. "You don't go in for darknet handles, I take it."

"My father gave me my name, and I intend to use it. I would've just selected the handle 'Hank,' but eighteen Hanks already beat me to it. You got a real name?"

"Jon."

"All right, *Jon* no-last-name." He looked up at Ross's call-out. "I guess a twelfth-level Rogue's gotta be secretive. What the hell's a 'rogue' do on the darknet, anyway?" He slammed the tailgate closed. "I thought rogues were bad guys."

Ross laughed. "In the darknet we're more like scouts. We infiltrate systems and facilities, and we detect threats to the network. Move about unseen, that sort of thing."

"Oh, *reconnaissance*."

"You could say that."

"My boy's in a recon regiment overseas."

"I hope he comes home safe."

"So do I. And I hope we get this economic mess sorted out before then." He glanced up at Ross's call-out again. "Well, you've got a four-and-a-half-star reputation on a three K base—which means you must be doing something right. Hop in."

Fossen whistled to two younger men cradling scoped AR-15 rifles. They wore tactical gear and body armor— fourth-level Fighters with Scandinavian-sounding network handles. They had been busy talking to a young nurse at the aid station. They nodded to Fossen and came running, hopping up into the cargo bed.

Ross got into the cab with Fossen, and they were soon easing the old Ford stake bed through the tent city crowd.

Ross gestured to the truck. "Biodiesel?"

"No. Dimethyl ether. They split the water in Greeley with wind turbine electricity and add the hydrogen to something to create hydrocarbons. Makes a pretty good diesel fuel. I still don't quite understand it. I had no idea half this stuff existed until a few months ago."

"So, the guards . . . Are you expecting trouble?"

He shook his head. "No. The town council requires armed escorts down to the city. A lot of desperate folks out here. But there's a darknet recruiting station to the right. Hopefully it'll get people sorted out in the next few months."

Ross looked over to see a series of motor homes resembling bookmobiles. Dozens of call-outs clustered around them. Lines of civilians were waiting to be interviewed by the automated recruiting bot of the Daemon—what was known as The Voice. Ross had gone through a similar process, just not with such a crowd.

"This is just the first wave, I think. A lot more people are about to fall out of the old economy."

"You think so?" Fossen brought the truck slowly through the crowd, people making way. He nodded to them genially. "I mean, how could we let this happen here in America?"

"It's no accident. I've seen it before in other countries. It's all about control. The powerful scaring people into submission."

Fossen nodded. "I've had some experience with that. Just not on this scale."

"This is nothing. The real shock is coming. Believe me."

Fossen gestured to the tent city out the window. "*This* isn't the real shock?"

"No. It'll be much, much worse. They'll try to psychologically traumatize the public into accepting a new social order."

"And you know this because . . . ?"

"Firsthand experience."

Fossen raised his eyebrows. "I can tell you're going to be a barrel of fun on the way."

After a few minutes Fossen finally brought them out of the crowd. As the old Ford picked up speed, the cab got much noisier, especially with the windows open, and they drove for a while without talking.

Eventually Fossen turned to his passenger, shouting, "So what brings a rogue to Greeley?"

"I'm looking for someone."

"They in trouble?"

Ross shook his head. "No. I got word a few days ago that an old friend I thought was dead is actually alive."

"That's good news. Does he know you're coming?"

"He moves around. He's hard to get in touch with."

"Maybe I've heard of him. What's his name?"

"The Unnamed One."

"That's his *name*? 'Unnamed One'?"

"You might know him better by his real name: Detective Pete Sebeck."

Fossen just frowned. "The Daemon hoax guy? He's not really dead?"

"You didn't see the news feeds on his quest?"

"I don't read news feeds much. Not enough time in the day lately. How do you know he's in Greeley?"

"I've seen feed reports that say he's in the area."

"That's new to me, but like I said, I don't read the feeds much." Fossen seemed to be pondering something. "I'm no expert, but can't you just search for his coordinates if you know his handle?"

"He keeps them unlisted—I suspect because of all the press he's been getting. A lot of people are following his quest."

"So he's on a *quest*—as in, heroic journey and all that?"

"They say he's searching for something called the Cloud Gate. A portal that may unlock a higher level of the darknet."

"Well, best of luck to him."

"Apparently he's also been appearing in places where paramilitary units have been operating—helping to develop a smart mob-alert system."

"Well, we haven't had any of that stuff occur near us. It's been in Nebraska and Kansas mostly."

Ross looked at the landscape and rows of abandoned houses with FOR SALE signs in suburban subdivisions. "They're still foreclosing on houses out here?"

"No. I think people are just abandoning them. Off to find work or public relief facilities. Driving is no longer an option for most people, and there's nothing to live on out here."

"Is anyone swallowing the 'illegals gone wild' story?"

"I don't know. I think people would have noticed armed gangs if they really existed."

"Oh, they exist. They're just not what the media claims."

"Then what are they?"

"Paramilitary units. Terror squads."

Fossen just gave him a look. "I think we would have noticed that, too."

"Not if they move at night by helicopter."

"Helicopter?"

Ross nodded. "They fly in low and fast. Drop in teams, advance on foot, then ex-fil by chopper. They've hung people. Burned houses. On television the next day you usually hear how gang violence is behind it. Senators calling for martial law. And checkpoints."

"How do you know all this?"

"I've been tracking their movements for the last several months."

Fossen just gave Ross a sideways look. "Are you pulling my leg?"

Ross pointed to Fossen's call-out. "You joined the darknet recently."

"Yeah. My daughter convinced me. She's really something."

"You have a farm?"

"Fifth generation—a 'horticulturalist' now, I guess. My daughter has made a lot of positive changes to our operation. You should come by and see it."

"I'd like that."

"Jenna's rising fast in the Greeley holon. She's leading

two projects now—a biodiversity initiative and an education program."

"You must be proud."

"I'm proud of both my kids. Life is starting to make sense again for us. I just hope we can get other folks on the new economy in time."

Fossen turned the old truck onto a county road and soon they were heading out into a veritable ocean of green corn plants stretching unbroken to the horizon. This road was even louder in the old truck, so Ross just watched the landscape roll by.

They occasionally passed through small, downscale towns. Ross was able to spot them at a distance not by their church steeples but by the local grain elevators—invariably a row of concrete tubes a hundred to a hundred and fifty feet tall looming like missile silos at the end of Main Street.

Between the towns they passed several abandoned farmhouses, crumbling in the prairie. The clapboard ruins were choked with bushes and collapsing in on themselves.

Ross shouted over the engine. "That doesn't look recent. Why all the empty houses?"

Fossen leaned close. "Been happening for decades. Farms had to get big or go out of business. Market forces. The population of this county has dropped about a third in the last fifteen years or so. It's coming back now, though."

He slowed the truck down, and they turned this time onto a gravel road that was ramrod straight. They were traveling slower now, and it was much easier to talk.

"The fields look healthy."

Fossen waved him off. "Those plants have as much to do with agriculture as a weight lifter on steroids has to do with physical fitness. See that?" He pointed out tiny plastic signs spaced ten yards apart running along the edges of the fields near the road. The signs stretched into the distance and all bore the image of a green leaf with a single dewdrop dripping from the tip. The text HALPERIN ORGANIX—MITROVEN 336 was written in a bold sans serif font beneath the logo. The signs looked cheerful, healthy, and inviting. "They're all clones designed to maximize kernel production. In fact, ninety-eight percent of the crops grown in this country a century ago are now extinct.

"This is just a big green desert. You'd starve to death out here. This corn is inedible—it's just starch; it needs to be processed in an industrial stomach, with acids and chemicals, to break it down into processed food additives. We're up to our eyeballs in corn here in Iowa and we can't even feed ourselves."

"I gather that's the plan."

Fossen nodded. "Damned right. Big business was screwing over farmers in the 1890s, too, and my grandfather's father didn't put up with it back then, either. There was an uprising. You might not think it, but it was always the farmers who raised hell in this country. They worked for themselves, were self-reliant, and weren't about to take shit from anybody. But then some clever bastard figured out how to make crops inedible. My family's been doing industrial farming for forty years and all it produces is debt, pollution, and water shortages. It ruins the land and the people on it."

Ross nodded to the uniform fields out the window. "You think these other farmers will change?"

"They'll have no choice. Gas is, what—eighteen bucks a gallon now? Industrial farming and the global supply chain gobble up fossil fuel." He peeled off each item with his fingers. "Natural gas in the fertilizers, petroleum-based pesticides, fuel for the tractors, more fuel for transport to food processors, fuel to process the raw crops into food additives, then to manufacture them into products, and then to transport the products across the country or world to be consumed—thirteen hundred miles on average."

"What made you finally change?"

Fossen stopped for a moment, then laughed. "When I started educating myself on why farming no longer made sense. We basically used oil and aquifer water to temporarily boost the carrying capacity of the land, all for economic growth demanded by Wall Street investors. It's a crazy system that only makes sense when you foist all the costs onto taxpayers in the form of crop subsidies that benefit agribusiness, and defense spending to secure fossil fuels. We're basically paying for corporations to seize control of the food supply and dictate to us the terms under which we live."

They continued down the gravel road, sending up a cloud of white dust behind them. The road curved up toward a slight rise on the horizon. They came over it, and a dramatic shift in the scenery occurred.

Now in the fields on either side was a patchwork of

crops and fences, along with rows of saplings, the occasional chicken coop, and a few cows grazing in a meadow. It was, in fact, the first sizeable area of prairie grass Ross had seen in many miles.

Before long Hank slowed the truck and came to a halt at the intersection with a paved road. He pointed to their right. "Greeley's down that way about a quarter mile."

Ross could see a wooden sign alongside the road. It read WELCOME TO GREELEY with Rotary Club and Kiwanis Club badges bolted just below. Above that, floating in D-Space, glowed a virtual sign that read: *Iowa's first dark-net community.* Ross knew it meant that all of the town's civic functions and officials were darknet-based. Judging from the widespread construction going on in the countryside, they might have been the most advanced, too.

"Our place is up ahead a few miles. You interested in a tour, or should I take you straight into Greeley?"

Ross nodded across the road. "I'd love to get a tour."

Hank nodded and brought them across the road and down the gravel lane beyond. After a few minutes Ross saw barns, outbuildings, a traditional farmhouse, and a new-looking prefab house among some trees up ahead. There were also a couple of shipping containers and a few modern turbines turning in the breeze a ways off.

Fossen nodded to the view. "This is ours."

Fossen turned into the farm's long gravel driveway. There was an ornate D-Space 3-D object in the shape of a cornucopia bursting with vegetables and fruits hanging above the entrance. It was labeled *Fossen Farm.*

Dogs with D-Space call-outs above them ran out, barking to greet the truck. Two of them were black Labs named *Blackjack* and *Licorice*, and the third was a Golden Retriever named *Hurley*.

Ross smiled. "That's clever."

"Well, they're always getting into trouble. This way we know where they are." He stopped the truck near the barn, and the Fighters in back quickly hopped out.

Ross looked around just as a woman called from the porch of the white clapboard farmhouse. She was a stout-looking woman in her forties or fifties in work clothes and a garden hat. She had no call-out or HUD glasses. "Everything go okay at the clinic?"

Hank nodded. "The crowd's getting bigger." He took off his own hat and gestured to Ross. "Lynn, this is Jon. Jon, this is my wife, Lynn."

"Oh." She extended her hand. "Pleased to meet you, Jon."

"Likewise."

"I'm giving Jon a ride into Greeley, but I thought I'd give him the tour."

"Well, don't bore him to death. You know how you get. Let us know if you need anything, Jon."

"Thanks, ma'am. I . . . Are you a member of the darknet, too?"

"Not my thing. I'm not into all that social network mumbo jumbo."

Fossen pointed toward a group of half a dozen people not far off—men and women of various ages and ethnicities at the edge of a large vegetable garden. They all had D-Space call-outs above them and were focused on a young woman talking.

Fossen waved. "There's my daughter, Jenna." The young woman waved back.

"Lovely girl. Who are the others?"

"She's teaching hybridization and genetics to some newbs. Part of her civic reqs."

Mrs. Fossen frowned. "I wish you wouldn't call them that, Hank. They're students."

"My wife teaches in the middle school in Greeley." He jabbed his thumb. "Here, let me show you the big project we've been working on."

They walked over to a fence line with the dogs following them, tails wagging. Ross petted Hurley on the head as he gazed around.

There were a few more people out in the fields doing chores, and they all had D-Space call-outs. "You've got a really nice place here."

"Yeah, thanks to Jenna and the other students it's really coming along. We're one of the most sustainable farms in the county. Which isn't saying much." Fossen led them up to the fence and looked out to several acres of grain and other plants, waving in the breeze. "We use a mix of crops and animals to recharge fertility. Here, we've planted beans with wheat and a little mustard to fix nitrogen without resorting to chemicals." Fossen kneeled down and pulled up a handful of soil, letting it drain through his fingers. "We've been farming this land for five generations. I need to fix the damage I did to it. We've been relying on artificial fertilizers for a long time. It'll take a few years to get where it should be, but it'll come around."

He stood and pointed to the distant cows. "We're raising the animals on grass—not corn. We put in a good blend of natural prairie grasses. Big bluestem, foxtail, needlegrass, switchgrass. It grows naturally here on the prairie, so it's turning solar power into beef—no fossil fuels necessary. And we rotate animals through the fields. Chickens follow the cows out to pasture, picking bug larvae out of the manure and eating bugs and worms from the broken turf left behind by the cattle. The chicken dung, in turn, makes the field fertile for crops. It's all an integrated, sustainable system."

Ross leaned on a fence and nodded. "It *does* look more like a farm than the other ones did."

Fossen nodded to the edge of the property. "Got two ten-kilowatt wind turbines and some flywheel batteries to store the power. Every other darknet farm in this holon is working for the same thing. Regional energy and food independence. We rely on Greeley for our critical manufactured goods—printed electronics, micro-manufactured precision equipment, tools, software. They, in turn, rely on us, along with other farms, to provide their food and raw materials. It's a symbiotic relationship. We need each other."

Ross felt the breeze and looked out over the sunny, bustling farm. "I've been so caught up in this fight, I sometimes forget what the end goal is."

Fossen nodded. "I know what that's like." They started to walk back toward the house. "You're staying in Greeley?"

"Yeah, I have a room at a motel in town."

Fossen slapped Ross on the back. "Well, hell, when was the last time you had a home-cooked meal?"

Ross grimaced. "Probably fifteen years."

Chapter 25: // Black Ops

Hank Fossen lay in bed in the darkness, listening to the gentle breathing of his wife, Lynn, next to him and the ticking of the clock in the hall. He wondered where his son, Dennis, was at that exact moment. Was he on some mountaintop observation post? Convoy escort? They hadn't heard from him in nearly a month, which usually meant he'd been posted to a remote observation post.

What would his son make of all the changes on their farm? And in town? Dennis had never shown any interest in staying close to home. Although, who could blame him? Fossen had drilled into his kids at an early age that they were going to college and getting white-collar jobs. The day his son sat him down and explained that he was joining the military so they wouldn't have to borrow money for school . . . well, Fossen felt both shame and pride at the same time. Shame that his son had to make such a choice, and pride that he had.

Fossen prayed for his son's safety—even though he wasn't very religious, he tended to become so on certain occasions.

The dogs started barking outside. Fossen knew the pattern. If it was a raccoon, a skunk, or an opossum, they'd be run off pretty quick. Stray dogs were another matter, but his dogs were in a fenced enclosure. They'd be safe.

The barking didn't subside, though.

Fossen sat up in bed. All the exterior lights were off. And the motion detector lights near the barn hadn't come on either. *Strange.* But the dogs were going crazy. Certainly the hired hands and students in the prefab unit must have heard this racket. He threw off the covers and listened more intently. There was movement downstairs. Creaking of boards on the staircase.

Was it Jenna? *The dogs wouldn't be going crazy.*

Adrenaline spread through his bloodstream like warm water, and he slipped off the bed. He reached underneath it for the pump Remington shotgun.

The barking of the dogs suddenly stopped. Silence.

Then he heard a terrified scream in the hallway. *"Daddy!"*

He just started to get to his feet with the shotgun when the bedroom door kicked in and a blinding white light pierced his eyes. He felt something hard and blunt slam him in the stomach and he doubled over. He couldn't get any breath in his lungs.

He heard his wife screaming as the shotgun was yanked out of his hands. People thundered around his bedroom shouting in some foreign language.

"La pamant! La pamant!"

"Acum! Fa-o, acum!"

Still sucking for breath and blinded by the lights, Fossen heard struggling and breaking glass. He was then thrown to the ground by powerful hands.

Paramilitaries. The word kept going through his mind.

He'd been told Greeley had developed an early warning system. But then—he hadn't been linked to the darknet while he was sleeping. He didn't know anyone who did that.

He heard more screaming in the house. And he finally found breath to speak. "Jenna! Lynn!"

The powerful hands pulled his arms behind his back and he felt a zip tie cinched tightly around his wrists. He'd just begun to get his vision back as someone strapped duct tape across his mouth and pulled a hood over his head.

He heard muffled screaming and shouting now. He was hauled up painfully by his arms and dragged, he assumed, out of the room. He felt his feet thudding down the stairs and across the living room, and suddenly he felt the night air on his legs and arms. He was dressed only in boxers and an undershirt. It was a warm summer night.

He could hear crying and whimpering, and suddenly the hood was pulled from his head. He was shocked by what he saw.

Dozens of heavily armed men in black ski masks, jeans, and casual shirts surrounded them in the moonlight. They had AK-47 assault rifles slung across their chests and wore body armor over their clothing, along with vests of spare clips. Night vision goggles covered their eyes.

They had gathered their captives in the yard behind the farmhouse, and Fossen could see his wife and daughter, as well as three hired hands and the four visiting students in their underwear or pajamas, kneeling, bound and gagged on the grass nearby. Only Fossen was still standing among all the men. Behind them, he could see the still forms of his dogs, Blackjack, Licorice, and Hurley, lying on the dirt of their pen. Dead.

A tall, thickly built masked man stood in front of Fossen and rested his weapon in the crook of his arm. He spoke with a thick accent.

"Mr. Fossen. You have lovely farm." He reached down and, laughing, grabbed Jenna by her hair. "And lovely daughter."

The other men laughed.

Fossen struggled to speak—to beg them to leave his family be. To take only him. But the duct tape over his mouth prevented it. He struggled with all he had against his bonds.

The big man grabbed Fossen's face in a viselike hand. He pointed to one of his compatriots, who tossed one end of a rope up over a thick branch of the old oak in their backyard. At the other end of the rope was a noose.

Another man held a digital video camera in the moonlight, taping the action.

Fossen's wife let out a muted scream from behind her duct tape gag, and Fossen continued to struggle against his restraints and the arms holding him fast. They put the noose around his neck, and again he heard the others trying to shout from behind their gags. Fossen could see his wife in anguish as men behind her held her face up, smacking her and pointing in Fossen's direction—shouting, *"Uite! Uite!"*

Other men were trying to cut the pajamas off his daughter as she struggled. The rope was cinched firmly around Fossen's jaw, and Big Man was in Fossen's face again, laughing through his mask, his night vision goggles looking buglike in the darkness.

Then a welcome sound came from somewhere out in the night—the angry shouts of hundreds of people approaching through the fields—the rattle of weapons and equipment as they approached underlined their angry shouts. Big Man made several hand motions and his men spread out, concealing themselves behind vehicles, trees, and walls. They all focused on the darkness with their night vision goggles, whispering. . . .

"A se vedea ceva?"

"Nu, șefule."

"Nimic."

The massive crowd was approaching from somewhere out in the darkened fields. Fossen stood on his tiptoes, the noose cinched tightly around his neck. He didn't dare turn to look.

Big Man motioned abruptly, and his band of raiders fled into the night—disappearing in the opposite direction from the advancing mob. They didn't fire a shot, apparently hoping they could slip away unseen. Leaving their victims behind.

Fossen could hold his precarious balance no more. He fell to the side and was greatly relieved when the rope, no longer being held by anyone, simply unwound as he collapsed to the ground.

He tried to get a glimpse of the approaching mob, which was almost upon them now. But suddenly there was complete silence. Fossen rolled over to look for his wife and daughter and could see a shadowy form dressed head to toe in black kneeling over them, swiftly cutting their bonds. Their rescuer handed a knife to one of the students, then moved over to Fossen, drawing yet another knife.

Fossen could now see the man clearly. He wore some sort of formfitting black body armor with a hood and what appeared to be advanced night vision goggles over his face. Weapons and equipment were secured in pouches integrated into the suit.

The man turned Fossen over and tore the duct tape off his mouth with a sting. "Are you hurt?"

"No. Thank god you got here in time." Fossen could see his wife and daughter hugging each other, crying. The students and farmhands were also embracing in relief.

The man cut Fossen's bonds, then pulled off his own hood and night vision gear.

"Jon!" Fossen smiled and grabbed his arm. "I don't know how to thank you."

"We can't stay here, Hank. Townspeople are on the way, but the death squad might return."

Fossen looked around for the large crowd he'd heard moments before but saw no one. "I thought they were here already."

"They will be soon."

"But I just *heard* them."

Jon pointed at a device affixed to his forearm. "Hypersonic sound projector. I created the impression of an approaching mob." He looked up. "We should get to cover."

"Jesus Christ! It's only you?"

Suddenly they heard automatic weapon fire crackling in the distant fields. The students and farmhands ran for cover along with Fossen's wife and daughter.

Jon put his night vision goggles back on and nodded to himself. "Cover your eyes, folks . . ."

"What . . . Why?"

In answer the fields erupted in mind-blasting bursts of light and skin-crawling eruptions of sound that seemed to be tearing apart reality.

Fossen turned away and covered his ears. "My god, what is that?"

"Sensory assault. You might feel some nausea. Battle armor is synchronized to cancel out the effects." Jon helped Fossen get to his feet.

The gunfire had stopped.

"Then we're safe?"

Jon nodded toward the darkness. "We've got friends close at hand now. I see call-outs approaching."

"Hank!"

Fossen turned to see his old friend Sheriff Dave Westfield at the front of a dozen armed townspeople from Greeley, all of whom wore HUD glasses. They were running up from the darkness behind them. "God, am I glad to see you guys."

They lowered their weapons as they arrived. "Well, don't thank us. Thank Jon. He's the one who detected these bastards and sent out the alarm."

Fossen looked at his wife and daughter, then back to Jon. "I don't know how I can ever repay you."

"That dinner was plenty."

"Look . . ."

The crowd turned to see a group of darknet fighters coming out of the night from the direction the paramilitaries fled. The fighters were led by a darknet soldier in full composite body armor and enclosed helmet. He had an electronic pistol in one hand, and was guiding a dazed-looking prisoner with the other. Fossen knew at a glance that the prisoner was the Big Man who had tried to hang him.

The townspeople cheered and clapped as the party came in from the darkness. Jon pulled off his night vision glasses again.

The heavily armored soldier passed his prisoner into the custody of the sheriff. Then he just stood nodding to himself as he beheld Jon. He twisted his helmet to remove it, revealing a vaguely familiar face and a shaved head. He smiled and laughed hard as he grabbed Jon into a backslapping hug. "I can't believe it! Jon Ross!"

"It's been a long time, Pete. I'm glad you're still alive."

They exchanged world-weary looks. "Likewise."

"How's your quest going?"

"It's hard to tell."

He turned and shouted, "Price!"

A voice in the darkness answered. "Yes, Sergeant."

"Make sure this prisoner gets brain-scanned. Let's find out who sent him."

As Fossen, the sheriff, and the others looked on, Jon and the bald-headed soldier walked off. "There's a lot we need to talk about, Jon. . . ."

Chapter 26: // Privacy Policy

It had been twenty-one years since Stanislav Ibanescu had worn the uniform of the Securitate, but he had never stopped making a living as a soldier. The world over, war was a growth business, and he knew he'd never go unemployed like his brothers. And earlier in the evening he had thought that no one back home would have believed that he was invading America. It had all been a dream come true.

But that was three hours ago and a long drive down

dark roads into unknown captivity. Who these people were who held him was anyone's guess—but they sure didn't seem like a ragtag group of terrorists.

He considered the night's events. The op had gone off without a hitch, and they were about to kill the target subject and leave. But a counterstrike team had assaulted them out of nowhere. The lookouts hadn't reported a thing. In fact, Ibanescu hadn't seen more than half a dozen of his men since they'd been captured.

Were they U.S. Army? Socom units? They were supposed to have free rein in this area. That's what they'd been told by their contact, but it must have been a setup. Now he knew half his men were either dead or wounded, and the other half had been divided up and trundled off to god knew where. Now the tables had turned, and men who looked like science-fiction convention warriors in plastic armor and full headgear with mother-of-pearl faceplates were marching him down a white hallway glowing with light. Ibanescu was strapped to a backboard—even his head had been completely immobilized, and he knew what was coming next was torture. They were going to waterboard him, like he'd heard the Americans did. He was just hoping that this was a professional crew—one reachable by logic. One not doing this for kicks. He could then clear up this mistake. Because that was what it must be. Perhaps they were a local unit—one that hadn't been informed. One thing was sure: this was going to cost extra. In any event, it couldn't be worse than what he'd received at the hands of the Chechens.

The two armored soldiers brought Ibanescu into a

strange chamber filled with what looked to be medical scanning equipment—like some sort of MRI or CAT scan equipment—cold and efficient. And even though he didn't see anything around that could be used to torture him, he didn't imagine it was far away.

Mercifully, he didn't see anyplace where they could waterboard him without getting some expensive equipment wet.

The guards lifted the backboard holding their prisoner up onto a platform beneath the scanning equipment, and then lashed the board to the scanner bed.

Here we go.

He was suddenly sliding with the whir of electric motors, moving deeper into the scanning machine. Were they perhaps checking him for injuries? That seemed odd.

The backboard jerked to a stop, and Ibanescu soon heard the telltale sound of MRI magnets hammering, chirping, and pinging for one or two minutes. He'd gone through this before in Switzerland after a head injury while skiing.

As the scanning continued, a soothing female voice came to his ears, speaking English. Inbanescu knew some English, and he was able to decipher it.

"Do you understand what I'm saying?"

It was an oddly synthetic-sounding voice. He decided to pretend he didn't understand and just kept staring up at the interior of the scanning machine.

"Yes. You do understand me."

They were bluffing. He felt certain.

"Is English your primary language?" A pause. *"No. It isn't. Let's find your primary language."*

This was strange. It definitely sounded like an artificial voice. Like something he might hear from a credit card or airline customer-service line. Very strange. He wondered if this was some sort of automated interrogation system. *Leave it to the Americans.*

The soothing female voice spoke in a dozen different languages, waiting five or six seconds between each. Ibanescu didn't understand any of them, although he thought he could detect French and German. Also Czech. Eventually she came to Rumanian. . . .

"Is your native language Rumanian?"

He was damned if he was going to answer. He just lay there like a statue.

Her voice responded differently this time. *"Yes. You are Rumanian, aren't you?"*

He frowned. *How the hell . . . ?*

The rest of her words came to him in slightly stilted, synthetic-voiced Rumanian. *"This machine is a functional magnetic resonance imaging scanner. It monitors the blood activity in your brain to identify patterns of deception, recognition, and emotion—such as fear or anger. You will be unable to evade my inquiries. So please relax and enjoy your interrogation."*

Ibanescu just frowned at the machine around him.

"Please speak your full name and place of birth."

Were they serious? He wasn't about to tell them anything. He just lay there silently.

"It appears you are either unable or unwilling to respond."

Suddenly a map of the globe was projected onto the ceiling of the scanning chamber. It looked a lot like a

Web mapping program, with the globe spinning slowly in space. The map zoomed in on Rumania as the globe stopped spinning.

"Where were you born?"

Asking again wasn't going to help. It did feel comforting to see the map of his homeland, however. It was a detailed, physical map, showing the mountains and lakes. He could see a dot on the map for his hometown of Pitești, northwest of București.

Before he knew it, the view of the map centered on Pitești.

Holy shit. Was this system tracking his eyes? Did it sense that he was focusing on Pitești? What an idiot he was to fall for that! The map was zooming in now to a full-screen satellite view of Pitești. He shut his eyes.

"You are from Pitești, aren't you?" There was a pause during which Ibanescu clenched his eyes tightly. *"Yes, you are. This is where you were born, isn't it? Do you still have family there?"* A pause. *"Yes. You do."*

He was starting to lose his mind. How was this hellish machine discovering these things? It was obviously reading his neural activity or something. This was a nightmare.

"I have access to records from this ... nation state. Let's discover who you are. Does your last name begin with an ... A?"

Ibanescu realized that closing his eyes wasn't going to help. He opened them again and just stared at the detailed aerial view of his hometown. This was insane. He was being processed by a machine that was sucking the information through his ears.

"Does your name begin with B? C? D? E? . . ." And on it went.

He just stared in numb disbelief as the machine finally came to "I" and then halted. It asked again. *"I?"* A pause. *"Good. Now the second letter. Is it A? B?"* Another pause. *"B? Good. Now the third letter . . ."*

And so it continued with relentless precision until it had teased Ibanescu's name from his mind. It finally said in a stilted, machine mispronunciation, *"Mr. Ibanescu, what is your legal first name?"*

A series of names scrolled slowly across the ceiling in front of him, but he no longer tried to close his eyes. What was the point? He knew it would simply speak the letters into his ears—which was even more excruciating.

Sure enough, as the list scrolled down through the S's and centered on "Stanislav," the scroll slowed. Then stopped. "Stanislav" was highlighted in bold. *"Stanislav Ibanescu. Is this your legal name?"*

He knew there would be a pause, followed by the inevitable, *"Yes. This is your legal name. Are you Stanislav Ibanescu of Trivale bloc 25A?"*

Now he did close his eyes. This machine had in a matter of ten minutes completely identified him. It now knew who his family was, his history, everything. What a nightmare technology was. Then he thought, *If we had had this technology in the Securitate, we would never have fallen from power.* Whoever was doing this was someone he wanted to be part of. These people were *winners*.

Just when you think America is finished . . .

Now he was looking at his official state identification photo, his employment history, and his military history.

It showed that he was currently employed by Alexandru International Solutions. His most recent tax copayments were from his employer, and this system seemed to have access to all of it.

"Were you sent here by your current employer . . . Alexandru International Solutions?" There was a pause. *"Yes, you were."* Another pause. *"Did your job responsibilities include perpetrating acts of violence against unarmed civilians?"* Another pause. *"Yes. It did."* Yet another pause. *"The financial resources of . . . Alexandru International Solutions . . . have just been deleted."*

He tried to shake his head in disbelief, but couldn't even manage that in the viselike grip of the head restraints.

"Now let's determine your social network. What is the primary means you use to contact your handler? Is it e-mail?" A pause. *"No. Is it phone?"* A pause. *"Yes. By phone. What is the first digit of your contact's phone number? Is it 1 . . . 2 . . . ?"*

Ibanescu sighed deeply. His career, if not his life, was over. He stared intently ahead.

"I would like application. Yes? Is this the word? *Application?*"

Chapter 27: // Reunion

For those of you tracking Unnamed_1's quest, ask
yourself: why has his thread been leading him in circles in the Midwest? What's there that might justify
our freedom to the Daemon? Is it the paramilitaries,
or are those bastards looking for the same thing?
C'mon, upvote this post, and let's get some resources
on this problem.

Arendel****/ 793   9th-level Horticulturalist

Pete Sebeck and Jon Ross sat in an outdoor cafe on
Greeley, Iowa's Main Street. Around their table sat another half-dozen people, various locals who had been following Sebeck's quest on the darknet feeds, as well as his
recent exploits against paramilitaries. Introductions were
long over, as was the meal, and the group was now talking
animatedly. On the far side of the table, Laney Price was
debating with an online gaming economist named *Mo-
dius*, while their hosts laughed uproariously. Today, Price's
T-shirt read: "What would Roy Merritt do?"

Sebeck sipped his espresso and chuckled. He turned to Ross. "Laney's kept me sane. I don't know what I would have done without him."

"I guess it was luck of the draw that the Daemon selected him to revive you."

Sebeck grew somber. "My past life seems like a thousand years ago, Jon."

"I know the feeling."

"I think about my wife and my son every day, but contacting them would only put them in danger. And what would I say?" Sebeck raised his hands dramatically. " 'I'm not a mass murderer and by the way, the Daemon is real'?"

Ross had no response.

Sebeck leaned back in his seat. "So there I was in federal prison and imagine how I felt when they told me you were an imposter all that time we were working together on the Sobol murder case."

Ross grimaced. "Yes, you probably wanted to strangle me."

"I thought you'd *framed* me, Jon." He took another sip of his espresso. "So what do I call you now?" He pointed up at Ross's call-out. "It's not really 'Rakh,' is it?"

"No."

"What the hell does 'Rakh' mean, anyway?"

"It's Russian. Look, one advantage of the darknet is that no one needs to know who you *were*. Because they know who you *are*."

Sebeck gestured up to Ross's darknet reputation score. "Meaning you're someone people can rely on."

Ross nodded. "That's what matters, isn't it?"

Sebeck pondered the question. "Well, you sure were right about Sobol in those early days. We should have listened to you."

"Should you have?" Ross gestured to the bustling small town around them.

Unlike many Midwestern towns, Greeley appeared to be undergoing a renaissance. Main Street was lined with recently renovated brick storefronts and micro-manufacturing shops with their rolltop doors opened to reveal machinists and customers poking at D-Space objects, negotiating and ordering 3-D plans off the dark-net. CNC milling machines hummed in the workshops beyond.

In the street dozens of young adults, young families, and even middle-aged folks with call-outs over their heads walked, clicking on one another's data, interacting in multiple dimensions as though it were a natural extension of reality. Already second nature.

It reminded Sebeck of something Riley said to him months ago in New Mexico about social interactions where race and gender didn't matter. They were all members of the network here, and Sebeck had found himself increasingly looking at people's call-outs to really know who they were. Reputation mattered more than physical appearance, and he was shocked at how quickly his brain had made that transition. Everyone had the same color call-out in the darknet.

Sebeck dialed down the number of layers he was looking at and reduced the range of his D-Space vision to prevent call-out overload. He wondered how long it had been going on like this. Judging by the scaffolding and ongoing construction, it hadn't been long. Most of these folks were probably new arrivals from suburbs and cities. Or perhaps *returning* from suburbs and cities.

Ross was watching the people of the small town, too. "Given what we both now know—it's sometimes hard to tell whether it was for better or for worse. If society continues to come apart, who's to say this won't wind up saving lives *and* civil society?"

"So, what made you finally decide to join the darknet?"

"Have you ever heard of a sorcerer named Loki?"

Sebeck shook his head.

"He's possibly the most powerful Daemon operative alive. He nearly killed me. He killed just about everyone I worked with."

"And that convinced you to *join* the darknet? I'd expect the opposite reaction."

"If this new network is going to have a future, it can't be ruled by bloodthirsty sociopaths like Loki. And there was another person on that task force—a man they call The Major—who made me realize the existing order is even worse."

Sebeck nodded. "I've heard of The Major. Hell, people are looking all over for that guy. He's the one who shot Roy Merritt—the Burning Man."

"I *knew* Roy. I worked with him. He's the one who got me onto the government team. We were both betrayed by The Major."

Sebeck raised his eyebrows. "So you've got some powerful enemies."

"Here's what I'm worried about, Pete: the darknet is an encrypted wireless mesh network—constantly changing—but it's got to have some elements that tie it together, and I'm worried that some very advanced minds are working on a means to hack into the Daemon and take control of it."

"You think that's possible?"

He nodded. "This new spring of freedom might be short-lived if that's the case. And I've lived through false springs before."

"So this Major guy is . . ."

"Part of a financial system that rules behind the scenes. They seem to know the global economy is faltering, and they view the Daemon as a way to retain control. Darknet news feeds are recording a rise in violent repression around the world—focused on resilient darknet communities. They don't want people to be like this. . . ." He gestured to the town.

"You mean self-reliant."

"Exactly. Democracy is a rare thing, Pete. You hear how democracies are all over the place, but it isn't really true. They call it democracy. They use the vocabulary, the props, but it's theater. What *your* Founding Fathers did was the real thing. But the problem with democracies is they're hard to maintain. Especially in the face of high technology. How do you preserve your freedom when the powerful can use software bots to detect dissent and deploy drone aircraft to take out troublemakers? Human beings are increasingly unnecessary to wield power in the modern world."

"Laney calls it 'neofeudalism.'"

Price's voice rose across the table. "And it's happening already, Sergeant. Mark my words."

Ross turned to Price. "What do you mean, Laney?"

"See, in medieval Europe a mounted knight in armor could defeat almost any number of peasants." He jabbed a fork in Ross's direction. "The modern elite warrior is much the same—they can mow down mass conscripted armies with superior technology. So what happens when small elite forces can overwhelm citizen forces of almost any size? We return to feudalism—landless serfs and a permanent ruling class. Just look at the fortified upscale neighborhoods now being built with their own private security forces. It's neofeudalism, man."

Ross turned back to Sebeck.

Sebeck shook his head. "I'll never understand how we let this happen."

"Democracy requires active participation, and sooner or later someone 'offers' to take all the difficult decision-making away from you and your hectic life. But the darknet throws those decisions back onto you. It hard-codes democracy into the DNA of civilization. You upvote and downvote many times a day on things that directly affect your life and the lives of people around you—not just once every few years on things you haven't got a chance in hell of affecting."

Sebeck finished the last of his espresso. "Look, I can see distributed democracy working in holons like this, but can we really run an entire civilization off something that was essentially a gaming engine?"

"Can you name anything else that's as battle tested? It's been attacked nine ways to Sunday by every leet hacker on the planet. Sobol basically used an army of teen gamers to beta test the operating system for a new civilization. I guess all those hours gaming weren't a waste of time, after all."

Price laughed. "Right on, man."

Sebeck glanced at the Scale of Themis at the center of his HUD display. Locally, power was leaning a bit to the left—widely distributed. "Jon, humor me: look at the Scale of Themis."

"Okay." Ross started clicking on D-Space objects. "What about it?"

"I've been noticing this. Dial it back to look at the global distribution of darknet power."

Ross did so, and Sebeck already knew what he was seeing; the Scale of Themis had moved dramatically to the right—nearly three-quarters of the way. It meant that darknet power in much of the world was concentrated in relatively few hands.

"Is this really an improvement over what we have now? You'll find the reputation ranking per level is below average also—two stars out of five. So there's a concentration of power among people of questionable character."

Ross confirmed this with a few clicks and stared at the objects in D-Space. "The darknet is still new in many places—and being taken up first by misfits and outsiders—like most new frontiers. That was the case here in the beginning as well—just look at Loki's reputation score."

"But let's not just drink the Kool-Aid here. We should always be asking ourselves if—"

"Excuse me. I don't mean to bother you. . . ."

Sebeck looked up to see a man in his early thirties, with his wife and their infant in a stroller. The man's call-out identified him as *Prescott3*, his wife as *Linah*. "Sorry to interrupt you, but I couldn't help notice your quest icon. Are you Pete Sebeck?"

Sebeck nodded.

"I've been following your quest for months. It's an honor to have you here in Greeley. I wonder if we could get a picture with you?"

Sebeck could see the man was a sixth-level Architect with a three-star reputation score. He looked back down at the man himself, and suddenly realized how the world had changed. "Sure. Happy to."

"Oh, that's so nice of you. Here. . . ." He picked up his infant and extended him for Sebeck to hold in his lap. Sebeck accepted the child uncertainly—it had been a long time since he'd held an infant. As he looked down at the child, he couldn't help but think of his own son, Chris. Sebeck had barely been seventeen when he became a father.

The parents moved in on either side of Sebeck's chair. "I want to have this picture to show Aaron when he grows up."

Ross was standing now looking at the four of them, aiming his HUD glasses. Sebeck remembered that most HUD glasses had built-in cameras. It was the source of all the many millions of photos and videos people were uploading to the darknet—the eyes of this distributed society.

"Smile. . . ."

Everyone smiled.

Ross then slid the virtual photo across D-Space over to the parents, and then he slid a copy over to Sebeck as well.

The parents were cooing as they collected their son. "That looks great. Thank you so much, Rakh. Detective Sebeck. The very best of luck on your quest—for all our sakes."

The parents started moving off, the father holding his son in his arms.

Ross watched them go. "Let's talk about this quest of yours."

"What about it? The Thread has been leading me in a circle around the town of Greeley for a week now. There's something here I'm supposed to be doing or getting or understanding—and I'm not."

"Do you think the Cloud Gate is here in Greeley?"

Sebeck shook his head. "The gate is supposed to appear after humanity justifies its freedom to the Daemon—not before."

"And Sobol gave you no indication how we were supposed to justify our freedom?"

"No. He was annoyingly vague."

Ross pondered the question. "This Thread has been leading you to *events*—not places? Correct?"

"Yeah. For the last seven months Price and I have found ourselves at the center of just about every major change now under way. I've seen the rise of the new power infrastructure, the new economy, the new fMRI legal system—you name it. That's how my reputation grew so fast. We just always seemed to be in the right place at the right time."

"Well, then we do know one thing."

"What's that?"

"Something big is about to happen in Greeley."

Chapter 28: // Sky Ranch

Natalie Philips shared the Cessna Citation III business jet with only one other passenger as it flew high above . . . well, somewhere. The destination was classified. In the absence of reading materials or a laptop, she had difficulty keeping her thoughts from wandering. She wasn't even permitted a pad of paper or a pen. So instead she used her prodigious memory to recall her exploit code line by line—searching for flaws.

The interior of the plane was roomy and reasonably comfortable, but there was no easy way for her not to be in view of the other passenger. He was a disheveled man in his sixties with unruly gray hair, a sizable belly, a cheap suit, and a wide, striped tie in a careless knot. He smelled of alcohol from the moment he got on the plane. He was staring into space—or so Philips had thought.

"You mind if we turn that on?"

Philips looked up at him and then toward the front of the cabin where a flat-panel television screen was set into the bulkhead. "I don't think we can get television. It's probably for video."

The man sighed and got to his feet, grabbing a remote from a low table. "I saw the HD satellite antenna on the fuselage. They always want to know what the media is saying. If we're gonna be here for a while . . ."

He clicked the television on, and it was already set to a news channel. On-screen newscaster Anji Anderson was talking, while behind her video played of masked gunmen looting a shop in a town somewhere in Kansas. The Chiron read, "Illegals on a Rampage."

Anderson's voice came through clearly even over the jet engine noise. ". . . another night of violence. Armed gangs of men—believed to be undocumented laborers and drug dealers. Local residents have taken up arms in defense of their property, but the problem seems to be growing ever worse as the economy continues to crumble."

The guy sighed, nodding to himself. "You gotta hand it to 'em." He looked at his watch, then continued clicking through the channels. . . .

News followed by news, and all of it showing mayhem in the streets of middle America. One of the graphics bore the title "Rape Counseling Center" in bold letters, followed by addresses and phone numbers in several states. He kept clicking—cartoons, a shopping channel, and more disturbing newscasts.

"Can we just watch one thing, please?"

"So, why'd they call you down?"

Philips turned to him. "I don't discuss my work."

He smirked. "I used to be like that."

"Well, I'm still like that."

He muted the television as burning houses filled the screen, and put the remote down. "Too bad they don't have a bar on this thing. I could really use a drink."

Philips tried to ignore him.

"Name's Rob, by the way. You are?"

Philips just looked at his extended hand. "Rob, no offense, but we're not intended to socialize. There's a serious crisis under way. I suggest you use this time to concentrate on what you'll do about it."

"Ah." He retracted his hand. "So you already accepted an offer, then."

Philips felt suddenly irritated. "I didn't *accept* anything. I've been loaned to Weyburn Labs from a government agency."

"And that's how it goes." He sat down across from her. "I was in government work. But after a while you just . . ." He looked around the cabin. "Christ, I could use a drink!"

She said nothing and tried to return her focus to her remembered code.

"You know, I did tours in some real shithole dictatorships, let me tell you. We helped build a huge commercial empire overseas. Hell, we were facing down communism in those days. A lot of questionable things were done to contain the Soviets. We installed a lot of dictators who were business-friendly. But we didn't give much thought to what would happen after."

"I don't think you should be talking about this, Rob."

"Why not? I've got nothing to lose anymore. Did you ever feel like that?"

She just stared at him.

"Do you know why it was possible for the *Krasnaya mafiya*—the Russian mafia—to spring up, fully formed, organized, and financed so soon after the fall of the USSR? Didn't you ever wonder where those guys came from?"

Philips considered it and realized she hadn't.

"The intelligence sector. The KGB. Those guys were spread around the world. They had covert communications, bank accounts, and knowledge to move and launder money. They had useful skills like eavesdropping, weapons, assassination, and they had incentive—lots of enemies.

"After the Cold War, some of our own guys didn't come home either. They helped to keep in place the system built overseas to hold back communism, and it became the system we're all a part of now."

"Are you referring to a conspiracy to betray the United States?"

Rob shook his head. "Betraying America doesn't require a conspiracy. That's what Sobol figured out. It's why he was able to hack into it. The free market is just a system of positive and negative reinforcement with a few interchangeable fixers to maintain it. The sole purpose of that system is to maximize profit. For whom the returns are made is irrelevant. Those who make the profits might turn around and become great philanthropists—who knows? Who cares? Because there's always another set of investors who want in. Who want to work the split-second fluctuations of the markets to get very rich, very fast. They might not ever know what's done in their name. That was the secret Sobol knew. And what he did was create a new system that leveraged a broader human will. That's what freaks these guys out. The Daemon is the first true threat they've faced."

"But what they do overseas has no legal authority here in the States."

He stared at her for a moment—then laughed. "International trade agreements are equivalent to constitutional amendments. They're the 'supreme law of the land' according to article four, paragraph two. That means we must meet foreign trade obligations or face reforms—and I've seen firsthand what those reforms do. They create a have and have-not society. The rich are bunkering down. It's not a conspiracy, just a reaction to a process set in motion. You don't even have to know what the goal is. That's why systems *work*—because they don't rely on individuals."

They sat for a few moments in silence, listening to the drone of the plane's engines.

"If this is what you believe, why are you on this flight?"

He shrugged. "Eventually, you come to realize it's inevitable. What's about to happen can't be stopped."

Philips stepped from the jet into withering humidity and a merciless prairie sun. She looked across a stretch of sun-bleached tarmac—fear turning her feet to lead.

Two dozen heavily armed soldiers in MTV body armor patterned in universal camouflage, Kevlar helmets, and ballistic goggles stood in ranks, cradling M4A1 rifles with full SOPMOD hardware. They just stared, face-forward, without acknowledging her existence.

Philips walked toward the reception committee.

At first she couldn't tell what division or corps the soldiers belonged to, but as she came within thirty feet she could make out a nondescript logo above their breast pockets—where an American GI's last name would normally go. It read simply: "KMSI." She knew it well; Korr Military Solutions, Inc.—the private military arm of its parent, Korr Security International.

She glanced around the airfield. A modern control tower with a rotating radar dish stood above an American flag drooping lazily in the torpid heat. Beyond stood hangars and row after row of gleaming aircraft—Bombardiers, Gulfstream Vs, a mammoth Boeing Business Jet. A couple billion dollars in private aircraft. In the distance, she could see squads of soldiers marching double-time toward distant hangars from the belly of an unmarked C-17 cargo aircraft. Hundreds of soldiers were in her field of view. A corporate army. What the hell was this place?

Suddenly a nearby non-com shouted in a hoarse voice, *"Pochodem vchod! Zrýchlené vpřed!"* and the soldiers responded in unison with a guttural *"Hah!"* and began to march off double-time.

Philips watched as the troops moved in formation across the tarmac, toward a distant, taxiing transport plane. For a moment she wasn't sure what to do next.

But the soldiers' departure revealed a square-jawed man in a sweat-soaked shirt and a photographer's vest moving briskly toward her. A KMSI photo ID badge wagged on his lapel as he walked, and he was completely absorbed in flipping through papers in a dispatch case.

He finally looked up to reveal mirrored sunglasses and smiled broadly. "Dr. Philips, Clint Boynton, Sky Ranch Services." He offered his hand.

Philips just glared at him. "What is this place, Boynton?"

He started flipping through folders in the dispatch case again. "I've got that here."

"I don't think you have to look in there to tell me where we are."

"An undisclosed location." He pulled a thick Mylar envelope from the case. It was stamped "Top Secret" in four places. He handed it to her. "The decision to bring you here was made at the highest level."

"The *White House* is involved?"

Boynton laughed, then apparently realized Philips was serious.

She took the envelope from him and felt the weight of it. There was a thick report inside. In her experience a document this heavy meant somebody had just spent several hundred million dollars.

Boynton pointed. "I'm told you'll find answers to your questions in there. There's a cover letter."

She sighed and ripped the seal on the envelope, pulling out the contents. There was a thick bound report inside entitled "Project Exorcist," with an attached letter, addressed to her. It was on Pentagon stationery. "Chairman of the Joint Chiefs of Staff." As she had been told, she was being loaned out to Weyburn Labs—for Operation Exorcist. She maintained a poker face.

"I've been instructed to—"

Philips just interrupted him with one upheld hand,

then started flipping through the fifty-page bound report at great speed.

"Doctor?"

Philips ignored him and continued flipping pages. In half a minute she'd reached the last page. She looked up again. "Very, very interesting . . ."

Boynton pointed at it in disbelief. "You just read that?"

"Only the useful parts. Some of the estimates are overly optimistic, but still . . ."

Boynton snapped his dispatch case shut. "In any event, you're now part of the Weyburn Labs team." He looked at his watch. "We've got a forty-mile drive ahead of us, Doctor, and time is tight."

"We're going to this Sky Ranch?"

"You're already on the ranch, and we won't be leaving it." He raised his arm and curled the four fingers of his hand.

Several vehicles emerged from a nearby hangar: a rose-colored Mercedes Maybach limousine followed by a couple of Chevy Suburbans with blacked-out windows.

The Maybach rolled to a stop in front of Philips and Boynton. The passenger door bore a family crest, as though it was some Renaissance coach and four horses. The crest was a riot of cattle, rifles, and oil derricks.

She'd seen it once in a library book when she was a child. *Great American Families.* "The Aubrey coat of arms."

Boynton smiled. "I'm impressed, Doctor. The Aubreys no longer own an interest in the property, but the holding company still uses their coat of arms as a logo."

Philips nodded. "They owned the largest contiguous parcel of private land in the United States—784,393 acres. Larger than the state of Rhode Island."

Boynton grinned. "If we play Trivial Pursuit, can I be on your team? In all fairness, it's more like two million—not that anyone would know." He motioned for her to approach the waiting limousine.

"Why such a large piece of land?"

"Privacy. We're seventy-five miles from the nearest town. The outer perimeter is ten miles from where you're standing and ringed with the latest seismic sensors and cameras. The sky is swept by radar, and we've got a battalion of crack troops in garrison—including an artillery section. The Daemon would have difficulty sneaking up on us out here."

Philips nodded.

Soldiers wielding what looked to be metal detection or radio frequency wands emerged from the Suburban and approached Philips. Other soldiers moved to take her luggage.

"What's this?"

"Necessary, I'm afraid. No outside electronic devices or weapons of any kind are permitted on the ranch. The Daemon is cunning and the secrecy of this operation is vital. Your understanding is greatly appreciated."

She had left her phone and laptop back in Maryland, but they riffled through her purse and carry-on bag with gusto.

They also started scanning her body.

In moments, they detected her watch and the silver amulet on a chain around her neck. They scanned both closely, then nodded to Boynton that they were okay.

A soldier now strapped a small gray plastic bracelet around her wrist. He fastened it into place with a rivet gun and ran tests on it with an electronic device.

Philips looked at it. "You're strapping a transponder on me?"

A soldier snapped a digital photograph of her.

Boynton held up his hands reassuringly. "RFID tag for tracking purposes. Don't try to remove it." He pointed to the one on his own wrist. "It's your identity while on the ranch. It'll send an alert if it's tampered with. Sensors at the entrances to most buildings will go into alarm if you enter without one. Likewise if you enter restricted areas. And alarms are responded to with lethal force. These RFID tags let the troops know that you're friendly, and we've got quite a few snipers out there—so please wear it at all times."

Boynton opened the door to the first limousine and gestured for Philips to get inside.

She lingered at the open car door. "Why is the airfield so far from the house?"

"The FAA restricted the airspace within a twenty-mile radius of the mansion."

Philips nodded. "I guess after 9/11 you can't be too careful."

Boynton looked confused.

"Planes as weapons."

Boynton thought for a moment, then nodded. "Oh, right." He gestured again for Philips to get inside the car. "If you please . . ."

She got inside.

The drive to the main house was a blur of grass and scrublands. For all the signs warning of cattle and the dozens of cattle guards they rumbled over, Philips never saw one. Instead she saw military units and antiaircraft missile batteries.

Even though she remembered every word of what she'd read of the Aubreys, she was still stunned at the sight of their mansion. After World War II they'd purchased an English manor house from one of the grand estates of central England—one that had gone bankrupt as the British Empire started to collapse. They'd had the house dismantled stone by stone and reassembled here in south Texas. A hundred-room neoclassical mansion done in solid granite blocks, replete with acres of ornamental gardens and statuary.

It was as if Philips had just rolled up to Castle Howard in Regency-period England. The cobblestone courtyard in front circled around a massive Italian fountain, blasting water thirty feet in the air from a dozen cherubic lips—with a muscular stallion rearing up over it all. It looked as though the Aubreys had sacked Europe. For all Philips knew, they had.

Linked to the back of the house by a covered causeway was what looked to be a sizable modern conference facility, done in smoked glass and granite.

The Maybach stopped under the shadow of twin marble staircases rolling out from the massive front door of the house. Philips stepped from the limousine as a valet in a red livery coat held the door for her.

Boynton had exited the Suburban and walked past them. "This way, Doctor."

Philips followed Boynton through a maze of ornately furnished hallways dotted with armed guards. With every room they entered, she heard a *beep* as radio frequency sensors along the doorways logged her movements.

They passed people in impeccable suits and diverse military uniforms walking in groups of two or three, all hurrying off somewhere.

"So you have more than KMSI troops on this project?"

Boynton nodded absently. "We've had to gather several dozen corporate military providers to deliver the needed manpower. Not to mention the expertise."

Philips followed Boynton into the center of an echoing ballroom and was dumbstruck at its size. It was dotted with sets of ornate furniture on islands of carpet and bustled with activity. People of various ethnic extractions, either military or smartly attired civilians, moved in and out, talking in hushed tones in English, Mandarin, Arab, Tagalog, Russian, and several other languages she didn't recognize. The ceiling was easily forty feet high. Philips craned her neck to look up at the murals. She had visited Versailles once, before joining the NSA, but the Sun King's palace exuded a neutered magnificence. This palace was still alive with authority.

"Doctor."

Philips turned to see Boynton gesturing to a rich

damask divan. She hadn't noticed him moving on without her. She caught up.

"Please have a seat. You'll be called soon." He nodded toward a distant buffet table with uniformed staff. "Feel free to have a bite. I hear the quail is excellent. Hunted locally."

"Thank you, no."

Boynton raced off, checking his watch, and Philips sat on the sofa. Her eyes swept the walls, taking in the dozens of massive paintings. They seemed like a cross between royal portraits and roadside billboards, depicting eighteenth-century battles from the Continent, landscapes, and portraits of nineteenth-century railroad barons leaning on walking sticks. Their gold-leaf frames were so ornate they looked like collections of medieval weaponry, dipped in gold paint and glued together.

Philips glanced around at the knots of people talking softly and in earnest. Military officers nodded and pointed at satellite photographs—all in the open. What was this place? It was the NSA without internal security and with a decorating budget gone out of control.

Philips leaned back and recalled the details she'd just read of Operation Exorcist. The complete, simultaneous extermination of the Daemon from critical data centers throughout the world. A Daemon-blocker patch, capable of interdicting the self-destruct signal on infected networks. An ambitious plan, but notably not one that destroyed the Daemon—one that simply blocked the Daemon from destroying selected targets.

The question was how she'd be able to use *their*

resources to carry out her own plan: to destroy the Daemon.

Philips was dozing an hour later when a booming voice nearby suddenly shook her awake. A tall, loose-jowled Texan in his sixties wearing a bespoke suit was slapping a nearby Chinese statesman on the back and speaking with a powerful Southern drawl. "How y'all settlin' in? They treatin' ya a'right, Genr'l Zhang?" He smiled broadly and broke into Mandarin. *"Ni hao ma? Wo fe-ichang gaoxing you jihui gen nin hezuo."* He smiled and shook the man's hand.

The Armani-suited "general" nodded back grimly and exchanged a firm handshake just a shade removed from an arm-wrestling match.

"Mr. Johnston, health to your family."

Philips caught Johnston's eye. "Excuse me, Genr'l." He strode toward Philips, turning his powerful voice on her. "Dr. Philips. Why don't you come on in here for a chat?" He grabbed a uniformed servant by the arm, but kept his eyes on Philips. "You want something? Coffee? Tea?"

"Nothing for me. Excuse me, have we been introduced?"

"Damn me, we haven't." He extended his hand and nearly crushed hers with it. "Aldous Morris Johnston; I'm fortunate to be senior legal counsel for several companies backing Operation Exorcist." He turned to the servant. "Get us a pot of coffee and some finger sandwiches in here."

"Sir, no offense intended, but time is wasting. The

news I saw coming in was quite dire. When can I meet with the Weyburn Labs team?"

"Doctor, that's what we're here to talk about." A nearby door opened, and several suited men could be seen rushing about inside. A security man in a navy blazer and gray slacks held the door. An earphone wire ran down into his collar.

Johnston was leading Philips along. "Now that you're part of the team, we want to get your input on the overall direction of the effort."

They moved into a sitting room warmly furnished with more human-scale sofas and chairs and wall-to-wall carpet. The security man closed the door and stood, hands clasped in front of him. Paperwork was everywhere on the coffee tables, and several suited men were tapping furiously on laptop keyboards. A bank of towering windows filled the far wall and bathed the room in diffuse light. The frames were arched into gothic points but the glass was smoked—keeping out much of the daytime heat. Beyond the windows lay vast grasslands dotted with horses.

"It's something, isn't it? Our group owns it all as far as the eye can see."

Philips nodded at the view. "Including the sky, apparently."

He didn't seem to notice. "It's a rare joy on horseback—especially at dawn."

Johnston patted a large upholstered chair. Philips bristled at this potential display of social rank and sexism combined—but realized she was being childish and sat where invited. Johnston sat on the arm of a nearby sofa.

Someone shoved a bone china cup and saucer into her hand, and a servant in a dinner jacket and white gloves poured steaming coffee from a silver pot.

Johnston gestured toward three other men sitting nearby—lots of symmetrically graying temples and impeccable tailoring on display. "Dr. Philips, this is Greg Lawson, Adam Elsberg, Martin Sylpannic."

They nodded in turn as people came and went from various doors in the background.

"Are you gentlemen with Weyburn Labs?"

Johnston laughed. "No, no, Doctor. They're with one of our Houston-based firms. They're here to represent the interests of key partners."

Philips placed the coffee cup on a nearby table. "Gentlemen, why am I sitting here? I need to speak with the Weyburn Labs team. Events are unfolding in the streets right now. Action needs to be taken."

"Understood, understood." Johnston nodded, while the other men looked questioningly toward him. "But first we want to hear your thoughts, Doctor. Did you have a chance to read the briefing paper on the way in from the airfield?"

"Yes."

"What do you think?"

"I think there are weaknesses. First, this Daemon-blocker mentioned in the report—I don't see how you can insinuate it into all infected networks. Especially in the time frame indicated. Not to mention the risk of storming all these data centers simultaneously around the globe."

One of the trio of Johnston's aides was furiously tapping at a keyboard as she spoke.

Philips stopped for a moment. "Look, I've had more than a few difficulties working with private industry against the Daemon in the past. I need to know who is—"

Johnston nodded genially. "Yes, I know there was some unpleasantness—that some of our representatives might have taken wrongful actions."

"*Wrongful actions?* My DOD liaison shot key group members, and destroyed our task force headquarters with demolition charges—killing everyone and destroying all our work. That's more than a little unpleasant."

"I understand, Doctor. But this is a war. And in war mistakes are made. It's whether we learn from those mistakes that spells the difference between victory and defeat. We've tightened up the chain of command. You weren't aware of it at the time, but the Daemon Task Force was just a pilot project. A proof of concept. And thanks to you, a successful one. Operation Exorcist is the result—a multibillion-dollar effort. It will take all of government and private industry resources to defeat the Daemon. We truly need your help."

Philips still eyed Johnston. She figured acquiescing too quickly would seem suspect. "What about The Major?"

"He's no longer on the project."

"But neither is he in Leavenworth."

"The Major needs to be kept on a short leash, but we need all hands right now, Doctor."

"He murdered Special Agent Roy Merritt."

"Understood, but nothing about this situation is personal. This is national security, and Deputy Director Fulbright assures me that you're familiar with making leadership decisions. We think you have a bright future in the private sector, Dr. Philips. We see leadership potential in you."

She paused as long as she thought necessary to make it appear that she was wrestling with her conscience. In actuality she was wrestling against the desire to spit into his face. "Who's calling the shots?"

"Joint public-private advisory committee. Sounds bad, I know. But doesn't matter—they're back in Washington and we're all out here. I want to hear your thoughts."

"Who came up with the Daemon-blocker?"

"Weyburn Labs folks. Some Chinese fella."

"The code sample in the report—it bears a disturbing similarity to some of the API calls I discovered in the IP beacon. Those API calls are not safe."

Elsberg responded. "You needn't worry, Doctor—"

"Don't tell me what to worry about."

Johnston motioned for her to calm down.

Elsberg continued. "They didn't use the Daemon's API. We all know it's a trap, Doctor. Weyburn reverse-engineered the Destroy function. They found that it's susceptible to what I believe is called a . . . a buffer overrun, and they developed a countermeasure. A 'vaccine,' if you will, against the Daemon's data-destruct command."

"And this works?"

"It's still in testing, but the tests were very encouraging."

"How do you know your test case is realistic?"

"We didn't use a test case."

"You mean you tested on *real companies*?"

Johnston nodded. "Owner's prerogative, Doctor. Sever a gangrenous limb to save the patient."

Lawson put his two cents in. "We were hoping to have you perform a review of the Weyburn Labs code, Dr. Philips. To ensure that only code in line with the spec is present."

"You mean you don't trust them?"

"This is mission-critical, Doctor. There can't be any slipups. The more trusted, expert eyes that see it, the better. We were hoping you'd be willing to help."

"Why wasn't I briefed and then asked to come on board—instead of being packed off on a plane with almost no warning?"

He grimaced. "I know you must feel poorly used, but again, it's national security and couldn't be helped."

"And my lab facilities?"

"We've got everything you need. You've got a blank check, Doctor. Any expert in the world—you need 'em, we'll find 'em. Any resource, we'll get it for you. Just ask."

"I'll have access to all the data this time? For real?"

"You'll have full access to our research, and vice versa. We won't micromanage you. We've got some sharp people, though, Doctor: Litka Stupovich, Inra Singh . . ." Looking to Lawson. "What's that other gal's name?"

"Xu Li?"

"Right, Dr. Li—a Taiwanese, I believe."

Philips nodded appreciatively. Top private industry crypto folks—some previously with the Soviet government—but world-class experts nonetheless. Philips considered the chance to work with a truly international team. It was an unheard-of opportunity for someone who rarely got to leave Fort Meade. An NSA-lifer with umbra-level clearance. She almost wished it weren't an evil plot.

"I'm surprised at the degree of government and private industry cooperation. It's certainly a sign of how seriously this issue is being taken."

Johnston laughed a booming laugh. "My gawd, Doctor, this Sobol fella's got us over a barrel. That's for sure. We've got a saying in South Texas: 'Common enemies make for uncommon friends.'"

Philips sat back in the chair, thinking. "I'd like to discuss this with Deputy Director Fulbright."

Johnston grimaced. "Well, Deputy Director Fulbright doesn't report to me, Doctor, but we'll request a conference call if it'll put your mind at ease."

"I'd like to make the call."

Johnston appraised her for a moment, then nodded. "I understand. You're careful. I respect that more than you know—especially now. I'll arrange with Fulbright's office for them to expect your call, Doctor. And we'll get you access to a secure line. Won't be until tomorrow, I expect. I hope this won't prevent you from commencing review of Weyburn's code. Time is, as you say, of the essence."

Philips considered this, then nodded. "I see no problem with that."

Johnston smiled and extended his hand. "Excellent, Dr. Philips. We're glad to have your assistance. We'll get you settled in your new quarters. I think you'll like them very much, and I'll have some Weyburn folks come by and collect you. Whatever you need, you just ask. Hell, don't hold back. Give it to us straight. If we don't already make it, we'll buy it."

Johnston and his colleagues stood, signaling the end of the meeting. Philips stood also, and Johnston once again grabbed her hand in a crushing handshake.

"Doctor, welcome aboard. We look forward to much success together."

She nodded. "Thank you, gentlemen."

With that, they turned to meet their next appointment as they shunted Philips out a side door.

Chapter 29: // Scorched Earth

The Major stepped off the rear loading ramp of a C-130 transport plane and onto the tarmac of a deactivated U.S. Army airfield near the town of Rolla in northern Missouri. It was hot and humid. Three uniformed KMSI soldiers stood ready to greet him with sharp salutes—the center one stepping forward, extending his thick paw.

The Major knew him well—a towering, powerfully built South African, handpicked for this operation. They'd fought in more insurgency campaigns and covert wars in more countries than The Major cared to remember.

"Major. Everything is in order, sir."

"Colonel Andriessen." The Major shook his hand. To the uninitiated it no doubt seemed odd to hear a colonel giving deference to a major—but The Major's nom de guerre was just that. He had long ago outstripped his last formal rank.

"Your undergarments are showing, sir." He pointed.

The Major glanced back into the cargo hold at the closest of ten identical pallets covered in green canvas tarps. A corner clasp had broken during landing, revealing the bricks of twenty-dollar bills beneath, wrapped in cellophane. One hundred and eighty million dollars a pallet—one point eight billion dollars in all.

The Major nodded. "Get some forklifts out here." He started them walking briskly toward a white Toyota Land Cruiser waiting nearby.

"Shall we cover it first, Major?"

"Don't bother. It won't be valuable for much longer." He turned to the Colonel. "So get the payments out to the strike teams soon."

"Yes, sir."

A driver in KMSI BDUs was standing next to the Land Cruiser. He opened the rear door and saluted. "Welcome to Missouri, sir."

The Major ignored him and got in, the Colonel right behind him.

As they drove across the airfield The Major could see three C-130 cargo aircraft parked near hangars, either loading or unloading equipment with forklifts. It was hard to tell the way logistics teams were milling about and pointing instead of actually doing something. *Soldiers.* Private or government issue, they were always bitching about something.

There were also scattered squads of heavily armed men in civilian clothes standing around near civilian vehicles. He'd much rather they stayed under cover, but it was tough to keep these guys in hangars on a hot summer day like this. It was probably over a hundred inside those metal buildings. With a seat-of-the-pants operation like this, best to let the mercs cool off.

Before long the Land Cruiser pulled up to a tired-looking brick administration building done in art deco style. Some of the windows were boarded up, but there were several generator trailers nearby with thick black cables running out the edges of the front door—which was propped open. Two guards with Masada rifles stood in the entryway in full-body armor—the KMSI logo on their breast pockets.

They saluted The Major as he walked into a musty-smelling hallway, the Colonel leading the way.

"Ag, you caught me just coming back from an inspection on those Slovak bastards. They got shot up pretty good. We're missing a few."

The Colonel brought them down the vandalized but recently patched hallway, gesturing to the far end. "We're back here. Not much to look at."

They passed several sets of uniformed guards, and each office they passed was filled with command staff and lots and lots of laptops, radios, and satellite phones. Officers were busy orchestrating the movements of strike teams and making sure all necessary materiel was arriving as and when needed.

"Did they ever find that Loki fella who kept messin' with your schedule?"

The Major shook his head. "He's still MIA, but it's too late for him to stop this—even if he has any power left."

In a few moments they reached the end of the corridor and entered what was most likely the old base commander's office, replete with a secretarial anteroom. There, a uniformed male assistant was pecking away at a laptop, while two high-strung-looking men in immaculate casual business attire stood up from folding chairs the moment the hulking South African colonel stepped through the door.

The first of these men had on an expensive-looking, large-faced chronometer and an impressive tan to go with it. He extended his hand to Andriessen. "Colonel Andriessen, I'm Nathan Sanborn, chief executive officer and chairman of Halperin Organix." He offered his embossed business card and pointed to the other man, who carried a small black attaché case. "This is Sanjay Venkatachalapthy, our senior counsel."

The Colonel laughed. "Ag, you're bloody joking, right? This kefir's got more name than a German viscount." He looked to his assistant. "Corporal, are we letting *anyone* into my office now? How did these men find me?"

"Colonel, these gentlemen are well-connected in Washington."

Sanborn interjected himself. "Look, I've been speaking with General Horvath and Admiral Collins—I think there's a grave misunderstanding, gentlemen. I've been trying to get someone on the phone or to reply in e-mail for a week now, and I don't appreciate having my calls dodged." He gestured to the office. "Can we speak in private, please?"

The Colonel looked to The Major. The Major didn't budge or respond.

The Colonel turned back to Sanborn. "We've got urgent business to attend to, Mr. Sanborn. Everyone here is cleared top secret. Everyone but *you*."

Sanborn looked like he considered getting angry, but decided against it. With one more glance around he threw up his hands. "All right then. I've been given to understand that the blatant patent infringement being perpetrated against my firm is being used as a pretext for what can only be described as a paramilitary police action."

"It's not your concern, Mr. Sanborn."

"No. That's where you're wrong—and by the way, I'm not entirely comprehending why you're South African. Why is a South African in charge of what's going on here? This is Missouri, not Capetown, Colonel Andriessen."

"I wouldn't have pegged you as a racist, Mr. Sanborn. We Africans have had a long struggle against such prejudice." The Colonel chuckled and looked at The Major.

Sanborn fumed.

The Colonel continued. "The global economy provides for efficient competition. You of all people should appreciate that."

"So what I'm not understanding is whether this is a government operation or—what is going on here?"

"Get on your fancy jet and leave, Mr. Sanborn."

Sanborn got into the Colonel's face—or at least his neck, given the Colonel's height. "I'm not some pipsqueak you can push around, Colonel. I've got a thirty-billion-dollar company and a fiduciary responsibility to defend both its brand and its reputation." He gestured to the nearby lawyer. "Both of which we fully intend to protect."

"So you're going to sic your lawyers on us then, Nate? Is that it? Every syllable of Mr. Venk-kachanky-whatever here?"

"I am deadly serious, Colonel. We have significant influence in Washington."

The Major looked at his watch. "We've got a timeline to meet, Colonel."

Sanborn pointed. "Who the hell is *this* guy?"

The Colonel interposed himself. "Surely this conversation can wait, Nate."

"No. It cannot wait. Our investigators tell us that there are armored cars coming in by rail. There are military helicopters without markings being stationed at retired air bases like this across the Midwest. I've been watching the news—watching what's been going on out here. This is insane. This is America, not some crackpot dictatorship. People in government have told us that a justification is being made for these operations in defense of intellectual property held by Halperin, and I'm here to tell you that yes, we do have claims, and we are mounting lawsuits, but legal action is the course to resolve this problem. This is not a police matter—or whatever the hell you're making it into. I'm telling you that what you're doing is not authorized by us in defense of our business interests."

The Major pushed the Colonel out of the way and got right back into Sanborn's face. "*Not authorized?* Listen, you Ivy League prick, you don't determine what is and isn't authorized. Halperin isn't *your company*; it's the investors' company. The last time I checked you didn't found it. You're not even a scientist. You're just a trained business monkey that someone hired to crank an organ handle. So get back on our company jet like a good little monkey before someone sells you off for medical experiments."

Sanborn's face had gone from tanned to burning red as The Major's fearsome visage got up close and personal—like a drill sergeant in basic training. Sanborn stepped back a pace. "I'm not a person who gets treated like this. You are making a mistake. I don't know who you are, but your career is over. No one speaks to me like that."

"Get the fuck out."

"You have not—"

"OUT!"

Several armed KMSI soldiers suddenly appeared in the doorway, and the Colonel nodded toward Sanborn and his silent Indian attorney. The guards made way and Sanborn led the way. "You haven't heard the last of me."

The Major said nothing, but only shut the office door behind them and proceeded toward the Colonel's office. He stopped in the doorway and turned around.

Andriessen raised his eyebrows inquisitively.

"Colonel. Mr. Sanborn was ambushed by domestic insurgents on his way back home. Insurgents who were no doubt enraged at the lawsuits that he's mounting against darknet communities throughout the Midwest. I'll see that a psy-ops officer contacts your people for the proper news spin on his untimely death to ensure maximum usefulness to ongoing operations."

The Colonel nodded. "It's a bloody tragedy. Mr. Sanborn will be missed." He nodded to his assistant, who picked up the phone.

The Major entered the office, let the Colonel enter, and then closed the door behind them. The Major looked the place over as an aging air conditioner labored to keep the place cool in the stifling Midwestern heat. There wasn't even a computer or a map in the place.

The Major sat down on the edge of the desk. "Rules of Engagement for darknet communities are as follows: kill everyone you find, burn every structure, and destroy every vehicle. Without exception. The knowledge and equipment that makes these communities work must be eradicated. The cultural memory that they ever existed must be erased. Is that understood?"

The Colonel nodded, poker-faced. "Yes, sir."

"Don't forget storm cellars and culverts. Any hiding place."

The Colonel nodded solemnly.

"As for tactics, the irregular forces will prevent civilians from escaping, while your forces move through town destroying everything in their path. Psy-ops units will be filming as needed. It's important that they get some footage that resembles an operation to dislodge an insurgent occupation. I expect the residents will oblige us by resisting with force, but if not, your men should facilitate that imagery."

"That's a formal objective?"

"It is. One other thing, Colonel."

"Yes, sir?"

"I'm sending a special unit into one of the target areas. It's a detachment out of Weyburn Labs. No one may inspect their equipment. Their mission is classified and reports directly to me. It takes priority over any other objective. Do I make myself clear?"

"Crystal clear, sir. I'll make sure the men understand. What target is your team being sent to?"

"Greeley, Iowa."

Chapter 30: // Quarantine

Pete Sebeck stood in a fabrication shop in Greeley, Iowa, watching a selective laser sintering machine print a tractor part out of metal powder. The car-sized machine used laser-generated heat to fuse the powder into a metal solid based on a digital 3-D model. The proprietor of the shop, a thirteenth-level Fabricator named *Hedly,* monitored the process through a tinted window.

Sebeck stood behind him listening to *Diving Bruce,* an "Ozzie" eleventh-level Entrepreneur, who'd come all the way from Melbourne to see what was going on in towns like Greeley. Sebeck found himself in more and more of these demonstrations as he and Price scoured the town for some idea of why the Thread brought them here.

The Australian talked with passionate intensity. "When the Daemon infected our networks, I saw it for what it was, yes? A bloody opportunity."

Sebeck raised his eyebrows. "Even though it was stealing from you?"

"Stealing? Yes, but it was a wake-up call, too. It changed the game for everyone, didn't it? Not just me. I realized I couldn't have long supply chains. It would punish me—and my competitors—for doing that. That's a level playing field. The Destroy function it installed in our network is like a hand grenade pin that anyone can pull—a ticking clock forcing us to migrate to a more sustainable, less complex system. And besides . . ." He gestured to the machines around them. "This is the future. It makes no bloody sense to transport parts thousands of miles. Creating them to-order like this from raw materials—metal powders or Arboform granules—that's the market, mate. There are other machines that can produce circuitry from printed, flexible material. It's a bloody third Industrial Revolution, isn't it?"

Sebeck saw Jon Ross approaching from the shop's open-bay entrance. Ross passed a D-Space object to Sebeck and nearby Laney Price. It appeared as an aerial photo floating next to them.

Bruce was still talking, apparently unable to see their private layer. "I'm no bloody tree-hugger. I have no intention of living in an effing yurt and milking cows each morning. Just look up at that colossal energy whore in the sky and tell me there's an energy shortage. The sun uses up more energy in a second than mankind has used in all its history. We just need to get at it." He ticked off items on his hands. "Solar carpet—replacing expensive platinum catalysts with metal oxides—gallium solar paint—copper indium gallium selenide—"

"Sergeant . . ." Price frowned as he examined the aerial photo.

"Excuse us, Bruce. I think something's come up."

Bruce extended his hand and shook Sebeck's and Price's enthusiastically. "Brilliant! Best of luck on your quest, and don't forget if any darknet reporter asks you, we're going to be replicating this shop in Queensland come December. Cheers, mate!"

Price pulled Sebeck away and they joined up with Ross near the doorway.

Sebeck shrugged. "What's going on?"

Ross jabbed at the photo that was following them around in D-Space. "Just look. They're encircling us."

"Who is?"

"Serious people."

Sebeck studied the image. "Where did you get this?"

"We have two security drones orbiting this county, and we've come under aerial surveillance ourselves."

"What am I looking at?"

"Let's find a more private place to talk." Ross motioned for them to follow. They exited the micro-fabrication shop and moved along the crowded sidewalk. Everyone looked busy on some private errand, but even as they walked, they could see news was traveling quickly through the townspeople. Photos, videos, and messages were flying through the darknet.

Ross stopped in mid-sidewalk. "News travels fast."

Sebeck could see the feed alert appear in his HUD display: *Greeley Blockaded by Security Forces.* It was a highest-priority alert, quickly getting upvoted. He knew that soon the system would automatically put someone in charge of dealing with it. "We've been surrounded?" He more closely examined the virtual photo floating in D-Space.

Ross pointed at creeks, rivers, and roads at the edge of the county. "Three-mile radius. They're setting up checkpoints on all roads, and they've got unmanned surveillance drones watching the terrain. They're cutting power lines, communications—all connection to the outside world. And we're not the only ones. . . ."

Ross presented a digital map of the Midwestern U.S. "There are news feeds reporting similar blockades of towns in Missouri, Kansas, Nebraska, Ohio, Indiana. . . . It's a carefully orchestrated campaign to isolate darknet communities."

Sebeck studied the map. "And we're at the center of it."

Ross tilted his head. "So we are." He looked up. "Does that mean the Daemon had advance notice of this?"

"You mean because the Thread was keeping me here?"

Price shook his head sadly. "Dude, why the hell wouldn't it just warn us? Now we're trapped here—surrounded by . . . ?" He looked to Ross.

"Corporate military would be my guess."

Sebeck was at a loss. "But they can't just—"

"Check your history, Pete. This wouldn't be the first time corporate combinations attacked people in the United States. Based on the brain scans of that so-called insurgent you brought in, and the scans of others captured elsewhere, it looks like we're facing a who's who of mercenary companies that have supported repressive regimes around the world." Ross was clicking on D-Space, examining feeds and quickly reading. "Here's a high-rep journo with pictures of armored cars coming in by train, at night under tarpaulins. Light attack helicopters . . ."

Sebeck leaned in to look. "How can they get away with this? Where the hell is the U.S. military? Where is the government?"

Price leaned in as well. "Check out the media blitz they've been putting on nonstop. 'Anarchy in rural America'—the economy spiraling downward. They're making people desperate for security."

Sebeck pondered their situation. "We need the National Guard."

Ross shook his head. "I don't think we can count on government intervention to help us, Pete. Something's going on behind the scenes. Something we can't see."

Price threw up his hands. "So what does *that* mean? Internment camps? Worse?"

Sebeck sat down on a nearby public bench and put his head in his hands. "So they cut the power, but we still have electricity because we've been using local sources."

"Right."

"And we still have communications with one another and the outside world because we're using a wireless mesh network."

"Yes—although, I imagine they'll have electronic warfare people trying to locate and destroy all the nodes on our perimeter as soon as possible."

Price interjected. "But the factions outside the quarantine will keep throwing down more to keep us connected. And infrastructure defense factions will get involved in this at some point."

Sebeck sat up straight. "Yes, but my point is that the darknet gives us some resilience. We're not reliant on those things—they know that—so why are they bothering to cut them off?"

Ross shrugged. "There are still a lot of people in this region who aren't on the darknet. Those folks have been plunged back into the Stone Age by this—no power, no cell service, no Internet. These guys want to control the message coming out of this region. The general public can't read darknet news feeds. They won't hear the truth, so it'll be like this never happened."

Price sat down next to Sebeck. "Just the official story. Which will no doubt be of the valiant private security forces containing looting and anarchy in the Midwest."

They all stared at one another.

Price crossed his arms. "We are fucked, man!"

"We'll be all right, Laney. We've been in tighter spots before."

Price narrowed his eyes at him. "No we *haven't*!"

Just then Sebeck sat up straight, and stared in complete astonishment.

Both Ross and Price noticed the look on his face.

Ross asked first. "What's wrong, Pete?"

"The Thread is back."

Price concentrated as if he could see it by squinting. "Why now?"

Ross considered the question. "It must be linked to this news event. Maybe that's what you were here for?"

Price shrugged. "Well, it's not like we have much of a choice. Where's it leading us, Sergeant?"

Sebeck pointed at the horizon. "Straight through enemy lines."

In the predawn of a moonless night, Sebeck, Price, and Ross moved along the edge of a field. A chorus of frogs and crickets filled the stillness. Sebeck wore his suit of ceramic composite armor and enclosed helmet. He held a multibarreled electronic pistol with a suppressor attached and scanned the path ahead with white phosphor night vision. He then signaled it was clear.

Sebeck lifted his visor as Price and Ross ran up and knelt next to him. "I still say this is a mistake, Jon. These townspeople are going to need all the help they can get."

"Pete, the Thread was what brought you here in the first place, and if what Sobol said was true, then recent events have redirected it."

"But it could wait. I could stay here and help fight first."

"Do you really think you're going to make a difference here?"

They exchanged grave looks in the dim light.

"*You're* staying."

Ross nodded. "I don't have a high quest to complete. It would be wrong for me to go. Besides, the town will badly need my surveillance drones."

They just looked at one another.

Ross grabbed Sebeck's armored shoulder. "I'll catch up with you later."

Price and Sebeck didn't look convinced.

"Personally, I don't envy you for having to slip

through the blockade. I have your coordinates on my listing now, so I'll know when you're clear. Be careful. And good luck."

They shook hands and slapped backs. And then Sebeck and Price moved along in the darkness again—Sebeck following the Thread as it led down into a tree-shrouded creek bed and into the night.

Chapter 31: // Extermination

Central_news.com

Private Military Contractors to **Restore Order** in **Midwest**—Beleaguered local residents in six **Midwestern** states cheered the arrival of private security forces, Saturday. William Caersky of Patterson, **Kansas,** felt the cavalry had arrived just in time. "It's been a nightmare. With sky-**high food and gas prices, armed gangs** have ruled the streets for days. The **government did nothing.** Thank god for these guys...."

Henry Fossen looked up from cleaning a rifle barrel as the wail of tornado sirens pierced the night. He stood up and glanced at his watch: *3:42 A.M.*

He dropped the barrel onto a cloth on the kitchen table and vaulted up the back stairs, shouting. "Lynn! Jenna! We've got to go! Hurry, hurry, hurry!"

As he ran down the upstairs hall, Jenna was already exiting her bedroom, dressed and clutching a backpack. She looked rattled. "They're moving in, Dad."

"Who says?"

"I just read it on the town alert feed. There are soldiers headed this way right now." She shook her head in incomprehension. "How could this be happening?"

Fossen's wife, Lynn, appeared in their doorway holding a case as well. He grabbed her by the shoulders. "We've got to go, hon. I've got my things downstairs. Let's move!"

He brought them down through the kitchen, where he rolled up the cloth containing pieces of the Korean War–era, M1 Garand rifle he'd been cleaning—the one his father had given him. He also grabbed a sealed can of 30.06 ammunition dated from 1958.

"C'mon, out the door!"

As his wife and daughter headed out the mudroom door, he took one last look at the family house, then turned off the lights and joined them out in the drive near the garage. It was still dark out, but as Fossen and his family got into the crew-cab pickup, they could hear the rattling of distant machine-gun fire.

Lynn covered her mouth. "God help us. . . ." She looked at her daughter.

Jenna looked back at them both, slowly shaking her head. "I didn't mean for this to happen. . . ." Tears started flowing. "I'm so sorry. I didn't mean for this to—"

"Jenna, let's not even talk like that."

Both of them got in and he rapidly had them moving down the long gravel driveway. "Jenna, I need you to give me some idea where these people are. Are there reports of them between us and downtown Greeley?"

She wiped her tears and started clicking on D-Space as Fossen drove at high speed down to the road.

"If we move quickly, we'll be fine. They're coming in from the east and south. . . ." She paused. "But there's also another force reported coming in from north and west."

"Yes, all right, but we can make it to town?"

"Yes."

Fossen glanced to them both. "We're going to be all right. We'll get to the storm cellars at the elementary school just like we planned. We're going to be all right."

As he looked down the road, he could see the lights of Greeley just a few miles ahead. There was thunder in the distance and the lights suddenly went black.

At the sound of tornado sirens Ross sat up in the motel bed and reached for his HUD glasses on the nightstand. He tried to turn on the lights, but they didn't work. A glance at the digital alarm clock confirmed that the power was out.

So much for local power generation.

He threw on his black Nomex flight suit and computer belt as the system logged him on. The sirens were winding down now, and he could see hundreds of darknet call-outs beyond the walls and hear the voice of Floyd_2, an ex-army officer that the darknet had automatically selected as civil defense commander, based on his reputation score and skill set. His voice came in over the public comm channel in midspeech. . . .

"*—need everybody to those storm shelters. Security drones show helicopters and a light armored force converging on Greeley from all four compass directions. Everyone,* *please get to the middle school storm cellars. Ex-military folks and hunters, you have your assignments. We've only got a few minutes. I'm going to project the location of the choppers onto layer six, and I want all tagged enemy objects placed on that layer, too."*

Four bright red call-outs appeared some ways off to the east, identified as *Helo 1, 2,* and *3.*

Floyd_2 paused. *"Everyone move quickly but calmly to the middle school storm shelters. You can see the video surveillance overlays on layer five. It looks like these people are heavily armed. We've got summons in for infrastructure defense and equipment, but it looks like there are a lot of darknet towns under attack tonight. So I think we're on our own for the time being. Let's look out for one another now."*

Ross could hear the voices of people outside moving through the darkness. The hushed voices of parents. The worried, high-pitched voices of children.

Then Floyd_2's sudden urgent shout over the channel. *"Incoming!"*

An explosion tore a hole in the air nearby. Its shock wave hit the front of the motel like a solid object, blasting out one of Ross's windows and shaking the whole building. Ross hit the floor and pulled blankets down on top of himself from the bed as glass continued to rain down. A layer of previously unseen dust had lifted off of everything and hovered in the room as a choking cloud. There was another explosion somewhat farther away that made Ross realize his ears were ringing. Dogs were howling and car alarms had gone off throughout the town.

The second explosion was followed by the crackling of distant gunfire in an indeterminate direction. Possibly every direction. Ross peered up at the jagged edges of the front window with its imitation, snap-on window frames. He could see guttering orange light and shadows across the street. Flames. But the sky between the curtains looked tinged with its own glow. Possibly dawn— or more flames farther off.

Ross listened in the darkness of his room to the gunfire, between which he could hear people screaming. And now the sound of helicopters. Not the deep, booming thump of Bell Rangers that he remembered from Building Twenty-Nine. No, these choppers had a high-pitched buzz to them that was soon followed by the sound of ripping fabric. Then more screams.

He could see the call-outs of dozens of nearby operatives racing past beyond the walls. Obviously headed for the middle school. He could hear their voices over the public darknet comm channel as well, and a series of jagged lines adorned each call-out as they spoke. It was like a surreal first-person game.

[Beavertail]: "Three Helos coming in from the east. They're using miniguns!"

[Yardil]: "Thanks for the fucking news flash, Darrol!"

[Floyd_2]: "Cut useless chatter, Yardil!"

[Knockwurst]: "ASVs coming in across the fields. East and west. Half a mile off."

[Needleman]: "I'm on the west side. What's an ASV?"

[Knockwurst]: "M1117. Armored car. Gun platform."

[Needleman]: "Holy shit, I'm pulling back to B-twelve."

[Vorpal]: "Sniper fire at the barricades on the thirty-eight. North and south. We've got casualties!"

[Beavertail]: "Get stragglers into the storm shelters. We've got snipers on the east and south sides. They're taking up positions in the abandoned cars on the edge of town."

[Vorpal]: "I knew we should have moved those fucking things!"

None of it sounded good. Before Ross was fully dressed there was a pounding on his motel room door. Through the wall he could see a call-out that read *OohRah*. It was Sheriff Dave Westfield, a recent member and second-level Constable. He had also been a marine in his youth.

"Rakh! You okay?"

Ross grabbed his things and opened the door. "Yeah, I'm fine."

OohRah held an M16 rifle. "The feed says we're being hit with Hellfire missiles. It's time to get to the middle school."

Ross could see that the building across the road was engulfed in flames. It had been a machine shop—one of the local fab labs. A family lived on the second floor. Now there was no second floor, only a ground floor with doors and windows belching flames.

The sound of a helicopter was approaching.

OohRah rushed into Ross's room. "The feed says the missiles are coming from a gray Cessna 208 Grand Caravan that left a decommissioned army airfield north of St. Louis." The tearing sound was heard again. Then the chopper passed low overhead.

Ross leaned out the motel room door to look up into the sky.

The barest glow of dawn showed on the eastern horizon, and an AH6 Little Bird helicopter raced low along Main Street, its twin miniguns blazing. Tracer rounds streamed from them like orange lasers. He could see the phosphorus-coated bullets ricocheting in a shower of sparks into the predawn sky farther to the west—over by the American Legion Hall. There was more shouting and gunfire as a second chopper zipped overhead, launching rockets.

"Jesus Christ!" Ross ducked back into the motel room. "No markings on them."

"We saw the photos of those rail yards. But I don't think it really sunk in."

The rockets exploded in a series of deafening booms. It was followed by a large volume of gunfire erupting from the western edge of town. It sounded like a couple hundred people were involved in an intense firefight—an odd assemblage of large- and small-caliber weapons crackling like green pine in a fire. The sounds of women and children screaming among the refugees and the shadows of dozens of people racing past the open motel room doorway gave a sense of rising panic.

OohRah rushed to the doorway and shouted, "Get out of the street! Get out of the street! Come in here!"

He ushered a dozen people inside, men, women, and children—people of all ages. Carrying backpacks and suitcases.

One woman kept screaming at Ross, "What's going

on? What's going on?" These people weren't darknet operatives, so they appeared to have no idea what was happening.

OohRah grabbed the woman by the shoulders. "Get ahold of yourself. We're going to get you to a storm shelter."

One of the other refugees pulled her back into the group, where she quickly broke down sobbing.

"Let's get these folks to the middle school."

Ross was already busy flipping through an array of D-Space street cameras in his HUD view. Most of the town's public cameras were still functioning. They showed a series of buildings ablaze and bodies, or parts of them, in the streets. People were rushing around retrieving wounded. Others were firing out toward the edge of town at attackers Ross knew must be there. "Looks like the route to the middle school is still clear. Here . . ." He slid the prepared camera layer over to OohRah.

"Thanks. So we've still got network power, anyway."

Ross nodded. "The bank was hit, but they've got ultrawideband transmitters and fuel cells in the vault. It's pretty thick concrete."

OohRah was already looking out the doorway and motioning people to follow. "Let's go, folks! Follow me!"

A dozen frightened people ran after him. Ross brought up the rear, sprinting beneath the porch roof along a line of motel room doors. Some of the doors were open, but he didn't see anyone inside the rooms. Another chopper zipped overhead startlingly low and fast, guns *braapp*ing down the street. Empty shell casings rained down in a jingling cascade of brass that bounced in all directions.

Ross looked out at the call-outs ahead of him. He could see lots of names he didn't recognize, and he heard frantic voices over the comm lines.

[Barkely_A]: *"We've got wounded over here! We don't have anything to stop these armored cars."*

[Creasy]: *"Jack, about two dozen infantry coming through Courtney's field."*

[BullMoose]: *"Near the propane yard?"*

[Creasy]: *"Ten-four."*

Ross reached up and dialed down the volume on nearby chatter not directed to him. OohRah brought the civilians down an alley behind Main Street. It was cluttered with Dumpsters, pallets, and cars that had been idled by gas prices. As they crossed to the next block, they saw a car burning in the middle of Main Street. The car's side and fenders were riddled with bullet or shrapnel holes. The silhouette of a person was still sitting in the front seat, enveloped in fire. Someone with the call-out *DoctorSocks* raced past the flames, and then headed off into the night.

Another huge explosion ripped the dawn air, and Ross turned to see what he suspected was the propane yard going up in a roiling fireball a couple hundred yards away. Metal and wood debris spun into the air in a wide arc. Ross ducked around behind the nearest building.

"Up ahead!"

The sheriff brought them across the street to the arched granite-and-brick entryway of the Eisenhower Middle School. Mercifully, the steps led down to a cellar door lined with sandbags and away from prowling choppers.

Ross stopped in the entryway and let the others go in. He stood next to farmers with assault rifles as they watched the skies.

One of the other volunteers, a thirtyish, heavy-set operative named *Farmster* in a Halperin Seed hat, pointed to Ross and grabbed a scoped AR-15 rifle from a table just inside the doorway. "You know how to use this?"

"I'm better with an AK."

"An *AK*?"

Ross shrugged. "Russian army."

That brought out gales of laughter amid the distant gunfire.

"Well, I'll be damned. I never thought I'd be handing a gun to a Ruskie to shoot up the town with."

The guy fished through the pile of weapons and came up with a scuffed AK-47. He also grabbed a satchel into which he stuffed several thirty-round clips. "We can't let them reach this school."

Ross looked up at the choppers crisscrossing the sky in the distance and realized that this was just the beginning.

In the darkness Sebeck and Price peered at an abandoned, crumbling farmhouse from the shelter of a creek bank. The new Thread led directly toward a weathered barn behind it. The entire place was choked with weeds and bushes.

The sound of frogs and crickets filled the night, but miles behind them they heard loud explosions and the zipping sound of helicopter miniguns.

Price gazed back over his shoulder as the horizon flashed and flickered. "They're really getting pounded back there, Sergeant. Whatever we're supposed to find better be worth it."

Sebeck nodded. He'd been surprised they made it past the blockade, but then, whatever powered the Thread might have been able to create a path . . . somehow. He'd seen the Daemon do stranger things.

"Stay here."

"No problem."

Sebeck climbed up from the creek, and started moving through the tall grass, electronic pistol at the ready. He kept scanning the darkness for trouble but made it the couple hundred feet to the barn door without incident.

The glowing Thread proceeded right through the twin doors. Sebeck looked down and noticed fairly fresh tire tracks in the mud. He nodded to himself. Whatever the next segment was leading him to was apparently inside, and recently arrived.

Sebeck pulled open the right barn door partway. Stealth was not an option because it sagged on its hinges. He peeked in and noticed a dark late-model panel van with dealer plates. The Thread continued straight through the closed back doors of the van itself.

Sebeck scanned the interior of the barn and saw nothing except old stalls, a workbench, and piles of rusting equipment on either side of the van. Above he could see stars through the gaping holes in the barn roof.

He moved inside and came up to the shiny van doors. No sounds came from inside. He held the pistol in one hand, stepped aside, and tried the handle. It clicked open. He slowly pulled it open, peering in with the pistol aimed and ready.

"It's you."

"Me?" Sebeck stared at an oddly dressed man sitting on a folding chair in the cargo bay of the van. Mirrored sunglasses and a balaclava obscured the man's face, and he wore a camouflage outfit with knee pads and body armor. Before him he held what looked to be a transparent video panel or glass screen through which he was viewing Sebeck. It gave the effect of carrying a huge set of spectacles in front of him. The Thread led right to the tip of a wand he was clutching in his gloved right hand. A nearby call-out identified him as *PangSoi*, a first-level Weaver with a two-point-five rep score on a base of three.

Sebeck was puzzled. "What the hell are you supposed to be?"

"I'm PangSoi."

"I can see that." Sebeck clicked his pistol into its holster and opened his visor. "But why the hell did the Thread lead me to you? And cause me to leave all those people to get attacked?"

"It's hard to say."

"You're not a high-level, high-rep operative—you're a weaver-trainee for chrissake. And what's with the panel?"

PangSoi gazed at him, following Sebeck as he shifted on his feet.

"Why are you doing that?" Sebeck noticed wires running down from the panel to a large box draped in black fabric. It sat next to PangSoi's chair like an end table and gurgled from some tiny motor.

"We must hurry."

"What the hell . . . ?" Sebeck flipped up the fabric covering the box and came face-to-face with the severed head of a young Asian woman wearing HUD glasses—bolted into a metal frame. Her dead eyes looked forward, the lids pinned back. Tubes ran into her neck and wires into her HUD glasses. A tiny pump was burbling on a frame. "Oh my god . . ."

Suddenly what felt like an entire football team tackled him from behind. He felt rough gloved hands prying at his face, but the van he was pressed against kept him from falling down. "You son of a bitch!" He pushed his open helmet visor against the van door to close it, and the weight of several people pulled him backward, where he fell onto the muddy floor. Several strong bodies piled onto him, shouting, "Get him! Hold him!"

Sebeck spoke the keywords to electrify the surface of his armor. The tangle of men fell off him yelping, as he rolled free and stood.

Now he could see that he faced half a dozen commandos in full tactical gear. Some of them carried beanbag guns and Tasers. Clearly, they hadn't expected Sebeck's Armor of the Warrior—the gift of a faction supporting Sebeck's quest.

He eyed them through his mirrored faceplate. "I could say I don't want to hurt you guys, but I'd be lying. . . ."

He turned and jumped up into the back of the van, past the severed head of the young woman in the box. The soldiers pursued him. Sebeck grabbed the ghoulish PangSoi and drew his electronic pistol. "She was practically a child, you sick . . ." He fired a short burst into the man's chest and watched him fall.

Price.

Sebeck suddenly saw Price being dragged in through the barn doorway—a gun held to his head.

"Detective Sebeck! We'll kill him if you don't put the gun down and come out peacefully!" The man had a vaguely Asian accent, but like the others his face was covered.

Sebeck kicked both of the panel van doors open to get a clear view of the situation.

Price looked very muddy and very irritated.

"Laney, they're hired guns here to capture us. They're not gonna kill us. We're both too important to them."

"Oh for chrissake, Sergeant . . ."

"They somehow figured out a way to hack into my quest Thread. No, there's something big going down." Sebeck noticed a row of several plastic ten-gallon jugs of gasoline in the cargo bay. "I guess with gasoline so expensive and hard to find, you guys planned ahead. Smart."

The man with the gun pressed it into Price's temple. "Don't do anything you can't undo, Sergeant!"

Sebeck grabbed a magnesium flare from his suit belt. "You gonna tell your commander you killed an irreplaceable prisoner because I fucked with your van?" He sparked the flare. "I don't think so."

He dropped the flare onto the gasoline jugs and jumped from the van as everyone ran for their lives.

Sebeck was clear of the barn doors by the time the gasoline flared up and filled the entire barn with a rolling fireball that lit up the night, destroying the van and all the hellish things in it.

The moment he came out of the barn he was faced by several dozen commandos charging at him from several directions simultaneously, trying to knock him down. He emptied his pistol at them, wounding several, but he got struck from the side and slammed into the mud. Someone stepped on his weapon hand, pinning it to the ground, and then two men aimed fire-extinguisher-like devices at him, spraying thick white foam all over his legs and arms.

One of them shouted, "Why didn't you use the foam to begin with, asshole?"

"It's impossible to clean up!"

The white gooey material quickly turned rock hard—trapping Sebeck in place. Then they knelt around him and twisted to pull his helmet off.

"You bastards, I'm going to—"

Something struck him on the back of the head, and he blacked out.

Chapter 32: // The Burning Man

Darknet Top-rated Posts +2,995,383↑

The corporatists want to make it impossible to live independently without having to become hippies in a commune. But we've proven the people can create a high-tech, sophisticated society that's both connected to the land and to the world as a whole. Darknet communities everywhere *must* be saved. We must upvote the importance of these attacks as a priority one threat to the entire network.

Vitruvius_E*****/ 4,103   18th-level Journalist

Jon Ross stared with a deep sense of dread at the two messages that had just now popped up in his HUD listing:

Chunky Monkey—logged off 08:39:36

Unnamed_1—logged off 08:40:33

Ross had added Sebeck and Price into his friends list so he was alerted to changes in their network statuses.

He'd been checking the progress of their call-outs across the county every few minutes. They'd gotten through enemy lines, but their call-outs disappeared a mile or so later.

He let out a deep breath and held his head in his hands, unable to conceive of a scenario where this wasn't bad news.

It was midmorning and the situation in Greeley had become dire. The sun was up now, and it was another burning-hot day. Almost all the outlying farms had been burned to the ground; columns of black smoke striped the horizon. Likewise, the homes on the edge of town were being razed.

Ross knew that darknet video of this event would get out to the Web sooner or later. He wondered what people in the outside world were going to make of it. But then it occurred to him that he'd seen a hundred hours of footage showing violent conflicts in various parts of the world. What would the world think? Probably that America had finally lost its mind. But otherwise things would continue as they always had.

In the brief lulls in the fighting, Ross had used his HUD display to follow the unfolding farce that was mainstream news coverage. They were apparently being "liberated" from an insurgent occupation. Someone had created a darknet feed of mainstream news beyond the blackout.

Ross and a group of forty or fifty other men and women had spent much of the morning moving the ample numbers of abandoned cars from the fields in town to create blockades around the downtown perimeter, while the mercenaries busied themselves razing outlying areas. He also helped fill sandbags that were apparently intended for floods and packed them outside the walls of the middle school.

One mercy was that the helicopters had gone away some hours ago and not returned. The Cessna with Hellfire missiles had also flown off. They'd either gone to re-arm or had finished their role.

Luckily the mercenaries had not seemed to care about the unmanned surveillance drones Ross had brought with him. Neither had they been able to jam darknet radio communications. Ultrawideband was proving quite resilient. But then, the mercenaries appeared more interested in killing everyone than jamming their radios.

The chattering of gunfire punctuated by the louder cracks of hunting rifles filled the air. Ross leaned out from behind a masonry support pillar, looking both ways down Greeley's empty Main Street.

It was littered with broken glass, debris. A burning car stood in the middle of the road at the end of the block. Bullet holes had chipped the concrete and bricks, and several of the buildings on Main Street were already burning from rocket and missile attacks. Beyond that was a wall of roiling black smoke and flames. Burning houses. Every few moments he heard another deafening *boom*, and debris would fly hundreds of feet into the air.

They were destroying the town block by block.

Ross looked to the center of the road where a fenced green with a World War II memorial and benches stood. The street ran around it to either side. The memorial was a tall granite obelisk with a thick square base about the width and height of a man and was flanked by defunct cannons plugged with concrete.

Ross could see OohRah and Hank_19's call-outs behind it. He clicked on their call-outs and spoke into the comm channel. "Hank! You guys need me?"

OohRah's call-out flashed as he replied.

[OohRah]: "We could use another set of eyes behind us. Come on over. Move quick and stay low. We've been sniped."

Ross took another glance and ran to the center of the street at a crouch. He hopped the low iron fence at the edge of the green, and dove behind the monument, using the smaller Vietnam memorial nearby to provide cover from the opposite direction.

Hank and the sheriff nodded to him.

Ross brought his AK-47 to bear, watching their flank. "Where are they?"

The sheriff was pushing rounds into a spare clip while Hank kept watch down Main Street. "Pick a direction and start walking. You'll find 'em soon enough."

Fossen nodded. "Crazed gang members to the east, professional military to the west."

"Or so the costumes tell us. . . ."

Ross examined the memorial stone. "This should be good cover."

The sheriff shook his head. "Not from a grenade it won't be. We can't let them get close in."

Another ear-stabbing *boom* sounded from the east end of town.

"What the hell are they doing?" Ross brought up a D-Space video panel that showed an overhead view from a surveillance drone. He could clearly see the line of advance and the wasteland the private contractors were leaving behind them.

The sheriff ground his teeth. "They're tossing demo charges into houses. Shooting flamethrowers into cellar windows. Burning everything."

Ross could clearly see it when viewed from above. Then the drone flew into a cloud of smoke and the image was lost. He nodded behind him. "What happens when they reach the middle school? There must be six hundred people in there."

The sheriff peered through his M16 scope over the rim of the memorial. "We'll either have to stop them from reaching it or die trying. Everyone else is digging in, too."

Hank_19 kneeled down and nodded grimly to Ross. "My wife and daughter are in there. I don't care about losing the farm. You can always rebuild buildings, but . . ."

Ross tapped him. "If you need to go back and be with them, I'll understand." Ross looked to the sheriff.

The sheriff nodded.

Fossen shook his head. "No. If we just hold out, we might still have a chance. Look at the darknet feeds. My daughter says they're going haywire. These attacks here in the Midwest are a threat to the whole network. I'll bet no single thing has ever been upvoted this high." He looked to Ross. "The world is watching what happens here."

The sheriff shrugged. "So what? So what if everyone *cares*? What does that do for us? The situation we're in isn't going to be solved by angry posts and best fucking wishes. *Public outrage* has never stopped these bastards."

Fossen looked determined. "Jon, we're just second-level. What can a twelfth-level Rogue do that could help us?"

Jon cleared his throat. "I can get into and out of places and networks without being detected, but in this type of situation . . ."

There was suddenly a deafening explosion that broke the last of the windows along Main Street.

They all ducked down, but peered over the rim of the memorial to watch the far end of the street. An M1117 armored vehicle flanked by twenty or thirty well-equipped soldiers on foot suddenly rounded the corner. The ASV swiveled its top turret and fired grenades into the upper-story windows. The walls and windows erupted with flames and flying debris.

A camera crew in helmets and body armor rounded the corner as well, filming the action as soldiers fired grenade launchers into the doors of shops on either side and raced through the openings while their comrades raked the walls and streets with gunfire.

Tracer bullets whined past and Ross and the others ducked down as stone fragments rained down on them. Metal whined into the sky.

"Jesus Christ!"

"I see the propaganda unit is here to film our saviors in action."

Fossen crawled on his belly to look down the side street. "They're coming down the next block, too."

There were more explosions in the buildings down the street. Ross snuck a quick glance to see the ASV turret and its coaxial machine gun focused in their direction. The rest of the soldiers were nowhere in sight.

The sheriff stuffed newly reloaded clips into pouches on his web harness. "These fuckers seem to know what they're doing. They're following the number-one rule of street fighting."

"What's that?"

"Stay out of the goddamned street. They're blasting through walls and destroying the buildings behind them as they go."

Suddenly the ASV rolled forward, firing indiscriminately. Then a colossally loud explosion echoed across the town and they could hear masonry walls collapsing and wood snapping as a whole building avalanched into the street. The ASV's diesel engine was still advancing.

The sheriff clenched his gloved fist. "Fuck it. We've got to do something. We can't just lay here."

Ross could now see more troops coming in from the next block as he stole a glance over the Vietnam memorial Fossen was hiding behind. "Heads down, Hank. About twenty more and an ASV on that side."

"Time to fight." The sheriff crawled over toward Fossen. "Let's hit the second group while they cross the street." He took a breath. "Ready?"

Ross nodded.

Fossen nodded as well.

"On three. Two. One . . ."

They leaned around and over the edges of the solid-rock memorial and opened fire at a squad of mercenaries running across the street about a hundred meters away.

Ross fired his AK in semi-auto mode trying to focus on a line of men dressed in black body armor and tactical gear. The soldiers immediately scattered and hit the deck. At over a football field away, it was hard to tell if any of them got hit or just dove for cover.

But moments after they opened fire, the turret of the ASV escorting them swiveled in their direction and opened up with a .50-caliber machine gun.

All three of them ducked down and hugged the ground as powerful, high-velocity rounds slammed into the back of the stone memorial, eating away at the far side. Ross felt the sting of stone chips like needles on his exposed skin.

Then loud explosions erupted on the far side of the larger, World War II memorial next to them—grenades impacting with deafening concussion. Then stopped just as abruptly.

The sheriff crawled to the far side of the green, pulling a metal canister from his harness. "Far side of the street! Behind the bank columns!"

Hundreds of rounds of small-arms fire raked their position in addition to .50-caliber bullets.

The sheriff shouted over the roar. "When I pop the smoke, give it a few moments, then . . ." He jabbed his thumb toward the bank. He pulled the pin and tossed the canister over the fence halfway between both enemy forces. After a few moments, billowing clouds of white smoke began to rise—immediately raising hails of gunfire that whipped the air above them.

The sheriff led the way, rolling over the low, cosmetic fence around the green. Ross and Fossen did likewise, and followed as the sheriff half-slid and half-crawled toward the steps of the bank across the street.

They were halfway across when they heard grenades exploding among the monuments where they'd just been. Ross could see another one arching in from down the street, blasting the obelisk and toppling it. Machine-gun fire still zipped and sizzled through the air overhead, and then Fossen shouted and toppled onto the asphalt.

Both Ross and the sherriff went back and grabbed him under the armpits, leaving behind his rifle and his HUD glasses as they dragged him to relative safety behind the pillars of the bank building.

Ross reloaded his AK-47 as he stood behind a pillar.

The sheriff reloaded as well. He just shook his head and shouted over the deafening thunder in the street. "They've got too much firepower!" He eyed the stone walls and heavy wood door behind them. "I don't think we're getting out of this corner!"

"I don't think they saw us pull back." Ross looked down at Fossen, who was lying against the back wall, trying to sit up. A pool of blood was expanding around him.

"Damnit!" The sheriff crawled over to Fossen and put down his gun. "Hank, let me see where you're hit!"

Fossen shook his head. "I'm in trouble, Dave. My guts are on fire."

A bullet impacted the wall three feet to the right of him and ricocheted around the vestibule.

Fossen didn't even flinch. "Get back to the school. Look out for Lynn and Jenna."

The sheriff took off his HUD glasses, too, and looked into Fossen's eyes. "We're gonna stay right here. We're on our own goal line, Hank. You hear me? No room to lose ground." The sheriff grabbed Hank, and for the first time Ross noticed the dark cloth of the sheriff's shirt was stained with blood as well.

The sheriff held on to Fossen, stopping him from sliding down the wall. "You remember, when we were kids? You remember the heat lightning? And the creek?"

Fossen nodded weakly.

There was another deafening explosion outside and the sound of shattering glass.

Fossen looked up. "Bury me next to my dad, okay, Dave? And you look out for my girls, okay . . . ?" And then his head slumped and the sheriff held him tightly, sobbing.

Ross still stood with his back to a pillar. Outside he could hear the ASVs moving down the street, troops blasting apart nearby buildings.

The sheriff let his best friend's body slide to the floor. He left his HUD glasses as he stood with some difficulty. Then he picked up the M16 and came up behind one of the pillars.

"I'm sorry about Hank, Sheriff."

He just shook his head and wiped his nose on his sleeve.

"Let me see your wound."

"Fuck it. That's not gonna be what kills me today."

"If we're going to try and stop them from reaching the school, then it's pretty much now or never."

The sheriff nodded and looked at Ross.

They nodded to each other, and then suddenly Ross saw a very strange series of D-Space alerts running through his HUD listing—all highest priority. They indicated the launch of a number of different processes he'd never heard of, but one of which caught his eye: *Burning Man Instantiated*.

"Wait a minute. . . ."

The sheriff frowned at him. "What?"

Ross was tracking something moving along Main Street—a D-Space call-out unlike any he'd seen before. It was wreathed in flame and bore the name *Burning Man*, a two-hundredth-level Champion. Ross had never heard of such a level before.

It was coming their way.

"Get your HUD glasses on, Sheriff. Something's up."

He looked like he'd had enough games, but he moved out of Ross's sight, while Ross tried to peek out into the street.

Ross could see two ASVs in the street, drawing fire from other townspeople in nearby buildings. Just then the building across the way detonated in a massive explosion, sending brick, wood, glass, and clouds of dust out into the street.

But through the dust an avatar approached with a confident walk that seemed familiar. It was headed directly for Ross, walking straight through mercenaries and the hull of an intervening ASV like a ghost and emerging from the other side.

The avatar appeared to be dressed in a tactical operations suit, with a bulletproof helmet and mask as well as
body armor. He had twin .45 pistols in combat holsters,
but was otherwise unarmed. As the avatar came to the
foot of the stairs it turned to Ross and flipped up its
faceplate.

Roy Merritt nodded to him and spoke in his familiar
even tone. *"Everything's going to be okay, sir. I need you to
stay calm and tell me where the bad guys are. . . ."*

The Major stood in a command-and-control trailer lined
with dozens of LCD screens and control boards. Board
operators and drone pilots in headsets sat at each station
monitoring every aspect of Operation Prairie Fire from
above.

The Argus R-7 surveillance blimps were barely eighty
feet long, but they could loiter over a theater of operations for up to two weeks using the solar cells covering
their upper surface. One of the aerospace firms in their
group had developed it and had sold hundreds to dictatorships in Africa, Asia, and the Middle East.

Flying at sixty thousand feet with no telltale contrail,
they were all but invisible to the naked eye, and their
sensitive long-range cameras could pinpoint and monitor
individuals or entire communities, especially when combined with telecommunications and purchasing records.
They weren't invisible to radar or other sensors, but it
was the public they were meant to monitor, not military
opponents.

On the screens before him, the Argus cameras
showed FLIR and color imagery of civilians in darknet

communities in several Midwestern states. The forms on-screen were fleeing, fighting, hiding—but in all cases losing as the private military contractors squeezed them ever closer to their final stand.

Standing next to him was the towering South African colonel Andriessen. "Good news from your special unit."

The Major nodded. "Yes, but they've lost their transport."

Short, loud beeps and red lights activated on several control boards.

"And it looks like this will be wrapped up fairly soon as well."

The Major nodded as the beeping continued to spread along the flight line. Several flight officers pulled off their headsets and started talking urgently with their tech officers. Some LCD screens nearby were no longer showing stable close-up shots of street fighting, but instead showed whirling blurs, then blackness, then blurred lights again.

The Major walked over to a nearby flight officer who was struggling with his controls. "What's going on? Why have we lost video?"

The officer turned off the alarms and pointed to another screen showing a row of red numbers next to critical measurements. "The temperature readings on our avionics system just red-lined. I think we've got a fire on board."

The tech officer leaned in. "Our fire suppression system did activate. So, give us a moment. . . ."

The Major looked in both directions down the line of

drone pilots. There were red lights flashing on half the boards now.

The Colonel gave him a concerned look.

He started walking down the line, seeing more and more black screens. Temperature readings and pop-up messages reading *Fire!*

Within a minute virtually all of the control stations were blinking red. The video screens black. What started out as a frenzied chorus of urgent talk had turned into a reading room of technicians flipping through three-ring SOP manuals.

The Major shouted down to the Colonel, still standing where he'd left him. "What the hell's going on, Colonel?"

The Colonel looked at all the blank screens and said nothing.

"How the fuck can this happen? The Daemon penetrated our encryption somehow and overrode our avionics." He grabbed a headset sitting on the nearby board and hurled it onto the static-free tile floor with all his might, shattering it into several pieces. "Goddamnit! What is this, fucking amateur hour? I thought we put together the best goddamn electronic countermeasures team possible."

The Colonel apparently thought it wise to just listen until he was asked a direct question.

The entire line of board operators was now looking up at The Major. They were shut down—blind to a complex multidimensional operation that required close coordination across six states.

The Major burned holes into them with his stare,

and then stormed out of the trailer. "Colonel, get these drones back on line or get more."

"They won't get here in time."

"Then get amateur astronomers with binoculars in a fucking Piper Cub—but get me real-time information on my battle space. Is that understood?"

"Yes, Major."

They were now walking among several large trailers placed within an aircraft hangar—thick bundles of power cables running from each.

A Korr Military Services communications officer stuck his head out of a nearby trailer. "Major! You need to hear this."

He extended a pair of radio headsets.

"It's coming over all our encrypted channels."

The Major hesitated before putting them to his ear. He heard a vaguely familiar voice speaking over the comms. . . .

Ross listened to the booming voice, echoing across the town. It seemed to be coming from the sky and was loud enough to be heard over the sound of nearby machine-gun fire. . . .

"Attention enemy force: you have unlawfully invaded this community. Drop your weapons and surrender and you will not be harmed."

The gunfire and explosions had paused. There was sudden calm as the voice in the sky spoke again, this time in a foreign language that sounded vaguely Slavic— yet not Russian. It was nonetheless a voice Ross recognized as that of Roy Merritt.

The sheriff meanwhile had his HUD glasses back on and frowned in confusion. "Where is that coming from?"

Ross pointed into the street. "Him."

They both looked down and saw the Merritt avatar with his hands at the edges of his mouth "shouting" his terms to the entire town.

"But it's coming from the sky."

"Hypersonic sound." On the sheriff's look, he explained, "High-frequency audio beam projection. I'll show you later—just listen. . . ."

They could now hear laughter emanating from the private military contractors arrayed around the town, standing behind their ASVs or crouching in nearby buildings.

"You have violated the popular will of a critical mass of the population—which empowers me to take you into custody—by force if necessary."

A distant shout. "Fuck you!" Followed by gales of automatic weapon fire.

"You have been warned."

As Ross watched, Merritt's avatar raised its hands and looked up into the sky—where Ross suddenly saw a grid of numeric D-Space call-outs appear and slowly grow larger. As they did, physical objects came into sight— what could only be described as shimmering mirrored "dots" or tiny spheres coming down from above. It was impossible to say how large they were because he had no scale reference, but from his limited view looking up from between bank pillars, he saw at least five—arrayed in an orderly pattern. Merritt's avatar lowered his hands, bringing the dots even lower. They appeared to be spinning very fast, shimmering.

The sheriff looked up, too. "What are they?"

Ross clicked on one of the call-outs and read its properties. "Hot mirror . . . faceted high-rotation inertial gyroscope . . . see FireStrike. . . ." He clicked a link. "One-hundred-kilowatt solid-state laser . . . infrared." He looked back at the sheriff. "I think the shit is about to hit the fan. . . ."

A bullet whined past and ricocheted off the wall.

Ross ducked but then heard Merritt speak again. *"Network citizens! I need your help to identify the enemy. Aim any D-Space pointing device at enemy units until they throw down their weapons and raise their hands in surrender. You must respect their surrender. You will be scanned for honesty after this is over. Please keep pets and small children indoors. Thank you."*

Ross and the sheriff exchanged puzzled looks, but Ross put down his AK-47 and clicked on his D-Space pointer. It appeared much like a laser dot, but was visible only in D-Space. He cautiously peered out from behind the pillar and aimed his finger at a machine gunner sitting in the turret of the nearest ASV, bringing the dot to bear on the man's head.

In moments, a discernable beam—like an intense ray of sunlight—shot from the nearest mirror ball and burned through the particle-filled air, becoming invisible by the time it reached the ground. But the soldier leapt up and tore off his helmet, screaming, and rolled off the turret. Other soldiers looked at him and ran to assist. Ross turned his pointer to them, and each time he brought it to bear, they quickly stopped what they were doing and fled several yards.

"Sheriff, do you know how to use your pointer?"

He was already pulling his haptic glove on. "Hell, *everyone* does. . . ."

In a few moments other rays of energy were zapping down from above, and the soldiers were scurrying around like ants under a magnifying glass. It didn't take long for dozens more darknet members behind sandbags and shutters to join in.

Nor did it take long for the mercenaries to focus their gunfire up at the distant mirror balls that were raining down terror upon them. Tracer bullets started spraying skyward. But the devices were apparently more distant than they seemed, or durable. And even though one eventually did falter, wobble, and spin out of control into the streets below. There were many more of them.

In minutes the soldiers were fleeing their positions. Even soldiers in windows weren't safe—the array of mirror balls always seemed to provide a vector that could zap them. They pulled back into the shadows.

Meanwhile the sheriff showed the intensity of an all-night gamer. "Fry, you bastards!"

The Merritt avatar stood apparently observing the action. *"Enemy force, you may not leave this area. You must surrender. If you lay down your weapons and surrender, you will not be harmed."*

The remote turrets of the nearest ASV were spraying the buildings as the soldiers retreated by the dozen down the streets—unable to find cover because they'd destroyed every structure between here and the edge of town.

Ross and the sheriff focused on the firing ASV, and they saw many other pointers do likewise—clustered on its engine vents, or big rubber tires. Burning rays of heat fried airborne smoke particles on the way down their target, and before long the engine compartment on the vehicle began to smoke.

The sheriff stared intently at it. "God help you when you get out of that thing, you sons a bitches. . . ."

Now more than a few soldiers were kneeling in various places in the street, their arms raised. Several assault rifles were lying on the pavement. One of the retreating soldiers opened fire on them, cutting several down before they got involved in a firefight among themselves. They, too, were quickly subdued, and to Ross's amazement, he was soon looking at a staggered array of kneeling mercenaries extending down the street.

The other ASVs in town were roaring back where they came from, soldiers trying to grab on.

Merritt shouted again. *"You may not leave. You will be stopped if you try to leave. Surrender!"*

There no longer appeared to be any resisting soldiers in view. The enemy was in full retreat. Ross couldn't help but smile at the apparition of Roy Merritt standing firm in the public square.

Ross turned to the sheriff, who was now leaning back against the pillar.

"About that bleeding. I think I'm gonna need a doctor, after all. . . ."

Chapter 33: // Epic Fail

Central_news.com

Insurgent Reprisals Against **Civilians**—In a disturbing development, **terrorists** in **Midwestern states** have taken to **burning** entire **towns** in retaliation for resistance by hometown militias. Officials speaking on condition of anonymity were confident that **martial law** would be **expanded** to bordering states to halt the spread of the **fighting**, and that private **security forces** would be given an **expanded** role.

"**M**ajor, something powerful came out of the darknet—something we could not have anticipated." The Major walked briskly toward a private Gulfstream V jet—one he had recently acquired. A knot of uniformed private military officers followed him.

"This is a colossal intelligence failure, Colonel. I was told these communities had no significant weaponry or defenses, and we developed our force posture from that assessment. Now I've got a client who, instead of facing a compliant population after the crash, might be facing a general uprising."

"Ag, they didn't have significant weapon systems when the assessment was done."

"Sobol was devilishly clever. Perhaps too clever. Now we'll have to come back and bloody carpet bomb these towns from the stratosphere."

The Major shook his head. "Sobol wasn't behind this."

"What do you mean, Major? Of course he was: it's the Daemon."

The Major stopped at the foot of the jet stairway. "Roy Merritt has become a folk hero to the darknet community. Why—who the fuck knows? But he has, and that 'powerful' system avatar that came out of the darknet today was patterned on Merritt."

"How do you know this, Major?"

"I have my methods. But suffice it to say, Merritt's legend—and the video to prove it—is bouncing all over the darknet tonight."

The Colonel was speechless.

"Let there be no doubt, Colonel: the Daemon is evolving. Sobol apparently provided a mechanism to permit the user population to change it. And it's that mechanism that's going to help us bend the Daemon to our purpose."

"Then, the loss of our forces is . . ."

"Still a colossal fuck-up. Any word on the number of men lost?"

"We've lost the entire damned force, sir."

"And their equipment?"

The Colonel just shook his head.

"Goddamnit. Now we're going to have to redraft the entire psychological operations program. And reshoot all those news broadcasts we taped—goddamnit to hell!"

"That the entire security force was wiped out by supposed gang-bangers isn't going to help the privatization sales pitch, sir."

"All of this can be dealt with. We just need Operation Exorcist to succeed, or all of this will come back to haunt us."

Sebeck returned to consciousness as he was being dragged across a field by his elbows. It was daylight, so he must have been unconscious for a while. He felt groggy, as though he'd been drugged. His hands were zip-tied behind his back, and tape covered his mouth. His HUD glasses were long gone. His armored helmet was gone. The crackling of automatic weapon fire could be heard some ways off, punctuated by soldiers speaking into radio headsets.

"Tango. Delta, Zulu. Five, six, three. We are *go* for extraction. Repeat, go for extraction. Over."

Sebeck craned his neck back to see what was behind him—but it was too difficult. As they dragged him forward, he passed a dozen mercenary soldiers leering and laughing. The situation was starting to become clear.

His quest was finished. He had failed. The soldiers carried him toward the tailgate of a waiting pickup truck, where they tossed Sebeck into the cargo bay. He landed face-first on the corrugated steel alongside an unconscious Price. He had never been happier to see Price's puffy red face and flaring nostrils. At least he was still breathing.

The tailgate slammed shut, and the pickup lurched forward. Sebeck tried to turn his face away from the rough, scratched metal of the cargo bed. He managed to turn on his side and saw trees racing past overhead.

Before long the pickup truck was racing down a road so fast that the soldiers on either side of him kept tensing their muscles to deal with the impact of bumps. They occasionally opened fire on unseen targets, but otherwise, Sebeck just listened to the roar of the truck engine.

In a few minutes the truck lurched off the road and moved across quieter ground—grass perhaps. The truck skidded to a stop, and the soldiers piled out. Sebeck was then grabbed by the ankles and yanked off the truck, causing his face and shoulder to hit the ground first. He was dragged across several yards of meadow grass, struggling to get his face out of the dirt. They finally let go of his feet and pulled him up by his elbows again.

As Sebeck looked around, he realized these men didn't view him as a human being. He was like a piece of meat. An objective. Nothing more.

He could hear another mercenary behind him speaking on a radio. Sebeck couldn't understand why the soldiers suddenly had radio communications. Didn't the ultrawideband emanations of the darknet disable other radio communications? He was probably misunderstanding it. Or perhaps the heavyweight defense people were starting to get involved. Someone had invented ultrawideband, after all, and Sebeck didn't think it was Sobol.

Glancing around he saw there were twenty or thirty soldiers in the field, all dressed as farmers or laborers—some with bandages on their arms and legs, real or faked. They were a mix of races. So their bond was the mission. Or their contract.

A few soldiers approached Sebeck with what looked to be a parachute harness. They roughly grabbed him and wrapped it around his torso. As they worked, he could see two other men unwinding a steel cable from a spool.

One of the soldiers, a Latino with a teardrop tattoo under one eye, grabbed Sebeck's jaw. "You're goin' for a ride, *hombre*!" He laughed and turned Sebeck so he could see what looked like a weather balloon being lofted skyward, dragging a steel cable up with it. As Sebeck looked farther up into the sky, he could see another elongated, translucent balloon already ascending with a cable beneath it. Just then Sebeck saw Laney Price lifted up and hurtled skyward.

What the hell?

Then a steel cable lifted up off the grass nearby, coming taut just as the harness around Sebeck yanked tight. He suddenly launched up into the air, too, rapidly ascending. Sebeck twisted in the wind, watching the ground recede beneath him. In just a few moments he was hundreds of feet in the air with a view of the distant town of Greeley, still shrouded in columns of black smoke. He could also see torched farmhouses dotting the landscape—a scene of devastation. The only hopeful sign was the variegated landscape of grass, crops, and the saplings of recently planted orchards.

However, as Sebeck kept ascending, rising thousands of feet into the air, his view broadened, and he could see the bigger picture was the larger ocean of corn in which this island of variety was planted. The monoculture of corn stretched from horizon to horizon—and none of those farms was burning.

Sebeck hung there realizing the vastness of his failure. They hadn't even made a dent in the old system. And here it was carrying them away—to disappear forever.

Sebeck kept rising, listening to the slap of the steel cable against the back of his harness as he swayed in the wind. He wondered why he wasn't afraid of the height. Between his feet he could see thousands of feet to the broad plain below. He was actually level with the nearby clouds.

Then he heard the roar of approaching aircraft engines. He wriggled his body to turn enough to see— and there, some miles away, he could see the head-on view of what looked to be a C-130 cargo plane, chopping at the wind on a collision course with him. He watched it with silent amazement. *No effing way . . .*

As the plane approached he could see what looked to be a V-shaped fork extending from the nose of the aircraft and running some ways away from the fuselage. It was a collection fork, and, as Sebeck watched, the C-130 headed straight for the balloon. He winced as the plane roared past only fifty feet overhead.

As it did so, the steel catch fork grabbed the balloon, instantly yanking the cable and accelerating Sebeck so violently that he blacked out again.

Chapter 34: // Cold Reality

Pete Sebeck sat strapped to a thick wooden chair in a brightly lit holding cell. The chair was bolted to the concrete floor with L brackets. They'd taken his clothes and left him nude. He felt vulnerable. Helpless.

That was no doubt the purpose.

Just then the steel door of the cell opened and a man he recognized from darknet news feeds entered. It was The Major. In person he was more intimidating—a stern man with buzz-cut hair and a firm jawline. He appeared to be in excellent shape for his fortysomething age, and wore full combat fatigues in a shades-of-gray urban warfare pattern. He carried no weapons, however.

He closed the cell door behind him and examined

Sebeck without betraying emotion. No surprise. No irritation. Nothing. "Detective Sebeck."

"Major."

The Major narrowed his eyes and dragged a heavy wooden chair across the concrete floor to sit across from Sebeck. "Sergeant, I must say that I'm surprised to find you, of all people, serving the Daemon."

"I don't serve the Daemon. Where is Laney Price?"

"Tell me about your quest, Sergeant."

"I don't know what you're talking about. Where is Laney?"

"He's safe nearby—telling us everything about nothing we care about."

Sebeck stared into The Major's cold eyes. "What are you doing to him? He doesn't know anything."

"Tell me about the quest Sobol gave you. You're supposed to justify the freedom of humanity, is that it?" The Major studied Sebeck's bonds. "How is that going so far?"

Sebeck said nothing.

"What are you supposed to accomplish to achieve this quest of yours, Sergeant?"

"When are you people going to leave me alone?"

"Answer the question."

"Are you with the government?"

"It doesn't matter."

"It matters to me!"

"Don't shout. Shouting will only make you hoarse. And it won't change anything. A lot of prisoners make that mistake. Now, let's get back to your quest. How many darknet operatives are tracking the progress of your quest? How many are donating darknet credits toward its success?"

"I don't know what you're talking about."

"Don't play dumb, Sergeant. We're already creating darknet objects—like the quest Thread you followed to us."

Sebeck stared at the floor.

"We have a complete breakdown of your activities from darknet news feeds, and we know your circle of operatives. You've been on quite a journey."

Sebeck shook his head slowly. "You evil prick . . . you're carving up young people to—"

"Yes, we've infiltrated the darknet, Sergeant. We're more creative than you imagine. And unlike you, we'll do whatever's necessary to win."

"I've seen what you're capable of."

The Major looked at his watch. "Belief is malleable. All one has to do to gain access to the darknet is *believe* in its purpose. The teenage runaways I introduce to the Daemon consider me their dear friend. A friend who rescued them from life as a sex slave in some brothel—one who showed them a world they never dreamed existed. And once they're in, they become very useful to me."

"You cut off their heads and hijack their accounts!"

"Soon, we won't even need to do that."

"I thought I knew what evil was. But I was wrong."

The Major just shrugged it off. "I don't care, Sergeant. There's no shortage of unwanted people in the world. Now let's get back to this quest of yours. What happens if you succeed? What Daemon event are you trying to trigger?"

"Fuck you."

"You won't answer?"

"I don't know. That's the answer. Sobol gave me a quest, and I have no idea how to accomplish it."

"What about this D-Space Thread you're following?"

Sebeck realized with a pang of loss that he no longer could see the Thread. He no longer had HUD glasses, and D-Space was invisible to him. "I can't see it anymore."

"And what if we brought your HUD glasses? Would you lead us on the path of this Thread?"

"It wasn't meant for you."

"If you cooperate, I can give you your old life back. I can undo this curse Sobol cast on you. Make Detective Sebeck live again. Clear his name. Turn him into a hero."

Sebeck just shook his head. "I'm not the person I was then, and I don't want to be. I've seen the truth now."

The Major nodded grimly. "Why would you help the same system that took so much from you?"

"This 'system' will help people take back control—from bastards like you."

"'Bastards like me' serve a purpose. People need order, Sergeant. They need to be told what to think, what to do, what to believe, or everything will fall apart. This miracle of modern civilization doesn't just happen. It requires careful management by professionals willing to do whatever is necessary to keep things running smoothly. . . ."

"Is that what you tell yourself?"

"It's the truth, even if you don't want to hear it."

Sebeck shook his head. "I don't have to believe you. I've seen the truth with my own eyes. The people don't need to be protected from themselves."

The Major glanced at his watch again. "You disappoint me, Sergeant. You really do. I would normally have taken a more patient and deliberate approach with your case, but time is of the essence, and I must be off." He stood and pulled the chair back along the wall. "And you—along with your DNA—were officially cremated many months ago. We can't have you popping up and ruining the official story. Not now." He rapped on the metal door. A portal slid open with a clack. A moment of recognition and then the door opened.

Two beefy soldiers in ski masks with stun sticks and metal whips on their belts entered.

The Major pointed to Sebeck. "Take him and his friend out to the dump at Q-27. Put their bodies through a wood chipper. I don't want anyone to find a shred of evidence that they ever existed."

"Yes, sir."

Sebeck glared from his chair. "You motherfucker."

The Major regarded him. "Look at the bright side, Sergeant. Your quest is over." He exited as the guards pulled out their stun sticks.

Sebeck rode in the passenger bay of a heavy vehicle. A diesel engine rattling somewhere beyond steel walls. He could feel his hands lashed behind his back as he lay facedown on a hard, cold diamond-plate floor. He was still nude. Road vibration circulated through his bones.

He turned over to see several sets of combat boots nearby and looked up into the masked faces of soldiers with M4A1s slung across their chests. They looked back down menacingly.

The closest of them pointed a gloved hand in Sebeck's face. "If I get any trouble from you, I'm going to make it painful. You hear me?"

Another soldier on the opposite row of benches kicked Sebeck. "You hear him!"

Sebeck had the wind knocked out of him for a moment. As he got air back into his lungs, he turned to the man. "I'm an American. I'm one of you. Why are you treating me like this?"

"Shut the fuck up, you commie prick!"

He landed another vicious kick to Sebeck's ribs, sending him rolling.

That's when Sebeck noticed Laney Price nearby. Price was also nude, and he sat slumped with his back against the front wall of the vehicle. Price was staring into space with unseeing eyes. He rocked back and forth, muttered silently to himself. Sebeck was horrified to see Price's body. He expected that it would be overweight and just as hairy as the young man's face and arms, but instead what he saw along Price's chest, stomach, and legs was a solid mass of burn scars. Sebeck was horrified.

"Laney. Laney!"

One of the soldiers leaned into view. "Tough little fucker, that one."

Another soldier chimed in. "Yeah, you're not going to reach him. He knows how to deal with torture. Don't you, boy? You're an old hand." He smacked Price's head.

Sebeck crawled closer to Price. "Laney." Price's eyes remained unseeing as his lips moved in a repeating rhythm. The scars all over his body looked old.

"Curling iron would be my guess."

Sebeck turned to face the soldier who said it.

Another soldier shook his head. "This fucker had some sick parents."

Sebeck felt his heart dropping. He remembered Riley's words to him back at the Laguna reservation: *You never asked about Price's suffering.* How could he never have realized? It nearly swallowed him with grief. He looked to Price. "Laney. Listen to me, Laney!"

The vehicle suddenly slowed and lurched into a steep turn.

The lead non-comm stood up and grabbed an overhead handrail. "Let's finish this and get back in time for chow." He wrapped a cloth around his nose and mouth, as did the other men.

The vehicle came to a complete stop and the back wall lowered like a drawbridge. Before he could react Sebeck felt himself grabbed by the feet and dragged roughly across the diamond-plate floor. He felt the pain of a dozen small cuts, and then he was unceremoniously dumped onto the dusty ground. All he could smell was the stench of death—so thick that he tasted it as much as smelled it. He heard the squawking and shrieking of birds.

Sebeck sat up and surveyed his surroundings. They'd been traveling in some sort of six-wheeled, armored personnel carrier and arrived at a series of tall wood chip piles—probably from brush clearing at the ranch. Nearby was what looked to be a well-worn wood chipper on a trailer, its chute aimed at the smallest pile of wood chips. Just beyond the blower, crows and buzzards fed noisily on carrion already splayed in a long streak of red-brown covered with chunks of gelatinous meat. They bickered over the scraps.

The whole place reeked of dead flesh. As he glanced around he saw nothing for miles in any direction. It was just flat scrubland.

Sebeck felt Price thrown against him, and as he sat there next to Price in the dust he leaned in once more to look Price in the eyes. He got up close. "Laney! Laney, it's me, Pete! Talk to me. Please."

There was a flicker of recognition in Price's eyes, then they focused on Sebeck.

Sebeck looked around him as a squad of soldiers stared at two others pouring gasoline into the wood chipper's fuel tank. Another was preparing a video camera with a ghoulish grin on his face.

Sebeck turned back to Price. "Laney, I'm sorry. I'm sorry that it ended like this."

Price's brow contorted. "It's not your fault, Sergeant. Sometimes things end badly."

"I want to thank you for everything you've done for me. I know you didn't have to be here—and now I've gone and failed everyone."

Price shook his head slightly. "Your quest wasn't about *you*, Sergeant. It was about how people reacted to it. It was *their* quest. You're just carrying the flag."

Sebeck stopped. The truth of it hit him. It was the effect his quest had on others that was the purpose. He was just an icon. It made his burden suddenly easier to bear.

Just then the wood chipper's deafening engine roared to life, and the birds lifted off in panic, fleeting shadows against the sun. Two soldiers walked up to Sebeck. One pointed first to Sebeck, then the wood chipper. They both nodded and slung their weapons. They grabbed Sebeck by the elbows and started carrying him to the bloodstained maw of the roaring machine. Sebeck felt primordial fear grip him as he struggled and dug his bare heels into the dirt. "No!"

They dragged him, twisting and shouting.

But then it suddenly became much easier, and he fell to the ground. Oddly, he was also sopping wet. He turned up toward the man carrying him on his right, but saw that the soldier was missing from the waist up. The man's severed arm still tightly gripped Sebeck. He stared at it in disbelief. It was not the sort of thing a civilized mind readily computed.

Sebeck then realized no one was holding him to his left anymore either, and when he turned he saw his other executioner's torso had emptied its contents across the dirt. The rest of the man lay farther on.

And now Sebeck noticed that the roar of the wood chipper was punctuated with crackling gunfire and the roar of more powerful engines. He turned to see several unmanned, blade-covered motorcycles wielding twin swords, slashing at the soldiers as they raced past. Already, one of the mercenaries lay on the ground, screaming and legless. Several of the soldiers were in prone positions, firing on the motorcycles to little effect, but then clutching their eyes as green laser light played across their faces. Blinded, they tried to grope their way back to the troop carrier, but got cut down.

One of the guards managed to make it through the open armored car door, but a motorcycle followed him up the ramp and chopped him into sections with a couple swift sword slashes.

Soon their captors lay in pieces on the ground, blood everywhere, and a score of automated motorcycles slammed down hydraulic kickstands and started preening themselves like praying mantises—spinning their sword blades to clean the blood off.

Sebeck looked to Price, who sat in stunned silence, spattered in blood, but otherwise apparently okay. The only sound was the piercing drone of the wood chipper engine. Sebeck glanced around but could see only fallen bodies and pieces of bodies. He crawled on his belly toward Price, who was trying to sit up.

Price shouted. "Are you hit?"

Sebeck shook his head. "No! This is someone else's blood!"

Just then the pack of unmanned bikes parted to make way for a lone rider in a black helmet and riding suit. He drove directly up to Price and Sebeck and looked down at them. He dismounted his bike, and suddenly all the engines turned off. A gesture of his hand sent a bolt-straight arc of electricity into the wood chipper, killing its engine as well.

As the chipper wound down, the rider removed his helmet and riding gloves, revealing an unnerving sight. It was a young man, early twenties, but his eyes had been replaced with black lenses with flat black rims. Wires ran from drill holes in his bruised temples to an enclosure at the base of his neck. All of his fingers appeared to have been replaced with titanium or silver prosthetics, topped by gleaming claws. He moved stiffly, as if in pain.

The rider knelt down in front of them, staring right into Sebeck's face with his lidless, metallic eyes. An artificial voice, deep and menacing, spoke an inch or so in front of the man's mouth—without his lips moving. It was apparently hypersonic sound. "Where is The Major?"

Sebeck shook his head. "I don't know, but I just left him. They took us out here."

The rider's expression was unreadable with his metal eyes. He stood and stared at the horizon.

"Thanks for rescuing us. Who are you?"

Price answered. "He's Loki Stormbringer, Sergeant." Price leaned close and whispered. "You remember—Jon Ross mentioned him. . . ."

Sebeck did remember. The most powerful sorcerer on the darknet. And almost as ruthless as the Major himself. Sebeck couldn't help but think they deserved each other. He twisted to reveal his tied hands. "Can you please untie us, Loki?"

Loki gazed at the horizon with his dead eyes. "You should leave this place. Everything here is about to die. . . ."

With that Loki walked to his bike, and started it. His two dozen razorbacks started up as well. Then an even larger swarm of razorbacks swept past—at least a hundred strong—and Loki merged into it. A flock of dozens of microjet aircraft also howled low overhead in close formation. The entire retinue thundered into the distance, back the way the truck had brought Sebeck and Price. Back toward the center of the ranch.

Price nodded. "He's even scarier in person."

Sebeck started crawling toward nearby bodies. "We can probably find a knife on one of these."

"Hey, look."

Emerging from the edges of the wood chip piles were a couple dozen armed men in Ghillie suits. As they got closer Sebeck realized their poncho-like suits were more than just physical camouflage—they appeared to reflect whatever was on the other side of them. They were translucent.

He could see their telltale HUD glasses. They had electronic multibarrel rifles slung across their chests and gave the thumbs-up sign to Sebeck and Price as they approached.

Several of them watched the horizon and skies as a tall, muscular-looking darknet operative came up to them and flipped up his bulletproof mask to reveal that he was African American. "Are either of you hurt?"

Sebeck shook his head. "No."

"Are you The Unnamed One and Chunky Monkey?"

Price exhaled deeply. "That's us, man."

"I'm Taylor. An operative named Rakh sent us to get you."

Sebeck nodded. *Jon Ross.*

He made motions with a gloved hand in D-Space as several other darknet operatives cut Sebeck and Price's bonds. They also offered canteens to them.

He called to the others, "Morris, let's get them some clothing and gear!"

"We're on it."

Price rubbed his wrists. "That was calling it pretty goddamned close!"

"Loki Stormbringer has gathered an army of machines. He's going to attack. Many others are going to follow him in."

"Attack? What attack?"

"We came to stop Operation Exorcist. Unmanned vehicles are opening up the roads. We're pushing in overland."

"You're here for The Major and his men?"

"Yes. Have you seen him?"

Sebeck felt his temper starting to flare. "Yeah, and if you're going after him, we're going with you."

Chapter 35: // Infil

Only on the Texas prairie could a three-thousand-square-foot home be called a bungalow. Natalie Philips's quarters were located in a cluster of other bungalows, all done in Southwestern style—tiny Alamos of white plastered brick with flat roofs and a cosmetic bell tower. It was part of a subdivision of corporate residences located about a mile from the main house across landscaped grounds with fountains, ornamental gardens, and rows of poplars. Beyond the complex the prairie extended unbroken to the horizon. It was peaceful out here. Actual solitude.

The interiors of the bungalow were first-rate—hardwood planks, adobe walls, and hand-hewn beams. High ceilings, handwoven rugs, and expensive-looking Southwestern art adorning the walls. The entertainment centers for each bungalow were insane. Seventy-inch plasma televisions with surround-sound stereo systems linked to an impressive music and movie library drawn off of some central server—but no Web access. No outside phone service, only in-house room service. There was a fully stocked bar and a small kitchenette with a microwave, as well as a disproportionately large dining room that could easily seat a dozen people. There was a separate servants' entrance with a ramp for bringing in carts, connected to concealed servant paths that ran between the homes behind hedges and fences—as though they were modern Mad Ludwigs, unwilling to countenance the serving staff.

Philips sat alone at the dining room table looking at a powerful laptop linked in to the ranch's expansive network. A laptop they'd given her and which she was certain was riddled with spyware.

Aldous Johnston had named half a dozen world-class cryptanalysts and software scientists working on Operation Exorcist—but she hadn't actually *seen* any of them. She'd just been here, waiting. Even though this was supposed to be an emergency, they hadn't asked her to do a damn thing. She'd left a dozen messages with Johnston's admin assistant to find out when she'd be able to get an outside line to talk with Deputy Director Fulbright back at the NSA—as they agreed she could—but no one had gotten back to her. All she had was 24/7 access to food, music, and a huge library of movies.

With representative democracy about to be subverted, kicking back and watching television wasn't high on her priority list. However, she'd turned on the news to give the impression that she was behaving normally. Recent experience had shown that predictable patterns of behavior were more likely to keep the data gods off her back, and she wanted to foster the belief that she could be trusted.

The news was all bad—civil unrest in the Midwest,

the dollar had fallen to record lows against the euro and yuan, and stock markets around the world were incredibly volatile, spiking and falling. Chaos.

And the resounding theme of the media blitz was unmistakable: *you are not safe—you need security.*

Philips listened to the news as she sat at the dining room table examining the plastic RFID bracelet affixed to her wrist. She held it up to the light to try to see through the thin plastic band. Boynton had said it was tamper-resistant, and she assumed this meant it had a wire antenna braided into its length that would be severed if the bracelet were broken. The whole ranch complex was littered with RFID readers—she'd spotted no less than six here in the bungalow. The sudden loss of a signal would undoubtedly put her unique RFID number into alarm and summon security to investigate.

Unless she could slip this digital leash, she wasn't going to be able to escape or do anything else without their knowledge. It was becoming apparent that she was under house arrest—at least until Operation Exorcist was completed. By then it would be too late. They would have taken over the Daemon and solidified their control.

Philips knew an RFID tag was just a circuit attached to an antenna. It used energy from a radio wave to activate the circuit and broadcast its unique ID on a specific frequency. That's how it could broadcast its location to Sky Ranch Security without needing a battery.

The ISO 15693 standard common for RFID proximity cards and mobile payment systems meant this bracelet was probably operating at 13.56 MHz—which was a commercial frequency.

Philips had attended conferences where hacker groups demonstrated homemade devices able to harvest and spoof RFID tags at will. The question was whether Philips could build something similar with the materials here in the bungalow. If she could make them think she was home when she wasn't, she might be able to trip up their plans.

The place was packed with consumer electronics—but not a lot of them wireless. She'd gathered the few wireless devices she had onto the dining room table to examine their FCC labels.

There was the cordless phone handset and its base station—a 1.9 GHz DECT unit. Not much use. Likewise, all of the television and stereo remotes were infrared, not radio based. There was the 2.4 GHz Wi-Fi transmitter in the laptop. This was a decidedly more crowded spectrum here on the ranch, but also useless for interacting at 13.56 MHz. Of course, she also had her Acura TL car remote entry key, which she recalled worked somewhere in the 300–400 MHz range, but attached to the same key chain she had her RFID gas payment fob, which she had disassembled to reveal a tiny clear plastic bulb containing a spool of copper wire connected to a small circuit board. It was the proper frequency, but there was a problem: its code was burned into the circuitry at the factory. Unchangeable—at least theoretically. And she had no specialized tools.

Philips looked back up at the cable news playing on

the television. Now in addition to the fighting in the Midwest, a series of major Internet outages had begun to "grip the nation"—or so the media claimed. It was being blamed on sabotage. On domestic "terrorists" blowing up critical fiber-optic lines at vulnerable junctions. The very things they were doing to stifle dissent were being used as the justification for making draconian measures permanent. And everywhere was video of smartly attired private security forces rushing to rescue besieged towns, to restore service. How was it possible that they could do all this? How could they possibly get away with it?

Philips sighed in exasperation—but then stopped cold. On the wall next to her a message was spelled out in brilliant red laser light:

Your room is bugged.

The butter knife she was planning on using as a screwdriver dropped from her hand with a clang. The glowing message changed to read:

Open the service door and do not speak.

She turned around.

There at the rear service door stood a man dressed in a black Nomex flight suit, body armor, and utility vest. A balaclava covered his head and advanced-looking night vision goggles covered his eyes. In his gloved hands he held a laser pointing device aimed at Philips's dining room wall.

She recovered from the shock and walked to the service door. After a moment's hesitation she opened it.

The intruder ducked past her and closed the door, holding a gloved finger to his lips.

He pulled a wandlike device from his utility harness and started scanning the walls, light fixtures, and furniture with it.

As she watched, Philips listened to the news playing in the background, continuing its litany of financial and social woes. Philips turned up the volume.

Anji Anderson was on-screen as part of a panel with other pundits. She spoke authoritatively for someone who had a few short years ago been a lifestyles reporter. *"People can't simply blame others for their plight. They need to lift themselves up by their bootstraps, but it appears that some people don't want to do that. They want to take from others in pursuit of what they call"*—air quotes—*"'fairness.'"*

The stranger meanwhile was teasing a small bugging device out of her dining room lamp with tweezers. He held it up for Philips to see, then placed it in one of several chambers in a small metal box.

He continued scanning for bugs as Philips followed him

It took nearly twenty minutes, but by the time he was done, he had located eight bugs in all—from the bar to the bathroom to the bedroom. The stranger then sat down on a changing bench at the foot of the bed and removed his hood and goggles. Jon Ross sighed in relief and smiled at her. "There we go."

"Jon! My god . . ." She rushed to hold his face in her hands. There was that slight crinkle at the corner of his eyes when he smiled that she missed so much. Before she had time to think about it, she was kissing him passionately. After a moment she pulled back to look at him.

He gazed back, and then pulled her close, kissing her harder, longer, and with a strength that almost squeezed the breath from her.

He eventually relaxed his hold. "I thought I'd lost you."

"How on earth did you find me?"

He tugged on the silver chain around her neck, coming up with the amulet he'd created for her.

She scowled. "You gave me a tracking device? How romantic . . ."

"It's more an amulet of protection."

"Protection from what?"

"From Loki—and people like him. I didn't want his machines harming you."

She studied the amulet and then turned back to him. Philips pointed to the metal box on the nearby table. "You're sure they can't hear us?"

Ross nodded. "Bug Vault. It produces generic sounds of human habitation—footsteps, television, stuff like that. It'll make them think their bugs are still in place."

"How the hell did you get past ranch security? This place is surrounded by the best surveillance system money can buy."

"Yeah, they're using the latest technology—a Beholder Unified Surveillance System designed by Haverford Systems. State of the art."

She looked puzzled.

"Let's just say it has some flaws built in, compliments of the Chinese people."

She sat down next to him. "I was worried I'd never see you again." Philips looked at him gravely. "But why would you take such a stupid risk to come here?"

"I came to get you, Nat."

"What made you think I needed rescuing? This is where I need to be. They're about to launch Operation Exorcist, and unless I can stop them, they'll take control of the Daemon."

He contemplated her words. "The Weyburn Labs people have expanded on the work you and I did at Building Twenty-Nine. They're starting to crack their way into the Daemon's darknet. I don't know how they did it, but they've started spoofing people and creating darknet objects. They used it to capture Pete Sebeck, and he's here on the ranch now."

"Where did you hear that?"

"From Pete Sebeck."

"Peter Sebeck is *alive*?"

"Yeah, look, it's a long story, but Sobol rescued Sebeck from his execution and sent him on a quest to justify humanity's freedom. The Major just kidnapped Sebeck and brought him here. There's about to be a serious showdown, Nat, and I need to get you out of here."

"I'm not going anywhere."

"Loki Stormbringer is headed this way with an army of machines. There are two dozen darknet factions on his heels. Once Loki's army is gathered, this whole place will be a war zone."

"*The* Loki?" She sat on the arm of a nearby sofa and shook her head. "I can't leave, Jon."

"Why not? This isn't your—"

"Look, you have no idea how happy I am to see you, and I can't tell you how much it touches me that you risked your life to rescue me. But I can't go. The plutocrats are planning to execute some sort of cyber warfare attack. Physically storming this ranch won't stop it. I need to figure out what they're really up to and stop them. Luckily, I have some clues." She brought him over to a huge stack of documents on a nearby desk. "They've given me tech documentation on Operation Exorcist—but something about it doesn't make sense."

"Operation Exorcist?"

"Yes. Remember the Destroy function of the Daemon—the command that destroys all data in a Daemon-infected corporation? Well, they've come up with a blocker."

"How the hell did—?"

"They figured out that if they use a format-string hack, they could inject executable code through the tax ID function parameter. It puts the Destroy function into an infinite loop so that it doesn't return a value."

"Meaning the Destroy command won't be issued . . . making the Daemon harmless to them."

She nodded.

"Can they really inject it into all the Daemon-infected networks?"

"The *Ragnorok* module is a Web API. They can invoke the function from anywhere."

"Jesus . . ."

"They could do it with a *script*. They're using the Daemon's own high availability against it."

Ross gestured to the piles of technical documents marked "Top Secret." "But you said something's not adding up."

"Yes. I've spent the last forty-eight hours examining all this, and it just looks too rosy."

"A ruse?"

She nodded. "Jon, they're planning on launching their Daemon-blocker attack from thousands of machines, and then they're going to send in police and paramilitary strike teams to seize tens of thousands of data centers around the world—all at once. It would easily be the largest covert operation launched in the history of mankind—by several orders of magnitude—and I don't see how an international operation this size could be kept secret."

"You mean from the Daemon?"

"I mean from anyone."

She picked up a sheaf of documents. "So how am I supposed to believe this? It's not credible."

"So Operation Exorcist is a lie."

"Or we don't know what the real Operation Exorcist is. They've basically put me under house arrest here to read through propaganda—so when things go to hell, I can attest to some congressional subcommittee how diligently Weyburn Labs and Korr were working toward defeating the Daemon."

She threw up her hands. "But I saw *armies* of corporate soldiers down at the airfield. Something serious is about to go down."

Ross grimaced. "Darknet news feeds have noticed private security forces moving into position to defend property—office towers, media centers, telecom infrastructure, and utilities. Also high-end gated communities."

They sat for a few moments contemplating what that meant. The sound of murmuring television voices came from downstairs.

Ross looked at her. "So I can't convince you to leave?"

"I care about you more than you know, but my duty is here."

He grinned slightly in respect of her choice; then he moved over to the fifty-inch plasma screen mounted in a hutch in front of the bed. He pulled the television away from the wall on its swivel mount.

"What are you doing?"

He produced a small electronic device from one of his harness pockets, and uncoiled an HDMI cable, which he used to connect the device to the television.

"I'm opening the surveillance system's back door to other darknet operatives so that they can help us collectively keep an eye on what's going on here on the ranch. We'll have a better shot at finding anything important with tens of thousands of people searching with us." He spoke into D-Space. "Rakh, requesting high-priority Thread: review all camera imagery at Sky Ranch for evidence of complicity in current social disturbances. Publicize findings, ASAP."

In a few moments, the screen showed an hourglass with a label reading: *Number of Respondents*. The number rapidly incremented into the thousands, gaining speed by the second.

"So . . . *thirteen thousand* people are searching the surveillance system for suspicious activity?"

He nodded. "This ranch is on a maximum-priority Thread—we're all concerned about it. And it doesn't hurt to have a good reputation score when summoning a smart mob." He peered at the screen. "Past twenty thousand now."

She was stunned. "This is amazing." She closely watched the screen.

Almost immediately a "suspicious" item came up on the screen as a link. It read simply: *Broadcast News Set— by dPooley.*

"They found something."

"Thanks, dPooley. . . ." Ross clicked on the video link and brought up a live surveillance feed of a full-sized television sound stage, complete with green screens. The set looked quiet.

"A news studio."

Ross clicked out to an overhead map of all the cameras in that location, bringing up a 3-D model of the building it was in. "Hang on a second, I have an idea."

Philips pointed at the overhead map. "Look, they've got a satellite farm. This is a complete broadcasting facility."

Ross brought up another view—this one of the producer's control room. It showed an array of large screens as well as a window onto the studio beyond. "Do you think they're creating the news here at the ranch?"

Philips shook her head. "It's just one studio, and the

news is running 24/7 on a dozen channels at once. This has some other purpose."

"Let's roll this back in time."

"We can do that?"

"Yeah. One of the big selling points of the Beholder system was detecting recurring patterns over time—people casing embassies, that sort of thing. It can store *huge* amounts of video. Here . . ." Ross moved his hands, interacting with invisible controls. "I'm going to run backward to the last time there was activity in this control room."

The image of the control room stayed relatively unchanged, even though the lighting changed very slightly, indicating a passage of time and voltage fluctuations in the overhead lights. Suddenly the room sprang into life, and there were several people in the control booth. Ross slowed down the rewind and kept rolling it back until there was a hand signal being given to a distant anchorperson sitting at the green screen desk. He clicked the video into play mode.

Suddenly audio came through and they could clearly see the computer-enhanced image of the anchor on the central control board screen.

Philips shot a look at Ross. "Anji Anderson!"

He nodded. "So it is. . . ."

"Then she's here at the ranch."

On-screen Anderson was delivering the news next to a disturbing graphic with the word "Cybergeddon" in bold, terrifying letters. She was in midsentence. . . .

"—responsible for this unprecedented attack on modern civilization. It appears that a cataclysmic loss of corporate

data has occurred. The New York and American Stock Exchanges have been closed, along with most other world stock exchanges. Again, we have no word on whether this happened during the blackout, before the blackout, or just before. But if you're just now joining us, there has apparently been a cyber attack of unprecedented magnitude against the world electrical grid. Most of North America, Europe, and parts of Asia have been without power for the last seventy-two hours."

They were showing video of looting and fires looming over downtown areas throughout the world. Some of the scenes were at night.

"These are images of some of the looting and sporadic violence that's unfolding worldwide. The U.S. government has declared martial law—and there's talk that perhaps the domestic terrorists in the Midwestern United States were behind the attack. In all, the death toll may number in the tens of thousands. No one knows whether the perpetrators have been apprehended or are still at large. All that's known is the data of thousands of public companies has been destroyed in what might have been an electromagnetic pulse weapon attack coordinated to cause maximum damage to Western economies. Security forces are securing key facilities and launching humanitarian missions at this hour. Certainly, this is the biggest shock to hit the world since 9/11, and I don't think I'm wrong in saying that. Let's pray that someone can help put a stop to—"

Ross clicked the STOP button. He then sent the video out to the darknet, flagged *maximum priority*. Then he and Philips stared into space for several moments in silence, her hand over her mouth in horror.

Philips spoke first. "They're going to deliberately invoke the Destroy function against everyone else. And in the chaos, they'll seize control."

Philips just held her head in her hands.

"We can still do something, Natalie. People know about this now." She stood up and walked through a pair of French doors to get some fresh air. There was a patio just off the bedroom on the second floor, and it overlooked the grassy plain leading up to the huge main house in the distance. It was lit up like Cape Canaveral. Baroque music could be heard coming softly from the mansion, Vivaldi's *Four Seasons*, and she could see shadows of party guests moving about on the terraces among ornamental lights.

Ross followed her outside, and they both stood at the railing.

Philips spoke matter-of-factly. "The Weyburn Labs team is preparing to hijack what's left of the Daemon. They're going to use it as a means to control people—just like Sobol did. Only this time, for their personal benefit."

"Nat—"

"Even if we stop their plan, they'll still seize control of the Daemon."

The music in the background didn't match the grimness of their predicament.

Ross gazed at the distant party. "The plutocrats' ball."

She nodded. "Celebrating their victory."

Philips turned to see Ross come up alongside her and put a hand on her shoulder.

She shook her head. "I gave it to them, Jon. We cracked

Sobol's code, and I gave it to the plutocrats. The same API they'll use as a weapon against the world. How many generations will be reduced to slavery because of me?"

"You couldn't have known."

"I'm supposed to be able to find the real message in the noise, Jon. That was my gift."

"You had faith in democracy, Natalie. There's nothing wrong with that."

Tears started to roll down her face. "Not you, though. You were the smart one. You never had faith in anyone but yourself."

He grimaced. "You know that's not true." He leaned against the stone wall, his back to the distant soiree. His eyes settled on her.

Philips shook her head. "It all seems so clear now. Corporate intrusion into public institutions. Corporate domination of culture and media. It happened in plain view, with us cheering on their success as if it reflected well on us. As if it *was* us."

"By now millions of people know the truth. In a couple of hours, we'll have enough people mobilized to stop them. We can still beat them, Nat."

She laughed ruefully. "*How*, Jon? They own everything. They're not a stupid computer program. They can't be hacked. And the Daemon *can* be hacked."

She felt ashamed imagining the gargantuan social, financial, and commercial networks arrayed against them. Their opponents were so numerous. So powerful. "We can't beat them."

They sat in silence for a few moments, the music providing a backdrop.

He sighed. "You always wanted to know my real name."

She looked up at him in surprise.

"If you want to know my name, I'll tell you. . . ."

"Jon, I—"

"I am Ivan Borovich. My father was Aleksey Borovich. He died on October fourth, 1993, after Boris Yeltsin dissolved our democratically elected legislature. My father went to defend it, but he was killed when tanks shelled the Russian White House and Yeltsin's troops stormed in shooting. Media in the West called my father a 'communist holdout.' But he laid down his life for democracy. Not for himself—but for *me*, and my brothers and sisters. And his countrymen."

Philips moved closer to him as he spoke. "Jon . . ."

"They may beat us, Natalie, but as long as there's another generation, there will always be hope."

She kissed him tenderly, forgetting for the moment her anguish and doubt.

Chapter 36: // Downtime

In the Sky Ranch Ops Center, Weyburn Labs network analysts calmly spoke instructions into headsets while the chief operating officer of Korr Military Solutions, General Andrew Connelly, and senior partner, Aldous Johnston, stared at a huge media wall. Television news feeds from every channel in the Western world were tiled along the wall to either side. Live spy satellite imagery from a dozen locations around the globe were tiled on screens all along the bottom row.

But the large central screen was a wonder to behold. Spread across its thirty feet was an awe-inspiring image of Earth—live high-definition video from twenty thousand miles in orbit. The day-night line cut diagonally across the eastern edge of Russia, with North America in a band of daylight that stretched to the Western seaboard of Europe. Most of the Southern Hemisphere lay in darkness. Great swaths of Europe were woven with intricate filaments of light, blending into the glow of metropolitan sprawl. Knotted clumps of light daisy-chained across the landscape. Japan glowed like a tear in a lampshade down in the Pacific.

Connelly could see the lights from the vast night-fishing fleets in the Sea of Japan. The lights of Seoul bringing back fond memories of the DMZ. Beijing, Hong Kong, and Mumbai glittered. Indonesia blazing in the South Seas. Wildfires raging in north-central Australia. More traceries of light stretching along the Trans-Siberian rail line into Russia's heartland. Natural gas burn-off smoldering in the blackness of Siberia.

Connelly felt an adrenaline surge verging on euphoria. What would Napoleon have given for the power he now held? He turned to Johnston.

Johnston nodded solemnly back.

Even he's hushed by it. They were gods.

Red lights were still flashing on dozens of other sensors. Connelly concentrated on the task at hand.

Suddenly a Klaxon warning sounded. Johnston jumped in his seat. Connelly turned around to face a nearby Korr board operator. "Report to me."

The board technician was clicking through monitors. Images on the big board changed. He brought up an overhead view of the massive ranch with its concentric rings of fencing. Hundreds of flashing red points arrayed all around the ranch—in a 360-degree arc. "Seismic sensors have gone off on the fence line all around the ranch, sir."

"Along four hundred miles of perimeter? Unlikely. No one would scatter their forces like that. What are the chances that our security system has been compromised?"

"We're on it, sir."

Johnston scowled. "If our security system has been breached, then that might mean Daemon operatives know about our plans."

"Unlikely. But even if they did, it's too late to do anything about them. We're going to move ahead on an accelerated schedule."

Connelly was motioning to gather subordinates around him, but he spoke to Johnston.

"A Daemon counterattack was anticipated, but much of the darknet's bandwidth should disappear when we conduct the blackout."

"What the hell are we waiting for?"

Connelly ignored him and instead barked at the control board operators. "What are we seeing from our surveillance drones on the perimeter? I want live visuals."

"Yes, sir."

In a few moments the central screen showed black-and-white infrared imagery of the prairie floor from a few thousand feet. The fence line was clearly visible running into the distance. Nothing unusual. The image jumped to another drone aircraft. Then it flipped to a third. Then a fourth. This one showed a rail spur stretching out to the horizon. The plain was empty.

"Looks clear on the perimeter, sir."

Connelly nodded. "If false alarms are the worst it can throw at us, then we can manage. Lieutenant, seal the ranch and put the base on high alert. No one enters or leaves as of *now*. I want Kiowas in the air in a thirty-mile radius, and I want perimeter roads watched closely."

"Yes, General."

A piercing air-raid siren slowly wound up to a long mournful wail somewhere outside the bunkerlike building.

Connelly and his assembled staff officers gathered around a plasma-screen table displaying a satellite still image of the ranch. He pointed with a pocket laser light as he spoke. "The seismic sensors along our perimeter have been compromised. Ignore them. However, we can't rule out that this is the beginning of an attack. We have six surveillance drones airborne, but since we can no longer trust our perimeter alarms, that gives us too much terrain to cover. Have the garrison pull back to the secondary perimeter and establish kill boxes at the service gates here, here, and here, and at internal ranch road junctions here and here. Keep a garrison at the south airfield."

"What are the rules of engagement, General?"

"Fire on anything that approaches our lines by land or air."

"Anything?"

"Let me make this clear: if a horse and buggy filled with orphans and nuns approaches a gate waving a white flag—open fire at four hundred yards and keep firing until those bitches are down. Sobol was devious enough to conceive of the Daemon and devious enough to build it. If his agents get into this compound, they will sabotage our systems and sow confusion in our ranks. That must not be allowed to happen."

"Do we pursue retreating forces?"

"Don't get drawn out from our perimeter. Keep your forces concentrated around what matters: the inner perimeter, the airfields, and the power station. Call in an air or artillery strike if you've got them on the run."

"What about the rail spur?"

"We'll blow the tracks at Snake Bayou if outside rail traffic appears." He scanned the faces of the gathered officers. A tough bunch of career warriors. Veterans of many secret wars. "You will not be forgiven for allowing the enemy to enter our perimeter. The mission is simple: hold your positions until the tech folks give the all-clear. At that point resistance should stop." He looked at them all. "Any more questions?"

A one-star frowned at the board. "Who is it we're expecting?"

"Intelligence reports indicate elements of Daemon militia are en route. They're going to be lightly armed civilian irregulars—susceptible to electronic countermeasures and disbursement by heavy weapons. However, we all know what happened to Operation Prairie Fire. So we can't assume anything. The difference this time around is we're on our home turf."

Another officer gestured to the map. "What about unmanned vehicles?"

"High likelihood."

"What about unmanned car bombs?"

"They'll be easy targets out here in the prairie—particularly for the Bradleys guarding these interchanges, here and here. Instruct the crews to engage with their cannons. I don't want TOW missiles wasted on Toyotas."

He paused for any further questions. "You have your orders. Dismissed."

The officers scattered to the exits. Connelly called to the nearby analysts. "Have you traced the fault in the seismic sensors yet?"

The analysts conferred briefly. One of them looked up. "We've lost contact with our aerial drones, General."

"Where?"

"Northeast sector, near gate two."

"The north road." He examined the map. "Have the remaining drones increase their altitude, and scramble a Kiowa chopper to the northern sector. I want aerial imagery ASAP."

"Roger. ETA roughly twelve minutes on the chopper."

"Twelve minutes?"

"It's thirty miles, General."

"Damnit." He turned to Johnston. "But we don't need to outsmart the Daemon. We just need to keep it busy long enough for the techs to cut its claws off." He pointed to the analysts. "Get me some intelligence about what's on my perimeter. Send out scout teams if necessary—but get it. In the meantime, let's keep in close radio contact with the perimeter gate teams."

Johnston sat in a leather chair at the edge of the video table. The ranch map spread out before him, showing the placement of forces. "How long until we execute Operation Exorcist, General?"

"Not long now, Mr. Johnston. Not long."

Korr Military Solutions captain Greg Hollings stood next to his Humvee inside the north gate of Emperor Ranch. Arrayed around him in foxholes on either side of the road his squad lay in ambush, watching the large, wrought-iron estate gates, chained shut fifty yards away. Three concrete highway dividers had been dropped in front of them—blocking the way. A fifteen-foot-high stone perimeter wall on either side of the gate stretched into the darkness in both directions, but Hollings knew it was largely cosmetic and only extended a few hundred yards before yielding to barbed-wire fencing and seismic sensors. Sensors that were all in alarm.

What was to prevent attackers from outflanking them way down the perimeter—coming in from behind and reconnecting with the ranch road miles south? HQ lost a surveillance drone seven or eight miles north of here. Those were his eyes in the sky. It didn't bode well.

"We're meat-on-a-stick out here, Chief."

"Keep it together, Priestly." Hollings scanned the perimeter with a FLIR scope. He had already ordered the exterior lights on the guardhouse extinguished, plunging the area into darkness. "Give me a status report."

Lieutenant Priestly spread a map out on the hood of the nearest Humvee. They both flipped down their night vision goggles. "We've got a sixty and a Javelin crew in that guardhouse and another here in ambuscade. Two fire teams entrenched alongside with SAWs. Interlocking fire on the gate centerline. Ten sets of Claymores guarding the north road beyond the gate, starting at one hundred yards out and spaced ten yards apart. Motion activated." He gestured into the darkness right and left. "We've got Humvee-mounted M60 teams on both our right and left flanks, a hundred and fifty yards out—at the ends of the gate walls. They'll serve as artillery spotters."

"What about Lopez and Tierney?"

"Their vehicles are in reserve. I figure we'll move 'em wherever they're needed."

Hollings nodded. "Face them rearward. I'm concerned we'll be attacked from behind—these walls don't go far. The moment we make contact, I want remote fire support. Any word from the Kiowa they sent up?"

"Negative, sir."

"Goddamnit. I'm blind." He pointed back at the map. "We do not fall back to the guardhouse—it's a death trap. Not enough windows, and it looks highly flammable. If we get overrun, we mount up and join MRTP a few clicks south. Understood?"

Priestly nodded as he folded the map.

Hollings surveyed the area. This would not have been his first choice for a defensive position. He'd rather dig in somewhere in the prairie with his men deployed in a ring. They'd be able to see anything coming a long ways off. But here, the broad expanse of a fifteen-foot perimeter wall thirty yards ahead of them blocked their view of the road north—and it was worthless as a defensive position; too tall to fight behind and too thin to stop much. Only two courses thick with no parapet. It was for show only. Like the guardhouse. Apparently, corporate military brass was just as dumb as the government kind.

Hollings looked at the large, log-cabin-style guard building just to the left, inside the gate. It had an overlarge, peaked slate roof with field-stone chimneys and log-cabin walls. Some billionaire's idea of pioneer style. It blocked his field of fire to the east, and it had no windows on that side. He couldn't have designed a more useless building if he'd tried. And yet he'd been ordered not to demo it.

This was a civilian security layout. All-out assault wasn't contemplated. The guardhouse was the largest structure for miles, and was intended as a rest stop for guests and employees starting the thirty-three-mile drive toward the center of the ranch. Restrooms, refreshments, and house phones next to a small parking lot.

And then there was the guard shack outside the gate, used for greeting vehicles as they drove up to the closed gates. More Davy Crockett–style nonsense. A small pedestrian gate beside it lent access to the guard shack from the main building.

"Priestly, we bring any C4?"

"Yeah, some."

"I want to take down these curtain walls near the gate. It's just blocking our field of fire."

"Already asked, sir. Not approved."

"For chrissakes . . ."

Suddenly a shout from the guardhouse went up, and then along the line. "We've got company!"

Silence prevailed for a moment. Then they all heard it. The sound of distant tires wailing on pavement, coming from the darkness of the north road. The noise of many engines also came in on the breeze.

"All right, places, ladies! Wait for the claymores, and keep an eye on our flanks!"

The Korr soldiers adjusted their night vision goggles and hunkered down in their foxholes around M249s and M60s. Another readied a Javelin anti-tank rocket launcher. They were all trained professionals here. Steady fingers rested near trigger guards as last-minute radio calls squawked in the blackness.

"There, sir!" Priestly pointed.

Hollings trained a FLIR scope into the darkness through the bars of the wrought-iron gate. He could see them coming—a long line of cars racing in at over a hundred miles per hour, only a half mile out. He didn't see any end to them. "Vehicles one thousand yards! Coming in fast!"

Gears creaked in the dark as hands clenched around pistol grips and straps were pulled taut.

"Give 'em hell, gentlemen!"

The roar of approaching engines took center stage now, echoing off the outer face of the estate wall. Suddenly a booming wall of sound hit their eardrums—followed by a shower of sparks and flame. Quickly followed by several more sharp explosions and the screeching of metal.

There were hoots in the ranks. "Yeah!"

A flaming, twisted piece of wreckage slammed into the wrought-iron gates, knocking one gate off its hinges and filling the grillwork with fire. Another flaming wreck slammed into the first, toppling the gates completely.

They crashed down onto the highway dividers, sounding like a xylophone tumbling down a staircase.

"So much for our gates." Through the flames Hollings could see that the claymores had taken out another dozen AutoM8s, which were burning in the ditches alongside the road.

But there was now a veritable roar of racing car engines. The flames revealed dozens more cars coming in from the night.

Just then a staccato *boom* echoed and tracer fire flicked out of the guardhouse—tracer rounds bounced off the distant prairie and metal wreckage. The M60 near Hollings opened up, too, as another sedan plowed through, smashing into the burning wreckage filling the arch and sending the whole pile over the highway dividers. The deafening crash washed over them, flaring into a brilliant fireball as the wreckage cartwheeled into the corner of the guardhouse. Another car blasted through. And another—which tumbled into the ditch alongside the road—partially blocking their field of fire to the gate.

"Jesus H. R. Pufnstuf Christ!"

"Priestly, put some arty on that road!"

"All I've got is static, Captain. Comm just went down!"

"Goddamnit, get on the landline in the guardhouse. And bring some fire down!"

Priestly saluted and took off at a run toward the guardhouse. Flames and tracer fire silhouetted him against the surrounding blackness.

Soldiers around Hollings were flipping up their night

vision goggles. It was getting bright in the kill zone with all the flames.

A rocket streaked out of the guardhouse window and disappeared through the gate opening. A flash and *boom* echoed out there. Another rocket raced in from the foxholes and detonated against the stone wall. Rock splinters blasted back, dinging against the Humvee fenders as Hollings ducked down. "Damnit!" He stood back up and had a much better view of the road now. Good thinking. They could build a new fucking wall. . . .

A whole row of SAWs on his right opened up through the new opening—tracers screaming toward the sound of a NASCAR race approaching them out of the darkness to the north. Ricocheting off of unseen targets. Another rocket raced out of the guardhouse. An explosion. The burning wreckage of a car knocked down a section of wall to the left of the gate.

Machine-gun fire rattled from the extreme right and left flanks—out by the ends of the wall.

"Keep on them! Keep firing!"

Several more cars raced into the meat grinder, crashing into the barriers and pitching up. But by now the barriers were partially pushed aside or smashed in two.

He could see Priestly racing through the guardhouse door. The guardhouse was starting to catch fire now. Soldiers raced up, pulling pieces of burning wreckage away from the wall. A Humvee with the .50-caliber on top roared past Hollings and slowed near the wreckage— nudging it from the building.

"Good job, Lopez!"

Lopez waved and opened up with the .50 into the

maw of the gate. The deep, slow booming of the .50 was a kettledrum section to the crackling of small-arms fire.

Another rocket streaked out of the guardhouse and nailed a car on the approach road.

Hollings looked around at the carnage. Good lord . . . Flaming wreckage littered the prairie. It looked like something from Revelation.

The gunfire was crackling less intently now. Soldiers were changing drum clips. Barrels were smoking hot. Their field of vision was now the radius of light around the flames. Their night vision and FLIR scopes were useless so close to this light and heat.

But the sound of approaching engines only got louder—and there was a deeper one among them. Hollings stood up and shouted. "Truck! Incoming truck!"

Just then another two sedans smashed through the opening, and tracer fire ripped through them. One caught fire and tumbled over the foxhole nearest the road. Shouts and screaming. Nearby soldiers ran to help their trapped comrades.

"Goddamnit!" Hollings could see Priestly rushing out of the guardhouse, waving his weapon over his head. He sprinted down the road toward Hollings's position among the Humvees.

"Captain! Phone line's been cut. We have no communications! They must be—"

Just then a steel-plated concrete truck plowed through the wreckage, filling the mouth of the gate—sending burning wreckage, concrete dividers, and stone blocks flying. It continued on into Lopez's Humvee, crashing into it and plowing it through the front wall of the guardhouse. The truck followed, crushing the front wall and collapsing the rest of the structure under the weight of the enormous peaked roof. The nose of the concrete truck was buried under debris. Lopez, his driver, and the guardhouse team were gone.

"Goddamnit!" Hollings cupped a hand to his mouth and shouted. "Fall back to the Humvees! Fall back! Bring the wounded!"

Bullets ricocheted off the cement mixer as it caught fire, but now the gate opening was clear. Two more AutoM8s—domestic sedans—raced through the opening and quickly took fire from retreating soldiers. But the fire wasn't intense enough to stop them and one locked on to Priestly in the road. Before he could duck into the nearby ditch, it nailed him at sixty miles per hour with a sickening *whump* and sent his body twirling off into the darkness beyond the flames.

"Lieutenant!" Hollings jumped onto his Humvee's hood, as the grenade launcher Humvee roared past. "Fuck!"

It fired a burst of grenades at both AutoM8s, ripping off their fenders and roofs—quickly shutting them down.

Hollings jumped off his hood and shouted again. "Fall back!!! Fall back!!!"

Then he heard a howling engine coming up from behind. He turned just in time to see the gleam of a blade in the moonlight. It was the last thing he saw.

Chapter 37: // Logic Bomb

General Connelly ignored the alarms sounding all around him and beheld the central screen again, with its orbital view of Earth. He breathed deeply, savoring this moment.

A nearby analyst interrupted his reverie. "General. I've got direct confirmation that we are under attack by darknet factions. Kiowa choppers have been engaged by what appear to be microjet aircraft. We have at least one chopper down. There are thousands of enemy troops moving in from every direction."

Connelly nodded calmly. To be expected. "It will do them no good. Do we have confirmation that all strike teams are in place and ready?"

"Affirmative, sir. All strike teams in place and ready."

Connelly kept his eyes on the screen. The world lay before him. "On my mark."

"Standing by."

"Commence Operation Exorcist."

"Commencing Operation Exorcist."

It was a facet of the modern world that the most important events now occurred unseen by human eyes. They were electronic bits being flipped from one value to another. Connelly knew that somewhere in this command center one of the network analysts was now, with a single keystroke, destroying the data of almost 80 percent of the world's most powerful corporations. It was a command script that sequentially invoked the Daemon's Destroy function, using as a parameter the local tax IDs of thousands of Daemon-infected corporations throughout the world. The net effect was that they were using the Daemon's own followers to destroy that data along with the backups. Sobol had warned his Daemon would do this if they tried to retake control.

But why wait for the Daemon?

With an encrypted IP beacon beaming out the Daemon's *Ragnorok* API to the entire Internet, it was only a matter of time until some other national power or corporate group had access to the Destroy function as well. There was no other choice.

Why not be the first? That's what finally convinced Connelly to join this effort. Nuclear war was unthinkable—but all-out cyber war was not. They could finally unify the world under a single all-encompassing economic power. One that could achieve miraculous things. Countries didn't matter anymore. The world was just a big market. It needed to be unified.

At the same moment Weyburn Labs was invoking the destruction of vast amounts of corporate data, they were also running a second script—one that invoked the Destroy function with a malformed parameter. It was all Latin to Connelly, but the big brains in Weyburn Labs had come up with a way to overstuff the Destroy function somehow, putting it into an infinite loop that would prevent it from destroying data, even if Daemon operatives somewhere in the data center tried to invoke it later manually. This malformed command would make these companies—and these companies alone—immune to the Daemon's wrath. And it was these companies in which they had invested their wealth. It was a mix of corporations that would give them control of nearly every productive commercial activity and the right to rule since they alone had been smart enough to survive "Cybergeddon." There would be a period of civil chaos in most countries, but they'd already taken steps to physically secure their facilities.

Connelly gazed at the dozens of television monitors showing the news of the world—financial meltdown. Violence in the Midwest. He glanced also at the ranch surveillance screens showing explosions and tracer rounds tearing across the prairie. It was high time for a cleansing fire.

"Got to hand it to the bastards. They're really giving it their all. I wouldn't have thought they could organize something like this. Where did they all come from?"

"Looks like the Daemon found a use for all those unsold cars."

"When this is all over, we'll need to take out those logistics people. Otherwise they'll make trouble later."

A nearby network analyst spoke into a microphone. "We have successfully deployed the Logic Bomb. Tests show the Daemon's Destroy function is no longer responsive in all protected sites."

A small cheer went up among the Weyburn Labs team.

Connelly nodded. *That was fast.* Apparently digital warfare was lightning war. They'd destroyed most of the corporate world in less than a minute. He knew it would plunge the world into a vast depression, but the end result would be worth it. What was the alternative, after all? Surrendering control of the civilized world to an uneducated mob?

He looked back up at the image of Earth on the big board. The view was centered on Western Europe, whose cities still glowed in the darkness.

Connelly imagined his father, the Southern Baptist preacher. What would he think of his son now? Even that hard-hearted bastard would have burst with pride. He would finally have been forced to admit that his son was a success.

"Commence the blackout."

"Commencing blackouts, sir."

Suddenly, like hitting knife switches, lights throughout Europe started tripping off—vast stretches of the continent plunged into darkness. Then Japan disappeared into the blackness of the sea. Beijing disappeared. A graphic depiction of the power of the merchant kings lay before Connelly as he beheld Earth. No one had ever fully realized just how much control they held. He trembled slightly with the power at his command. Two billion people had just been returned to the Middle Ages. Nearly a third of the human race. And most of the rest never had electrical power to begin with.

The Daemon was now a tiny shadow of its former self. It never stood a chance.

"Launch the data center strike teams."

"Strike teams are go! Repeat: strike teams are go!"

The board operators chattered into their headsets, spreading Connelly's command around the globe in seconds via private satellite networks.

Sebeck and Price had found clothes, body armor, and weapons quickly among the darknet factions moving in from the east. There was a wide diversity of equipment and armaments among the groups. They looked more like a high-tech militia than a true military force, but then, they were following in the wake of Loki's automated army.

Some operatives wore composite armor with full helmets, personalized with band stickers and ironic buttons; others just had hunting rifles.

The crowd drove a random assortment of civilian SUVs and Jeeps. However, they were a sizable force, spreading out toward the horizon in both directions and moving fast across the prairie. Someone had raided dealerships or something because most of these vehicles looked new. With gasoline going for eighteen bucks a gallon, Sebeck guessed there wasn't much market for them anymore. Examining the call-outs extending over the horizon, Sebeck estimated this group to number in the thousands. The operatives varied in level from the numerous first-level Newbs, such as himself, all the way up to fifteenth- and twentieth-level Operators. There were tech factions, micro-manufacturing factions, logistics factions, and the most formidable groups of all—the infrastructure defense factions. They were the folks in full-body armor with darknet electronic weaponry, packs of razorbacks, and flocks of microjets.

Wherever Sebeck went, operatives came up to him and shook his hand—asking to take pictures and pose with him. It was like some sort of macabre convention. Have your picture taken with the Unnamed One. . . .

Immediately after obtaining a loaner pair of HUD glasses and a computer belt, Sebeck opened a link to Jon Ross, finding Rakh's call-out ten miles west of him— right in the center of Sky Ranch. He was glad to hear his voice over the comm line.

"Jon, thanks for saving our asses. How did you locate us?"

"Loki has eyes everywhere. And other people were looking for you, as well. It's that quest you're on."

"You found Dr. Philips?"

"Yes, and she's here with me. We're safe for now. Is Price okay?"

"He's fine. What's the latest news?"

"Loki's smashing through the ranch defenses. He's got an army of . . . god, thousands of AutoM8s. Four or five hundred razorbacks. He must be spending every power point he has for this."

Sebeck nodded. "If you saw him, you'd understand why. He looks only half-human. I wouldn't want to be The Major when Loki catches up with him."

"Pete, you were right about Weyburn Labs. Smart mobs scanning the surveillance system have discovered their facilities. I won't show you the worst of it, but here . . ."

Sebeck saw an object zip toward him through D-Space and land in his HUD list. He opened it and sucked in a breath.

"There are dozens of young women still in cells there. It

looks like The Major's people were perfecting darknet identity theft."

"Jon, we need to send forces to those labs first— before the researchers can destroy the evidence. Those girls are in serious danger."

"I'll put the word out."

"Look, we're closing in on the inner perimeter. I'm told that we'll face resistance, if Loki hasn't wiped them out, so I'm going to get off the line. I'll need to be heads-up as we go in."

"Give my best to Laney, and be careful, Pete."

"You too, Jon. I'll see you on the other side."

Sebeck could already see explosions ahead. It looked like artillery airbursts. The thunder of detonations followed a second later. The vehicles were routed around the barrage and moving fast now, bumping across the prairie at fifty or sixty miles an hour. They passed distant burning wreckage riddled with shrapnel holes, broken bodies nearby, but the overwhelming majority of the force moved on—too spread out and moving too fast to be easily targeted by artillery.

The driver of their Jeep pointed ahead and shouted to Sebeck and Price. "We're going in a mile or so to the south of the ranch roads. There are ambush points with missiles and armored vehicles there. Loki's forces are taking them out."

Sebeck nodded. He looked back at Price.

Price stared back. "What?"

"I'm glad you're okay. I thought we were done for back there."

"Yeah, well, the day's not over, man."

And then it hit.

Out of nowhere the darknet disappeared as Sebeck's HUD glasses went dead. All of the call-outs around him disappeared as well. "Aw, shit!" He removed his glasses. "No wonder someone was willing to loan these to me. They're broken."

He turned back to face Price but was met with a confused stare. Price also removed his HUD glasses. "Oh shit . . ." He tapped the driver, who was frowning himself. "Dude, can you see D-Space?"

The driver looked worried. "No." He pointed at the nearby vehicles. "Look!"

Sebeck and Price followed the driver's gaze, and they could see hundreds of darknet operatives removing their HUD glasses and calling out to one another. The column of vehicles wasn't slowing down yet, but now they were suddenly without a unifying system of control or direction.

They were blind.

Sebeck turned back to Price. "What the hell just happened?"

Price looked lost—as though he'd just lost an old friend. "They've somehow knocked out the darknet, Sergeant."

General Connelly stood next to Aldous Johnston at the central console of the command center. Half the television monitors on the big board were filled with electronic snow. The Great Blackout had begun. The modern world was undergoing a cold reboot.

Johnston pointed at the screen. "So the data centers all still have power?"

Connelly nodded. "Of course. It's standard for data centers to have battery and backup generators. They can run for as long as they have diesel fuel. Some even have local power generation facilities."

"Then why the blackout if it doesn't bring the servers off-line?"

"The blackout isn't meant to cripple the Daemon, General. We already eliminated it as a threat with the Destroy function calls. No, the blackout is a psy-ops action. It's a demarcation between the old order and the new one for the general public. People need to be shocked into accepting their new situation. Revealing just how vulnerable they all are accomplishes that. They will seek protection."

"But *three days* without power?"

"Our social psychologists told us the panic should make people eager for strong leadership."

A nearby board operator looked up. "I've got Colonel Richter with a status report on the darknet militias, General."

"Put him on."

"Go ahead, Colonel. You're on speaker."

A slightly distorted voice came through the speakers. "General, this is Richter. Darknet militias are stopping their advance on a broad front. They appear to have degraded command and control."

Control room crew chuckled among themselves and clapped. Connelly and Johnston exchanged looks.

The general nodded. "That's good news, Colonel." He turned to Johnston. "Apparently the blackout has affected the bandwidth of these local operatives." He turned back to the speaker. "Once we finish up Operation Exorcist, Colonel, I want you to prepare a counterattack to wipe out these local militias."

"Understood. Do we take prisoners?"

"No prisoners. Now's our chance to get these bastards out of the way."

The line clicked off.

Johnston took a seat nearby. "Which brings up the code injection. Now's as good a time as any to let the Weyburn folks see if they can control the Daemon."

General Connelly's face was unreadable. "Our secondary objective is just that. Let's achieve the primary objective first."

"But a modification of the Daemon's code base needs to happen, General."

"Once we've solidified our beachhead, Mr. Johnston."

The control board operator looked up, frowning. "General, we're getting some strange reports back from the data center strike teams."

Connelly cast a look at Johnston. "We're not done yet." He then turned to the board operator. "What sort of reports?"

"There don't appear to be any people in the target data centers, sir."

Connelly pointed to the monitors on the big board. "Put up some video, goddamnit. I want eyes."

Board operators started working switches. Images

of the white snow on major news channels and the lull in fighting outside on the ranch grounds were replaced by head-mounted cameras on distant mercenary strike teams. These images were variations on a theme—racks of servers that appeared damned near identical all around the world. The grainy video showed heavily armed soldiers in black body armor and helmets moving through aisle after aisle of computer racks.

The screens showed hundreds of soldiers. There were Asians, Latinos, Africans, and Caucasians—mercenaries from a hundred different global firms. But none of them was finding human targets.

The board operator looked up again. "I think we found something you should see, sir."

"Put it on this screen." He pointed to the closest one on the control board.

The board operator nodded and clicked a few switches. Suddenly a grainy video from a soldier's head-mounted camera appeared there. It showed commandos milling about a fifty-inch plasma television sitting atop a Romanesque pedestal. The television displayed the logo for Daemon Industries, LLC, and the message:

Click to play . . .

Johnston frowned. "What the hell is *that?*"

The board operator looked up again. "They're finding them in a lot of the data centers, General."

On the big board they could see more and more of the small monitors displaying strike teams arriving at the center of each data center and finding a similar plasma-screen television. All of them showed the Daemon Industries, LLC, logo with the message "Click to Play."

Johnston closely studied the bank of monitors on the wall. Soldiers half a world away were pulling up their masks and giving the all-clear signal. "General, were we expecting to find these?"

Connelly ignored him and spoke to a nearby Weyburn Labs analyst. "Is our data still intact?"

"Well, the Destroy function is still looped for these companies."

"What about the corporate *data*, damnit!"

The analyst shrugged. "That's going to take some time to determine. We're running on the proven evidence that invoking the Destroy function destroys a given company's data. Blocking it blocks the destruction sequence."

"But can't we just check these servers?"

"It's hard to tell where code is executing nowadays, sir. With a global blackout in place, we won't be able to use the public Internet to connect."

"Jesus Christ." Connelly studied the screen.

Suddenly sections of the world started coming back to life on the large center screen that displayed Earth from space. Lights across Europe, Russia, and Asia were clicking back on in sections.

"Goddamnit! Why is the blackout ending? I didn't order an end to the blackout!"

The board operator looked up. "We're not doing it, sir."

"Then who is?"

Just then they could see video on the distant plasma

televisions automatically start as the Daemon Industries, LLC, logo was swept away in a colorful animation.

"Bring one of those onto the big board! *Now!*"

The board operator spoke into his headset and suddenly grainy video of an Asian Korr Military Solutions special forces captain moved into view and saluted into the camera. "Sir!" His image pixelated momentarily by the satellite delay. His voice came through fuzzy with satellite distortion. "Overlord, we've secured objective four-thirty-nine."

"Get the hell out of the way, damnit! Let me see the screen. Have that soldier focus his camera on that television screen!"

The captain dodged out of the way and the helmet cam focused on what looked to be an infomercial already in progress. Cheerful music accompanied a montage of images showing darknet operatives working together. Smiling young faces, wearing HUD glasses, working with fab lab equipment, fiber optics, agriculture, and alternative energy.

"Bring up the sound!"

The distant infomercial music crackled as it filled the speakers in the big command center. The montage faded out and to everyone's horror dissolved into a familiar face—Matthew Sobol. He was sitting in a wing chair next to a roaring fireplace and looked healthy. Words appeared at the bottom of the screen:

Matthew A. Sobol, Ph.D.

Chairman and CEO, Daemon Industries, LLC

Sobol nodded to the camera as the music came to a close. "Hi. If you're watching this video, it means you just tried to take over the world. Now, you all know who *I* was. But until now, I couldn't be certain who *you* were. Thankfully, your recent actions helped to clarify things." He took a moment to place another log on the fire, and he stabbed at the flames with a poker.

Connelly, Johnston, the Weyburn Labs team, and the entire data strike force watched the video playing in every data center in simulcast.

Sobol looked up again after putting the fire poker away. "I knew it would only be a matter of time until you broke into the darknet. No system is completely secure. Of course, you would scour my code for flaws. So I gave you some good ones." Sobol smiled amiably. "As we sit here, the companies you attempted to harm are perfectly safe. However, the Daemon is deleting *your* personal and business wealth, and is, in fact, destroying all the data and backup tapes of the companies you sought to protect."

He held up his hands reassuringly. "Now, please don't get agitated and head for the doors because it's already too late. Your greed caused you to concentrate your investments in a very specific way among a handful of companies—companies that someone just tried to defend with a lame-ass format-string hack—even while the rest of the corporate world was targeted en masse with the Destroy function. That's what we call an *anomaly*, and it has a signature that can be detected. The private individuals who were involved in this activity are now known to the Daemon. And what's more, most of your wealth, the source of all your power, no longer exists. Money, after all, is just data, and yours has been erased."

Connelly looked up at the network analyst. "Damnit, if the power's back on, get on the phone with our people and find out if this is just nonsense!"

The network analyst got busy, but a lot of the other people in the room were looking concerned.

Sobol was already talking again on-screen. "What's more, the Daemon will continue to destroy the resources of these individuals wherever they appear—in whatever form. And a log of your recent actions will be submitted to pertinent law enforcement agencies and the companies you were targeting. And as for the people who helped make all this possible? The assistants, lawyers, brokers, programmers, accountants, and security forces? To those people I say: your employers *have no money.* So do the smart thing—and just walk away."

The cavorting corporate Muzak returned, along with manic studio audience applause. Sobol waved. "Thanks for invoking this event, and remember, if you're not playing the game, it's playing *you.* Bye-bye now!"

Credits began to roll at double-fast speed.

"Turn it off!"

The screen went black and Connelly looked up at the nearest network analyst. "Well? Can we confirm if our networks are intact? Have our companies been affected?"

The analyst just cast a look at Connelly, then picked up his coat and hurried for the door.

"Where the hell do you think you're going?"

"We don't work here anymore. And neither do you."

Connelly turned to Johnston.

Johnston just shook his head. "That's ridiculous!"

Suddenly one of the board operators turned on the broadcast and cable news stations again, and there, on almost every channel, was Anji Anderson. She was sitting at a conference table. It looked to be surveillance footage as seen from up near the ceiling—but the individual on-screen was unmistakably Anji Anderson, the famous newscaster.

Connelly stared at the screens in confusion. "What the hell is this?"

The board operator was grabbing his coat, too. "It's playing on every station. Someone hijacked the emergency uplink we were going to use after the blackout. They somehow got footage from the surveillance system."

Everyone in the control center looked up at the camera pods mounted on the ceiling.

"Good god . . ."

"I advise that you try to escape as best you can, General. We have no secrets anymore."

Connelly looked back at the live television monitors. On-screen Anji Anderson was nodding, as what looked to be consultants conferred with her.

"—but the change needs to be sold to the American people with a sudden disruption. Otherwise they'll resist strongly. It needs to be the penultimate event that marks a demarcation between what came before and what must come after. It's a psychological transition."

Anderson nodded. "And the blackout does that?"

"Our studies show that a period of general anarchy as brief as forty-eight hours would make the public willing to accept severe changes in exchange for security."

Another market consultant held up sample graphics on a foam core board. *"We're calling it Cybergeddon."*

"That's catchy. . . ."

Chapter 38: // Ghost from the Machine

After the darknet came back online, Sebeck got busy examining darknet video streams from the thousands of operatives swarming over the ranch. He grabbed Price and hopped on a pickup truck loaded down with darknet Fighters brandishing automatic weapons. As they drove the final miles past wrecked military equipment and dead mercenaries, Sebeck watched D-Space video clips of Loki's mechanical army smashing through the defenses. Swarms of his razorbacks, AutoM8s, and microjets were spreading through Sky Ranch's network of roads, tearing into every soldier or worker they came across. As the private military's disorder spread and their radio communications disintegrated, the mercenaries retreated back toward the main ranch house, only to encounter a wave of mercenaries going in the other direction—telling tales of bankruptcy and trying to escape the ranch.

But thousands of darknet operatives were storming the ranch from every direction now, breaking into large complexes and warehouses filled with luxury consumer products, barrels of wine, pharmaceuticals, and racks upon racks of spare machinery and parts. As darknet journalists posted their reports, it became increasingly clear that the residents of Sky Ranch were planning on being here for a while. Perhaps waiting out an unfolding chaos they'd helped to cause in the outside world.

Darknet troops had begun accepting the mass surrender of mercenaries from dozens of companies, stripping them of weapons, and taking iris scans and fingerprints. No longer employed, the multinational army of mercs wasn't up for a fight—especially when it was outnumbered forty to one.

But at the center of the ranch Loki's machines were still marauding. Razorbacks, AutoM8s, and low-flying microjets were crisscrossing the gardens around the house, parking lots, roads, and kitchens, killing any nondarknet member they found—without exception.

There was sheer terror around the central compound as surrendering household staff members pleaded with darknet operatives—who could not prevent the bloodsoaked machines from hacking their captives to death.

Sebeck and Price reached the grounds of the mansion and joined a large crowd of operatives already surrounding it. All eyes were on Loki Stormbringer, as darknet feeds denounced him. People everywhere downvoted him, but Loki's reputation score already could go no lower. In the broad plaza before the mansion, Loki stared with lifeless eyes from a position on his Ducati street bike. He had formed hundreds of razorbacks into a ring around the main house, where the international financiers with their wives and children had barricaded the ornate doors. Loki appeared to be sensing the world through the eyes of his numberless minions, through their sensors, scouring every inch of this place, every culvert—searching for people in hiding. He seemed ready to tear down every brick of the place until he found The Major. And in the process was apparently going to kill every one of the plutocrats who cowered in the massive house—along with their trophy wives and their pampered offspring. Loki seemed ready to make them all pay.

Sebeck watched a video feed even now when a group of bankers tried to escape to the airfield to board their private jet and resume their lives as if this never happened. But Loki's distant razorbacks were shown forcing their Bentley off the road, dragging out the screaming occupants, and . . .

Sebeck closed the video inset in his HUD display. He'd seen enough death.

Hundreds of darknet members had gathered around the mansion to watch in dismay as Loki prepared his attack, while women and children held out surrender flags and pleaded for mercy.

Loki's new booming, synthetic voice tore into the air. "Major! I'm going to kill you—and every man, woman, and child who's hiding with you!"

The crowd booed, and Loki turned to face them, his voice truly booming now. "What can you do about it? None of this would have happened if not for me! I *am* the darknet!"

Ross and Philips arrived, apparently using D-Space coordinates to locate Sebeck and Price in the crowd.

Ross shouted over the noise of the razorbacks. "Sergeant! What is Loki doing?"

Sebeck pointed at Dr. Philips. "Jon, get her out of here! Loki's killing every civilian he finds."

"It's okay. . . ." He gestured to the amulet she wore, which gave off a soft D-Space glow. "Amulet of Protection. She's safe." Ross regarded the scene of Loki's swarming razorbacks.

Sebeck turned back toward the mansion. "Loki's getting ready to kill everyone in the mansion. He's hunting for The Major."

"Has anyone seen The Major?"

"No, I don't think so."

Philips just sucked in a breath at the sight of Loki amid a hundred razorbacks, while still more circled the mansion. "This is what I was afraid of, Jon. "

Ross, Sebeck, and Price turned to her. Sebeck asked, "Afraid of what?"

"The darknet is no different from any other social system. The powerful ignore the weak. Look at him. . . ." She gestured to Loki.

Sebeck ran his hand over his scalp. "She's right. You

saw the feeds; the plutocrats are bankrupt. We've taken back our freedom already—so then why hasn't my quest been satisfied? Why don't I see the path to the Cloud Gate?"

Price leaned in. "Do you see your quest Thread, Sergeant?"

Sebeck shook his head. He hadn't noticed it in all the insanity, but he no longer had a Thread to follow. "No. Which means this is where I need to be. It's not finished yet." He looked to Price and the others. "Stay here . . ."

"Sergeant, where are you going?"

Sebeck pushed through the crowd, making his way across the wide plaza that surrounded the house. As he came into view, with his well-known high-quest icon, the crowd roared their approval and parted to let him pass.

He finally reached the line of razorbacks, and as he tried to slip by, they moved to block his path. He knew they couldn't attack him—he was a member of the darknet—but neither would they let him through.

Loki's booming voice spoke in the air nearby while Loki watched from a hundred feet away. "What do you think you're going to do, Sergeant? You'll never get near me."

"Whether you like it or not, Loki, you're one of us." Sebeck could see the darknet feeds in his HUD display going haywire with news of the defeat of the plutocrats— but also at the rise of Loki. Hundreds of thousands of network members responded as they saw live video of Loki facing down the Unnamed One, and no one able to constrain him.

And then a D-Space light flashed and a familiar form

emerged from the network. Roy Merritt's avatar started walking through the swarms of razorbacks—straight toward Loki. His two-hundredth-level call-out was burning above him. The crowd went completely silent.

Loki just stared, obviously trying to figure out what to do, but still the Merritt avatar walked on.

Merritt's avatar walked past Sebeck, who stared in shock.

Video of the encounter was being taken by a hundred darknet cameras in the crowd and simulcast throughout the network. The crowd listened closely as Merritt came alongside Loki. Merritt's voice appeared in the air as well, calm and in control.

"Sir, I need you to stop what you're doing and come with me."

Loki looked around to the crowd. "What is this?"

"Sir, a critical mass of network citizens strongly disapproves of what you're doing. I need you to stop immediately and come with me. It would be much better if you cooperated. Would you do that for me?"

"Fuck you! Roy Merritt . . . you're a toy, an AI puppet that all these little users have put together."

"Sir, prosody tells me you're upset. I came here to help you."

"Help *me*? I don't need help!"

"Please, sir—"

"What are you going to do to me, Roy? You're a fucking ghost!" Loki turned to the crowd. "No one's powers can be turned on me. That's part of the *peaceful* nature of our new society, isn't it?" He laughed. "I'll do what I damned well please!" Loki sent a command that caused his army of razorbacks to surge forward, smashing at the mansion doors.

"You leave me no choice, sir. I'll need to hold on to these. . . ." Merritt's avatar reached up its hand and actually pulled the level numbers off of Loki's call-out—suddenly dropping the numbers down from sixtieth level to merely tenth level. *". . . until you feel better."*

The Merritt avatar was no longer two-hundredth level—he was now only one-hundred-fifieth level, and it was immediately apparent to all that the Burning Man had sacrificed his own levels to disable some of Loki's.

Loki watched in mute terror as all of the razorbacks around him and the microjets in the sky suddenly turned and departed. He got off his bike and staggered, finally falling to his knees in the realization of all he'd just lost—and the price he'd paid as well.

Even as people watched, Merritt's levels started to rise again, as people from around the darknet donated hard-won levels—at a ratio of a thousand to one—to replace those Merritt had tied up.

In just a few moments, Merritt was back to his maximum two hundred levels.

Merritt stood over Loki. *"Sir, we all need help from time to time. That's why there's more than one of us. . . ."*

Loki stared up at an avatar created out of the popular will of millions of people—programmed to react in times of dire need. It was apparently part of the darknet. And what the darknet was evolving to become.

Loki collapsed onto the ground, silently wracked with sobs, his metallic eyes unable to shed tears or look away.

The crowd, no longer hostile, gathered around him. A nearby woman placed her hand on his shoulder.

Merritt turned to the crowd. *"Everything's okay here, folks. Nothing to see. . . ."*

And suddenly Sebeck heard a chime. He looked to see a gold-colored Thread wind away from him, leading north, toward the distant horizon. "Price!"

"I'm right *here*, man."

"We need to find our gear. *Now.*"

"Can't it wait?"

"No. We've got to leave right away."

"To *where*?"

Sebeck was already pushing through the crowd. "To the Cloud Gate."

Chapter 39: // End Game

Reuters.com

Global Blackout Linked to Bankrupt Financial Groups—The FBI has conducted dozens of raids and made hundreds of arrests at prestigious brokerage houses and investment banks in connection with last night's sweeping power outages.

Pete Sebeck's final Thread led him north to Houston, and then east toward a once bustling container port at Morgan's Point, Texas. The glowing, golden line ran toward a massive shipping container facility that lay alongside a stretch of shipping channel named Barbour's Cut.

In recent days the dollar had slowly begun to rise from its historic low—no doubt in large part from Sobol's vengeance against the plutocrats. But as Sebeck brought their newly assigned Lincoln Town Car through the vast industrial wasteland and utterly subjugated landscape of Morgan's Point, he wondered if this place would ever thrive again. The days of ten-thousand-mile supply chains might have gone for good.

He turned to see Laney Price sitting in the front seat

next to him, wolfing down chicken nuggets and sipping a jumbo soda. Sebeck just laughed and shook his head.

"What?"

"You have no sense of irony, Laney. Do you know that?"

"I told you, I was hungry."

"Well, I guess you've earned the right to eat crap."

A female voice came from the backseat. "Leave him alone, Sergeant. Each of us celebrates in our own way."

"She's right, Pete."

Philips turned to Jon Ross. Their look lingered longer than necessary.

Price scowled. "What the hell kind of name is 'Ivan Borovich,' anyway? I just got used to calling you Jon."

"Call me whatever you like, Laney. I won't be listening anyway."

Philips leaned against Ross. "I like the name Ivan."

Price chuckled and spoke in a Russian accent. "Yeah, I'm sure the NSA will like Ivan, too."

Philips waved him off. "Defending the U.S. government against a hostile takeover should be worth a green card."

"I don't know. I hear the requirements are getting tougher."

Sebeck slowed the car. "Here we go. . . ."

"We're there?"

"No, but I think were running out of land pretty quickly on this peninsula."

They were now heading down along a wide concrete road apparently made to deal with a high volume of container truck traffic. The traffic seemed much reduced.

They had the place mostly to themselves—although a veritable skyline of multicolored shipping containers rose to their left across several lanes of highway.

Philips studied them. "What is the Daemon's fascination with shipping containers?"

Ross looked as well. "They helped spread the consumer culture virus to every corner of the world. It's no wonder the Daemon found them useful."

Sebeck slowed the car again as they came alongside a truck yard, and he turned across the highway to a frontage road.

Price nodded. "A container yard. You're going to open a container that contains *something*. Something Sobol sent to himself. Or—"

"Price, would you please? I can't hear myself think."

"Then think *louder*, man."

Sebeck pulled into a driveway that surprised everyone. As he followed the golden Thread down the narrow lane, they all gazed through the windshield.

Ross looked puzzled. "A *cemetery*? In the middle of all *this*?"

Before them stood a rusted metal sign that read MORGAN'S POINT CEMETERY. The parcel was perhaps a couple of acres in size, and stood at the end of a long drive that placed it in the middle of a massive container yard. It was surrounded on three—and very nearly four—sides by towering container stacks. However, the driveway and the cemetery beyond looked green. Trees and shrubs covered the grounds, and a barbed-wire fence separated it from the surrounding shipyard.

Sebeck sighed. "Well, this is where it's leading me."

He came to a stop in a small, empty parking lot. Everyone got out and glanced around.

"This place is positively surrounded." Philips gazed up at all the containers looming above them.

Price pointed at the names on the sides of the center container in each wall. In big blue sans serif letters was the word "HORAE" painted along the corrugated steel. "Sergeant. Just like Riley told us." He turned to Philips. "Doctor, you've read some Greek mythology, yes?"

"Yes, quite a bit. In native Greek."

"Prove to us you are deadly boring: What are the Horae in Greek mythology?"

She shrugged. "They were the three goddesses who controlled orderly life. Daughters of Themis. The word means 'the correct moment.' And the earliest mention is in the *Iliad*, where they appear as keepers of the cloud gates."

Price just threw up his hands. "Well, that's pretty damned impressive."

"Is it a code?"

Ross stood alongside her. "Or an arrangement, perhaps. Like tumblers in a lock."

"You mean these containers need to be arranged precisely like this to unlock something?"

He shrugged. "You tell me, Doctor. You're the code breaker."

Sebeck was already walking forward. "It's no code. It's symbolism. And as you know by now, Sobol's worlds are chock-full of symbols."

Price followed. Ross waited for Philips, and soon they were all walking down a cracked sidewalk toward an ornate, wrought-iron gate. It, too, was somewhat rusted, but the iconography of the gate was unmistakable— three female guardians holding long spears loomed in bas-relief on either side, wreathed in ironwork clouds. The gate was closed.

As Sebeck approached the gate, D-Space avatars of three towering female forms in robes and enclosed, plumed helms materialized from the shadows, holding tall golden spears.

Philips looked puzzled as all three men in the group backed away from the shadows. "What is it?"

Ross held her hand and tapped his HUD glasses. "Female avatars. The Horae, I gather."

One of them spoke in a booming female voice. "Only the quest-taker may pass through the gates."

Price held up his hands. "No problemo."

Ross nodded. "I guess we'll wait for you here, Sergeant."

Sebeck glanced to Price as he stood with his hand on the gate. "You know, Laney, I don't think I would have made it here without you."

Price shrugged. "Well, let's wait to see if it's good or bad before you go thanking me."

Sebeck shook his head and entered the gate. It closed and locked behind him with an audible *click*.

As he continued to follow the golden Thread along the cemetery path, he noticed the graves were widely spaced. It was more like a shady garden—albeit one with colorful shipping containers as a backdrop.

Before long Sebeck's path brought him to another D-Space apparition: a young, healthy-looking Matthew

Sobol, sitting on a stone bench beneath a tree. There was an identical bench across from him.

As Sebeck approached, this younger, healthier Sobol nodded to him in greeting. "Detective. I'm very happy that you're here."

Sebeck couldn't get over how vibrant and healthy Sobol looked, with his tousled hair, khakis, crisp button-down shirt, and suit jacket. He looked the very image of a successful man with his whole life ahead of him.

"Please, join me." The avatar gestured to the open seat.

Sebeck swept off some leaves and dirt and sat.

"You might be wondering why I look different from the way I will . . . or *did* . . . earlier." He sat back in his seat. "It's because I started here at the end. Where you are now. I have no idea where here is or now is at the moment. But I did know that if I started from the end of the story and moved to the beginning, then the Daemon couldn't begin unless it was complete. So really, your beginning is my end, and my end is your beginning."

Sobol gazed directly at Sebeck's eyes. "When I realized what our world had become, how humanity had become cogs in its own machine, I resolved to do something terrible . . . perhaps one of the worst things ever done. To exploit the automation of our world in order to plant the seed of a new system is reckless and irresponsible. But I didn't see any other way we would change. Or could change.

"But now that humans have accomplished this quest, and you have arrived to tell me of their success, the question I need to ask you is this: was I right or wrong,

Sergeant? Should I *destroy* the Daemon? Should I undo everything I've done? Yes, or no?"

Sebeck felt the shock work through him. He was speechless.

"You of all people would know, Sergeant. Should the Daemon be ended? Yes, or no? I will wait for your answer."

Sebeck took a deep breath and looked back toward the gate. He could see no one. Just himself and this long-dead genius-madman. He sat recalling the entirety of his journey, from the point he received the Sobol murder case up to this very day. It had been years. He thought of his lost wife, Laura, and their son, Chris. Of his colleagues and friends who were dead or to whom he was now dead. He recalled all the people he had met who were building new lives on the Daemon's darknet, and all the people who had perished in its birth—and in its defense. A procession of faces came to him. What was society, after all, but a group of people making up rules? At least on the darknet, it was a large group of people making up the rules instead of a small one.

Sobol had waited patiently, but when Sebeck met his gaze again, the avatar repeated the question. "Should I destroy the Daemon, Sergeant?"

Sebeck took a deep breath. Then shook his head. "No."

"Let me confirm your answer. Should I destroy the Daemon? Yes or no?"

"No."

There was a flicker in the image, and Sobol looked grimly relieved. He gazed directly at Sebeck again. "You don't know how much I dream for this to be the ending. There are so many ways for it to end. If you're really there, Sergeant, good luck to you. Good luck to you all. And don't be afraid of change. It's the only thing that can save us."

Sobol stood, nodded farewell, and walked toward the nearby gardens. In a few moments he vanished into thin air.

Sebeck sat in the garden for an unknowable time by himself, contemplating what had just occurred. Until finally he received an alert in his HUD display. It was from a network handle he was too afraid to recognize. He read it over and over: **Chris_Sebeck**

After bracing himself, he opened the message and read it slowly . . .

Dad, I sent you this message triggered to open when you're ready for it. I know the truth, and can't wait to see you. Your son, Chris.

Sebeck felt the tears come forth from him—coming from some place he thought hadn't existed in his heart. He had a family. He was a father.

He was going home. . . .

Chapter 40: // Exit Strategy

It had taken over a century for Sky Ranch to evolve from the ancestral home of a wealthy family into the heavily fortified executive retreat and End-Times bunker complex it ultimately became. However, The Major knew these things didn't happen overnight. They accrued in layers over decades—and so they had secrets.

It was *knowing* those secrets that set The Major apart from his colleagues. He planned for the worst, and was seldom disappointed. His brand of "black sky thinking" had kept him alive on more than one occasion when all around him had perished. Even now as he looked through a 1960s-era periscope at the cleaned-out storage rooms beyond his secret hiding place, he realized that, once again, paranoia had prevailed.

It had been ten days since Sobol's Daemon had bankrupted the merchant princes of the world. Ten days since thousands of darknet operatives had scoured the five-star luxury survivalist lodge that was Sky Ranch. They'd cleaned out the warehouses and storerooms, dismantled the weapon systems, and raided the vaults. They'd gone through the floor plans and databases to find everything there was to find.

But they didn't see The Major's Cold War hiding

spot on the blueprints. Rumor had it that the room was a tryst location for a philandering banker—built to Cold War bomb shelter standards to mask its true purpose in the books and to muffle loud music. The entrance was concealed to keep out the uninvited.

True story or not, the place looked a lot like the swinging pad of a midcentury banker—long sofas, bar, pool table, and card tables. It was also musty, covered in dust, and unaccountably cold. But it had kept him alive. Living on canned goods gleaned from the storage room outside before he closed himself in, The Major once more checked the periscope. All was quiet.

He'd grown a slight beard over the past few days and wore a hooded sweatshirt and jeans pilfered from the nearby laundry. He opened the heavy door and listened. He heard nothing.

He turned up the hood and poked his head out, looking both ways. There was daylight coming through an open fire-exit door at the corner of the room, wagging in the wind. Trash skittered around the floor with each breeze.

Disarray. A good sign.

He shouldered his scoped Masada rifle, then grabbed his daypack of canned provisions and water in liquor bottles, and took one more precautionary glance before exiting the bomb shelter. He got to the open fire door and peeked through the gap between the hinge and the door.

It was a cloudy day, but he cursed under his breath as he saw what obviously were darknet sentries still moving about on the walkways near the main house. One of them wore the telltale armor of a Daemon champion. They were all carrying darknet weaponry. There was no way he could exit unseen. And night would be no better, since he knew they'd have night vision. In fact, he'd be at a disadvantage.

The Major remained calm. He reached into his pack and produced a pair of quality HUD glasses along with spooled wire that led to an electronic enclosure.

In the closing days of Operation Exorcist, the Weyburn Labs team had made significant progress cracking into the encrypted Daemon darknet. Partial credit was due, of course, to Dr. Natalie Philips for her work at Building Twenty-Nine—where she proved the concept of darknet identity theft. But in order to use this network, they needed to own it. They had been well on their way to doing that—and The Major might soon be again.

His researchers had advanced past the need to keep a darknet operative medically alive in order to spoof them—they'd done better. They digitized the biometric data and created a unit that injected it into the standard darknet HUD glass sensors, replete with pulse sensor. All that was needed to steal a darknet operative's identity with this system was their biometric data—fingerprints, iris scan, voice.

And The Major had given just that to the lab team.

As he powered up the unit and slipped the glasses on, he became Loki Stormbringer. He suddenly saw the HUD display first-person, instead of on a projection screen, and he saw darknet objects moving in a plane of augmented reality. They were all over the place. This was going to be a very interesting new world.

He walked with purpose out the storeroom door, ignoring the guards, and then kept walking briskly toward the distant guest bungalows. He gauged the houses were two miles away across slightly unkempt gardens and uncut lawns.

He kept his back turned to the guards and just kept walking. As the minutes ticked away and he estimated he was hundreds of yards from the main house, he felt the tension draining from him. He looked up at the sky with his new glasses.

He saw the call-outs of surveillance drones up there, thousands of feet in the sky. But he was one of them now. A member of the darknet. He also had four hundred thousand euros in his bag. It would be much needed since his accounts had all been emptied by Sobol's Daemon. If only he hadn't been greedy. But he still had some safe-deposit boxes in Zurich and Dubai.

And he could now steal all the darknet identities he needed. He suddenly frowned at Loki's reputation score. It looked surprisingly like a half-star out of five. And what was this? It now looked like Loki was only a tenth-level Sorcerer.

What the hell?

No matter. This was only a temporary identity. The sky was the limit now. He was almost to the bungalows, and he could either head out on foot for the power station or try to obtain a vehicle legitimately from the darknet.

He risked a glance behind him, but there was no one in sight any longer. He was more than a mile from the main house.

He kept walking and chuckled to himself. Once he was clear of this place, he knew some hackers who could make very good use of this darknet identity theft technology. Very good use.

"Excuse me, Major."

The Major stopped cold. The voice came from *right behind him.*

The Major clicked the safety on his Masada rifle and spun around even as he crouched. Then, in utter astonishment, he slowly came to his feet again.

"It is 'Ze Major,' is it not?"

Only a few feet away, impossibly, stood a spectral image of a Nazi officer in a full black trench coat, monocle, and filter cigarette. He looked real, except for the fact he was a ghost. The Major was so stunned he kept the gun aimed at the ghost's head.

It knew who he was.

"I zought I recognized you." The apparition tapped his cheek just under the eye. *"From your eyes. I can tell zees zings."* He took a deep drag on his cigarette. *"My name is Heinrich Boerner."* He started taking off his leather gloves as he spoke.

Meanwhile, around him, The Major heard a rising whine, like electric motors. He turned to see a line of razorbacks coming over the grass toward him. Why hadn't he heard them?

"Fuck!" He turned to run and saw another row of razorbacks moving toward him from the bungalows—like lions approaching in deep grass. There were at least a dozen closing in from all directions. He opened fire with the Masada. The bullets whined off the front cowlings harmlessly, and the machines all unfolded their swords as they advanced across the grass on electrical power.

Soon The Major's gun was empty. And there right next to him was Boerner, smoking calmly.

Boerner began to remove his heavy leather coat. "Your guns are qvite useless, Major. Zis is an unstoppable event. Struggle vill only prolong ze inefitable."

Now the razorbacks were all around The Major—trapping him in a circle of swords.

The razorback nearest Boerner raised one sword, and Boerner hung his leather jacket upon it. He rolled up his shirtsleeves and grinned at The Major.

"I do so enjoy my vork. . . ."

FURTHER READING

You can learn more about the technologies and themes
explored in *Freedom*™ through the following
books:

Omnivore's Dilemma by Michael Pollan, Penguin Press
The Shock Doctrine by Naomi Klein, Metropolitan
Books
When the Rivers Run Dry by Fred Pearce, Beacon Press
The Shadow Factory by James Bamford, Doubleday
When Corporations Rule the World by David C. Korten,
Kumarian Press & Berrett-Koehler Publishers
The Transparent Society by David Brin, Basic Books
Wired for War by P. W. Singer, Penguin Press
The Populist Moment by Lawrence Goodwyn, Oxford
University Press
Wikinomics by Don Tapscott and Anthony D. Williams,
Portfolio
Brave New War by John Robb, John Wiley & Sons

ACKNOWLEDGMENTS

This book was quite a journey. Dramatizing the sweeping socioeconomic and technological transformation of civilization required a little research. I'd like to extend my profound gratitude to: James Bamford, David Brin, Ian Cheney, Curt Ellis, Deborah Koons Garcia, Lawrence Goodwyn, Naomi Klein, David C. Korten, Fred Pearce, Michael Pollan, John Robb, and P. W. Singer, whose published works informed this story in ways both great and small.

The research and innovations of the following groups and institutions also aided greatly in the creation of this book: the National Renewable Energy Laboratory, Sandia National Laboratories, California Institute of Technology, the people and State of Iowa, and the Ames Research Center.

Thanks also to Stewart Brand and the entire Long Now Foundation for promoting long-term thinking in our institutions and culture.

Thanks to Dan G. and Don T. for giving me an interesting forum for my crazy ideas.

Thanks as well to Adam Winston for his much-appreciated insights on early drafts of this book.

Also, sincere thanks to my wonderful literary agent, Bridget Wagner, at Sagalyn Literary Agency, and also to my editor at Dutton, the saintly and talented Ben Sevier.

And finally, heartfelt thanks to my patient and loving wife, Michelle.